dead north

Published in the UK by Beacon Books and Media Ltd
Earl Business Centre, Dowry Street, Oldham, OL8 2PF, UK.

www.beaconbooks.net

ISBN: 978-1-912356-80-5 Paperback
ISBN: 978-1-912356-81-2 eBook

Cataloging-in-Publication record for this book is available from the British Library

Every effort has been made to identify material quoted from other publications and to acknowledge its sources in the text. The publishers will be glad to do likewise for any other such quotations brought to their attention.

Cover graphics and concept by Bryan Dawe

dead
north

Sandy McCutcheon

BEACON BOOKS

Dedication

With thanks to Sue Bail for her advice and feed-
back. Also thanks to Lisa Lark in Tasmania for
superb proof editing and belief in the novel. To
Bryan Dawe for his continued support and creative
vision. Finally, to the good folk at Beacon Books
for their great work.

Introduction

At the heart of this novel lies the Finnish epic *The Kalevala*. Of ancient origin, it was assembled from oral records collected by the scholar Elias Lönnrot and published in its final form in 1849. Since then it has inspired Finnish culture – nationalism, literature, the music of Sibelius and the work of many Finnish artists.

The quotations from *The Kalevala* that are not translated as part of the narrative are accompanied by footnotes. The translations are mostly adaptations from the work of Kirby (1907) but also owe much to the splendid work of Keith Bosley (1989).

Pronunciation of Finnish is not difficult, as it is almost completely phonetic with emphasis on the first syllable. Double vowels are long and double consonants are both sounded. Examples; Aino (*I know*), Auli (owl-lee) and the first syllable of Väinämöinen rhymes with 'say'. 'j' is pronounced as in the German 'ja'. 'h' is always sounded. 'y' is as in the German 'ü'.

Prologue

Mitä itket, tyttö raukka, tyttö raukka, neito nuori?
Why are you crying, poor girl, poor girl, young lady?
– *Kalevala (Neljäs runo)*

Later she wouldn't remember, she knew that. Yet she wanted to remember these moments. For each was a gift. Every precious second a triumph. Each second she remained alive was a victory. She didn't understand why, but knew she was right.

She felt no panic – no fear. They had given her something for the fear, or for the nausea. It seemed to be working.

A liquid warmth surrounded her, comforting, supporting her. It occurred to her that she was under water. Not Ophelia floating amidst the weeds, but deeper down, beneath the surface. She opened her eyes and saw above her a coruscating light. Not golden, not the sun. Then she saw a shadow that was not a cloud – more solid, more determined. She watched as a hand entered the water and came towards her.

Far away, she felt the hand touch her shoulder. I am being rescued, she thought, pulled to safety. The touch was strong. A man. I must remember him, she thought, knowing she wouldn't. He pushed her deeper and that was the moment she knew with certainty that she was about to change. Now, she thought, now I must become a salmon.

She wanted to remember, but knew, even as she thought it, that the dead don't have memories. In the last moment, as she felt herself transform, she smiled and watched a bubble of air rise slowly to the surface. I wonder, she thought, if a salmon has memories.

They waited until she was unconscious, barely breathing, and then stripped away her clothing. With the solemnity of undertakers, they laid her naked body out in the wooden rowboat. Then they stood back while the photographer added the finishing touches to the scene with the precision of an art director.

In the pre-dawn gloom she looked like a figure from a pre-Raphaelite painting: her pale skin translucent, eye sockets ringed poppy-purple. Her long, straight, ice-blond hair was arranged neatly down her body, leaving her breasts exposed, the nipples contracted with the cold. Beside her they laid the switch of birch twigs. Finally, they laid her hands one across the other, on her stomach.

The man with the camera stepped forward and took several shots, then grunted that he was done.

Their work complete, they pushed the boat out into the fast-flowing River Thames. The tide was going out and the current would carry her a fair distance by the time it was light enough for pedestrians on the riverbank or on bridges to see the boat's occupant. She would be long dead by then.

By the time they reached their car and looked back, the boat had vanished.

As they neared the embassy the passenger alighted and waved the car off. He took out his phone, typed a short message and sent it. Then, wrapping his coat around him against the dawn chill, he lit a cigarette and strolled to the embassy. A good night's work, he thought, and one that would send a clear message. Hopefully the English press would pick up on the story, but that was not essential. It had been like tossing a pebble in a pond, he mused. Those for whom the message was intended would notice the ripples. That others would see the message was of little concern. Or so he thought.

Part One

Chapter One

Nicole Parry took off her glasses, peered at them, and, pulling the tail of her blouse out of her trousers, polished them again. It made no difference. It never did. For a moment she held them up to the desk lamp. They seemed clean. She put them on, and with her finger pushed at the bridge. It also made no difference, for the moment she looked down at the file they slid irritatingly down her nose. She reminded himself again that she should invest in a new pair. She had been telling herself that for weeks.

The real problem was not her sight. Nor was it the glasses. The culprit was a crepuscular gloom that cloaked the space, not just in the evenings, but day and night. Her desk lamp threw a small circle of light onto her desk but failed to add much to the overall atmosphere. The glow from her computer simply added a cold quality to the surrounds. The ancient neon strip lights in the ceiling no longer functioned and the small grilled window high up on the wall allowed some air in but provided little illumination.

Nicole couldn't see anything from the window and though the room needed the air, she regretted having pried it open, for men returning from the pub regularly pissed against the wall. She supposed it gave them an odd satisfaction to piss on a police station.

The crypt, as the basement office at the Hammersmith Police Station was commonly known, was her domain, not by choice but as a penance. Questioning the male officers' judgment came at a cost. Not that she was a bolshie bitch or a flag-waving feminist; she was too controlled, too methodical for that. What irritated the other detectives was her dogged determination to pursue every minor lead to its very end. A waste of time and resources, they would say. It's going nowhere. But Nicole would ignore them and carry on. Two or three times in the last year she had been proven right, but instead of relieving the tensions between them, it exacerbated them.

The final straw had been a murder investigation where the station's senior DI hauled in a suspect found in possession of a knife with the victim's blood on it. They quickly charged the suspect and built a solid case based on the knife and a long animosity between the victim and the accused. Nicole had thought it all too simple and despite being told to back off, had gone back over the case looking at every minute detail. The knife intrigued her. It was solid steel and yet the tip had a small bend in it. When she took it to Doctor Jacobs, who had performed the autopsy, he re-examined the dead man's ribs and rewrote his report saying that the knife in question could not have inflicted the clean incision he had discovered in the bone. Jacobs congratulated Nicole, but was alone in doing so. Her fellow detectives shunned her but had no option other than to release the suspect. With no further leads and more urgent cases to attend to, the case turned cold. It was eventually shelved along with hundreds of others in the crypt.

As a reward for questioning her superiors, Nicole was assigned the job of reviewing unsolved cases, then checking that the computer records of evidence, interviews, forensics and crime scene photographs were collated into a single file, and archiving them.

'With your attention to detail, you never know what you might find in some of those old cases,' Chief Superintendent Andrew Crawford said. If that had been an attempt to placate her, it failed.

'I've been banished to the crypt to bury the dead,' she wrote in one of her infrequent emails to her older brother, Harry, in Australia.

For the last three months, since September, she had spent every day of her working week in the crypt. The repetitive nature of the work suited her, as did the lack of interaction with her fellow officers. The gloom was depressing, but that aside, she would have been reasonably content with her lot had it not been for her well-developed streak of obsession. But though she examined every file in minute detail, she found little other than the odd procedural irregularity; nothing that justified reopening a single case.

In the first week of November Nicole opened a file that was to change everything. It was a very short file, the kind of thing she could normally read and dismiss in a couple of minutes before consigning to the computer. The case, one she had heard about but had not personally worked on, involved the body of a woman discovered in a boat stranded in the tidal mud downstream from Fulham Bridge.

The case was unusual in that it had been shelved with what looked like unseemly haste, after barely a month. The final report claimed that there was 'nothing to investigate'. Nicole read the file several times and decided that the final report was wrong, and she removed the 'archive' tag on the computer. By doing so, the file would automatically be restored to its status as an active investigation. She had no concern about her action being noticed because, without the input of new data, it would effectively remain dormant.

The case had started on the seventh of October with an anonymous phone call, not to 999, but direct to the Hammersmith CID switchboard. The caller claimed that he had been crossing Fulham Bridge and seen what looked like the naked body of a woman in a boat stranded in the low-tide mud. The call was switched through to DI McKay, who took a squad car to the scene and, after donning wadders and struggling through the silt, confirmed that it was a genuine call.

The crime scene description was clinical and well-written, but gave Nicole nothing, so she decided to go and talk to DI Evan McKay. She imagined that he liked her and would be forthcoming. McKay had a made a pass at her within days of her posting to Hammersmith and after a couple of weeks she let him back to her sparsely decorated home and, skipping any foreplay, took him straight to bed. Although he was a young, good-looking and powerfully built individual, his lack of sexual finesse was immediately apparent and she recalled that she spent at least half of the twenty-five minutes wondering just how long it would take him to finish and if it really was time to paint the ceiling and get some decent curtains.

Afterwards, she had thanked him perfunctorily and shown him the door. For his part McKay must have found it a satisfactory experience because he subsequently asked her out on a number of occasions, but Nicole had lost all interest in him. None of that mattered now, she mused. It was simply the fact that he had been first on the scene and it was his signature on the bottom of the report. Taking a deep breath, she pushed herself out of her chair, pocketed her glasses and went upstairs.

Rising from the crypt was always disconcerting, not only because of the brightness of rooms with real lighting, but the noise and bustle. Blinking, mole-like, she shouldered past a staggering junkie being escorted to a cell. A screaming match erupted in front of her.

'You stupid little fucker!' a well-dressed middle-aged woman yelled, her voice slurred by alcohol.

'Shut it, Mum.' The handcuffed boy was banging his head against the wall while a couple of policemen attempted to restrain him.

'Twice stupid!' the mother continued at the top of her voice. 'Stealing a motor is stupid. How many times have I told you? And then getting fucking caught. You're just like your fucking stupid father.'

Nicole manoeuvred around the fracas and ducked into the canteen. Evan McKay was in his usual chair, deep in what was obviously an intimate conversation with another female DI, Annie Compton.

Nicole didn't wait for a pause in their conversation. 'I want to know about the woman in the boat,' she said.

McKay looked startled. 'And good afternoon to you, DI Parry.' He made no attempt to hide his displeasure at being interrupted.

'What was your first impression?'

Annie Compton shrugged and got to her feet. 'You two obviously have a lot to talk about...' she said archly and wandered off.

'For christsake, Nicole, I was talking –'

'Just describe it, please.'

McKay heaved a sigh and, knowing from past experience that there was no escaping her insistence, opted for the line of least resistance. He gestured for her to sit. She ignored him and remained standing.

'The woman was naked and had been laid out like some sort of ritual.'

'How do you mean?'

'Like a Viking sea burial, you know... or a cult thing.'

'No, I don't.'

McKay sighed again. 'It was an old-fashioned wooden rowing boat; clinker-built, with rowlocks but no oars. The seats had been removed and a couple of planks laid stem to stern for her body.'

'Like on a slab?'

'She was on display. She had a pillow under her head, her hair had been brushed and her arms folded over her stomach.'

Nicole squinted, thinking.

'No covering?'

'*Nada*. Not a stitch. So, I called Dr Jacobs and a forensics team and while I waited for them I taped off the area and kept the on-lookers and press photographers out of the way.'

'Any external signs of trauma?'

'Nothing I could see.'

'I'll talk to Jacobs,' Nicole said. She turned on her heel and strode out of the canteen.

'Nice talking to you too, Nicole,' McKay muttered after her.

Before her fall from grace at Hammersmith, Nicole had vis-ited the police morgue in Horseferry Road a number of times and always found it enjoyable. There was something comforting about the quiet determination with which the staff went about their business. Although the facility, attached to the Westminster Public Mortuary, was officially called the Iain West Forensic Suite, it was known in the force simply as the morgue. Several times it had crossed Nicole's mind that she should have made the effort to gain a medical qualification and found work there.

The facility had a CCTV viewing area with a live link to the post-mortem room so investigating officers could watch forensic pathologists at work. Nicole's preference was to be in the room with the pathologist but most of them refused her on the grounds that she was a distraction.

The one exception was Jacobs, who had taken a shine to her and always allowed her to observe first-hand. The staff at the morgue were the best in their field, but as far as she was concerned Saul Jacobs was unparalleled. He was an artist. His dissection skills were second to none and his ability to describe his work with clinical accuracy, impressive. Nicole knew it was this last skill with which she would have struggled.

The pathologist informed the front desk that DI Parry should join him and that she knew the way. As she came in, he looked up from a corpse, slipped his mask from his face and greeted her warmly.

'Nice to see you, Nic. Getting ready for the Christmas break?'

'You too, Saul, and no, I don't do Christmas.'

Saul smiled. 'Funny, that; neither do I.'

She kissed him affectionately on the cheek. He was one of the few people who called her Nic. She hated diminutives but, as she had once told him, Nic was fine – Nicky never.

Saul nodded down at the slab. 'Meet Rosencrantz – real name unknown – a fascinating chap with an unfortunate habit of running into sharp objects. Twenty-two times at last count. There's determination for you.'

Jacobs, now in his sixties, was a short, rotund individual who always reminded Nicole of a male version of those Russian dolls, the *babushkas* that were sold as souvenirs. Since they had last met, she observed that the few remaining strands of hair had departed.

'How did you go with Abhorson?' Nicole asked. Saul had the quirky habit of giving unidentified corpses random names from Shakespeare. She didn't know a thing about Shakespeare but Saul had explained that Abhorson was the executioner in *Measure for Measure*.

Saul chuckled. 'Fascinating. It turned out it was a little sexual game that went wrong. There was, alas, no joy in his end. He hung himself without achieving his goal. No secretion, sadly.'

'I wanted to ask you about the girl in the boat.'

'Ah, Eleanor, Duchess of Gloucester,' he saw the frown on Nicole's face and added, 'the wife of Humphrey, Duke of Gloucester in *Henry Sixth, Part Two*. Eleanor dabbles in witchcraft with disastrous results.'

According to the pathologist, the scene had been extremely strange, verging on the bizarre. 'It was like something from a medieval fantasy movie,' Saul said. He rummaged in a filing cabinet, retrieved two photographs and slid them to her over the marble-topped morgue table. 'I shot these before... well, you know.'

Nicole took out her glasses and examined the first photograph carefully.

It was a wide-angle shot of the area, taken from the footpath above the river. The boat was clearly visible, stuck, as the report said, on the mud. There were two sets of footprints in the silt – DI McKay and his partner, she surmised.

The woman was not visible, masked by the high side of the boat.

Nicole turned her attention to the second photograph. It was a close-up showing the prone woman with her head towards the prow. Nicole guessed that the woman was probably in her early thirties. Not certain of her own judgment, she asked Saul.

'Between thirty-one and thirty-five, I would say,' he shrugged, 'I'm usually pretty accurate but with a margin of error, of say, two years at the top end.'

'You mean up to thirty-seven?'

He nodded.

Her face was pretty, Nicole thought, and then corrected herself; striking, not pretty. The woman's skin was extremely pale, as though never exposed to the sun. Alabaster was the word that sprang to mind. High cheekbones, small nose, almost snub. The most noticeable feature apart from the nakedness was her hair; straight, waist-length and, Nicole guessed, natural blonde. As DI McKay had said, the hair was brushed and neatly spread down the side of her torso. The breasts showed no sign of implants. Average size, firm... Probably not had a child, Nicole guessed. Small nipples, lightly ringed in deep pink. In the photograph the woman's pubic hair appeared light and downy. Cut short, trimmed, or maybe growing back? She pointed to something green beside the body.

'What's that?'

'Mmm, it's a bunch of twigs and leaves. They were tied at the stem. Could have been intended as a wreath, or maybe part of the ritual or whatever it was.'

Nicole took the photographs. 'I'll keep these.'

Saul shrugged. 'Why not? The case is closed. I take it you are sniffing around as usual.'

'I'm interested in what happened next and why it was never resolved.'

'Sure.'

'So, what happened?'

'There was nothing I could do without getting into the boat, so I had to wait while we put some sheeting down. Then we decided to pull the boat further up onto the bank in order to stabilise it. But one of the planks she was resting on must have shifted and she rolled off. The forensic team put a plastic sheet over as much of the boat as they could and I climbed in to examine her. As I did, I heard something. I'm used to the gurgling and whistling that corpses make, but I have never heard anything like that. It was a distinct cough. She had rolled onto her stomach and the jolt must have dislodged something. In any case, what I heard was a cough. Then, again to my surprise, she vomited. I crouched down beside her and turned her head. She was breathing. Not well, but enough.'

He paused, thinking, and then continued. 'Oh, and her eyes were dilated. I remember making a stupid joke to DI McKay that he should only call me out for the dead ones. It was a frivolous thing to say given the circumstances, but the woman's coughing had startled me.'

'No sign of bruising or lacerations?'

'Well, I could hardly do an internal, could I? McKay called an ambulance and I wrapped her up in a blanket from the squad car.'

'The report says you accompanied her to the hospital. Why did you do that?'

'Yes. It's odd, but I felt kind of protective towards her. Responsible for her being alive, I guess.'

'Did you talk to her?' Nicole asked.

'All the time, because I was concerned she might lose consciousness again.'

'But according to the report, she didn't say anything.'

Saul shook his head. 'That's not accurate. In fact, she talked all the way to the hospital. She may have told us a lot of things, but unfortunately the language she was speaking wasn't English.'

'What was it?'

'I have no idea. Neither had McKay or the ambulance officers. The same when McKay attempted to interview her at the hospital.

I've listened to the tape. It's possible that it may be a language, but it could just as well be gibberish, or Klingon.'

'What?'

Saul chuckled. 'Sorry, bad attempt at humour.'

Nicole removed her glasses and put them in her jacket pocket. 'What do you think had happened to her?'

'My best guess? I think she was drugged and then someone, probably the same person or persons, attempted to drown her. Somehow didn't die. The vomit was mostly water. And I remember thinking that maybe she had taken or been given something that had slowed her metabolism in some way. I talked with Edward Harris, the doctor who attended her at St Thomas's. He said he was going to do a blood test. Unfortunately, considering what happened next, it was pointless.'

'You never saw her after that?'

'As you know. Sometime during the night she vanished.'

'She discharged herself?'

'No, just disappeared. How she found clothes to wear, I have no idea, but I suspect someone assisted her.'

Nicole pushed her glasses back up her nose and jotted 'Edward Harris' in her notebook. 'Good. I'll talk to the doctor.'

She was at the door when Saul called after her. 'One other thing, Nic.'

'Yes?'

'When she rolled over in the boat, I caught a glimpse of the nape of her neck. She had a tattoo, a small seahorse. It's probably not important.'

'Everything is important,' Nicole said. 'God is in the details.'

'Flaubert? Or was it that architect fellow, Mies van der Rohe?'

Nicole shrugged. 'Heard of the first, but architecture isn't my thing.'

He was about to quip that 'the devil was in the detail', but thought better of it. 'Take care,' Saul called after her, but she had already gone.

Before returning to the crypt Nicole made a detour to visit PC Irene Wallace. Irene, or 'the bag-lady' as she was known, had for many years been in charge of bagging and indexing physical evidence. It was a comfortable niche in the force – a place that kept Irene, who had recently turned fifty, out of harm's way and allowed her to indulge in the great love of her life, an occasional nip of brandy. Irene had never sought promotion and was probably the only truly content person at the station.

She greeted Nicole with a smile. 'Hello, love. What can I do you for?' She handed Nicole a sticky-note pad and a pencil. 'You know the drill. Write it down, love. You know me, by the time I'm down the first aisle, I'll have forgotten it.'

Nicole wrote down the file number and handed it to Irene. 'I just need to take a look and check that everything on file is there.'

'So they still have you down in the crypt?'

'Out of sight, out of mind,' Nicole replied flatly.

'Just how I like it, love.' Her face, leathery from too much drink and too many cigarettes, cracked into another smile. She gestured to a bench against the wall. 'Pull up a pew, I won't be a jiffy.'

When she returned, Irene came around her counter, seated herself on the bench and placed two bags between them. 'Here you go.'

Nicole could smell the brandy on her breath. 'Thanks.'

The first bag contained a small duck-egg blue pillow. Nicole examined it carefully but could see nothing to distinguish it from any of millions that were, like it, 'Made in China'. There was a zip on one side and the stuffing was the normal artificial type. Still, she took it out.

'Nothing there,' Irene shook her head.

Nicole turned her attention to the second bag.

'Silver birch,' Irene said as Nicole pulled out a dried bunch of leaves and twigs. They were in a transparent plastic bag and most of the leaves had fallen off since they were bagged. The branches were all tip ends and were held together by having had one of the branches bent back and cleverly braided around the other twigs. It must have been done while they were still green, she concluded. Nothing special. Nicole peered at the leaves, some of which now had mould on them. 'Are you sure they're silver birch?'

'Same as in my garden, love,' she chuckled. 'At least they were. More like compost now.'

Nicole frowned. It was hard to imagine Irene being anywhere but here. The notion of her having a life in the outside world felt slightly odd. 'Well, that wasn't much.'

'Were you looking for something special?' Irene took out a cigarette, peered into the now empty packet, crumpled it and tossed it over her counter onto the floor.

'No. It's a nothing case. But I just wanted to see for myself.'

Irene, with complete disregard for regulations, lit her cigarette and then put the pillow back in the bag. She took the disintegrating bunch of twigs and was about to slip it into the bag when she stopped, reached in and produced a small manila envelope. 'Ah, hidden treasures!' she exclaimed and handed it to Nicole.

Inside was a CD. Someone, probably DI McKay, had used a marker pen to write *L.L. Interview*.

'L.L.?' Irene asked.

'It was a joke in the incident room. They thought the victim was dead, and called Dr Jacobs. It turned out she was alive so they called her "Lady Lazarus".'

'Funny. What was the crime?'

'That's the problem, there really wasn't one; attempted murder maybe. The woman vanished before she could be questioned.'

'So, what's on the CD?' Irene flicked her ash on the floor and scattered it with her foot.

'That's what I'd like to find out. May I borrow this?'

'No problem, love. You'll have to sign for it, though.'

'Of course.'

'Bloody bureaucracy.'

Back in the crypt, Nicole phoned St Thomas's and asked to speak to Dr Edward Harris. He was not available, so she left her mobile number and a request that he should phone her back.

For a while she sat, staring at the computer. Letting her mind wander. Eventually it struck her that there was something else about the case that was peculiar. The initial call was unusual. A majority of calls came through on 999. How did the person who reported seeing the woman in the boat happen to know the number of the direct line to the CID switchboard? She filed the question away in her mind. There was something else, but no matter how hard she tried she couldn't recall it. Let the little men look after it, she thought. It was a game her mother had taught her.

'You never forget anything,' her mother had said. 'It's just that sometimes it is difficult to recall what you want. So that's when you tell the little men to go search in the files while you get on with something else.'

It always worked. She would send mental filing clerks off to search for the lost memory and nine times out of ten they would pop up with the answer. Hopefully they would be hard at work while she listened to the CD.

Nicole slid the CD into her computer and waited for it to load. There was only a single MP3 file marked 'LL' – Lady Lazarus, again. Silly joke. She downloaded the file to her desktop and then removed the CD and placed it back in the manila envelope. She made a mental note to return it to the bag lady in the morning. She put on her headphones and clicked play.

'Can you tell us what your name is?'

The voice was that of DI McKay.

There was no response and he repeated the question.

This time the woman responded, but what she said was a series of sounds slurred together, rather than words. Or, if there were words in what she was attempting to say, Nicole couldn't recognise them. Gibberish, maybe, as Saul Jacobs had hinted.

'Do you know where you are?' McKay asked.

Again, the woman responded, but once again it was an unintelligible babble of sounds. This time she went on for several minutes.

Nicole thought she heard some sounds repeated, so she replayed the section several times. Yes, there were definable sounds, but she couldn't be certain whether they were words or simply nonsense; and if they were words, she couldn't determine where they began or ended. Maybe it was glossolalia, speaking in tongues. It was a possibility if she had been drugged. On the other hand, maybe she was psychotic.

'It doesn't make any sense to me,' said a voice in the background she recognised as that of Saul Jacobs.

'What is your name?' McKay spoke very slowly, enunciating every syllable carefully. He sounded like a parent talking to a recalcitrant child.

This time the woman's reply was more animated. Nicole sensed that she was frustrated by people's inability to understand her.

The woman made the same series of sounds and then stopped.

'We'll leave it there,' DI McKay said and the recording ended.

The entire thing was less than six minutes. Six minutes of nothing.

Nicole decided she would listen to it again at home so she emailed herself a copy of the file. She switched off her computer, pocketed her glasses and put on her coat. It was after seven and she hadn't eaten since before lunch. Time to go, she decided, and was about to turn off her desk lamp when her mobile rang.

'Edward Harris,' said a deep well-polished voice. 'You left a message.'

'DI Parry, Hammersmith CID,' Nicole said, and sat down again.

'What can I do for you, Detective?'

'Do you remember attending a young woman found unconscious on a boat in the Thames?'

'A while back? Yes.'

'You took a blood sample.'

'Yes, but she discharged herself, or something. No. She vanished. I remember there was a bit of a fuss about it.'

'That's her. What happened to the sample?'

'Nothing, Detective, because by the time the lab results came back she was gone.'

'Do you remember what the results showed?'

'Detective, it was months ago.'

'October the seventh.'

'I'm sorry. I don't recall.'

'Dr Harris, it could be important. Can you find the results and let me know?'

There was a pause and she heard him sigh. 'I can't do it now, but I'll see if my secretary can find them in the morning.'

'That would be a great help.'

She hung up.

It was then that her 'little men' returned with the thought that had been evading her. DI McKay had told her he spent the time waiting for Saul Jacobs by taping off the scene. Then he had said something about keeping the photographers back. Photographers? Did he mean the press? If so, how had they known about it in time to be down on the riverbank even before the pathologist had arrived?

She considered doing a search for media mentions of the case, but hunger intervened and she pushed herself out of the chair and climbed the stairs from the crypt.

'Another productive day, Nicky?' someone called down the corridor.

'The name is Nicole, so fuck off,' she muttered to herself and kept walking towards the exit.

Somehow, distracted by the day's events, she had forgotten it was Thursday, the one day a week she allowed herself takeaway. Turning in her tracks, she detoured to her weekly dilemma – the Lebanese *Taverna* or Golden Fry Fish. She opted for the fish, tucked the food into her backpack and headed for the underground. It was only a one-station hop, but the crowding still managed to annoy her. After spending most of her day alone in the crypt, the press of bodies was the last thing she felt like, so it was with a sense of relief that she got off at Putney Bridge.

The house in Edenhurst Avenue was not something she could have afforded, but her father had purchased it years earlier as a rental property. He had been smart like that. After he died, she and her brother Harry both inherited houses while their mother lived mortgage-free in the family home in Maidstone.

Harry had sold his house immediately and migrated to Australia. For her part, Nicole had removed every trace of the previous tenants and started stripping paint from the walls, with the intention of redecorating. However, the notion of interior design held too many choices, so she abandoned the paint stripping, equipped the house with a few essentials and postponed any further decoration. It was not pretty, but on the positive side, home was only three minutes' walk from Putney Bridge Station via Ranelagh Gardens.

After she had eaten the fish and chips from the box, she vowed never to do so again. It was a vow she made at least twice a fortnight.

Nicole washed the taste down with the dregs of a bottle of white wine and sat gazing at a half-stripped wall, pondering what to do next. She had a vague inkling that sex was on the agenda, but in the end her mind went back to the woman in the boat. Part of her could understand why the case had been dropped. Laziness really. Maybe she had someone help her vanish from the hospital. But it was also possible that she did not go willingly. What it needed was for her body to be discovered, or some explanation of where she was and why she was still alive.

She opened her laptop and downloaded the MP3 file of the interview. Listening to it again, she felt even less convinced that the woman was speaking gibberish. Maybe it was a language? Hindi? Urdu? No, not with that pale skin… Then she thought of Tom Myers. Tom, three years older than her, was an old friend of her brother's. The boys had gone to school together and after Tom had gotten over his disappointment that Harry wasn't gay, he maintained the friendship, but over the years had grown closer to Nicole.

Tom was one of those beings who was a true generalist, a renaissance man. Tom had a head full of amazing facts but early on he turned his back on what could have been a glittering career in academia, and with no real planning developed a voracious appetite for fine food and wine. Currently he lived in a gorgeous thatched cottage in the village of Long Crendon and each day made the thirty-five-minute drive into Oxford in his bright yellow *Deux Chevaux*. His chic gourmet delicatessen was a goldmine that provided him with an enviable party lifestyle and frequent trips to the continent for 'a little bit of foreign fun' as he put it, and to bring back European delicacies. Nicole liked Tom a lot and there were times when she deeply regretted his sexual preference. On those occasions she visualised his body and took care of business herself.

For a moment she considered ringing him but then decided she was too vulnerable for an intimate chat and that it would be difficult to keep it strictly business. She emailed him the file with a request to see if he knew whether it was a language, and if so, which one. Before sending it she changed her mind and suggested she might come visit on Sunday.

Later, she walked around the house trying to decide what colours would best suit her. Eventually she gave up and went to bed. As she fell asleep she tried to visualise the woman in the boat. There was something wrong, but she couldn't pinpoint it, so she sent the 'little men' off to seek it out and promptly fell asleep.

Chapter Two

She dreamed a familiar dream, one that had recurred since she was a teenager. She stood in a misty field, surrounded by ancient trees, their tops shrouded in haze. She was wearing mud-spattered wellingtons, the soil beneath her feet dark and damp with clumps of rich soil and grass greener than anything she had seen in her waking life. The soil smelled so sweet she wanted to bring her face close to the ground and simply inhale the moist air. And then, as she had done in countless dreams before, she walked to the cottage. The rough wooden door opened, spilling warm golden lamplight onto the ground. She went inside, into the comfort of a room that had a different smell. Here she was bathed in reassurance and the smell of smoke from the slow-combustion stove. Also yeast and hot bread… and somewhere someone was sitting in an old armchair beneath an oil lamp. And as in countless dreams before, though she longed to, she could never see their face.

Nicole woke early and with a single thought, not of cottages or mist but of the woman floating down the Thames in the dawn. She dressed, grabbed her phone, keys and bag, and then headed out the door. Instead of making her way to the underground, she walked to the Fulham Railway Bridge. Thankfully, the fog that frequently covered the river had dissipated in a chill breeze and she had an unimpeded view of the river and banks.

How far upstream had the boat been launched, she wondered. It surprised her that there were no other reports of a sighting. She filed away the thought that she must check where such a boat came from, who owned it and where it might have been moored.

Nicole walked to the centre of the pedestrian walkway and then retraced her steps so that she was standing at the closest point on the bridge to the crime scene. Nicole checked the view against Saul Jacob's wide shot of the boat. It was clear that the boat would have been visible from her vantage point, but not the body. In the photograph the boat had sunk in the sludge, but not noticeably tilted to one side or the other.

She looked at the photograph of the body. The woman was deep in the boat. There was no way she could have been seen from the footpath on the bridge. Someone was playing games, she thought, and retraced her steps to the Putney Underground.

Evan McKay had only just sat down at his desk when the phone rang.

'It's Nicole. What time did the call about the woman in the boat come through?'

'Christ, Nicole, why are you still banging on about that?'

'I just need the time, Evan,' Nicole said, wondering why he didn't understand that she was working.

'At about two-thirty or three in the afternoon, I guess.'

'Exactly.'

McKay took a deep breath and reached for his old notebook. 'The case is closed, Nicole.'

'Not anymore.'

'What do you mean?'

'Listen, I need to know –'

'Yes, of course you want to know the exact time. Here, I jotted it down... three-thirteen pm. Okay?'

'Was anything released to the media?'

'No, of course not, as there was no crime, nothing worth talking about. Okay, can I get to work now?'

There was no reply as she had already hung up.

After pulling up the tide times for the Thames she sat and pondered them. A high tide of 4.3 metres had been at 09:53 and the low of 0.1 metres at 15:56. The boat must have been stranded at the point below the bridge for at least an hour and a half. There had been only the police footprints, so it had obviously drifted downstream and become stranded at around two in the afternoon. Nicole jotted down the tide times and then turned her attention to the other quandary. How had the media photographers arrived at the scene so fast?

It only took a few minutes of searching for her to discover that both *The Sun* and *The Mirror* ran with the story. A story they didn't get from the police. The by-line in *The Sun* attributed the report to Gayle Morris, a woman Nicole had met a couple of times. She was a pain to deal with but reasonably friendly if she thought there was a sniff of a story. Nicole rang her and found her in a good mood.

'The mysterious dead girl in the boat? Yes, of course I remember it. There was no follow-up. One afternoon she's there and next thing nobody knows anything about her.'

'Gayle, did you see her yourself?' Nicole asked.

'And get my shoes covered in slime? Not likely. I sent someone from pictorial. Useless git came back with nothing. I couldn't do much with a picture of a boat in the mud, could I? Still, we ran it on the off-chance that the story developed.'

'When you say he came back with nothing, what do you mean? No picture of the boat?'

Gayle snorted. 'Pictures of the boat, like I said, but you couldn't see the supposedly dead woman.'

'Did he try to get a shot from the walkway on the bridge?' Nicole asked.

'Yes, but it was nothing I could run. Really. I mean, I was expecting naked. You know, like nude.'

'Have you still got the photographs?'

Gayle laughed. 'If you have the inside story on this phantom woman, then I have them. If not, I think they just got lost.'

'Gayle, listen. If I find anything substantial, I'll give you a call. That's a promise.'

'Deal. I'll email them this morning.'

'One last thing…'

'Yes.'

'Who told you about the woman in the boat?'

'Nobody I know. It was an anonymous call.'

'To you directly?'

'Actually, yes. It didn't come from the switchboard.'

'What time?'

'Hang on, it's in one of my old notebooks…'

Nicole heard the reporter riffling through a drawer and then flipping through a notepad.

'Here it is. Male voice. Five past three.'

So, Nicole thought, he rang the newspapers before he rang the police to inform them about a dead woman whom he couldn't see and who turned out to be alive.

'Are you still there?' Gayle asked.

'Thanks. I must go.'

Nicole hung up and sat staring up at the little window high in the wall of the crypt. She often did this when she needed to think. It might smell like piss and not let much light in, but once in a while it allowed a little inspiration to waft in from the street above.

The informant, Nicole reasoned, believed the woman in the boat was dead, and clearly wanted others to know. Was that it? He was sending a message, Nicole concluded, but not just to the police. He wanted media coverage. Find the caller and you would probably find the man who had attempted to kill her, and most probably spirited her out of the hospital.

Keep this up, woman, and you'll become a half-decent police officer, she muttered, and decided to reward herself with a coffee and a donut from the canteen.

The canteen donuts, she reminded herself as she returned to her computer, were like sex; great while anticipating, less so participating and – she reached for a tissue – leave you feeling sticky and vaguely queasy. She knew that was a description of bad sex, but there seemed no other variety on offer in the last few months. She wiped the sugar from her mouth, rolled the tissue into a ball, and flicked it accurately into the wastebasket. 'Goal,' she said out loud.

She avoided work for a few more minutes, making a detour into her own mail account. Tom Myers had replied to her email and was all 'a-tizz with excitement' about her visit on Sunday and, yes, he had found the perfect person to contact about the strange language on the file Nicole had forwarded. He signed off with a whole row of coloured emoticons – hearts, faces with sunglasses and, for some obscure reason, a crab-like thing with tiny claws that opened and shut.

Nicole flicked back a reply with a smiley face emoticon beside her name. Childish, she thought, a little too late. Sent is sent. Her brother had introduced her to Gmail and pointed out that there were a few seconds after clicking 'Send' when you could retrieve the email. Never mind, she consoled herself, Tom would probably love the smiley face.

The photographs Gayle had emailed from *The Sun* showed Nicole exactly what she had surmised; the woman's body had not been visible from the bridge. She scribbled some notes and decided to let her mind mull over things while she went back to her routine filing of old cases.

Her resolve didn't last very long before she found herself going over every detail again, but although everything she knew pointed to attempted murder, she knew it would need more if she had to justify opening the case again.

At four-fifteen her phone rang.

'You wanted to know about the blood sample on the unknown woman?'

Nicole mouthed the word *hallelujah*. 'Thank you, Doctor Harris, that would be very helpful.'

'I'm not so sure.' He paused, cleared his throat and then continued. 'Only traces, I'm afraid. But indications of a cocktail of drugs we can't identify.'

'What can you identify?' Nicole asked, trying not to sound impatient.

'Alcohol, propranolol hydrochloride and scopolamine are definite. But there are indications of other drugs. Not recreational ones. Given her condition at the time the sample was taken, I suspect there were also benzodiazepines, including flunitrazepam; but if so, they cleared from the system.'

'Why?' Nicole asked herself.

'What?'

'Sorry, I was talking to myself. Why would she have been given a cocktail of drugs like that?'

There was another pause.

'Doctor Harris?'

'Professionally, there is no way I can answer that...'

'But?'

'But to hazard a guess, I would say that whoever gave her the drugs did not do so with the specific aim of killing her, but more likely it was an attempt at rudimentary brainwashing. The probable outcome of such a drug regimen is likely to be amnesia. Also, her respiration would have been repressed which, interestingly, was a factor that may have saved her life.'

'How?'

'If someone attempted to drown her, the victim's shallow breathing could have been such that they might have thought she was already dead. And she would not have gulped for air as a fully active person might.'

'You think that is what happened?'

'You're the detective.'

'Maybe the drugs didn't do the job that was intended and so drowning was …' Nicole realised she had run out of thoughts. 'Sorry, one last question. You say there was no trace of flunitrazepam?'

'No. If they were given to her at an earlier stage, then they would have been untraceable within a matter of a few hours.'

'Just checking, Doctor, but isn't flunitrazepam the same thing as Rohypnol, the so-called date-rape drug?'

'Yes. But it doesn't deserve the name.'

'Why?'

'Check the statistics, Detective. The actual number of cases is minuscule. It's an urban myth and probably also an excuse for an alcohol-induced lack of judgment.'

'You mean sex?'

'I can see why you became a detective.' His laughter was friendly, not malicious.

'There is no chance the woman gave herself the drugs?'

'Self-administered? In order to do what? She ran a huge risk of chronic amnesia and a handful of other complications. Was this a suicide attempt? Definitely not.'

'Doctor Harris, thank you,' Nicole said, and meant it.

'My pleasure,' the doctor replied, then added, 'I'll send you a copy of the report. Good luck with getting to the bottom of it.'

I'll need more than luck, Nicole thought as she replaced the receiver. First, she needed to convince the Chief Super that there was still a case to investigate. Chief Superintendent Andrew Crawford had a reputation for good management and sticking to the letter of the law, though on the odd occasions, when officers under him had achieved results by non-conventional means, Crawford was first in line to congratulate them on their creative approach. Nicole rated her chances of convincing him as less than 50/50. I need something else, she thought. Maybe Tom Myers would have had some thoughts about the MP3 file she had sent. Suddenly impatient, she wished she had told him she would come on Saturday rather than Sunday.

Emerging from the crypt, she made her way up the stairs to the Chief Super's office. Fortunately, he was still at work, clearing his desk for the weekend. He gestured for her to sit and then listened as she detailed the information she had accumulated.

'I'm sorry, Nicole, but there is nothing in what you have to justify further investigation.'

'But –'

'Let me finish. I can see how it appears, but I cannot simply allocate resources that I don't have.'

Crawford's tone was friendly, but firm. The way he treated her had always been polite, just like my father, she thought. I'm a little girl and he is a grown-up.

'I'm not talking about resources. There's something strange about the case and I'm happy to work on it myself.'

Crawford shook his head. 'You have never lacked enthusiasm or talent, Nicole, but sometimes we simply have to have our priorities right.'

'Like keeping me locked away in the crypt?' she said a little too sharply. It came out before she could censor herself.

Crawford frowned. 'Listen, I'll see what I can do about that. But in the meantime, do the work, put in the hours and leave decisions about reopening cases to me.'

Crawford's response had been what she expected and part of her knew he was right. Still... she dismissed the topic and spent half an hour filing away the week's work. It didn't amount to much, but she offered herself the excuse that she had been distracted. The case was closed. The woman in the boat would float off into the mist and… Nicole looked at the open file on her screen. The file was still marked open. The right thing to do was change it back to archive status. On Monday, she told herself, after I see Tom Myers. She had also intended to return the CD to Irene Wallace, but that would have to wait as well.

Finally, around six-thirty, she switched off her computer. It was Friday night, and she realised she was feeling 'twitchy' and that it needed attending to. Nicole caught the Tube home, changed into her 'hunting gear' – short skirt and low-cut blouse. She glanced out the window and decided that she would also need a coat and umbrella. Then she headed to the Eight Bells.

After seven on a Friday night was officially the weekend, two hours into the weekend. All over the Babylon-on-Thames, the lights were going out. Filing cabinets were locked, combinations were set on the vaults, pot plants watered and offices empty of all but rostered staff. Quentin Grammaticus was not rostered on. He did not do weekends; did not approve of them. They were a complete waste of time and caused more problems than they were worth. Problems didn't take a weekend off. In fact, in his experience, weekends were when problems raised their grubby little heads. He glanced over his desk at Mitchell, who *was* rostered on. People like him needed a roster. Annoying little chap. Too damned handsome for his own good and with a reputation for being a bit of a lady's man. Irritating. Grammaticus rearranged the pencil and pen on his desk. He liked them just so, at thirty degrees. It looked neat; evidence of a tidy mind.

Chris Mitchell knew better than to say anything, so he stood quietly waiting for Grammaticus to honour him with a few words. Finally, his boss deigned to speak.

'Reclassified? Is that what you are saying?'

'Yes, sir.'

'I was assured that it was buried, archived.'

'It was, sir, but then someone changed its status. Luckily we had a silent flag on it...'

'Flags are not silent, Mitchell. They are invisible.'

'What I am saying is that the change of status came up as an alert.'

'I do know how the system works,' Quentin said.

'Of course, sir. What would you like me to do?'

Go away, Quentin thought, take yourself out of my office. No, throw the poor bastard a crumb. 'Good work, that. Attention to detail. The stuff on which we thrive, right?' He beamed convincingly. 'Now, I'll let you in on a little secret.'

'Sir?'

'A drill, Mitchell, it was just a little drill to make sure that a chap is on the ball. You passed with flying colours.'

'Thank you, sir.'

'What do I want you to do? I'll tell you what. Forget about the entire thing and don't mention it to anyone. I might want to test out some of the others.' He tapped the side of his nose, in what he imagined was a conspiratorial manner. 'Our secret, Mitchell.'

'Exactly, sir.'

'Now, be a good chap and see if you can rustle up some half decent tea.'

It was Mitchell's turn to beam.

'Right away, sir.'

Quentin watched him leave and then got to his feet and crossed to the window. The Thames was pretty enough with the lights reflecting in the water. The weather was foul. Scudding clouds, and rain showers visible in the lights on Vauxhall Bridge. Little people scuttled on slick pavements, plastic bags were sailing aloft, and in the middle of the bridge an umbrella blown inside out by the wind was dragging someone behind it. Quentin had no affection for little people, but he did take his job seriously – the task of keeping them safe from whatever might threaten their little lives.

He didn't categorise the Metropolitan Police as 'little people', but that didn't stop them being annoying. Quentin waited until Mitchell had delivered his tea. It needed a couple of minutes to cool, so he checked the time and, with the door shut, rang Crawford on his home number. In his experience an official call at home had more impact than one to a person's office where they were surrounded with their trappings of power. At home they were more vulnerable, more susceptible. Voices had to be kept hushed so that spouses or offspring couldn't overhear. For maximum impact, he believed a call to a person's home was best. Tone was important. Firm but affable; that was suitable, he decided. Yes, he would be affable.

'Andy! Quentin Grammaticus.' He didn't pause to let Crawford collect his thoughts. 'Little problem in your department, sorry to say.'

'Really? Look, surely it can wait until Monday,' Crawford interjected. 'I was about to sit down to...'

'Seems one of your bobbies has been poking around things best left alone.'

'I'm sure there is a good reason.'

'Oh, sure to be. But the thing is that no reason is good enough. Sleeping dogs and all that.'

'All right, hang on a moment, I'll go into my study and ring you back.'

Crawford sounded peeved, resentful. Perfect, Quentin thought. 'Fine, you do that.'

He hung up and took a sip of his tea. Mitchell had it about right. Not brewed too long and just the right dash of milk. Maybe he had underestimated the chap. He made a mental note to keep a close eye on him.

He let the phone ring five times and then picked up.

'Sorry, Andy, things are frantic here at the moment,' he said with just the right dose of exasperation.

'What's the problem, Quentin?'

'Ah, that's what I would like to know. You see, when a file is marked "archived", I trust your people to respect that. Of course, we could barge in and requisition anything sensitive, but frankly that would be an awful bother.'

'And highly questionable,' Crawford interjected.

Quentin sensed that Crawford needed more of a nudge. He switched from affable to professional mode. 'Listen, Andy, a file we had flagged as sensitive has popped up on our screens as being activated again. The change was made from a computer terminal at CID Hammersmith. The terminal is in the basement area your people charmingly call the crypt, and the detective involved is –'

'– DI Nicole Parry,' Crawford interjected. 'And before we discuss her, I want to register my objection to you tampering with or having anything to do with our IT systems. It is untenable that the Metropolitan Police should have to work with you looking over their shoulder.'

'Nobody is spying on the police, Crawford. But the case in question has far wider ramifications than simple police work.'

'And I suppose I am to accept that on face value and ask no questions?'

'*Auctoritas non veritas facit legem*, Superintendent, and I have the authority. You will close this down and send all relevant documents, physical evidence and anything else even remotely related to the case to Vauxhall Crossing by nine o'clock tomorrow morning. Then you will make certain that every computer record is wiped clean. Do I make myself clear?'

That was too much for Crawford and he made no attempt to hide his anger. 'Since when did you and your spooks at SIS tell my people what to do?'

Quentin let the question hang in the air as he took a sip of his tea. Then he switched back to affable. 'And Andy, keep an eye on that hoyden Parry, as we certainly shall.' He ended the call before Crawford could respond. The tea was now a perfect temperature so he swung his chair around to face the window and watched the rain lashing the glass. Not a nice night to be out but someone would have to. He buzzed for Mitchell.

'Two busy nights ahead, I'm afraid. But nothing is too much for keen chaps, eh?'

Mitchell wondered what he was letting himself in for, but nodded enthusiastically. 'No, sir.'

'A spot of surveillance and a little cleaning job may be in the offing. Tell the boys and girls to take their umbrellas and to rug up. It's beastly out.'

'And the job, sir?'

'Just get them assembled, Mitchell, and I'll brief them in an hour.' He was about to dismiss Mitchell when he had a thought. 'Wait.' The man had made decent tea, was always on call and seemed to share his distaste for weekends. Why not give him a bit of a run in the field? Not with the rest of the team, of course. New parts were never a perfect fit. But there was something. 'Mitchell, have you got a car?'

'Yes, sir.'

'Good man. Listen, we are stretched for resources on this, so if you would be happy to use your vehicle, then I have an assignment that is of vital importance. A job in the field.' He loaded the word with as much gravitas as he could. 'And this stays just between you and me.' He peered at Mitchell. The man was already standing taller, puffing up. 'Of course, the petrol will be on the firm. Okay?'

'Not a problem, sir. What is it you need done?'

'A spot of surveillance tonight and tomorrow.' He slid a file over the desk. 'All you need to know is in here.'

'Thank you, sir.'

'Keep an eye on comings and goings and report back Sunday morning. One important thing...'

'Sir?'

'No matter what you see, there is to be no intervention of any kind, understood?'

'Crystal clear, sir.' Mitchell tried not to let his enthusiasm spill over.

'Oh, and Mitchell, do rug up. It's beastly cold outside.'

She always enjoyed the Eight Bells and rated it her second most favourite pub in London. Not that she was a pub girl. The Bells was handy to home and normally full of an interesting mix of people. However, when she walked in she discovered it unusually quiet for a Friday night. The fact that Christmas decorations were already up was vaguely depressing. The upside was that Nicole had no trouble finding a seat with a view of the bar and as far from the flat screen TV as was physically possible.

By the time Nicole had removed her coat, chatted with the barmaid, Susan, and started sipping a half pint of London Pride, the Bells was warming up. Quite a few more people had scuttled in to escape the rain, and the noise level was now thankfully high enough to drown out the football on Sky TV.

Most of the people around the horseshoe-shaped bar she recognised as locals; there were a couple of football fans, a group of retirees and office girls from along Fulham Road. There were a few men she didn't recognise, including a couple of suits from the city. She wondered why they had picked the pub. Maybe the weather had blown them in. They and the Eight Bells were not a natural fit, because no matter how much you massaged it, the word *chic* was never going to fit the Eight Bells.

Yet, there was an eccentric and nostalgic charm about the old newspaper prints on the walls, the red rowing sculls hanging from the ceiling and the infamous carpet that contributed to the atmosphere. The carpet was something else. As one slightly inebriated soul had confided in her, the carpet was older than Stonehenge and had been soaking up spilled drinks since the days of the Druids. The only two people who appeared to value its alcoholic history were Nicole and the current manager. To everyone else it was simply 'that horrid carpet'. One thing everyone agreed on was that the Bells would not be the same without it.

'Buy you another?'

Nicole looked around to see a man smiling. He was tallish, maybe five-eight, wearing a mildly flashy Italian-style shirt but no tie. A black corduroy jacket was slung over one arm. Smart casual, she decided, a professional, but not a suit. His jeans didn't really go with the shirt, but she was in no mood to be picky. One of his expensive-looking leather shoes had recently strayed into a puddle. Nice smile, she thought, and smiled back.

'That's kind of you.'

He nodded, flashed her another smile and tossing the jacket on the seat opposite, turned and pushed through a gap in the now crowded bar.

Nicole watched him, reassessing her first impression. From behind the bar, Susan greeted him warmly. So he was a regular,

Nicole decided, and definitely a prospect. As he came back with the drinks she noted that while the jeans might have been a little too casual for the shirt, they fitted him extremely well.

It took two more beers and a shared plate of rather good pub food for her to decide that he would be fine. They had chatted in a relaxed manner and he hadn't raised an eyebrow when she told him what she did for a living. It was strange how the word 'police' could make even innocent people nervous. The thought flashed through her mind that the guilty ones had learned to hide their nervousness. She dismissed it. Everything was good. He was a man, he was good-looking, well-built, his name was Toby, he was an architect and, while she reminded herself that it was not her thing, there was nothing weird about him, nothing that she couldn't handle.

So as not to appear hasty or needy, she let the conversation meander along. When she did raise the subject, he agreed to her suggestion that he accompany her home for a nightcap.

He was good company, she decided as they walked to her house. There was something about unlocking the door and letting him in that changed the chemistry. They reached for each other at the same time and suddenly all thought of a nightcap was forgotten.

As it transpired, he was just what she needed and, judging by his noisy enthusiasm, she was just what he had needed as well.

When she awoke in the morning her twitchiness had gone, and so had he.

Chapter Three

After showering and eating the remnants from the bottom of an old packet of muesli, Nicole wandered around the house in another attempt to make up her mind about the colours she needed. In one corner she discovered the pile of items she had picked up from a hardware shop: tins of undercoat, sandpaper, scraping tools and two different sizes of paintbrushes. The optimistic mood she had felt when she purchased them had long since evaporated and now they just looked like reminders of how much more there was to do before she could even begin to contemplate colour.

She returned to the kitchen and pondered her next move. Her pragmatic side was urging her to don overalls and make some progress on the walls. She put it on hold while she made coffee.

Outside the weather had cleared and though it looked chill, there was no sign of rain. Not for at least an hour, she told herself. Then sensing that a day of decorating was all too much, she dressed and, grabbing her coat just in case, locked the house and got into her car. Sunday was too far away and she really wanted to talk to Tom. Being Saturday, he would be in Oxford at the shop; but sitting around chatting in between customers seemed preferable to stripping paint and waiting for it to start raining again.

It was as she started the car that she remembered that just before she went to sleep in his arms, Toby had mumbled something encouraging about her house.

'The half-stripped walls look really funky.'

She smiled at the memory. He was right, and after all, he was an architect, so he should know.

Nicole took the M4 and M25 route out of London and by the time she merged into the M40 it was still not quite ten o'clock. It had been a while since her old Saab had been taken for a decent run. Her father had always said that a car was like a dog; it needed to be taken out on a regular basis. How he had known that she never worked out, given that he had neither car nor dog. Yet from the moment she bought her first car, a third-hand Mini, he had been a constant source of mechanical advice. God knows where he picked it up.

Between London and Oxford there had only been a few minutes of rain. It was only a sprinkling but enough to remind her that the wiper blades needed changing and she needed detergent in the washer-water. Sorry, Dad, I forgot to check. She pulled down the sunvisor and grinned at herself in the mirror. Took myself out for a decent run last night, she mused. Maybe she would look Toby up again.

With a head full of pleasant distractions, the journey was enjoyable, and after arriving in Oxford in under an hour and a half, she had a momentary flirtation with the idea of simply keeping driving for a while. The decision was taken out of her hands by the sight of Tom's *Deux Chevaux* and the rare discovery of a parking space less than one hundred yards from his shop – *La Petite Épicerie*.

Tom Myers had never intended to end up running a gourmet delicatessen. His previous ventures – a combined bookstore and coffee shop and at another time a tiny French restaurant – had all run into a brick wall labelled reality. Loving rare books and coffee didn't attract enough people, and his restaurant couldn't seat enough patrons to make it worthwhile. In the end he opted for providing the ingredients and letting other people cook. Even the deli had begun badly. The original name, *L'Épicerie Peu*, had people either bemused or making crude jokes about 'spicy poo', or worse, 'pissy poo'. Now *La Petite Épicerie* was simply known by non-Francophone locals as 'Tom's Deli'.

It was fortunate that there were no customers in the shop as Nicole entered to the jangling of the small brass bell above the door. Tom gave a shriek of delight and glided from behind a beautifully arranged display of multi-coloured French *macarons*. For a big man, he moved gracefully, without effort, like a dancer. Though only thirty-six, his hair had turned prematurely grey, but he was one of those men for whom it simply made them look distinguished. His body was fit and healthy, with a still boyish, almost too perfect face. The same face that had fuelled her teenage fantasies, sadly to no avail.

'*Chéri*! Nicole! Nicole! *Quelle bonne surprise*!'

She managed to squeeze out a 'hello', before she was kissed on both cheeks and then lifted from her feet in an affectionate bear hug.

'You wicked thing! You look stunning. By the look of those cheeks you've been up to all kinds of naughtiness.'

'Sorry I am a day early...' she gasped as he set her back on her feet. 'And I'm not telling you a thing about what I have been up to.'

'Never say sorry for visiting me, *chéri*, you are *un rayon de soleil*!'

'I take it that is a good thing to be,' Nicole laughed.

'*Absolument*! We can have lunch. It's perfect. My tawdry little plans have all gone topsy-turvy anyway. I have a friend coming from Marseilles. It was to have been today, but the silly boy got side-tracked somewhere, so *aujourd'hui est parfait*.'

The doorbell jangled and Nicole was relieved to see two women come in. She had forgotten just how ebullient Tom could be when he was in top form. To be taken in small doses, she decided. Have lunch, talk about the file she had sent him and then head back to London.

The shop was busy over the next hour and for most of the time Nicole was content to sit watching a passing parade of shoppers, all of whom seemed intent on finding the most obscure ingredients. And, with Tom's charm and persuasion, almost every customer left the shop with far more than they had originally intended. The *macarons* she had noticed earlier were popular, but so too was a range of so-called Tibetan salt. It came in several varieties and colours, though most customers hedged their bets and took the mixed selection of pale cream and pink crystals.

'Crystal Balance Himalayan salt,' Tom said in a whispered aside to Nicole, 'it's really only clever marketing of rather impure halite from Pakistan. God knows what it has in it, iron oxide probably, but people swear to me they can taste the difference.'

That's why she liked him; he knew obscure stuff; stuff she didn't. 'Halite?'

'Common rock salt. You would be surprised the number of people who have bought it as Christmas presents for their gourmet friends.'

'And people pay more for it?'

'*Chérie,* you would not believe how much. The more expensive it is, the more popular. Salt from Timbuktu, Dead Sea salt and rare Persian Blue Diamond salt. I have the lot.'

'You made that last one up!'

'You think so?' He spun around, took a packet from the shelf and handed it to her. 'A little present, darling, and do read what it says on the label. It's a hoot!'

'Persian Blue Diamond has a confident taste that gently enhances the flavour of all dishes. Oozing sophistication and steeped in luxurious tradition, Persian Blue has always been sought after, and valued for its good looks and fine taste. A very rare breed of salt that is cautious at first, but delicious when tamed.' Nicole shook her head in disbelief. 'Who makes up the nonsense?'

Tom rolled his eyes. 'Gorgeous, isn't it – delicious when tamed – God help me, it is just halite.'

It was another hour before they could escape for lunch. Nicole had just got to the point of thinking that she had had enough. It was time to go before she arrested one of the middle-aged women simpering around Tom for the sheer pleasure of it. Fortunately, there was a lull and to her relief Tom winked at her, tossed a few provisions into a wicker basket and shooed her out the door.

'Where are we off to?'

'*Chez moi, Chérie. Suivez la petite bête jaune.*'

She punched his arm. 'Idiot! I don't speak Swahili!'

'Follow Fifi.'

'Tom!' She hit him again, only harder.

'Sorry. Follow my car. We're going home, I have something special to show you.'

Following Fifi was not difficult. Tom drove sedately and every few minutes he waved from the window. He's such a boy, she thought, thank God he never grew up.

Lunch turned out to be a gourmet affair, washed down with a bottle of very acceptable French rosé. When Nicole tried to talk about the case, Tom dismissed the subject. 'I've sent off an email with a copy of the MP3 to a friend who's a linguist. Don't fret, I'll let you know if anything turns up.' He grinned. 'Now tell me all about your love life.'

When they had finished eating and gossiping, he got to his feet, suddenly impatient to show her whatever it was he had hinted at back in Oxford. Warning her to duck under the old oak beams, he took her through a narrow door into a small room that reeked of turpentine. A couple of fresh canvases were stacked beneath a large bay window and in the centre of the room sat two wooden stools, and a large cloth-covered easel. Tom went straight to the easel.

'*Voilà!*' He made an extravagantly theatrical gesture and with a sweep of his hand pulled off the cloth. 'My latest work.'

To Nicole's amazement, the painting was superb.

'Your *latest* work?'

'Well, my first since I decided to become an *artiste*.'

'Jesus, Tom! You have always been an *artiste* and I knew you could do most things, but painting? It's not some paint by numbers thing?'

'Oh, ye of little faith! It's all my work and the only numbers involved were the ones I smoked. It's taken weeks. It's for my friend's Christmas present.'

She examined the canvas closely. The subject, presumably Tom's 'friend', a naked young man, draped only with a rough spun-wool blanket, had his head turned partially away. He was seated on a broken stump of a pillar in a ruin. He looked vulnerable, alone. Beyond the ruin, broken dry-stone walls disappeared off into a gloomy barren landscape, a vista bereft of any living thing.

She wasn't sure what Tom had intended to capture, but he had certainly captured something. It felt like loneliness. Nicole found herself surprisingly touched.

'The style…' she began hesitantly.

Tom coughed apologetically. 'Yes, I confess, a lot of Burne-Jones, Rossetti and those other naughty boys. But here is the difference. The style owes heaps to the Pre-Raphaelites, but remember they painted mostly women. Can you imagine a series of Pre-Raphaelite men? This could be a whole new thing.'

'The model?'

'Ah, yes, the divine Angelo? Lost somewhere between Paris and Calais, last I heard. But he promises to do the final sitting tomorrow.'

Nicole stared at the painting, perplexed. 'But it looks finished.'

'*Chérie,* you and I know that, but blissfully, he is unaware.' He looked wistfully at the painting. 'Mind you, I might add a briar rose climbing up a piece of the ruin.'

In a mellow mood, Nicole drove at a leisurely pace and arrived back in London just after six – thankfully too late to do any painting of her own. Having been sitting for most of the day, she decided on a short walk to the off-licence and on the way back bought a pizza. Not gourmet, but simple; *al fungi* with four cheeses. By the time she arrived home again and opened the wine, the four cheeses had melded into one. It needed a little salt and she opened Tom's gift intending to sprinkle a little on the pizza, but the crystals were coarse and would have meant an excursion to the kitchen to get a grinder. She tasted some on her tongue. It seemed as though this jarful had already been tamed. It tasted just like salt.

After she finished the pizza and half of the wine she sat back with a warm glow of contentment. For the first time in weeks she was feeling totally relaxed. The twin tonics of Toby and Tom had been just what she needed.

She made a desultory attempt to read in bed, but the novel, an Icelandic thriller, was either a bad translation or lacked a real plot and characters. In the end she decided it was all of the above and switched off the light.

It had been a good night's work and Quentin, despite having had very little sleep – if a couple of twenty-minute kips on the couch qualified as sleep – was in fine form. At nine in the morning he rallied his boys and girls into his office, greeted them with a beaming smile, and was fulsome in his praise. They had done splendidly. Action had been taken, a message had been sent and in addition, every file that ever existed on the case of the woman in the boat was now little more than a handful of ashes. Computer files had been erased and all the paperwork and a CD with an MP3 file on it, incinerated. And shortly, a certain meddling policewoman would find that her career had ended abruptly. All in all, it was a satisfactory outcome. Having concluded the debriefing, he made the generous suggestion that, since it was Sunday, they join him in a cup of tea and biscuits and then take the rest of the day off.

When his team had left, he called Mitchell in. The man had been sitting in a car all night and looked wrung out.

'It's like climbing Everest, Mitchell,' Quentin said, by way of consolation.

There were times when Mitchell wondered what his boss was on about but he had learned to simply nod and agree. If he said it was like climbing Everest, then it was. Of course, he felt nothing like it. Numb, yes, that would have described how he felt. Hours and hours watching a house in which and around which nothing happened. His only relief had been the very clear view of a couple having boisterous sex against a nearby sycamore tree. At some stage they had fallen to the ground, which necessitated craning his neck. Damn thing was a bit stiff now. But he had found it both enjoying and titillating. The man and woman had gone on for ages and as a connoisseur of such things he admired their staying power and their gymnastics. Finding their performance stimulating, he watched for the entire time. It had been an arousing diversion, which needless to say, he hadn't included in his written report.

'Yes, sir, as you say.'

'Like Everest. Up here we live in a rarefied atmosphere. The Sherpas have done the hard yards and now it's up to us.'

'Sorry, sir...' Now I am numb *and* confused, Mitchell thought. Not a good combination. He decided that capitulation was the best course. 'Like Everest,' he agreed.

'Exactly. We have to struggle on to the summit!' He rewarded Mitchell's look of non-comprehension with a glowing smile.

'And where is that, exactly?'

'At the top!' Quentin gave a braying laugh. 'No. It is time to let you in on a little secret. You see, Mitchell. There is no top. No summit. In our work we just gain a little ground and do what we can. There is no "there" to get.'

Mitchell gave up. 'You're right, sir. Exactly right.'

'So, I want you to collate all the reports from the last few hours.'

'And file them? Already done, sir.'

The smile faded from Quentin's face.

'No, Mitchell, I want them destroyed. Erased.'

Later, after Mitchell had scurried off to perform his task, he stood beside his desk waiting for the red telephone to ring. He let it ring once, then, straightening himself, he picked it up.

'It's all done, Ma'am.'

There was the usual grunt that he had long ago deciphered as a command to continue.

'I believe we will have the situation out of police hands by the end of today.'

'And out of our hands?'

'I understand that is what you requested.'

There was a long silence before she responded.

'Grammaticus. This never happened. No woman, no boat.'

'Understood, Ma'am,' Quentin said.

There was another long silence. Quentin knew better than to hang up. He wondered about her. Wondered what her office was like. Where it was. Wondered if he had ever seen her. There were no photographs, but she must come in and out of the building. Maybe they had shared an elevator at some time. Were others with her? He had pondered these things many times and knew he would never know the answer.

'Grammaticus…'

'Ma'am?'

'We never had this conversation.'

After a moment the line went dead.

He walked to the window. The sun was out. The little people were safe for a while. Yet it irked him that here in Babylon-on-Thames – or Legoland, as some of the plebs in the SIS building called it – there was another office where a woman wielded greater power then he, the *arcana imperii*. But he knew better than to lust for such secret power. It would come to him, because he remembered everything – especially the conversations that never happened.

At just after ten-thirty his phone rang again and his Sunday started to unravel.

The news of subsequent events in Long Crendon spread out like ripples in a pond. Information came to various people at different times. It reached London before the Thames Valley police were aware of anything. Later, from a telephone in Vauxhall Bridge, it reached Chief Superintendent Crawford.

It was inevitable the police would be called, but by the time that was being discussed the news had already reached them. At 09:00 on Sunday morning an anonymous call came in to Patrick Delany, Assistant Chief Constable and head of Operations at Thames Police in Greyhound Lane, Thame. He immediately dispatched a squad car, which took twenty minutes to arrive on the scene and verify the information. At 09:25 Sara Burnside, the Chief Constable, was brought into the loop. Her decision, after inspecting the crime scene, was made at 10:40. This was a local affair, she declared, and required no outside assistance.

Normally the matter would have rested there; the local police would get on with their job and for everyone else life would go on as usual. However, what ensued was far from normal. At 11:00 exactly, Sara Burnside was mildly surprised to receive a call from Chief Superintendent Crawford at Hammersmith. They were old friends, having worked together at the Association of Chief Police Officers committee on Terrorism and Allied Matters and the ACPO Intelligence Portfolio. However, it soon became clear that this was not a social call to renew their acquaintance.

'I'm sorry, Andy, but this case only just landed on my desk at around nine-thirty this morning. How in God's name do you even know about it?'

'We believe it is connected with a case we're working on.'

'That doesn't answer my question.'

'We had some eyes on the ground...'

'In my patch? Without informing me?'

'One of my officers, DI Parry, paid a visit to Long Crendon yesterday. But it's a bit more than that, Sara,' Crawford said as evenly as he could. 'It's sensitive. Way above my league... and yours.'

It was true, and that Crawford didn't like it had no bearing on the matter. His phone had rung at ten to eleven. He had heaved himself off the sofa and dutifully gone to his study and called back.

'If you are reminding me about sending you those files, I'll do it first thing Monday...' he began before Grammaticus interrupted.

'Related matter, I'm afraid, something to get the old heart pumping on a fine Sunday morning.'

Grammaticus sounded alarmingly cheerful. Nobody had the right to sound like that so damn early, Crawford decided. He didn't say anything, but waited for Grammaticus to continue.

'There has been a bit of a disturbance out in the wilds of the Thames Valley. Something I need you to take control of. I would do it myself, but *auribus teneo lupum*, as they say.'

'Sorry, Quentin, the Thames Valley is not my territory.' Damned if he was going to be ordered around by a toffee-nosed spook with a penchant for tossing up obscure Latin phrases.

'Then maybe you can explain why your charming DI Parry is nosing around down there? I hear she was in Long Crendon yesterday afternoon.'

Crawford had had enough of spooks and their silly games and he let it show. 'Quentin, for christsake, it's the bloody weekend. Maybe she was bird watching. If you have something to say, spit it out. Otherwise let me get back to the Sunday papers.'

Quentin was unfazed. 'I can think of nothing that would make me happier than you doing just that. Sadly, the world is all out of kilter. I have a serious problem. So, I'll tell you what you will do. Find that loose cannon Parry, and the two of you get to Long Crendon as fast as you can. The local plods have probably tramped all over the scene, but I would like your expert opinion and your assistance in shutting the whole thing down. Local contact is a friend of yours, I believe. Sara Burnside. I suggest you give her a call.'

Although she hadn't left home until after 10, Nicole had found a space in Truman Brewery car park on Brick Lane and wandered around Spitalfields Market with no aim in mind other than the sheer pleasure of having time to herself. She cruised through the food hall, and though tempted by the Tandoori Hut, decided she would rather go over the road and have a glass of wine at her favourite pub.

While the Eight Bells was handy to her home, her Sunday treat had a couple more bells to its name. The Ten Bells was an old pub that has retained its soul while changing its attire. The original blue and white floral patterned tiling was still intact, though the bar had in recent years moved sensibly to the centre of the pub. Its current landlord, John Twomey, had opened a fine eatery on the first floor and it was here that Nicole enjoyed coming to gaze out over the markets while she dined.

The weekend had been great. The drive to Oxford and seeing Tom had been fun and she still had some sweet images in her head of her night with Toby the architect. She decided to treat herself, so went up to the restaurant, ordered a glass of *Rosé d'Entrevon* and, feeling ravenous, a serving of braised beef shin, celeriac, broccoli and pickled walnuts. Life, she decided, was particularly good.

She was contemplating a second glass of rosé when her phone rang. It was Andrew Crawford.

'Yes, sir?'

'I just sent a car to your house to pick you up.'

'What? I'm not on duty, sir,' Nicole said testily. 'In fact, I'm out having lunch.'

'DI Parry, I don't give a damn what you're doing. Have you got your car?'

'Sir…'

'I want you to drive to Long Crendon as fast as you can. I'll meet you there.'

'Long Crendon? But I just –'

'I know. You were there yesterday.'

'How did –'

'Just shut up and listen. Tom Myers is dead. I'll see you at his house.' He hung up.

For a moment Nicole just sat there, her head spinning. It didn't make sense... Tom dead? It had to be a misunderstanding, but even as she thought it, she knew she was wrong. If the call had come from anyone but Crawford, she might have held out hope that it was a mistake.

In a daze, she got to her feet, paid for the meal and hurried to the car park.

Chapter Four

It appeared so normal. Tom's car was parked in its usual place under the sycamore. The house looked as it had the day before. That was if she could have ignored the crime scene tape around the front of the house, the three squad cars, an ambulance and the old Rover that Chief Superintendent Crawford had been driving for as long as she had known him. Tom is dead. It made no sense, but the phrase repeated and repeated in her head like a mantra. Tom is dead.

Nicole felt sick in the stomach but knew that somehow, she would get through whatever awaited her inside. She went to pull in beside Tom's car but a uniformed policeman signalled for her to move on. She ignored him and parked anyway. Nicole scrambled out of the car, flashed her ID at the policeman and ducked under the tape.

Chief Superintendent Crawford was waiting for her by the door of the cottage.

'Nicole…' he began, but she pushed past him and stepped into the living room.

She took a deep breath and steeled herself. Tom was dead. Tom had been cut down and his body transferred to a stretcher on the floor of the lounge room. The remnants of the rope were still tied to the oak beam in the centre of the room. Beneath it a chair lay on its side. She took in the scene before her but couldn't help seeing the two of them sitting, eating lunch. Laughing. Alive. He had been alive and now… Nicole forced herself to breathe one deep lungful, and then another. She ordered herself to concentrate on her job. The only way to get through this was to switch to professional mode and stay there. There would be plenty of time later to get sad or angry.

A man in a suit and wearing surgical gloves stepped up to her, barring her way. Behind him a woman in civilian clothes was examining the photographs on the mantelpiece. She was not wearing gloves.

'I'm sorry, I'll have to ask you to –' the man began.

'Tell me what happened,' she demanded.

The man looked affronted by her tone. 'And you are?'

Nicole produced her ID again. 'DI Parry, Hammersmith CID. And you?'

'I'm Doctor Mitch Mathews, pathologist.'

He was mid-fifties, balding. He had an air about him of someone used to being in command.

'Well, Doctor Mathews, could you please take me through what you know.'

The pathologist turned to the woman behind him, seeking permission or otherwise. 'Ma'am?'

'Go ahead, Mitch. DI Parry is with Crawford.'

The woman, late forties, her blonde hair cropped, was neatly dressed. She stepped delicately around Tom's body and extended her hand. 'Sara Burnside, Chief Constable.'

Nicole shook her hand. 'DI Parry, Ma'am.' She paused for a second and then gave voice to what had troubled her from the moment she stepped into the room. 'Why is nobody suited up? Or have forensics already cleared the scene? And why were you touching items on the mantelpiece without gloves?'

'No need,' Mathews interjected. 'It is a simple suicide. We estimate the time of death at around three in the morning. There is no crime to investigate and hence no need for pulling a full forensic team off more urgent criminal matters.'

'Suicide is not even a possibility,' Nicole said, a little too vehemently.

The Chief Constable took Nicole's arm and guided her to the side of the room. 'I am so sorry. I understand you knew Tom Myers rather well.'

'Ma'am, I have known him since I was at school. I had lunch with him yesterday.'

'Yes, so I understand. Nicole… can I call you Nicole? This must be very difficult, but I do need to ask. How did he appear to you? Was he depressed?'

Nicole forced herself to remain calm. 'He was very upbeat. We had lunch and chatted as we always do.'

'No mention of problems?'

'Quite the opposite, everything was going well.'

'Some women who had visited his shop in Oxford reportedly said he was over-excited.'

'Ma'am, he was a flamboyant, excitable, gay man with an appetite for the good things in life. It is illogical to think that between my leaving and three in the morning, Tom became suddenly suicidal. In any case he had just completed a painting and was looking forward to showing it to the model sometime today.'

The Chief Constable nodded sympathetically. 'Yes, the painting. I think you should see it.' She gestured for Nicole to follow her and ducked her head beneath the low door leading from the lounge room.

The painting was exactly where it had been the previous day, but in the intervening hours someone had taken a brush, dipped it in vermilion and written across it the words 'I am so sorry'.

'Tom did not do that. Not in a million years,' Nicole said dismissively.

The Chief Constable took her arm again. 'You must be dreadfully upset.'

The consoling tone was too much for Nicole. 'Yes, I'm upset,' she snapped, 'and I'll tell you why. If your people are treating this as a suicide then they have not done their job properly. He was not depressed and would not have defaced the painting. He was immensely proud of it. And Tom would certainly never have hung himself.' She stopped short as she registered what the woman had said. 'And tell me this, Chief Constable, how the hell did you know I was here yesterday?'

'DI Parry, I understand you are dealing with a lot right now, but I will not have you address me in that tone. I'll forget your outburst, but it must not be repeated.' Sara Burnside turned to leave the room and then realised that Nicole was no longer paying attention. 'I suggest you go outside and get some fresh air,' she said brusquely.

Nicole stood transfixed. 'This needs to be bagged,' she said almost to herself.

'What?'

'Has it been moved? Is this where it was?'

Sara Burnside moved past the easel to see what Nicole was referring to. 'I'm sorry, but I don't know what you're talking about.'

'This!' Nicole pointed to the floor at the foot of the easel.

'It is just a bunch of twigs and leaves…'

'It's silver birch.' Nicole squatted down and examined it carefully. 'Bound together by one of the branches being turned back and braided, exactly the same as the one we found in London.'

'I'm sorry. But I have no idea what you are talking about. It is most probably some leaves and so on for a flower arrangement. Maybe he was going to do a still life…'

'With all due respect, that is bloody nonsense. That is exactly the incompetence I'm talking about. Now, make sure it is photographed before its bagged,' she snapped and turned to the door. 'I'm going to look around the house.' I just gave an order to a Chief Constable, she realised. Well, tough. She was in no mood to play diplomatic games.

Sara Burnside was stunned. Nobody had talked to her like that in years. Well, she thought, Parry's a piece of work. It occurred to her that the person she most reminded her of, was herself back in the early days before she started climbing the ranks, before diplomacy became important. Maybe the young woman had a future, but unless she changed her attitude, it would definitely be outside the force.

Nicole spent the next hour going through the house looking at every detail. Tom had slept in his bed. The empty bottle from their lunch was down beside the kitchen tidy. The refrigerator was well-stocked. There was no sign of the basket he had used to carry their lunch from the Deli. Probably back at the shop, she surmised. It was obvious to Nicole that there was not the slightest hint of anything out of the ordinary. That is, if she discounted the bouquet of silver birch, the vandalism to the painting, the rope hanging from the beam and the fact that Tom was dead.

She returned to the living room to find that Tom's body had been removed. Crawford, Mathews and Burnside were in a huddle out beside Tom's car and the other police were preparing to leave. She marched up to the Chief Super.

'Excuse me, sir. A word please?'

Crawford frowned, heaved a sigh and then nodded. 'Alright, but be quick, I need to get back.'

'Sir, this isn't suicide. Not a chance in hell. And more importantly, there is something you should see.'

'I'm afraid we're all done here, DI Parry,' Crawford said with all the patience he could muster.

'There's a bunch of silver birch on the floor beneath the painting. It is exactly the same as the one found in the boat with that woman.'

'Yes, the Chief Constable mentioned it.' He stared at her for a moment. 'DI Parry, I will only say this once, so listen carefully. When I say we are done here, we're done here. This will be recorded as a suicide and that is the end of the matter. I appreciate he was your friend, but you are way out of line. What the bloody hell you were doing here yesterday is your own business. But let me be clear. One more word about this or that damn woman in the boat and you will be facing a charge of insubordination. Believe me, the Chief Constable will take a lot of placating, and at the moment she wants your head on a platter. I hope we understand each other. You are to go home and rest. I will see you in my office at nine on Monday.'

Nicole nodded. She was furious, but held it in. However, instead of going to her car, she stalked off down the road towards the centre of the village. Her mind was racing and she took no notice of where she was going. She just walked.

After a while she came to the village recreation ground, which she recognised from having come with Tom one summer afternoon the previous year to watch a local cricket match. Nicole found a seat and sat down. Her mind felt cold and hard like stone, but tears were running down her cheeks. She allowed herself to cry, but all the time she could feel the anger burning away inside. It was beyond comprehension that nobody seemed to care about finding out what had really happened. It was as though they had conspired to deal with Tom's death as quickly and quietly as possible. She knew she couldn't let that happen, but at the same time had no idea of how to proceed.

After a while the tears stopped and she walked, again with no clear destination in mind. She wandered down High Street. There were a few people about, mostly elderly. Along the street three youngsters on bikes were laughing as they rode in circles. Outside a shop a couple were chatting. Further on, locals carrying shopping bags made their way home from a Sunday market. In front of her a large matronly woman was shooing her toddler along like a mother hen with a chicken. It was all so bloody mundane, Nicole wanted to scream at them to wake up.

Then she came to a building she recognised. Bloody bells, she thought, why do I keep ending up in them? Why couldn't they have called it something else? The Eight Bells in Long Crendon was a world away from her similarly named local pub. The Long Crendon Eight Bells was kitschy cute, with whitewashed exterior and tiled roof. Tom had liked it and they had been there a number of times. Nicole went in, bought herself a double brandy, and continued on to the beer garden at the rear.

At first, she thought she had the place to herself, but then noticed a sullen looking young woman nursing a beer. Nicole ignored her and sipped steadily at the brandy. She knew she would soon have to drive back to London, but her immediate concern was to quell the anger she was feeling. Over on the far table the young woman lit a cigarette. Nicole had never smoked, but in that moment she decided it was a good idea. Regular smokers claimed that it calmed the nerves. Well, she thought, let's see if it's true. She got up and went over to the woman. She was younger than she had guessed, just a girl, probably no more than twenty. She was wearing rather grubby jeans and a hooded jacket. Nicole had never liked using the word 'hoodie'.

'Excuse me, can I be terribly rude and ask for a cigarette?'

The girl shrugged and fished out a partially crushed packet. She flipped a cigarette onto the table in front of her.

'Thanks.'

'I suppose you want a light as well?' the girl scowled.

'Thank you.'

Nicole lit the cigarette, passed the lighter back and inhaled. For a moment she thought her throat had caught fire and she doubled up with a fit of coughing and spluttering.

The girl laughed and took the lighter from Nicole's hand. 'You're not a fuckin' smoker, right?'

'Right,' Nicole gasped, and feeling dizzy, groped behind her for the nearest seat and sat down. Nicole, determined not to be beaten by a stupid cigarette, took another, more tentative, puff. She coughed again.

'I've been faggin' since I was ten.'

All Nicole could do was nod.

'Hang on, I'll get your drink.'

The girl fetched Nicole's brandy and slumped down in the chair next to her.

Nicole gulped at her drink then, without taking another puff, leaned over to stub out the cigarette. Before she could do so the girl had plucked it from her fingers.

'Don't waste it.'

'I'm bloody stupid. I'm sorry, I shouldn't have asked for a cigarette. But I've had a shit of a day. A friend of mind just got killed.'

'Shit, really? You mean the queer guy in the cottage? The one with that funny car?'

Nicole coughed again but not as severely. 'You knew him?'

The girl snorted. 'A queer guy in a fancy cottage with a freakin' bright yellow car? Living in this burg? Everyone knew him.' She paused and screwed up her face. 'I'm not saying I hate queers. Sometimes I think my brother is one.'

'Tom. Tom Myers. That was his name. I have known him since I was at school. I hated him being gay. He was two years older than me and I rather fancied him when I was your age. Fat lot of good it did me.'

'Tom Myers,' the girl sounded out his name. 'I never knew that.'

Nicole looked at her drink. It was empty. 'I'm Nicole. Can I get you a drink?'

'Brilliant. I'm Emma, but most people call me M-One and I'd love a rum and coke.'

Nicole returned with the drinks and for a while the two of them chatted about life in the village. According to Emma it was boring. If it weren't for the fact that her mother was sick, she would have been long gone.

'Where to?' Nicole asked.

'London. I love London,' Emma said and then added wistfully, 'I have a heap of friends there.'

'And your father?'

'He did a runner years ago.'

There was no malice in the girl's voice; it was just a statement of fact.

'So what do you do for entertainment around here?' Nicole asked.

Emma looked at her and then glanced away. 'If I told you you'd freak.'

'You think so?'

'Old people always do. They don't get it that things are different now.'

Nicole nearly choked on her drink. 'Old people? Christ, Emma, I'm not that old.'

'Sorry. But what I mean is, if you lived here you'd understand.'

'Try me.'

The girl looked away and then lit another cigarette. 'There's nothing to do here other than get drunk, stoned or have sex.' She glanced at Nicole. 'See, I knew you would think I'm rubbish.'

'Not in the slightest. I don't get stoned, but I like a drink and once in a while I even manage to drag a man into my bed.'

Emma laughed and then lowered her voice to a whisper. 'You know why they call me M-One?'

'Emma the first?'

'No. It's like the motorway.' Her voice was flat, as though recounting some old news. 'Everyone's been up me. It's a popular route.' There was no sense of shame in her voice; rather, resignation and slight bewilderment at where her life had brought her.

Nicole knew there was nothing she could say, so she remained silent.

After a time, Emma said quietly. 'I saw him, you know.'

'Saw who?'

'The perve that was hanging around outside your friend's cottage.'

Nicole sat up and put her drink down. 'You what? You saw someone outside Tom's place?

'When?'

'Last night. This is just between you and me, right?'

Nicole nodded. Between us for the moment, she thought, depending on what you say next.

'I went out there last night,' Emma took a drink and then continued. 'About one, it would have been. There was this guy in a car, watching the house. He wasn't local.'

Nicole was suddenly alert, with a tingling sense of anticipation. 'How do you know that?'

'Hell, I know every car in the village.' She sniffed and wiped her arm across her nose. 'It was an almost brand-new Mitsubishi Mirage. Purple, I think. It was hard to tell. Nobody around here drives one like that.'

Nicole was impressed. 'You know about cars?'

'Not a bloody thing,' she laughed. 'Garry does, though, and he said it was a Mirage. He reckons they're girls' cars.'

'Hang on, who is Garry?'

Emma snickered. 'The guy I was with. Christ, you think it's easy to find somewhere to fuck around town? There's a big old tree out by your friend's cottage and Garry and I go there. It's cold as hell, but at least it's out of the wind and we always take a blanket. Anyway, what I'm saying is this perve's eyes nearly popped out. It was fun. I didn't let on that I knew he was there and gave him a real show. Garry thought I had gone crazy, flashing my tits about and fucking like crazy, moaning and all that shit, you know, like in the pornos. The guy in the car even lowered his window so he could hear as well as see. By the time we finished, the perve was having it off with himself, dirty bastard.'

Nicole couldn't believe what she was hearing. Not the sex, but that this young woman had actually seen a car outside Tom's.

'Could you see the man clearly?'

Emma shook her head. 'Not all that well, but I could see he was really into watching.'

'Can you tell me anything else about the car?'

Emma hesitated and squinted at Nicole. 'Why?'

Nicole decided that at this stage it was best to lie. 'It sounds familiar. It might be someone that was bothering Tom.'

'I can tell you the number.'

'Really?'

'Sure. I was hopeless at school, but one thing I could always remember was numbers. I know all my friend's numbers. Don't need to write them down or nothing.'

'I'm afraid I don't have your talent,' Nicole said, and reached in her jacket for her notebook and repeated the number back to Emma to make certain she had it right.

'I can't thank you enough,' Nicole said.

'Then buy me another drink.'

'My pleasure,' Nicole said and she meant it.

'You're not so bad for an old person,' Emma grinned.

'Thanks.'

They sat in silence for a moment. Nicole was about to get up and go when the girl reached out and touched her arm.

'I'm sorry about your friend, about Tom.'

It was the first comforting thing that anyone had said to her all day. Nicole felt deeply touched and it was all she could do to stop herself crying again. She sniffed back the tears and looked into Emma's face.

'I want to tell you something about me, but first I want you to promise me you won't freak out.'

Emma shrugged. 'Whatever. Takes a bit to freak me.'

'I thought as much,' Nicole took one of her cards from her pocket and laid it on the table. 'Emma, I'm a police officer.'

'Shit.'

'And what you told me today is really important.'

The girl picked up the card and examined it. 'So you were just being friendly so you could ask me stuff?'

'No. But when you said you had seen a man in a car outside Tom's place, I couldn't ignore it.'

Emma looked dubious. 'And the other stuff. You know, me and Garry?'

'Emma, that is none of my business and I guess if I was stuck here, as you put it, I would probably be doing that stuff too.'

Nicole sensed the girl relaxing. She touched her arm. 'What I need to say is that I might have to get you to give a statement.'

Emma thought about it. 'I guess.'

'So will you give me your phone number?'

Emma took out another cigarette. She lit it, then nodded. 'Sure.'

After she had said goodbye to Emma, Nicole walked slowly back through the village. She made a conscious decision not to process any of what she had heard until she got back to her office. Let it mull over, she told herself. At the moment it all sounded too crazy. Give it time. Let it settle and then see if it makes any sense.

She was coming around the corner to Tom's cottage when she saw movement by the house. She slipped behind the hedge on the opposite side of the road and made her way along until she had a reasonable view of the cottage. It was nearly dark, but through the gloom she saw three men coming out of the house towards a black Chevrolet Impala. One of them carried Tom's laptop and another had the painting. The third man had nothing but a bunch of silver birch twigs bound together.

Nicole knew that if they were going back to London they would pass by her. So, she waited, crouched down, but with a clear view of the road. They left almost immediately, and even in the dusk she was able to scribble down the number on the plate.

Monday had never been her favourite day of the week. Nicole woke to this one with a sense of dread. She had slept fitfully and twice in the night had woken to find herself sobbing with anguish. Not just about Tom, but also about the frustration she felt with the police force and everybody in it. In direct contrast to her mood, the world that greeted her when she pulled back the curtains looked as if it was going to be fine and clear.

She went early to work, determined to make a list of every single point in favour of reopening the investigation into the woman in the boat and the possibility that somehow Tom's death was connected. This last point was troubling, carrying as it did, the implication that somehow she was the only possible link between the two, and her connection with Tom had somehow contributed to his death.

The minute she went down the stairs to the crypt she knew something was wrong. Her desk was a mess, her drawers spilled open and her computer switched on. Whoever had done this had made no attempt to clean up, making certain she got the message. With a rising panic she searched for the CD that contained the MP3 of DI McKay's interview with the woman. It was gone, as had the photographs. The file and all the previous data on the computer had been wiped clean. Then she remembered that she had emailed the sound file to herself. She logged on, but only to discover it had also been erased. Whoever was responsible had been thorough and skilled enough to hack into her personal email.

Nicole made a desultory start on cleaning up and then gave up. She allowed herself to sink into a lethargic haze and for ten minutes sat staring at the screen in front of her that was as blank as she was. Everything was gone and as far as anyone was concerned the case no longer existed and had never done so.

Eventually she roused herself, took her glasses off and laid them gently on the desk in front of her. Regroup, she told herself; that was what she must do. Figure out a strategy. She put her glasses back on, poked them up to the bridge of her nose and peered at her wristwatch. The glasses slid down again. She reminded herself yet again to replace them. It was just after eight-thirty. She had less than half an hour to prepare for what she knew would be an unpleasant meeting with the Chief Super. She opened a blank document and started typing.

Nine o'clock came, and though she felt under-prepared she knocked and stepped into Crawford's office. He didn't rise to greet her, but rather grunted that she should take a seat. He was making pretence of reading a file, a tactic to postpone their unpleasant confrontation. She knew that Crawford understood her well enough to know that she would not take a dressing-down lightly. Especially if she thought she was right. He said nothing for a while, then closed the file and looked at her.

'Jesus, Nicole, what on earth did you think you were doing yesterday?'

'Investigating a case, sir,' she said evenly, determined not to allow her anger to show.

'It was suicide. Nothing we can say or do will change that.'

'With respect, sir, I disagree.'

'Your behaviour towards the Thames Valley police and the Chief Constable was unconscionable. Do you understand that?'

'Sir, they were not following correct procedures. There was no forensic…'

'Nicole. Stop right there.' Crawford got to his feet. 'No matter how I try to see it otherwise, what you did amounts to gross insubordination. I might have overlooked it on the grounds that your friend had died, but unfortunately Chief Constable Burnside does not concur.'

It was exactly as Nicole had anticipated. She knew that she was in a struggle she couldn't win, so she nodded. 'I understand that, sir.'

'There will be a hearing in due course; but in the meantime, you are relieved of all duties and though you should be suspended, I suggest you sign this.'

He picked up the file he had been reading and handed it across the desk. 'It's an application for sick leave on the grounds of stress and bereavement. I will not fill in the duration until the date for the hearing is set.'

'Yes, sir.' Nicole took the form and without bothering to read it, placed it on the desk and signed it.

Crawford looked at her, perplexed. He had expected a fight. 'I am truly sorry about Myers…' he said gruffly.

'Sir,' Nicole rose from the chair and looked him straight in the eye. 'With respect, sir, I would like to say something.'

'Of course.'

She took the printout of her notes and laid it on the desk. 'This is a list of the discrepancies in the case. It lists the toxicology report on the woman's blood, the timing of anonymous calls to the media and the police, and the unlikely presence of silver birch twigs tied in a particular way at both crime scenes. You will find a description and the licence number of a car that was stationed outside Myers' place at the time he was supposedly committing suicide. The telephone number of a witness who observed the vehicle and its occupant is included. I have recorded the number plate of another car seen leaving the cottage yesterday evening. That car had three male passengers who were seen removing vital evidence from the crime scene, including the silver birch I mentioned, the vandalised painting and Myers' computer.'

'Nicole...'

'In addition, sir, I wish to report that sometime over the weekend my office was searched and both physical and computer files removed or erased. Photographs and an audio file of an interview with the missing woman were also removed.'

'DI Parry, are you finished?'

She shook her head. 'There is a list of the various lines of enquiry that were ignored during the initial investigation, including such basic things as ownership of the boat and checking CCTV footage in all locations pertinent to the case. I have added my own mobile phone number, should you require any clarification.'

Crawford shook his head. 'You really don't know when you should pull your head in and shut up, do you?' He shook his head in disbelief. 'You know, you could have been a great cop.'

'Sir.'

'Now get out of here.'

He watched her leave and then walked around the desk and picked up the report. Christ, he thought, what am I supposed to do with this? He knew that the sensible decision would be to destroy it. It would also, he realised, be what that bastard Grammaticus would want him to do. He had no doubt that he was responsible for going through Parry's office. Crawford folded the report and placed it beneath an unused diary in his desk drawer. The entire affair left a nasty taste in his mouth. Events were now way beyond his control, and to follow Parry's suggested course of action would certainly mean the end of his own career. He hated the fact that the whole damn business forced him to confront his own cowardice.

But worse still was the nagging feeling that it was possible that Nicole Parry was right.

Chapter Five

The following day Crawford rang and informed her that the situation had been taken out of his hands. He explained that his superiors had taken the decision after the Chief Constable had lodged a formal complaint of insubordination and misconduct against her.

'Sara Burnside was not happy with you simply being granted leave. She demanded your immediate suspension,' he said. He was going to add his own personal regret at the development, but Nicole had already hung up.

Tom's funeral was held on the nineteenth. Nicole, having nothing else to do, had started drinking heavily, but she pulled herself together so that she was sober enough to say a few words. Later she could not recall what they were. Afterwards she found the young girl, Emma, who told her that a man named Alejandro was staying in Tom's house, sorting out his affairs, so Nicole went and talked to him. He had arrived from France two days after Tom's death and was still in shock. There was, he swore, nothing about Tom's life that would have caused him to hang himself. He asked about the painting he had sat for.

Nicole didn't have the heart to tell him so she lied. 'It disappeared,' she said. Then she drove back to London to her empty house and another bottle of Stolly.

Later, when she tried to recall the next few weeks, all that remained was a Stolichnaya-induced blur. She had never been a heavy drinker, but there was something seductive in being out of control. She hardly ate; and once found herself waking up in a stranger's house in Clapham with the man taking photographs of her sprawled naked on his bed. She did remember taking the card from the camera before smashing it against the wall. Maybe she smashed him against the wall as well, but she couldn't be sure.

Eventually she put a stop to her self-destructive descent. She had a couple of days without a drink and decided it was time to get on with her life. The question that confronted her was – what life? Her life had taken a wrong turn, she decided, as she lay in the bath. Then she corrected the metaphor. She had failed to take a corner and run off the road. A turn suggested she was on her way to somewhere and at the moment the only destination she could envisage was unemployment. If she had had a life plan, changing careers at thirty-four had never been part of it. With a worse than useless arts degree and a Master of Studies in Applied Criminology and Police Management from Cambridge University, she was not exactly prepared for any other career than the one she had just screwed up. Her career looked less like a path and more like a dead end. The bath was cooling down, so she ran the hot tap for a while. In her present frame of mind, the bath was her second most favourite place. The first was her bed.

On the plus side was the fact that she was still on the payroll, though Nicole saw little hope of that lasting too long. She had a decent amount of money saved up, which was a good thing because the most likely outcome of a disciplinary hearing was a slide down the ranks and the pay scale. Given that she stubbornly held to her belief that she had been correct to criticise the behaviour of her fellow officers, she knew she would not accept a demeaning posting to Traffic or Community Liaison. 'Hope for the best but prepare for the worst,' her mother used to say. Well, damn that for a strategy.

She climbed out of the bath, used her towel to wipe the condensation off the mirror and examined herself. Thirty-four wasn't that old. She turned sideways and looked at her profile. Not too bad, she decided. Not having had children was an advantage. Her stomach was flat and her breasts were... what had Toby called them? Divine? Hardly true, but given her age... The thought of Toby was vaguely unsettling, so she towelled herself briskly and then dried her hair.

Back in her bedroom she weighed up her options. It was ten in the morning. It was a Thursday. Outside looked bleak. Inside looked in need of a great deal of work. She tossed aside the dress she had been about to put on and hunted for a pair of overalls. The decision, once made, seemed obvious. Until she regained some clarity, she would become a stripper.

By Friday afternoon she had concluded that being a stripper was not as easy as it sounded. There were at least four – and in places five – layers of paint in the upstairs bedroom. She chipped off a flake and examined it. The bottom coat appeared to have been pink, although it might well have been undercoat. Next came an extended blue period – duck egg blue over-painted with deeper cobalt. It had been a baby's room and then a teenager's, most likely a girl. The next layer was either burnt-orange or had become so over the years. It pointed to new owners with a teenage son. The last coat, the top one, was a bland cream, almost beige. Taupe, she corrected herself, having seen so many variations on it in the sample sheets she had collected from the hardware. Her father probably chose the taupe when he had done the house up for rent, all those years ago. The archaeology of the house, she decided, was not particularly fascinating.

She had tried a chemical paint stripper, but the necessity to wear goggles and gloves irked. Sandpaper and a scrapper were fine for cleaning up small areas, as was steel wool, but the large areas were daunting. In the end she decided the best solution was postponement. In reality what occurred was a relapse, and when she sobered up the following week and several bottles of vodka later, it was to discover that she had successfully missed both Christmas and New Year. Somehow during the interim she had managed to paint the hallway a rather bright orange. Hallelujah, she muttered to herself and went in search of coffee.

That evening, having successfully negotiated her way through an alcohol-free day, she cooked a decent meal and decided to reward herself with a long hot bath, something she realised she must have avoided for a while. She had just started to run the bath and was about to undress when, for the first time in weeks, her phone rang.

'Yes?'

'The Fulham Railway Bridge,' said a familiar and totally unexpected voice. 'Half an hour.'

Then the line went dead.

Nicole stood with the phone in her hand, temporarily unable to process what had just happened. She could think of no possible reason why he should call. Let alone want to meet her. She replaced the phone, turned off the half-filled bath and ran upstairs to change out of the overalls she had been wearing for a fortnight.

Half an hour, he had said. She was there with ten minutes to spare, so in an attempt to calm herself down, she walked slowly to the central span of the bridge. It was coming on dusk and the walkway was busy as people hurried over the bridge on their way home. Wrapped up in their own worlds, nobody even glanced at her. I could be invisible, she thought. The District Line train from Putney Bridge rumbled across the bridge towards East Putney. She turned and looked downstream. There was still enough light to see where the boat had been stranded, except now it was high tide and the exact spot was underwater.

'Grand old bridge. Four hundred and eighteen metres long. Nice latticework,' said a pedestrian as he stopped to lean on the railing and take in the view. 'Did you know it was designed by Brunel's former assistant William Jacomb?'

'I don't think I have heard of either of them.'

'Then your school teachers should be shot,' the man said, and gave a dry laugh. He peered at her. 'Happy New Year, by the way, and did you know you have flecks of orange paint in your hair?'

'I'm renovating, Chief Superintendent. And happy New Year to you too, sir.'

'Andrew. Please. I'm off duty and probably out of line as well.' He glanced along the bridge at the pedestrians. 'I have something for you.'

'Sir?'

'Wait…'

A couple involved in an animated conversation strode by. When they were gone he took a large envelope from inside his coat. But instead of giving it to her, he clutched it to his chest, as if reluctant to let it go.

'This is crossing a bridge in every sense,' he said, and peered at his watch.

Nicole had never seen him so tired and on edge. She didn't say anything.

'I've decided to retire –'

'But sir…'

'Hang on, let me have my say. This is difficult enough without you interrupting.'

Nicole nodded. 'Sorry.'

'I have been under a lot of pressure from our so-called MI6 friends at Vauxhall Bridge who seem to be under the misapprehension that I work for them. That incident in your office, I believe was their doing; and they certainly had knowledge of our computer files. God knows how they hacked in. And you are not their favourite person.'

'Jesus,' Nicole said quietly.

'For reasons best known to them, that damned woman in the boat was off-limits and from day one they tried to shut it down. It was the same with Tom Myers. Believe me, as far as the woman was concerned, I argued for a continued investigation, but I was left in no doubt that I had a choice between what they laughingly called patriotic duty and my career.' He reached out and touched her arm. 'I'm truly sorry, Nicole, but I was a coward. I try to convince myself that I could have made a stand right at the beginning. At first it seemed that we were sharing information but it quickly became a one-way street.' He heaved a sigh, shrugged and continued. 'I recognise that I made a lot of wrong choices.' He handed her the envelope. 'I hope this is the right thing to do.'

Nicole took it, slipped it inside her jacket and then looked at him, dumbfounded. He seemed older, worn out and more fragile than she had ever seen him.

'Andrew…'

He shook his head. 'Listen. You were right. Your disturbing conclusions about the timing of the anonymous calls to us and to the media are justified, and your instinct to follow up the toxicology report. Good policing.'

'Thank you.' Nicole felt a sudden sense of relief. 'And the licence plates?'

'I ran a quiet check on the plates. The details are there. You'll see that the black Impala does not officially exist, at least in the public records.'

'So, it's MI5?'

'Maybe, but given other connections it's more likely to be their big sister, SIS. The other car, the Mitsubishi, belongs to an individual who I am now certain also works out of Vauxhall Bridge.'

'What do you mean, "other connections"?'

'The demands on me came from a Senior Operations Officer, a senior SIS man. Whatever their game is, he appears to be the one running the show. His name is Grammaticus. Quentin Grammaticus. I hope you never need to have dealings with him. He is clever, charming and even witty at times. Probably more so if you have a degree in Latin.'

'But?'

'He's as vicious as a pitbull, only less trustworthy.'

'I'll keep that in mind if we run into each other.'

Nicole was still having trouble believing that the conversation was taking place. She pressed her hand to her coat to assure herself that the envelope was real. There were a lot of things she needed to know, but realising that Crawford's constant checking of his watch probably indicated he was not going to stay long, she went straight to the next item she had suggested investigating.

'Did you get someone on to the CCTV?' she asked.

'Checking the CCTV footage was harder. I was concerned about how secure our computers are and I didn't want to flag what I was looking for, so I asked for the relevant tapes and checked them all myself on a video not connected to the system. God knows, I had forgotten what boring work that is. It took hours.' A faint smile crossed his face. 'I did most of it by working late and I think my wife began to suspect I had a mistress.'

'And the footage?' Nicole tried to keep the impatience out of her voice.

They waited as another train rolled across the bridge. Crawford was obviously uncomfortable. He shifted his weight from foot to foot as though impatient to be somewhere else.

'The Impala was cruising around St Thomas's Hospital on the night the woman vanished. It went around five or six times over a couple of hours. The last sighting was just before midnight. I couldn't find it after that.'

'That's good work, sir,' Nicole smiled. 'So has the case been reopened?'

He ignored her question. Instead, he turned and looked down river. The water was a slow rolling ribbon of darkness. The tide was changing.

'Sir, what am I supposed to do? I'm suspended.'

'I revoked your suspension.'

'But the Chief Constable…'

'The Thames Valley police can go to hell as far as I'm concerned. I don't condone the way you spoke to Sara, but by God, I would have said the same in your circumstances. I think that your linking of the two incidents is credible and that the death of Tom Myers was probably not suicide. However, to take it further at this stage would be almost impossible due to the interference of those at Vauxhall Bridge.'

'What? Are you saying that MI6 put pressure on us over Tom as well?'

'I have said far too much already. What you do with the information is up to you.'

Nicole was exasperated. 'Jesus, Andrew! What the hell am I supposed to do?'

Crawford allowed himself a rueful smile. 'I have you listed as on leave. I checked and found you haven't taken a holiday for more than three years. Well, you're taking it now, all of it.' Then his tone changed. He looked her directly in the face and spoke carefully. 'What you do in your own time is strictly your affair.'

'Thank you, sir, but the case, sir…'

'The case does not exist, Nicole. It never did.'

He turned and without another word walked away into the gathering gloom.

The promotion had been a long time in coming. Now it had actually happened it seemed a good excuse for a party. His wife had been thrilled for him, so much so that they had sex for the first time in months. She was astonished by his vigour and to her surprise found the whole messy business enjoyable. Her enjoyment may have been diminished had she known his performance owed much to his visualising a couple having sex under a tree in Long Crendon.

Brenda Mitchell thought of her life as a success. Her husband was dependable, kind and understanding that she didn't want to have children, 'quite yet'. She had her circle of friends with whom she played squash and gossiped. Mostly they talked about other people because their own lives were all very respectable. When they talked about their husbands, she was always a sympathetic ear. In her own case, she was vague about what exactly Chris did in the office at the UK Environment Agency. All she knew was that he was concerned with making Britain cleaner, safer and free of Japanese knotweed. By the time she had explained that much, most people glazed over.

For his part, Chris was happy to share little titbits from time to time. 'It's not that it's hush-hush,' he would say, 'It's just a tad boring.' But to feed the legend he would spend an hour every week or so on the Agency website and then trot out anything that might be of interest. Japanese knotweed had been a winner.

In the rare circumstance that someone was inebriated enough to question him further about his work, he would launch into a description of his work on consultation and technical guidance for the registration of exempt small sewage effluent discharges from septic tanks and sewage treatment plants. It was the conversational equivalent of chloroform.

'I am now chief assistant to the head of research,' he announced to those assembled in his lounge room. 'Out and about in this still vaguely green and mildly pleasant land, rather than stuck in the office. No more drawing up guidelines, thank God!'

'No more Japanese knotweed, I hope,' Brenda tittered.

There was a flurry of congratulations and then people got down to the serious business of consuming Chris's generous supply of wine.

By the time the doorbell rang, Chris Mitchell was relaxed and happy. Grammaticus had given him the good news a couple of days earlier and he was still coming to terms with his good fortune. To make the leap from the corporate side to that of an operational officer had taken several years and a lot of hard work. This, however, was a promotion of a different calibre. To be appointed as deputy team leader under Grammaticus was something he had never envisaged. It held the promise of a lot more than preparing Quentin's cup of tea. He anticipated spending time in the field, learning the ropes, until the day far in the future, when he ran his own team.

He placed his drink on the hallstand and opened the door. It was not, as he expected, a late invitee, but a woman. She flashed her credentials, murmured her name and stepped into the hall. Her name sounded vaguely familiar.

'Just a routine enquiry, sir.'

'Look, can this wait? I've just been promoted and we are having a bit of a gathering to celebrate.'

The woman nodded. 'Congratulations, sir. This will only take a minute.'

'Quickly, then.'

She took out a notepad and flicked through it.

'Your car, sir, is a mauve Mitsubishi Mirage?'

'It's purple.'

She made a show of crossing out mauve and writing purple, sounding each letter out as she wrote it down. 'Okay, purple it is. Has it ever been stolen?'

'Never,' Chris snapped.

'You're certain of that, sir?'

'Of course I'm bloody sure,' he said with more than a hint of exasperation.

She read studiously through her notes. 'Good. Now… ah yes, a month ago, that would be November ninth. A Saturday night, I believe, and over into the morning of the tenth.' She looked up at him. 'You were in Long Crendon, sir. Is that correct?'

'Damned if I remember.' He felt a shiver as his exasperation turned to apprehension. 'Why?'

'Your car was observed parked, for a considerable length of time, outside a cottage at between one and three in the morning. Would you care to tell me what you were doing there?'

Suddenly sober, Chris knew this had to be shut down. First thing in the morning he would get Quentin to stamp it out, and this stupid bitch with it.

'I am afraid that is none of your business. My superiors will contact you in the morning and clear this up.' He gestured towards the door for her to leave.

She ignored him, and looked at her notes again. 'You see, sir, we have a complaint from two people who say you had parked at a well-known meeting place for teenagers. They allege you spent a long time watching them having sex. Is this correct?' She glanced down at her notes again. 'And that you subsequently performed an indecent act in the car. Are you a peeping Tom, Mister Mitchell?'

It felt like a kick in the guts. He imagined the futility of explaining to Grammaticus why he had not mentioned the incident in his report. He saw his promotion vanishing. The notion of this damn woman speaking with Grammaticus about this was no longer appealing.

'Listen…' he began. His mind was spinning and he floundered, lost for words.

To his surprise, the policewoman smiled.

'Look, I can see you are distracted, sir. I'll call back another day.'

Before he could say anything, she had gone, pulling the door shut behind her. He stood looking at the door, wondering what the hell he could do to avert a potential disaster to his career. When he returned to the crowd in the living room he put on a brave face, but the party spirit had left him. All that remained was a sick feeling in his stomach.

Outside, Nicole was grinning broadly. That scared the shit out of him; she congratulated herself. Well played! She could tell by his demeanour that she had him where she wanted. Okay, she thought, leave him to stew for a couple of days. Slow cooking was all the rage. Wait a while and then she had a chance of getting him to talk.

Andrew Crawford was at the entrance to the tube station when the man stumbled and bumped into him. Looking embarrassed, the man quickly apologised.

'No problem,' Crawford responded automatically, and was about to step around him. But the man bent over and picked something up from the ground.

'I believe you dropped this,' he said, handing him a small envelope.

'I don't think I did...' Crawford began, but the man had gone, merged into the crowd at the tube station entrance. He stepped to the side of the pavement, opened the envelope, took one look at its contents and swore under his breath. He looked around for the man on the off chance that he was awaiting a response. Seeing no sign of him, he pushed into the crowd and went as quickly as he could to the platform. Unfortunately, it was crowded and even if the man was still there, he had little chance of finding him. 'Fuck!' He hadn't meant to say it out loud.

Beside him an elderly woman snapped, 'Do you mind!'

He was in no mood to be castigated and glared at her. 'No, I don't bloody well mind!'

She was about to respond when, fortunately, the train came, and as the crowd on the platform surged forward he pushed ahead of her. The doors shut and through the glass he could see the woman mouthing something unpleasant. She was clearly furious. And fuck you too, Crawford thought as the train moved out of the station. He looked along the carriage, hoping that the man was on board but there was no sign of him. He desperately wanted to take another look at the contents of the envelope, but knew he was best to wait until he was somewhere very private. The train shuddered around a corner and he lurched sideways, almost losing his balance. 'Fuck everything,' he muttered.

At home he kissed his wife on the cheek and made a lame excuse about work. He poured them both a drink and, excusing himself, went to his study. Shutting the door behind him, he laid the envelope gently on the desk as if it were a letter bomb. Christ, he thought, it certainly has that potential. He sat, took a sip of his drink and then opened it.

There were three photographs. The first showed the blurred face of a woman in a crowd. The second was of the same woman. It was a better shot. The woman was in profile, standing in the stern of a boat, speaking with a man. Only his head and shoulders could be seen. They were wrapped in scarf and woollen hat. The third photograph was an enhanced detail from the first one. Crawford could not be absolutely certain, but if he had been a betting man he would have wagered it was the woman from the boat found stranded in the Thames. On the back of the enhanced photo was scrawled '11am Phoenix Garden'. He turned the other photographs over but there was no other message.

The right thing to do was to contact Grammaticus, but Crawford decided he was over doing the 'right' thing. He phoned Nicole. When she answered he simply repeated the message, but changed the time to an hour earlier. He hung up before she could respond.

Nicole had never heard of the Phoenix Garden but a quick Google search the previous evening had revealed it to be on Stacey Street in the heart of the West End, behind the junction of Charing Cross Road and Shaftesbury Avenue. While it had looked easy on the map, she discovered that there was no entrance from Stacey Street, so following directions from a friendly passer-by, she retraced her steps and turned down St Giles Passage.

The garden looked pleasant enough for a garden in winter, but there was no time to admire it because as she entered Andrew Crawford fell in beside her.

'Thanks for coming. I must say I had never heard of Phoenix Garden. Creepy history. Used to be a leper hospital. Lots of bodies buried here, I shouldn't doubt.'

'No wonder the trees look so healthy. Bodies are nourishing, so I've been told,' Nicole said, but she was in no mood for small talk. 'What are we doing here?'

Crawford checked his watch then recounted his encounter outside the tube station and his subsequent examination of the photographs. He fished them from his pocket and handed them to her. 'What do you think?'

Nicole took one look, shrugged. 'If it's not her, it is pretty damn close.'

'That was my feeling too.'

Nicole went to hand back the photos, but he waved her hand away. 'You had better keep them.'

She was surprised, but held on to them. 'So what happens now?'

'In about forty-five minutes' time, the man who gave them to me is coming here to meet me.' He took a folded newspaper from his coat. 'Here, I brought you this. Find a bench where you can read. If he turns out to be kosher, I will hand him over to you.'

'Why?'

'Because if he has something to contribute, I want to find out what it is before those bastards at Vauxhall Bridge get a sniff of him.'

Nicole shook her head. 'Sir, I mean Andrew, that doesn't make sense. Why don't you handle it yourself?'

'I think that Grammaticus and his team have eyes on me and I no longer trust that we're all playing from the same rulebook. Also – and you need to be aware of this – Sara Burnside at Thames Valley is on the warpath, demanding you be disciplined. I have headed her off at the moment by sending you on leave, but she's as stubborn as you and probably won't give up.' He coughed apologetically. 'First things first, I take it this place has no CCTV?'

Nicole looked around, suddenly wary. 'Sorry, I should have checked.'

Crawford laughed. 'No, I am confident we're fine here. I made damn certain I wasn't followed on the way. However, from now on, I suggest you start doing the same.'

'If you really think it necessary.'

'I do. Now go read the paper. If I don't send him over, then forget the entire bloody business and go back to your renovating.'

Nicole laughed. 'I'd prefer not to.'

Crawford humphed. 'I suspected that.'

From where she sat, Nicole had a clear line of sight both to the gate and across the garden to where Crawford was making an unconvincing display of appreciating what looked like a mixture of weeds and flowers; stinging nettles with pink geranium, blue comfrey and a carpet of attractive, pink dead-nettle. Overhead, the already weak sun looked as if it would shortly succumb to an invasion of clouds. Probably rain too, she mused. She turned back to *The Guardian*, but was too distracted and found she couldn't read half a paragraph without checking the gate.

When he did arrive, the man was a disappointment. She had imagined someone more interesting, someone less like an undertaker on his day off. He was of average height and his blonde hair had been combed to one side, with a hint of a cowlick. His face was unusually round and set with a small nose and slightly downturned mouth. He wore glasses that seemed on the large side and had unfashionably heavy frames. He looks like an owl, Nicole decided, a lugubrious owl. The pale skin suggested he was a night owl, or maybe he was ill. Her thoughts veered off on a tangent. Welcome to the leper hospital. Don't worry, you're among friends, we're all lepers here.

I'm bored already, she thought as she watched him stroll around the garden. He did not go directly to Crawford. Instead, he wandered, glanced at her, and continued his nonchalant inspection of the plants. He was giving the garden and its occupants a thorough checking. He got points for that, she admitted. As she watched, she realised there was something about him that was familiar. Then it came to her. The man's skin was like that of the woman in the boat. Almost translucent. Alabaster, that was the word. Had she used it, or had it been Saul at the mortuary? She couldn't remember.

When the man finally made contact, he and Crawford walked slowly around the garden, chatting like old friends. They looked like any keen gardeners, pointing out plants, stopping to squat beside small species.

Crawford and the man talked for about ten minutes before Crawford turned and nodded in her direction. The two men shook hands before Crawford left without a backward glance. Nicole resumed reading. If the man wanted to talk with her, he would make the move. Any observer would have thought it strange if she had been the first to do so.

'Do you know anything about plants?'

The man was foreign. His English clear but heavily accented. He stood directly in front of her, but his gaze was up into the trees, or maybe the nearby buildings. With a slow, natural movement, he turned so that he eventually took in all the buildings. Christ, she thought, he's looking for fucking snipers.

'Very little. I had a pot plant once but it died from too much love.'

He looked concerned. 'Too much love, how can that be?'

'Too much water.'

His face relaxed a little. 'Yes, too much water, I can see how that might be fatal.' He pointed to the seat. 'May I sit?'

'Please,' she shifted along a little to allow plenty of room between them. He sat as far from her as was possible without falling off the bench.

'You are Detective Inspector Nicole Parry, I believe.'

'Yes. And you are?

'My name is Pentti Toivonen. I work for the Finnish National Bureau of Investigation.'

Finnish? That explained two mysteries – the lack of a suntan and the awkward way in which he had sat on the bench. She had read once that Finns had the need for more personal space than any other nationality. Maybe it was true.

'Finland, I've never been there.'

A hint of a smile flitted across his face. 'Probably just as well, it is not very exciting; mostly dull and flat.'

It sounded like he was describing himself, she thought. 'And what exactly do you do, Mister...?'

'Toivonen. But please, call me Pentti.'

Not on your life, Mister Owl, not until I find out exactly who you are and what you want. Nicole nodded for him to continue.

'The National Bureau of Investigation, the KRP, is our equivalent of Scotland Yard.'

'The KR – what?' Had he said KRP? Either she was mishearing his accent, or that sounded the closest thing to 'crap' she could think of. She stifled a grin.

'KRP, the *Keskusrikospoliisi*,' he said. 'I'm a policeman like you.'

Christ, we're in trouble if that's true, she thought grimly. Well, Mister lugubrious Owl, we'll see about that. However, she decided to be a little more welcoming of a man who was obviously out of his comfort zone.

'What is it we can help you with?'

'The photographs Chief Superintendent Crawford gave you. Do you recognise the woman?'

Nicole nodded. 'I am pretty sure I have seen her before.'

'Is she the same woman who vanished from the hospital?'

Nicole frowned. 'Tell me, Mister Toivonen. How did you know about that?'

'Let me say that we have been searching for her for quite a while and had alerted everyone we could.'

She realised he wasn't about to divulge more, so she didn't press him. 'So who is this woman so many people appear to be interested in?'

He didn't answer.

Nicole looked at him. His round face vacant, his head tilted back, staring at the clouds gathering ominously above them.

'Mister Toivonen, I asked you a question.'

'I'm sorry. Yes, who is she? That is what we would dearly love to know.'

Nicole got to her feet. The man was clearly playing games. 'I'm sorry, but unless you have something more to offer, I don't see that I should waste my time or yours.'

He seemed unmoved. Then his face gave a half smile. 'Crawford said you could be a tough bitch.' He held out his hand. 'Give me the photos.'

A bitch? Had Crawford said that? She held her anger in but found herself handing him the photographs.

He took out the one taken on board a boat and pointed not to the woman, but to the man beside her. 'That is Matti Salomäki. She killed him on October the second last year and then disappeared. He was a fine officer and a dear friend. That's why I want to find her. And I'm sorry to say, but as far as I can see and from what Crawford tells me, you are about the only person in this country who would also like to find her.'

Nicole sat and stared at the photograph. 'Who took this?'

'It was taken by another police officer from the pier in Helsinki Harbour. At the time we thought she might assist us on another matter. We didn't know who she was but she had been seen with some people we had an interest in. Matti was chosen to make the approach. When she got on the ferry to Suomenlinna...' He paused and then explained, 'It's an island in Helsinki harbour, something of a tourist attraction.'

Nicole nodded for him to continue.

'He was seen disembarking from the ferry. Then nothing. We found his body a couple of hours later. He had been shot.'

Nicole thought for a moment. The man seemed genuine, but that was not her concern. 'I am sorry about your friend, but there is nothing I can do to help you. As Crawford probably told you, the woman was found laid out in a boat. She was revived and later escaped from hospital. That, I am afraid, is the end of the story. All the photographs of the crime scene and the recording of an interview with her have disappeared. I'm so sorry.'

'Doesn't it interest you as to why they disappeared?'

'Naturally. But there is nothing I can do about it.' She glanced at him. He was examining his fingernails, his expression unread-able. 'And as Crawford should have explained, I am not exactly in a position to help anyone.'

'Suspended or on indefinite leave. He was vague about your status. But yes, he mentioned it.' He sighed and took a card from his pocket. 'The woman we are looking for is obviously Finnish, so I will go back to Helsinki tomorrow. If you change your mind and think we could assist each other, or ever need to contact me, my number is here.'

'I'm afraid there is not the remotest possibility of that,' she said as bluntly as she could. But she took the card.

At the gate she turned. He was still sitting there, looking up into the clouds as though there was something there that would provide him with answers. What a sad individual, she thought. She walked out of the garden and caught a taxi, just as the rain began to tumble down.

Over the next week Nicole concentrated on Chris Mitchell. By the third day she had discovered him to be a creature of habit. Not, she thought, a good attribute for a spook. Most mornings he took the same route to work in his distinctive purple car. He arrived around nine and parked underground in a gated facility that he accessed by remote control. His routine didn't vary. The car remained parked all day and between seven-thirty and eight he returned to his car and drove home. The only exception was Wednesdays when, while his hours remained the same, he arrived and returned from work across the road at Vauxhall station. On Wednesdays, she discovered, his wife took the car for shopping and a game of squash.

Nicole chose a Tuesday because, as she had observed, it was a day when the cars parked nearby were, for whatever reason, departed well before Mitchell put in an appearance. She waited some distance away and only made her approach as he unlocked his car.

'Mister Mitchell! This is a surprise,' she said brightly. 'I was just on my way to your office.'

For a moment or two he was confused, peering at her, uncertain what to do. 'You're that bloody detective...' he began.

'That I am,' she smiled. 'And seeing as you won't cooperate, I'm going to also pay a visit to Quentin.'

She could see immediately that she had hit the mark, so she pressed home her advantage. 'I'm assured he will be more forth-coming. Have a pleasant evening, Mister Mitchell.' She turned and began to walk briskly towards the exit.

'Wait...'

Nicole stopped and turned back. 'Why? Is there something you want to tell me?'

'You are going to see Quentin?'

'That was the plan... unless you can think of an alternative.'

'If you know Quentin and know where I work, then you must understand that I am not supposed to talk to you.'

'Of course, I understand that,' Nicole walked slowly back towards him. 'But sometimes, as you are well aware, in the interest of the greater good, a few minor rules can be broken.' She allowed a pause for that to sink in, then added, 'And in your interests as well.' She watched him, a man flustered and confused, knowing that she had him. A trout on a bloody big hook, and there was no way she was going to let up.

'What is it you're after?'

'No, no, Chris,' she slipped in his name, a little intimacy between conspirators. 'Think rather what you're after. Our superiors think that Quentin has overplayed his hand, and strictly between us, he may be in for a bit of a tumble. Whichever way this goes, it will affect your career. It's up to you in what direction.'

'Christ!'

'Be strategic, Chris. Help me and I'll pass the word back up the food chain.'

'And Long Crendon?'

Nicole let him dangle for a moment, then reeled him in. 'I believe the young couple could be convinced that making their sexual exploits public is not in their best interests.'

Mitchell drew in a deep breath and then nodded. 'Then I think we have an agreement.'

'In that case, I suggest you tell me what the fuck is going on.'

'Honestly, I haven't any idea.'

Nicole looked at him sceptically. 'You'll have to do better than that, I'm afraid. Let's talk about the woman in the boat.'

'I swear, all I know is that every file on her is to disappear. It never happened.'

'And the removal of files from my office?'

'They were part of the case, and when Quentin says something is to be cleaned up he expects a thorough job.'

'So, your job was to make anything to do with that woman go away?'

'Listen. I am being as clear as I can. I had it all sorted and then you had to mess things up by sending that MP3 file to an unauthorised person...'

'Oh? Did I indeed? Unauthorised by whom? All I did was ask for assistance with a translation. My friend Tom Myers was killed because of it.'

Mitchell nodded. 'Yes, we also suspect that, but nobody is sure.'

Nicole squinted at him. 'Are you telling me that you and your spook friends didn't kill Tom?'

'I swear it. When our people arrived, he was already dead.'

'And you sat outside all night and did nothing.'

'It was what I was ordered to do.'

'You are serious? You don't know who killed Tom?'

'You have my word.'

'And Grammaticus?'

'I am sure he has no idea.'

'Then remember this. If you find out who killed him, or even have a vague suspicion, you will contact me immediately. Otherwise, I am afraid the little incident at Long Crendon will start causing problems.'

'And if I help you?'

'My superiors and yours will show their gratitude.'

Late that evening Nicole wandered home. Satisfied with the success of her fishing expedition, she had called in at the Eight Bells for a drink and bite to eat. A celebration of sorts, justified because the information Mitchell had divulged had been worth the effort. The next step, working out what to do with that information, would take time, but she was convinced she had the ammunition she needed to defend her position if Burnside got her way and there was a disciplinary hearing.

Nicole opened the door to her house and was relieved to find there was no smell of paint stripper. She was happy to be home, with only one slight disappointment. The detour to the Eight Bells had been what she needed in all but one respect – there had been no sign of Toby. Had he been there, the evening would have been perfect and she would have been rather absorbed in discussions about the architecture of her bed.

Out of habit she turned on her MacBook Air and checked her email. The spam filter had failed to clear an advert for a larger penis, Mister Gupta's offer of an investment opportunity that would make her rich overnight, and the welcome news that she had won ten million in a European Super Lotto – it was her third win in a week. She wondered what the scam-artists would think if she replied that she would personally come to Spain, or Luxemburg, or wherever they were based and collect her winnings. No, it was a silly idea, not worth thinking about. However, she missed all the Nigerian widows with their pleas to look after their late husbands' fortunes. But, she shrugged philosophically, life moves on. She nearly deleted the next email when she froze. She didn't recognise the sender – sirkka.mikkonen@helsinki.fi – but it was addressed to Tom Myers and copied to her.

Hei Hei Thomas,

Sorry about the delay but I have been marking examinations. Thank you for sending me the audio file. It is fascinating. My problem, and I suspect, now yours and your detective friend's, is that the language is not modern Finnish. For some strange reason (I suspect a joke), the woman is speaking in ancient Finnish (vanha suomi), which is not my field, but from what I do understand, she says her name is 'Aino' and someone has stolen the 'Sampo.' Very strange, I must say. I have a friend who could probably tell you more and I have sent her the file, so let me know if you need to know more. Over your way for a conference in February, so I look forward to catching up.

Yours affectionately,
Sirkka

PS – I have copied this to your friend.

Nicole read the email again, several times. Then she made a decision. She hunted through her jacket pockets and eventually found the card that Pentti Toivonen had given her. She rang the number on it and then, after a brief conversation, hung up. She had never been to Finland, but according to Pentti she would find it rather dull and flat. Well, she thought, as she climbed the stairs to start packing, at least I won't be disappointed.

Part Two

Ei sanat salahan joua eikä luottehet lovehen;
  mahti ei joua maan rakohon,
  vaikka mahtajat menevät.

Words shall not be hidden, nor spells buried;
  might shall not sink underground,
  though the mighty go.

– Kalevala (Seitsemästoista runo)

Chapter Six

Pentti Toivonen was worried. It had been a week since his futile trip to London, and now, without more than a day's warning, the rude English policewoman, Nicole Parry, was about to descend on him. And while he was as determined as ever to find the woman who the police suspected had murdered Matti Salomäki, he could see no possibility that this irksome woman could assist. However, on advice from his superior, he undertook to be welcoming, explain the complexities of the case in general terms, then after a couple of days sightseeing in Helsinki, put her back on a plane to England. Pentti's concurrence was somewhat reluctant for, as his superior was at pains to point out, it was an unofficial visit and hence there was no budget allocation for expenses. His boss added, by way of a parting remark, that this woman was under no circumstances to be given access to confidential material.

For an hour he scoured the Internet looking for cheap Helsinki hotels. They appeared to be an extinct species. It had been some years since the words 'Helsinki' and 'cheap' appeared in the same sentence. He walked over to the window and peered at the thermometer. The double-glazing was faulty and condensation, ice, or maybe simply grime, made reading the temperature impossible on cold days. It was a large thermometer but the mercury was only visible once the temperature reached 26 degrees. Sadly, that was not a frequent event.

It had been a bad winter so far, insomuch as it had been unusually warm. Not enough snow to make everything look beautiful, and what snow there had been soon reduced to slush. Hopefully they would get a cold snap and skating, skiing and ice fishing would be back on the agenda. He'd seen on the news that the regions further north had decent snow, but at the moment he wasn't in a position to take the time off.

The view from the window was less than inspiring, except when he looked up into scudding clouds that were offering more than a hint of rain or even more snow. No matter what the weather, he always found clouds interesting. Looking down, he could see the bookshop opposite and a glimpse of a tram travelling along Fredrikinkatu. That he had a view at all was something of a miracle, as most of his colleagues were crammed into spaces that in a decent world would have been closets. On the positive side the cramped conditions acted as an incentive to get most people out into the real world rather than remain behind a computer.

The thought of small, cramped spaces gave him an idea. He rang Heimo Harkimo. For more than ten years Pentti and his boss had enjoyed a close relationship, which extended outside the office. They enjoyed weekly visits to the public sauna together, drinking, and on occasion staying with Harkimo's family at his summer cottage near Punkaharju. He had no doubt that he could convince Heimo of the solution to his problem.

'Is the small apartment around the corner in Freda being used at the moment?'

'Hang on.'

In the short pause he could hear Heimo typing in a query. Like most of the senior officers, he was of a generation that had grown up pre-computers and like almost all of his contemporaries, was a two-finger thumper. He was convinced that unless he typed extremely firmly the computer would not respond.

'Yes, the safe house at Fredrikinkatu twenty is free. But if this is for that British policewoman...'

Pentti anticipated what the objections would be, but also that his boss knew he could be trusted.

'Heimo, it will only be for two nights.'

'Okay, but you had better make it look more like an apartment and a little less like a holding cell.'

Transforming the apartment was not as easy as he had first supposed. It involved two hours of shopping, just on one hundred euro, and several more hours of what he described to himself as 'set-dressing'. Fortunately, the washer-dryer was efficient and by seven in the evening the sheets and pillowcases no longer looked as if they had just come out of the packet.

He stocked the refrigerator, dusted the furniture and added the new cushions to the sofa. Knowing it would be a tedious process, he had taken the precaution of providing himself with food, so at around nine he cooked a salmon steak, and washed it down with a bottle of beer. Then, to give the lived-in atmosphere a little authenticity, he grabbed a spare blanket and slept on the sofa.

The following morning Pentti checked the flight times the Parry woman had emailed and realised he had the entire day to complete his preparations. Her flight was not due in at Vantaa until half-past ten at night, so he drove out to Espoo and visited his sister. Pauliina's husband was a wily French stockbroker whose ever-increasing good fortune managed to stay ahead of Pauliina's considerable ability to shop. They had chosen not to have children, preferring to spend their time travelling and enjoying the good life. While Pentti was not particularly fond of Pascal, whom he thought somewhat arrogant, he and his sister were extremely close and his strange request proved to be no problem.

Pauliina obligingly packed two suitcases with some of her and her husband's old clothes and, sensing an opportunity to get rid of some unwanted fashion magazines, loaded him up with far more than he needed. Pentti kissed her and drove back to Fredrikinkatu.

By the time Pentti had put the clothes in the drawers, hung a few blouses and shirts in the one small cupboard, and scattered a few magazines around, he was satisfied that the apartment looked lived in.

Nicole's flight arrived on time and he had only a few minutes to wait before she emerged from immigration. She was not in a talkative mood and responded to his enquiry about the pleasantness or otherwise of her flight with a non-committal 'so-so'. He was pleased to see that she had only carry-on luggage and had dressed for the weather. She was entirely in black, with a padded three-quarter length black coat, scarf, and small woollen cap pulled down over her short-cropped hair. And she had gloves. His offer to carry her bag for her was declined. Please yourself, he thought, following her as she trudged out to the car park. He supposed that some men would probably find her attractive – that was until they encountered her prickly attitude.

They drove in from Vantaa in silence. The temperature outside was minus two. It felt only slightly less chilly in the car. Eventually, as they turned into Fredrikinkatu, he grew sick of her silence and decided he would make another attempt to be friendly.

'Seeing it's your first time in Helsinki, I thought that tomorrow we could go for a drive around. The city is worth seeing and I have planned a route that will take in all the sights and then at lunchtime we could go to the Vanha Kauppahalli, the Old Market Hall, and have lunch. I thought I would pick you up around ten.'

Nicole loosened her seat belt and turned to face him.

'Mister Toivonen, we are interviewing someone first thing in the morning. I don't know how far it is from wherever we are to the Helsinki University, but I suggest you arrive in time to get us there at nine.'

He slowed the car down and pulled over. 'The university has several campuses…'

'It's the Department of Finnish, Finno-Ugrian and Scandinavian Studies. I can't pronounce the street name, but it is something like Union Street.'

'Unioninkatu. It will take us less than ten minutes.'

Pentti switched off the motor. 'We're here.' He got out of the car and led the way to the gate. 'If you get lost, it's number twenty. The apartment number is four, two. Apartment two on the fourth floor.' He swung the gate open, waited until she was through and then, after pressing the remote to lock his car, gestured to her to cross the courtyard to the yellow building. 'Thankfully there's an elevator.'

Once inside the apartment, Nicole swung her cabin bag onto the table, pulled out her laptop and switched it on. Then, while she waited for it to boot up, she turned to him. 'Is there Wifi?'

Crawford had warned him about Nicole's mood swings and irascible nature; he was right to do so, for Pentti was finding her very hard work. Crawford claimed it was some form of mild syndrome. Well, Pentti thought blackly, he was wrong about that. It was anything but mild. The next two days looked as if they would be very long.

'Yes, there's Wifi,' he said patiently, 'and the password *is bo-dominjärvi neljä. Bodominjärvi* is all one word, lowercase and *neljä*is the number four.'

To his amazement she ignored the hostile tone in his voice and smiled.

'Well, I won't forget that in a hurry.'

'Look, sorry. I have written it down with everything else you need to know. It's on top of the television. There's food in the cupboard and some things in the fridge. Please excuse the tiny apartment.'

'Not at all, it's sweet and very kind of you to find something other than a hotel.'

'It's nothing,' he allowed himself a smile. 'It's my sister's place. She lives in Espoo, but uses the apartment when she has to work late. She's very involved in fashion retail.' It was only a half lie.

After Pentti had left, Nicole explored the apartment. It was small, compact but functional. To her disappointment there was no bath and the shower was tiny. In the kitchen, which was really just an alcove off the main room, she found some tea bags and an electric kettle, so made herself a cup of tea. Then, not ready to sleep, she entered the Wifi password into the computer and logged on. To her relief the Internet connection was fast.

She ran a couple of Google searches, made a note of what she learned and then checked her email. The display on her computer claimed it was only eleven in the evening. Thankfully, she had changed her wristwatch when she landed. If her meeting was at nine and her internal clock said seven, she realised she needed some sleep.

After switching off her computer, she was going to brush her teeth when she remembered she had left the toothpaste behind, so as not to have it confiscated by over-zealous airport security staff. She made a mental note to buy some toothpaste in the morning, set her phone alarm for six, undressed, donned her pyjamas and slid between the sheets. Thankfully they were fresh and crisp; just like new ones, she thought as she drifted off to sleep.

Chris Mitchell had a problem. Normally he would have gone straight to Grammaticus, but the nature of the problem was such that he hesitated. Earlier in the day he had switched on the laptop that had been seized from the cottage at Long Crendon. After a cursory glance at the files, he went into Tom Myers' email. The man hadn't any security on it and the Gmail account opened without needing a password. He watched as over one hundred new emails loaded, then began to go through them, starting with the oldest. It was a tedious job, but Grammaticus had suggested it be done. 'Just to make sure there are no loose ends'.

Most of the correspondence was with suppliers – order confirmations and invoices. A terse note from an accountancy firm reminded Myers that his VAT returns were late. Mitchell smiled. They will be a lot later now. The first personal email was from someone named Derek who wanted to know if Tom could make it to a party in Brighton. Sadly not, and, Mitchell mused, anyone who still operated a Hotmail account was seriously out of date. There was nothing interesting in the emails up until the date of Tom's death. The day following, there had been a short message from someone called Alejandro, sent from an iPhone, saying that he would be delayed for a couple of days; a couple of days too late, as it turned out. There was nothing here, he decided. It was also boring... until he clicked on the next email.

Mitchell read the email again. The words 'audio file' and 'your detective friend' were alarming, to say the least. He had no doubt about what they referenced and also no doubt as to how Grammaticus would react. He was right.

'This was supposed to be buried,' Quentin muttered testily.

He spoke so softly that Mitchell had trouble hearing him, but he knew from experience that his boss's tone was a danger signal. It was, he imagined, like the quiet hiss of a viper; its energy coiled, ready to strike.

'It would appear not,' Mitchell said.

Quentin walked to the window and stood, motionless, gazing out into a sea of mist that had effectively blotted out London.

Mitchell knew better than to interrupt Grammaticus in moments like this.

After a time, Quentin spoke, his voice as cold and bleak as the view.

'I want you to find out where this Parry bitch is.'

'Yes, Quentin.'

Parry was another issue. Since his unfortunate meeting with her, he had shut her out of his mind. At the time he had said enough to get rid of her. Maybe he could find a way to shut her up permanently. Sadly, that sort of thing only happened in crime thrillers, or in America. We British are, he had decided a long time ago, too damn polite.

'I also want you to find out everything about this Sirkka Mikkonen.'

'Everything,' Mitchell echoed.

'In particular I want to know to whom she sent copies of the MP3 file. She mentions only one person, but it is possible she has also sent it to others.'

'Yes,' Mitchell responded. Grammaticus was still contemplating the mist. 'Quentin... DI Parry? What do we do about her, once we have her located?'

'Nothing until we see if she has decided to stick her nose in again. If she has, we will cut it off.'

'And the MP3 files?'

'To be deleted.'

'I don't know much about Finland. Do we have friends in their security service who could take care of that end?'

Quentin turned. 'Mitchell, get this clearly understood. In this job we have no friends.'

'So, I should go?' The thought was both exhilarating and perturbing.

Quentin studied him closely. 'Mitchell, if you doubt your ability to perform a simple task such as this, then I suggest you tell me now. Any one of a dozen young Turks would be happy to take your place.'

'No, sir, I am confident I can do the job. I was simply seeking clarification.'

'Then get this clear. You find Parry and make certain she is no longer a player. Then, when we are satisfied she has been quarantined, you will pack some warm clothes and take yourself off for a holiday in Helsinki. I understand it is particularly pleasant at this time of year.'

He recognised the joke and smiled dutifully. Quentin nodded slowly, which Mitchell knew was his cue to leave.

'I'll get on to finding Parry right away.'

He was just about to shut the door behind him when Quentin called him back.

'One more thing, Mitchell.'

'Yes?'

'Find out what the fuck a *Sampo* is.'

It had snowed overnight and the view of the rooftops from her window had been transformed from its previously bleak grey to pristine white. It was, she thought, decidedly pretty. She looked at her watch as she saw Pentti making his way across the courtyard, leaving footprints in the fresh snow. Mister Owl was on time.

Nicole had woken early, made herself a bowl of delicious porridge with full cream milk and brown sugar followed by a cup of coffee. It was a better breakfast than she allowed herself at home.

'Good morning, Nicole,' he said as she let him in, his glasses fogging up in the warmth of the apartment. He removed them, took out a neatly folded handkerchief, and wiped them clear. 'I hope you slept well.'

So, it was all politeness and first names now, very chummy. She only just stopped herself calling him Mister Owl.

'Morning, Pentti,' she said, pronouncing his name carefully; mimicking the pronunciation from the audio on the Finnish names site she had Googled the previous night. 'And, yes, I slept extremely well, *kiitos*.'

His face broke into a grin. 'Ah, I hear that you have been doing homework.'

'Far more than you imagine.'

'Meaning?'

'I'll save that for later. Now we must go.'

The traffic was light and it took them only ten minutes to get to the centre of the city. Nicole sat in silence, intending to go over the questions she needed to ask. However, she found herself distracted. The city was beautiful, with granite buildings topped by small snow-dusted turrets that looked as if they had sprung out of fairy tales. Then Pentti turned into a wide-open snow-covered square and she found herself surprisingly moved by the sight to her left. A broad sweep of steps led up from a cobbled square to a glorious building that was obviously the heart of the city.

'It's beautiful, and nothing like I expected.'

'And what did you expect?'

'Someplace dull and flat.'

'Okay, I exaggerated about the flat part.'

She looked up at the pristine-white domed building that dominated the square. 'And that, what's that place?'

'The Senate. The harbour is just a few hundred metres down there.' He pointed straight ahead. 'We can see it later, after Unioninkatu. What was the number?'

'Forty,' Nicole said, still entranced by the buildings. The thought popped into her mind that Toby, her one-night-stand architect, would love this place.

'I don't know anything about architecture, but there seems to be a real mix of styles.'

Pentti nodded, suddenly enthusiastic. 'So, you have been paying attention. There's a lot of what people call Nordic minimalism. Some people really like the Modernist functionalism, but me? I am very fond of *Jugendstil*. What our neighbours, the Russians, call *Modern*. I think you English say *Art Nouveau*?'

Nicole shrugged. She had been truthful saying she knew nothing, but she thought it rather sweet that someone would use the word 'fond' when describing an architectural style.

'Anyway, Helsinki has the biggest concentration of *Jugendstil* buildings in all of Northern Europe.'

'But that building back there, the Senate, that looks sort of Roman or Greek.'

'All around the Senate Square is Neoclassical.'

'I'll take your word for it,' Nicole laughed, but made a mental note to remember the conversation to recount if she ever saw Toby again.

Pentti slowed down. 'Number forty?'

'Yes.'

'This is the National Library? Is that where you want to go?'

Nicole dug into her handbag and extracted her notebook. 'No, it's a university department.' She squinted at her notebook. 'Hang on…' She fished around in the bag again, located her glasses, put them on, poked them up her nose and studied her notes. 'That's better. It's the Department of Finnish, Finno-Ugrian and Scandinavian Studies. A Professor Sirkka Mikkonen.'

'Okay.' Pentti pulled into a small car park. It looked to Nicole as if it was reserved parking.

Seeing her concerned expression, he shook his head. 'Nobody will tow my car away.' He opened his door. 'Please, just a moment, I will ask somebody.'

Two minutes later he was back.

'Well, we are in the right place. The university has access from this street and from Fabianinkatu thirty-three on the other side. The entrance to the Finno-Ugrian department is just back along the road. Twenty metres.'

The name on the department secretary's desk read: Anna Ericson. Looking up from her computer, the young woman smiled and glanced at her watch. 'Good morning,' she said and then added approvingly, 'You are exactly on time.'

Nicole wondered what the penalty was for being late. But she made a mental note that Finns preferred punctuality. She also wondered what it was about her that signalled the woman to address her in English. Then she recalled that she had emailed the department, requesting the interview. Of course the women knew she was English.

The secretary pointed towards a door. 'Please, go through. Professor Mikkonen is expecting you.'

There were two women waiting for them. The woman behind the desk was in her mid-thirties, with shoulder-length hennaed hair and high cheekbones. There was something about her that looked different from the faces Nicole had come to think of as Finnish. The second woman, seated on a chair to one side, Nicole immediately picked as being Finnish. She was strikingly beautiful and sat in a particularly upright way. She was older, maybe in her mid-fifties, her grey hair tied back in an old-fashioned bun. Her cardigan, buttoned up to her blouse collar, reminded Nicole of something her mother might have worn.

The woman behind the desk rose and came around to greet them.

'*Tervetuloa*! Welcome! I'm Sirkka Mikkonen and you must be Detective Parry.' She extended her hand. 'It is a pleasure to meet you.'

'Nicole Parry, please call me Nicole.' Nicole shook her hand and turned to Pentti. 'And my Finnish colleague...'

He picked up her cue and introduced himself before she could stumble over his name.

'*Pentti Toivonen, olen rikospoliisista.*'

'Two police in my office! Now I am feeling guilty about something.' Sirkka smiled and turned to the other woman. 'This is my dear friend, invaluable mentor, and my former professor, Kaija Rantaniemi.'

The woman rose, nodded her head and shook hands. 'She is too kind. I am afraid if I had been a better mentor, Sirkka would not be in such a small office.'

'It's very kind of you to see us,' Nicole said.

'It is a pleasure,' Sirkka said. 'Please, sit down. Anna will bring us coffee and cake.' She sat and spread her hands on the desk. 'First let me say how sad I was at the news of Thomas's death. We have been friends for over ten years, and since he opened his shop in Oxford I have been helping him get Finnish jams, smoked fish and so on. I will really miss him.'

'It was a shock,' Nicole said. 'He was a dear friend, and I feel dreadful that somehow I caused him to be involved in all this.'

'You think his death is connected to the tape?'

Nicole sighed. 'I'm struggling to make sense of it. The only thing I know for certain is that he did not kill himself.'

Sirkka shook her head. 'No. It is inconceivable.' She took a deep breath and composed herself. 'So, how can we help you?'

'You have heard the recording and although it may not help my investigation, it will certainly clear things up if I know what the woman was talking about.'

'Do you mind my asking what the case is?' Kaija asked. Her voice was soft and her accent only barely perceptible.

Nicole glanced at Pentti. He was sitting impassively and gave her no indication that he was going to volunteer anything, so Nicole explained what she knew.

'Someone had tried to murder her?' Sirkka asked.

'She was taken to a hospital where she gave the interview you've heard. Then she disappeared. That's all we know. If there was an actual crime, I would say it was attempted murder.'

'Poor thing,' Sirkka murmured. 'Do you think she is still alive?'

'I have no idea.'

Pentti leaned forward in his chair. 'The police are interested in this woman as well, but for a different reason.'

'Which is?' Sirkka asked.

'We suspect she killed someone.'

'Oh dear!' Sirkka exclaimed. 'Attempted murder on one hand and murder on the other; who is this woman?'

With a nod, Pentti deferred to Nicole.

'That's the problem. Neither the British police nor the Finnish police know who she is. We are hoping that the interview can tell us something.'

Sirkka shot a glance at Kaija, who shrugged.

'Yes, but maybe not what you need.'

At that moment there was a soft knock on the door and the secretary appeared with a tray of coffee and cakes.

'Thank you, Anna,' Sirkka said. 'On the desk will be fine. I hope you saved one of Kaija's *pulla* for yourself.'

The woman put the tray on the table.

'I have already had mine. It was delicious, Professor.'

The older woman was obviously pleased, but didn't respond until the secretary had closed the door behind her. 'I should hope I can bake *pulla*,' she said. 'I have had plenty of years to practice.'

'This is *pulla*.' Sirkka indicated some small round buns. 'Every Finnish woman knows how to make them but few do it as well as Kaija.'

'I make *pulla* the way my mother made it, but she called it *nisu*,' Kaija said.

'It has crushed cardamom on it. And the braided bread is *pitko*.' Sirkka poured the coffee into four cups and held up a jug. 'Milk? Sugar?'

'Milk, thank you,' Nicole said, 'just a splash.'

Pentti shook his head.

'So you listened to the audio file as well, Kaija?' Nicole asked.

'I found it most disturbing.'

'Why?'

Kaija thought for a moment, took a piece of *pulla* and dipped it in her coffee. 'The woman was speaking Old Finnish. I would have said *vanha kirjasuomi,* old literary Finnish, but she spoke it as if it was her native tongue.'

'And why is that disturbing?'

Sirkka edged the tray of breads across the desk to Nicole and Pentti. 'Because no living person speaks it, it's a dead language.'

'What did the woman say?' Pentti asked, 'I take it you could understand.'

'Old Finnish is not my area, though of course it does impact on my work. However, I could understand almost everything except maybe the nuances. That's why I asked Kaija.'

Nicole took a piece of *pulla* and following Kaija's example, dipped it in her coffee. It was not as sweet as she had imagined, but certainly delicious. 'What is your area?'

Sirkka laughed loudly. 'You may be sorry you asked, or arrest me for attempting to bore you to death.'

'I'll risk it if you will,' Nicole said, warming to the woman.

'The joke my colleagues have is that I only study two hundred or so words. In a way it's true. In general terms, I study Ugric languages. In particular I am working on the linguistic roots shared by

Finno-Permic and Ugric. Most philologists agree there are around two hundred words with common roots; mostly about fishing and reindeer.' She paused and took a sip of her coffee. 'Sorry, that was too much information.'

'Not at all,' Nicole smiled. 'So you are a word detective?'

Kaija smiled. 'With very few suspects.'

'What the woman said,' Sirkka continued, 'was basically what I told you in the email. Her name was Aino and the *Sampo* had been stolen.'

Pentti put down his coffee cup and turned to the older woman. 'You mentioned nuances?'

Kaija nodded. 'For a start, I don't think her name is Aino.'

'That *is* a Finnish name?' Nicole was scrambling to keep up.

'It is a made-up name. Elias Lönnrot, the man who compiled the Kalevala, invented the name.' There was something in Kaija's tone that suggested that whoever the man was, he was out of line.

'Hang on,' Nicole protested. 'Can we accept I know absolutely nothing. For a start: Kalevala?'

Sirkka laughed. 'Okay. The Kalevala is our national epic poem. Elias Lönnrot created it by stitching together a lot of oral poetry that he and others had collected. In the past children would study Kalevala much like you probably learned Shakespeare, but now...' she shook her head sadly. 'A lot of young people have never heard of it.'

Kaija returned her cup to the tray and gestured to Sirkka to top it up. 'In all the original variants there is no mention of Aino. In fact, the name comes from Old Finnish poetry.' She stood up and went to the whiteboard behind Sirkka's desk. 'Can I play at being a teacher again?'

'Could I stop you?' Sirkka laughed.

'Let me show you.' Kaija picked up a marker pen and wrote '*ainoa tytär*' on the board. 'This means "only daughter". If you look at it you can see the word "Aino" buried in the first word. So what Lönnrot did was to take away the final "a" and "ainoa" became "Aino", meaning "only". I'm not sure why he bothered.' She placed the marker down carefully and returned to her chair. 'For better or for worse, it has become a very popular name for girls. At present there are probably more than sixty thousand Finnish women named Aino, which makes a mockery of its meaning.'

'But,' Pentti interjected, 'to get back to what the woman said…'

'What Sirkka and I agree on is that though the woman claims to be Aino, it is not her name,' Kaija said. 'The way she stressed it was too emphatic, or rather, the emphasis was wrong. It was not "my name is *Aino*", but rather "my name *is* Aino". In a way it was like a child pretending to be Spiderwoman and insisting that was her name.'

Nicole felt as though she was back in school. She raised her hand. 'Could she have been emphasising "is" simply because she was frustrated that nobody understood what she was saying?'

'That is possible,' Kaija conceded, 'but the tone was not one of frustration, but rather of pleading.'

Sirkka nodded. 'When we listened to it the other evening, Kaija said something that struck me as true. The woman is desperate to convince the listener that Aino is her name.'

'And she says this over and over?' Nicole asked, 'For six minutes?'

'No, she claims to be Aino maybe seven or eight times and then she seems to drift off…' Kaija hesitated for a moment and then continued. 'Yes, drifts off, as if dreaming and she says, or rather almost sings… *Mitä itket, tyttö raukka…*' She nodded at Sirkka.

'… *tyttö raukka, neito nuori*?' Sirkka chanted, completing the verse.

'Well done,' Kaija beamed.

'Why are you crying, poor girl, poor girl, young lady?' Sirkka translated.

'From the Kalevala.' Kaija sounded suddenly jubilant as if somehow everything was explained. She turned to Sirkka. 'From?'

'*Neljäs runo*! The fourth canto, lines forty-one and forty-two.'

It was like watching a teacher and pupil playing a word game. Nicole suspected they had played it many times before.

'Sirkka was one of my better pupils,' Kaija said proudly, 'She could recite many, many poems from Kalevala.'

'And "Sampo", what is "Sampo"?'

For a moment Nicole thought she must have asked a sensitive question. The two women looked at each other with wry smiles on their faces. And Pentti, who had been particularly quiet, suddenly burst out laughing.

'Nicole, it's a mythical object, the Sampo, forged by the immortal blacksmith, Ilmarinen. And if we knew the answer to that question, we would be national heroes.'

Nicole looked at him coldly. 'It was a serious question.'

'I'm sorry, Nicole,' Sirkka said. 'But there are people who have built academic careers on trying to answer the question you ask. In truth, the Sampo is probably whatever you want it to be.'

'A mythical object, a mill that grinds gold...' Kaija shrugged. 'It is an object of power maybe. A lot of poems in the Kalevala deal with its making, its loss and so on.'

Nicole looked from one woman to the other. It appeared they were serious. 'Then why was this woman upset that it had been stolen?'

The women exchanged glances.

'It's certainly not my area of expertise, but I think you have to seriously consider the possibility that she may have been mentally ill, or on drugs?' Sirkka said.

'We have evidence that she had been drugged,' Nicole said. Then another question occurred to her. 'When she said her name was Aino, was that a direct response to the detective's question?'

Kaija thought for a moment, then nodded. 'Yes. Exactly.'

'Then despite the fact that she was speaking a dead language, it would be correct to assume she understood English.'

As they drove back towards the apartment, Nicole, feeling frustrated, mulled over what she had learned. Apart from a crash course in Finnish literature, linguistics and mythology, it amounted to nothing. She watched Pentti driving. His contribution to the conversation had been so minimal, he might as well have not been there. Not for the first time she wondered how good a detective he was. His temperament suggested he would be better filing lost property cases. She decided he would have been admirably suited to the job she had been doing down in the crypt. Maybe he was simply playing an investigator because of the murder of his friend. Pentti's silences and seeming lack of engagement annoyed her, so she decided to prod him.

'So what did you make of that?'

He grunted. 'Interesting.'

Nicole waited for him to elaborate, but he was not forthcoming.

'In what way interesting?' she asked, with all the patience she could muster.

'I find it interesting that people can spend their lives studying such things.'

'For christsake!' Nicole exploded. 'I am talking about my case.'

Pentti glanced sideways at her. 'Our case.'

'Oh really? And what case is that? You know everything about what happened in London and you have told me nothing about the murder here.'

Pentti shrugged. Then he suddenly swerved into another lane, turned hard left and accelerated in the opposite direction. She had no doubt he was exceeding whatever the local speed limit was. He turned into a wider street, a boulevard with a garden and trees that separated the traffic in each direction. His driving, though fast, was controlled; nevertheless, Nicole checked her seatbelt was secure, but decided against saying anything. It was the first time she had seen any emotion in the man, even if it was only expressed through his driving. It's a start, she thought.

At the end of the boulevard they came to the harbour. Pentti swung into a parking spot and switched off the engine.

'Come,' he said, indicating she should get out of the car. 'I will tell you about the murder of Matti Salomäki.'

Chapter Seven

DI Parry had vanished. In any other circumstances, that would have been a desirable outcome. However, having been tasked with locating her whereabouts, Chris Mitchell found the situation frustrating. Having co-opted two of Quentin's team to assist him, his assumption had been that the matter would be sorted in a matter of hours, not days.

When the paltry information they garnered did finally trickle in, it was confusing. According to one source in the Hammersmith police, Nicole Parry had been dismissed. Another claimed she had merely been suspended. Close observation of her house had revealed nothing other than that she had installed an automatic timer to switch a number of lights on each evening. She was certainly not at home.

Enquiries at the Eight Bells were initially promising. Mitchell had gone to the pub himself. Aware that his charms worked far better with women, he ignored the barman and waited until the barmaid had a break. Over a beer, Susan was only too happy to confide in this good-looking plain clothes policeman. He was, she decided, rather dishy.

Mitchell chatted with her for a few minutes then casually introduced the subject of an old friend he hadn't seen for a while. 'Nicole Parry,' he said. 'You may have seen her in here. I think it was the Eight Bells she mentioned.'

Susan looked at him blankly then her expression changed. 'You mean the policewoman?'

He nodded. 'Short hair.'

'Sure. Not a regular, but she drops in from time to time. She keeps to herself, mostly,' she added.

'Mostly?' Mitchell raised an eyebrow.

'Well, last time I saw her she was with a male friend, another semi-regular.'

'A boyfriend?' Mitchell pulled a forlorn expression.

Susan sniggered. 'Well, they certainly left together.'

'While you're stuck here pulling beers,' Mitchell said consolingly.

'Yes. All work and no play. But I get off at one.' She smiled, then reached out and laid her hand on his. 'You're nice to talk with. I'm sorry I have to get back to work.'

Mitchell squeezed her hand gently. 'Another time then?'

Susan mouthed a kiss. 'I would really like that.'

The 'male friend', an architect named Toby Branch, confirmed that he knew Nicole, but hadn't seen her for a while. While he claimed to have made no arrangement with Parry, he did express an interest in seeing her again.

'What joy?' Quentin asked. 'What news from the Rialto?'

Not a lot of joy, Mitchell thought glumly, and then briefed him on what they had found.

Quentin was less than impressed. '*Ceteris paribus,* you have found nothing.'

'Not exactly nothing, Quentin.' It was a feeble protestation and he knew it.

Quentin affected a weary sigh and held up his hand. 'Just a moment, Mitchell, let us hear what the Chief Superintendent has to say.' He picked up the phone and dialled Crawford's number.

'Andy, a quick word, if you don't mind. I am seeking to have a chat with your charming DI Parry.' He listened for a moment and then replaced the receiver. '*Et lux in tenebris lucet,* Mitchell. A little light in the darkness.'

'Good news, I hope.'

'DI Parry is on holiday,' Quentin spoke slowly, as if to a child. 'Now, please tell me you have run a check on border control to see if she has left the country.'

'It's being done as we speak.' It was a lie, but only a small one. The check would be implemented as soon as he could get out of Grammaticus's office. He hastened to explain that the woman, Sirkka Mikkonen, was a professor of linguistics at the University of Helsinki. 'I suspect she will be willing to divulge the translation of the MP3 file.' Mitchell, back on firmer ground, allowed his confidence to show. 'I'll take care of that myself, Quentin.'

'You will inform me the minute we have a translation of the interview and that the recording has been deleted.' He peered at Mitchell and not for the first time wondered if he had promoted the chap above the level of his competence. No matter, any stuff-ups and Mitchell would be back in the requisitions department, or whatever other sheltered workshop he had crawled out of. 'Oh, and this Sampo thing, have you established what it is, or am I forced to make another phone call?'

Thankfully he had done his homework on that score. 'No phone call necessary, sir.'

'Well?'

Thanks to the success of his research on the Internet, Mitchell was able to launch into the explanation with a sense of confident pride. 'It's a grinding mill used for making flour and gold and grinding salt. It's from Finland, and you know the most extraordinary thing?'

Quentin shut his eyes, as if praying for deliverance. 'Do enlighten me.'

'It's made from the oddest ingredients.' In anticipation of the question, he had written his notes on a slip of paper. He took it from his pocket. 'A Sampo is made from a swan's quill, the milk of a barren cow, a single grain of barley and some wool from a ewe born in summer. Quite extraordinary, wouldn't you say?' He looked at Quentin, seeking affirmation. None was forthcoming. Quentin had, however, opened his eyes and was regarding him with a look of disbelief.

'Of course, it's mythological, Quentin,' he added quickly. 'I, for one, very much doubt its existence.'

'For that insight, let us give thanks,' Quentin muttered wearily and rolled his eyes heavenward.

After striding briskly up from the harbour car park, Pentti ushered Nicole into a restaurant at the beginning of the esplanade.

Once inside he grunted at her to follow and led her through the café to a small circular space off the main dining area. The space, though somewhat cramped, was all glass and afforded a view out into the gardens.

'Nice place,' Nicole conceded, wondering how he was going to deal with his personal space issue in such a confined area.

'The Kappeli, it's been around since the late 1860s. The name means "the chapel". Very popular with locals and tourists.'

'Nice,' Nicole tried to keep the sarcasm out of her voice. 'If I want a tour guide, I'll get a professional. You are going to tell me about the murder?'

'In a moment,' he said. 'There's no table service for coffee. What would you like?'

'Not more coffee, maybe green tea.'

As he shuffled out of the booth, she murmured, 'Thanks,' and pulled her knees out of his way.

When he returned he was carrying a glass of beer and a cup of herbal tea that smelled like lemon verbena. He passed her the tea and squeezing in, placed his beer on the table. For a moment he sipped his beer and then he looked at her.

'So, I should tell you about Matti?'

He appeared reluctant to do so, for he sat there looking into his glass. After a time he took a deep breath and began.

'For the last two years we have been conducting an on and off again, low-level investigation into a group of individuals who are involved in what we suspect is money laundering. In such cases there are usually links to drugs, illegal gambling or prostitution. I think this is not unique to Finland.' He looked at her, awaiting a response.

Nicole shrugged. 'Not my area, but yes.'

'What was unusual was that we could find no such link.'

He paused and sipped his beer. Giving himself thinking time, she thought.

'Our attempts to trace the source of the money, have been similarly futile. Tracing it is like trying to unravel a tangled spider's web. Each thread is connected to another and then another. Some from off-shore tax havens and others from bank accounts in countries with a less than generous attitude towards information sharing.'

'Switzerland?'

'Among others.'

'Are people not required to declare their income, under Finnish law?'

'Naturally, but in this case, it was decided that to audit them would alert suspicion. It remains an option.'

Nicole sipped her tea. It was lemon verbena.

'Just so I am clear on this, what sort of money are we talking about?'

Pentti sighed. 'Hundreds of millions of euros.'

'Jesus.'

'Unfortunately, Jesus is not an international financial transactions expert.'

He lapsed into silence for a moment before continuing.

'We have a problem with this kind of crime in Finland.'

'You mean there is a lot of money laundering?'

'In fact, I mean quite the opposite. We have always had pride in officially being the least corrupt country in the world. My point is that we are unused to dealing with something of this nature and on this scale. And it's disconcerting that those who would normally assist us in such matters were surprisingly reluctant in this case.'

'Who do you mean?'

'Your government agencies, the Americans, the French, the Swedes...' He picked up his glass and looked at it as if somehow an answer lay within.

Again, he was silent, his attention seemingly elsewhere as he gazed out into the esplanade.

'And your friend, Matti?' Nicole prompted, 'He was investigating these people? So where does the woman fit in?'

'The investigation had lapsed, or at least was on hold until late September when we had a minor breakthrough. Over a period of a week the woman was seen meeting each one of the suspects.' Pentti took a drink and placed his glass down. 'Let me clarify that. The individuals we're investigating are all reasonably successful in their chosen fields and have known each other since university.

The odd thing is that they rarely meet in public and certainly never, to our knowledge, all at the same place at the same time. That she met all seven seemed significant, yet we didn't know if it had occurred in the past. So, it is possible this was not her first direct contact. For a while we had eyes on all seven, and had tried to record every contact and then find something that linked them. We found nothing. She is the only link we have identified.'

Nicole knew that what he described was a massive task and one that until it yielded results would have been painstaking, boring and expensive. 'It is odd that they didn't socialise together.'

Pentti nodded. 'It is as if they have an agreement not to meet. And we know that they don't phone each other.'

'No telephone contact at all?'

'And no emails.'

'You have electronic surveillance on them?'

'What we have…' Pentti faltered, and then frowned. 'That is strictly off the record.'

Nicole decided that was a 'yes'.

'And Matti couldn't find out her name?'

'Believe me, we were in the process of doing that when the murder happened.'

Nicole sipped her tea. There were so many questions and she sensed that there were certain things he was holding back. They would keep, she decided. 'Tell me about the murder.'

Pentti drained his beer and gazed out the window.

'It was a Tuesday morning. The surveillance team picked her up almost by accident, coming out of a shop in Aleksanterinkatu. They alerted Matti and when it became clear that she was walking in the direction of the harbour, he positioned himself there. The harbour market was busy as usual and he knew he would have trouble keeping an eye on her by himself. So he called in two of the surveillance team to act as backups. However, there was no problem because she circled the market, went to the ticket booth and bought a return ticket for the ferry to Suomenlinna.'

'That's the island fortress?'

'Yes.' Pentti nodded and glanced into the interior of the café.

Nicole realised that he had not been looking outside and now inside in a casual manner, but he was actually clearing the perimeter, checking who was nearby. Obviously, there was no problem because he turned his attention back to her and continued.

'Matti bought a ticket for the eleven-twenty ferry. While they were waiting for the vessel to cast off, he struck up a casual conversation with the woman. As you have seen, one of the remaining team took the photograph of them standing together.'

'And he wasn't wearing a wire?'

Pentti shook his head.

'And... after that?'

'Nothing. I mean, we didn't have eyes on her. According to a witness at the island terminal, they disembarked and she and Matti walked off together. There were no further sightings. Two of our team were on the midday ferry but by the time they arrived the woman had vanished and Matti was dead. He was shot at short range by a single nine-point twenty-one calibre bullet. According to the ballistic experts the gun was a SR-1 Vektor.' He looked over his glasses at her, questioning if she knew the name.

Nicole shook her head. 'Sorry, firearms identification is not my strong point,' she replied.

'It was developed by designer Piotr Serdyukov. It was known as the Gyurza, but the FSB call it the Vector.'

'The Russian security services? Are you suggesting he was assassinated by a Russian agent?'

'It's a strong possibility. On the other hand, it could be an attempt to divert our attention in the wrong direction.'

'But is it feasible that the Russians would be interested?'

'Those who have been untangling the financial spider's web believe that a great deal of the money has its origins in Russia.'

Nicole thought about that for a moment and then pressed on. 'So, let me get this clear. He is murdered on this island, and she, what? Simply vanishes?'

'She certainly did not get back on a ferry. The security cameras at the ferry terminal show her and Matti getting on but no trace of her getting off.'

'Then?'

'We searched the island. Nothing. We believe she must have had a boat waiting for her.'

'I would like to see all the security camera footage.'

Pentti shook his head. 'I am afraid that will not be possible.'

'I'm sorry? Did you just say no?'

Pentti heaved a sigh and got to his feet. 'We really must go. I have to drop you back and then do a couple of things at work. I can pick you up this evening. I have reserved a table at the Savoy, a very pleasant restaurant.'

'Sit down,' Nicole said quietly.

He glanced at his watch. 'No, really...'

'I said, sit down.' Nicole kept her anger out of her voice, but her vehemence was obvious.

He fidgeted uncomfortably then, sensing that she would not be above having a fight in public, held his hands up in a gesture of submission and sat down.

'If we are going to work on this case together, then you have to stop lying to me.'

If her words had meant to goad him, they failed. He sat, impassive as ever, prepared to let whatever unfolded flow over him.

'For a start, I don't believe you are police. Finnish Secret Service – now there's a distinct possibility. With an intimate knowledge of what pistols the Russian FSB uses? Yes, I'd say you're a spook. Secondly, stop treating me like a tourist who needs to be shown the sights. I don't give a fuck about the tourist treats this city has to offer. Also, while I'm on it, if you are going to put me up in a safe house and try to convince me it is an apartment belonging to your sister, well, you will have to do better.'

Pentti, rather than being intimidated, gave the best impression of a genuine smile she'd seen from him so far.

'I thought I did very well.'

'Oh, wonderfully well. For a start, all the food was unopened, everything purchased two days ago from...' Nicole fished out her glasses, slipped them on and then read from her notebook. 'Yes, the K-Supermarket Kamppi in Urho-something-or-other street.'

'Urho Kekkosen katu,' Pentti offered meekly.

'Whatever. You really shouldn't leave the receipt in the rubbish bin under the sink. Really professional, I don't think. And your sister's clothes would have been a nice touch, except they all had the smell of mothballs, and yet there are none in the cupboard.'

'You could make a good detective,' Pentti said. 'Now, are you finished?'

'No, I am not bloody well finished.'

'Okay, what else?'

'Your sister likes fashion, yes?'

Pentti nodded.

'Then I suggest that the password for her Wifi would be something like Zara, Prada or Desigual, not *bodominjärvineljä*. Correct me if I pronounced it wrong, but isn't that the name of a famous unsolved murder case? And the number four – the total number of people involved? Hardly the thing a dedicated fashion shopper would choose.'

'Okay, let me...'

'No, Pentti – if that really is your name – let me tell you what I think. You never expected me to show up and when I did, your superiors told you to put me in a safe house, keep me at arm's length, show me Helsinki and then pack me off home with a bunch of pretty postcards and happy memories of the friendly Finnish police.'

To her surprise, Petti laughed.

'You're wrong. They never thought of the postcards.'

Nicole found his openness disarming. She softened her tone. 'So, I'm right?'

Pentti nodded. 'On all counts, I'm afraid. Which is why I was instructed not to share any sensitive material.'

'So there is more?'

He looked away and Nicole sensed it was not the right time to push. They sat there in silence. Then Pentti did the thing she least expected. He reached out across the table and took her hand and lowered his voice. 'I'm sorry for lying to you. Just for the record, my name *is* Pentti; and you are correct, for the last five years I have been a *tarkastaja* – an inspector – working for SUPO.'

'SUPO?'

'The *Suojelupoliisi*; the Finnish Security Intelligence Service. Before that I was a specialist with the *Karhu-ryhmä*, the *Karhu* Team.'

'And what the hell is that?'

'The Bear Team; a nickname for a unit like… well, I guess, our equivalent of a SWAT team.'

'What kind of specialist?'

'A sniper.'

'With glasses like yours?' she said derisively before she could censor herself.

If he was offended, he gave no indication of it. 'I have my rifle sights calibrated to my eyesight and simply take my glasses off.'

He demonstrated, taking them off and blinking at her. He looked like a blind owl, she thought.

'Right,' Nicole said, remembering him back in London, checking the periphery for snipers. 'So where does that leave us?'

Apparently it was a question that Pentti couldn't answer. He rubbed his eyes and with a gesture of tiredness, or maybe resignation, put his glasses back on and sat in silence, his attention elsewhere.

Finally, sensing there was nothing more to be done, she came to a decision. 'Don't worry, Mister Sniper, I'll get a flight back to London tomorrow.'

Pentti gave no indication that he had even heard her. His head tilted back, he seemed lost in the few puffy clouds moving slowly above the city. 'You know,' he said eventually, 'you really should get out and experience Helsinki in winter. It can be very beautiful. So far this year it has been very warm, so there is not much snow and few lakes have frozen yet, but that will change. Hopefully a big freeze will come.'

'You can take me back now,' Nicole said.

He drove slowly back to the apartment and as she got out of the car Nicole concluded that she really didn't want to spend any further time with him. The case was going nowhere and she very much doubted that anyone would get to the bottom of it.

'If you don't mind, I think I'll pass on dinner this evening.'

Pentti gave no indication that he cared one way or the other.

'As you wish,' he shrugged.

Nicole shut the door and was about to turn away when he lowered the passenger side window and leaned over.

'There was a phone number.'

'What?'

'A phone number; Matti had a scrap of paper in his pocket with a phone number. Maybe the woman gave it to him.' He took a pen from the glove box, copied the number from his phone onto the back of an old envelope, and handed it out the window.

She glanced at the number – 017 523 526. Nicole was puzzled by his last-minute attempt to share information; too little, too late.

'It's a Kuopio number, zero, one, seven.'

'And?'

'It has never been issued.'

'Another dead end…' she began, but he had already raised the window and started the car. She stood watching until he turned off Fredrikinkatu. Then, deciding she needed a walk in order to clear her head, she asked a woman who was walking by for directions to the K-Supermarket.

The K-Supermarket was bright and surprisingly interesting. There was, she thought, something exotic about seeing products she recognised with names that she didn't. Toothpaste turned out to be *hammastahna,* a generous portion of salmon was *lohi* and when she discovered a small tub of ice cream called *Aino,* she couldn't resist. It was as she was beside the row of freezers that she saw something that gave her a start. She slid the freezer cover back and stood staring. There was not one, but dozens of them. And they were bagged, as if they were evidence.

'They are whisks for the sauna,' said a girl's voice behind her.

She turned and found one of the shop assistants smiling at her.

'For the sauna?'

'For beating yourself,' the girl took a clear plastic bag from the freezer. 'See? *Koivu,* silver birch. When it is not possible to get fresh ones, we have them frozen. We have two names for them. In the West they say *vihta* and where I come from in the East we call them *vasta.'*

'*Vasta,*' Nicole said. 'Thank you, I'll have one.'

It amused her that she had just bought a bunch of twigs to beat herself with. The bloody Finns obviously enjoyed it. It struck her as bizarre that they would sell them in the supermarket. But beneath her amusement was the image of Tom's body and of the identical bunch of silver birch twigs on the floor beneath his painting. And, the woman in the boat...

'Hello, Nicole!'

She was so deeply into her train of thought that it took her a few seconds to recall the woman's name.

'Kaija. So sorry, my mind was miles away.'

Kaija smiled warmly. 'Don't apologise, Finnish names take a bit of getting used to I'm afraid. I see you've bought a *vihta*.'

Nicole was pleased to have an opportunity to show off her just acquired local knowledge. 'No, I bought a *vasta*.'

Kaija frowned. 'Indeed? May I see?'

'Sure.' Nicole handed it to her and watched as she examined it carefully.

'Well, I am impressed! It is a *vasta*, though after such a short time in Finland, I am amazed you could tell the difference, or even know the names in the first place.'

Nicole was perplexed. 'It was a joke. I mean... I thought that there were two names for the same thing.'

'Usually I would agree,' Kaija said. 'In fact, most Finns wouldn't know the difference, but there is one. The method of tying them together in Eastern Finland differs from the way they do it in the West.'

Nicole suddenly wished she could remember how the two she had seen in England had been tied. It was only a small detail, but sometimes such little things can be important.

'Can you show me the difference?'

Kaija shook her head. 'It's the wrong time of year. To bind them properly they must be fresh and supple. But I have a better idea.'

'Yes?'

'You are probably in a hurry to get back to where you're staying...'

Going back to the cramped apartment and spending the rest of the afternoon and evening by herself was not particularly inviting and there were other things she wanted to ask the woman. 'Not at all,' she said. 'In fact, I was wondering what to do with myself.'

'But the case you're working on...'

'Was working on,' Nicole corrected. 'I have come to the conclusion that Inspector Toivonen can do very well without my assistance.'

'Then I have a plan. I live just around the corner and if you like, I can show you some sketches of the different ways to bind silver birch.'

'I would like that very much,' Nicole said.

'My apartment block has a sauna and tonight is women's night.'

'A sauna? I'm afraid I'm a sauna virgin.'

The notion seemed to amuse Kaija, who smiled and pointed to Nicole's purchase. 'Well, you have bought the *vasta*. It would be a pity to waste it, and afterwards I can cook some supper.'

Nicole nodded. 'I have some ice cream and a piece of salmon...'

Kaija laughed and held up her K-Supermarket bag. 'And I as well have salmon.'

'Then it sounds like a plan,' Nicole grinned. 'If I am going to have a sauna for the first time, then Finland would seem like the right place to start.'

He found it irritating that, despite the mist and occasional showers, the mid-morning crowds still flowed steadily along the Embankment. A group of Japanese walked in dutiful pairs in the wake of a rising sun held aloft by a tour guide. It was the only sun they were going to see all day, Quentin thought grimly, as he wove his way between a brace of brolly-wielding Belgians who had paused to take photographs of each other. Understandable, as there was nothing else to see, he supposed. A waffle of Belgians, was that the collective noun? If not, it should be.

Quentin Grammaticus detested having to leave his office. One had not scaled the heights of one's profession in order to mingle with the masses. Down here, one had to contend with them. He preferred the view from his office window. There he was in control, with the telephone and computer at hand when he needed to issue a command. That was why one had foot soldiers, minions, whose job it was to carry out one's instructions.

Ahead of him there was an eddy in the flow as a short, thickset man limped across the stream of people and stood still, his weather-beaten face impassive and his heavily lidded eyes squinting at the river. Then he moved on, walking beside the wall. Ahead of them the dome of St Paul's was barely visible through the mist.

The Russian's limp caused him to walk slowly. A childhood disease, or perhaps he had been born with it, Quentin mused as he adjusted his speed, adopting a more leisurely pace until he fell in beside the Russian. There was no hint of recognition.

Ahead of them a tourist turned and took a photograph of the view along the Embankment. Quentin disliked photographers at any time, but it was particularly annoying when he might have accidentally been in the shot. He waved his umbrella at the man, who simply shrugged and turned away.

When the limping man next to him eventually spoke, it was very quietly, taking his time with each word, making certain his pronunciation was understandable. 'Have you noticed that on maps the rivers are always blue? It is a shame. I have never seen a blue river. I expect I never will.'

'Life is full of disappointments, Andrei,' Quentin replied. He glanced at the man, wondering where the conversation was leading. Zaikov was normally more direct but he decided to let the Russian take the lead. Their meetings were, thankfully, a rare event, but his instructions were clear; an FSB asset is a rare commodity and in this instance the man was to be given whatever assistance he needed. It occurred to him that *he* was, in fact, the Russian's asset. It was not a comfortable thought.

'Take your river, the Thames. It is such a pity that it looks like shit, so full of rubbish. Why is that, Quentin?'

'It comes from the country and from what I understand the country is full of shit. Animals, I believe. They have animals that shit anywhere they like. Then it rains and the shit has to go somewhere. Sadly, in this case, that means London.'

'And the shit that comes? Who is to clean it up?'

'We do our best,' Quentin said tersely, knowing exactly which bit of shit the Russian was referring to. 'You see, that's where I have a problem. Some things should never be put in the river.'

The man raised his hands in a gesture of helplessness. 'Who are we to question the wisdom of our superiors? A message needed to be sent. And you were expected to clean it up.'

'We have done so.'

'That is not what I hear.'

'A few loose ends remain. I have it in hand.'

'My superiors very much hope so, Quentin. Your policewoman is keeping strange company in Finland.'

So she was in Finland. It was news to Quentin, but he shrugged nonchalantly, eyed the weather and opened his brolly. 'And what company is that, Andrei?'

'SUPO, so I am told. We have eyes on the individual involved and can render him non-operational if need be. We are quite experienced at dealing with Finnish Intelligence. The man is one of Harkimo's boys, one Pentti Toivonen.'

Quentin filed the name away. 'Some wag once told me that Finnish Intelligence was a contradiction in terms.'

The Russian frowned. 'Then your wag has never had to contend with them. We have fought wars with the Finns and know very well that they have a stubbornness that is to be admired. They even have a word for it – *sisu*.'

'I'm sure we all admire our Finnish cousins,' Quentin conceded.

'The question is, will you clean up your little problem?'

'As I recall, it is *our* problem. We both have much invested.'

'And our American friends?'

'They are being very American. They keep an interest in a positive outcome, but are reluctant to play an active role. If things go well they will claim the credit. Of course, at the first sign of trouble they will insist they knew nothing.'

They walked in silence for a while before Quentin stopped and leaned on the railing. 'I have a man in Finland. If it becomes necessary to clean anything up, he will attend to it.'

'I am pleased to hear it. I too have people there, experienced people. They would consider it their patriotic duty to assist you.'

'I will take that into consideration. However, she is a British citizen, best left to us.' Quentin looked at the river, watching the next shower of rain marking its passage across the surface of the water as it drifted towards them. 'May I suggest that next time you use one of your own rivers?'

'Alas, our rivers are fully supplied with corpses. Who would see such a message on the Neva?'

Mitchell was pleased with himself. It had been a splendid performance. As he dressed, he looked down at the woman sprawled across the bed. She was very attractive and if his agenda had been otherwise, he would have enjoyed spending more time with her. Under other circumstances she too would have praised his performance. But she would sleep for hours yet and when she finally awoke, it was almost certain that, sadly, she would remember very little. He took their wine glasses through to the kitchen and gave them a thorough rinsing. No fingerprints and no traces of what she had imbibed.

Returning to the bedroom, he sat on the bed and put on his shoes. Satisfied he had left nothing behind, he leaned over and kissed the back of her neck. She didn't stir. A job well done, he thought, congratulating himself not only on the sex, but also on the efficiency of the entire operation. In only a few hours in Helsinki, he had located the Mikkonen woman and the whereabouts of her office, then, waiting until she left for the day, gone in and chatted with the department secretary.

Anna Ericson had found him attractive, interesting and, importantly, available. She liked older men and they had few mature age foreign students. Derek, from London, was keen to learn about what courses were on offer and she was more than happy to convince him to enrol. When he suggested dinner, she had willingly accepted. From there to her bedroom had been a logical and almost unavoidable progression.

He leaned over and stroked her back. Her skin was beginning to cool down, so he pulled a blanket over her and tucked it in. Her office keys were on the hook inside the door where she had left them. Perfect.

Getting in and out of the university office had been no problem and the data removal even less so. Following the instructions given to him by the boffins in London, he inserted the USB stick first and then turned the computer on. As he watched, the program booted up and ran without a hitch. First it downloaded all her mail folders then set about wiping the computer. By the time it had finished, all that remained were the basic operating system and an animated and extremely pornographic welcoming screen proclaiming, in obscene language, another victory for the BHMH – Bulgaria's Heavy Metal Hackers. He removed the USB stick and switched off the computer. All in all, it was a good night's work.

The entire operation from the time that he left Anna Ericson's apartment until the time he returned took just under an hour and a half. Mitchell checked that Anna was still sleeping, replaced the keys, turned off the lights and shut the door quietly behind him.

Back in his room at the Glo Art hotel, Chris Mitchell opened a beer, toasted his success and applied himself to the task of looking for any email with an MP3 attachment. There were only two. One was the original email from Tom Myers and the second was addressed to a woman named Kaija Rantaniemi. It took him five minutes to find her address and two more to locate a number of photographs of her. He checked his watch. It was too late now, so he resolved to visit her in the morning. Hopefully she would go out at some stage. He would then take his USB stick and let it work its magic.

Chapter Eight

Kaija's apartment in Lönnrotinkatu was surprisingly light and spacious. Situated on the fourth floor, it was south facing, with a fine view across the city. For someone who specialised in ancient texts, the furniture was surprisingly modern. Nicole, thinking about the challenge of choosing décor for her own house, was immediately interested.

'All of it Finnish,' Kaija explained, with more than a touch of pride. 'The fabric is Marimekko and most of the tables and chairs are from Artek. I love the Alvar Aalto furniture because the designs never age. Most of the lighting comes from Aero.'

Nicole laughed, 'You've lost me with the names, but I love the way everything seems so clean and simple.'

'Just like we Finns,' she joked. 'But you are exactly right. Aalto's lines are so clean and the Marimekko prints are timeless,' she said, pointing to the bold colours in the curtain material and matching cushions.

Nicole wondered how her house would look if she did something similar. 'I'm about to decorate my own house and I have been totally stuck for ideas. That is, until now.'

'I often think I would have enjoyed being an interior decorator,' Kaija sighed. 'But life is just too short. Please sit, and I'll get us a coffee.'

Over coffee and cake, Kaija patiently took Nicole through the different ways of binding silver birch. Fortunately, she had some old prints illustrating each method. Nicole found it fascinating and, determined to compare them to the two in England, began taking detailed notes, until she remembered that the birch whisk from Tom's house had disappeared into the interior of a car and been driven away.

Around five-thirty, Kaija got to her feet and with a flick, released her hair from the bun. The change was dramatic. Suddenly she looked years younger. 'Time for the sauna,' she announced.

Nicole felt a sudden shyness at her lack of knowledge of sauna etiquette.

'What do I need?' she asked.

'Only these,' Kaija said and handed her a bathrobe and towel then pushed her gently into her bedroom. 'Just strip off and put the robe on.' She pointed to Nicole's necklace. 'I'd leave that here, along with your watch and earrings. They tend to get too hot. I'll get the shampoo and conditioner. Oh, and don't forget your precious *vasta*.'

Nicole was dubious. 'Strip off... completely?' she asked.

Kaija grinned and demonstrated. 'See? Completely.'

The sauna was in the basement and for Nicole the ride down in the elevator was unnerving, for even though she had the bathrobe on, she felt totally naked. When a man entered the lift on the third floor, she could feel herself blushing. The man, however, simply said hello and chatted to Kaija in Finnish. She couldn't understand a single word they said but they must have been talking about her. As he got out on the ground floor he turned to Nicole. 'I hope you have a good first sauna,' he said in English.

'Thank you,' Nicole responded, shyly clutching the *vasta* in front of her.

As she came out of the lift she felt the chill damp air of the basement on her face and shivered. The notion of someplace warm was inviting. They walked between some tables and chairs to a door in an unpainted concrete wall. Inside was more to her liking. The pine-lined changing room, filled with the scent of the sauna, was equipped with wooden benches, a small refrigerator and two showers. To the right of the showers a sturdy pine door led to the sauna.

'Just hang everything on a hook,' Kaija said as she removed her robe. 'Then have a quick cold shower.'

'Cold?' Nicole didn't like the sound of that.

Seeing the expression on Nicole's face, Kaija shrugged. 'You'll thank me, trust me.' She picked up a wooden bucket and stepped under the shower. 'It's really not that bad.'

Despite her assurances, Nicole noticed Kaija stepping away from the shower after only a few seconds, while leaving the bucket to fill. She took a deep breath, turned her shower on and ducked under it. The cold made her gasp and she jumped away too quickly and almost slipped over.

'Careful! The floor can be slippery,' Kaija cautioned. She picked up the *vasta* and placed it in the bucket. 'Ready?'

Nicole, shivering, followed her through the door into a dimly lit space and a very welcome wall of warmth.

'Welcome to the sauna,' Kaija said as she placed the bucket with the *vasta* on the floor. 'Come.' She climbed up to the top and patted the bench beside her. 'It is not too hot, so you should be fine.'

To her surprise she was.

As they sat in silence and Nicole slowly warmed up, she realised why the cold shower had been essential. Had she come in without it she would have found the heat uncomfortable.

After about five minutes Kaija climbed down and taking a ladle, poured some water on the stones of the sauna stove. 'Now for some *löyly*,' she said.

Nicole was about to ask what *löyly* was, when she was answered by a sudden burst of steam, so hot it made her flinch. It also burnt the tips of her ears.

'Jesus! That's hot.'

'Ah, but think of that super-heated steam cleansing every pore in your skin.' Kaija climbed back up and, moving away a little, stretched out. 'Believe me, it's good for you.'

'I'll have to take your word for it,' Nicole grimaced. 'Right now, I feel as if I am being slowly cooked.'

Kaija laughed. 'Boiled *and* basted. Don't worry, we'll take a break in a couple of minutes.'

If I'm still alive, Nicole thought grimly. It was the longest two minutes she could remember having to endure.

'Don't slip on the way down,' Kaija warned as she led them out of the sauna.

The sense of relief was wonderful. On their way to the chairs, Nicole grabbed her towel while Kaija paused by the fridge to take out two bottles of beer and open them.

She handed Nicole a bottle. 'Here, Lapin Kulta.'

'What?'

'Lapp Gold, one of our best beers, which, sadly, is no longer brewed in Lapland. Beer is traditional for the sauna.' Kaija indicated a chair. 'Relax.'

Nicole wasn't sure if the beer was exceptional or the sauna made it taste so, but in that moment, it was the best beer she had ever tasted.

The heat in the sauna had been almost too much and she would not have described it as pleasurable, but now she felt as if she was glowing all over and although the basement was cold, she felt surprisingly warm. She looked over at Kaija, who seemed totally relaxed, stretched out in her chair, eyes closed, sipping her beer. The woman hadn't bothered with a towel and seemed oblivious to the fact that she was totally naked.

Nicole found it fascinating that she seemed so at home with her body. She tried to imagine any of her female colleagues relaxing in such a manner. Even if they had found themselves in such a situation, they would certainly have had their legs firmly crossed and their arms folded about their breasts. Screw them, Nicole thought, why do I have to be so bloody English? She unwrapped the towel and enjoyed the cool air around her. She glanced again at Kaija. For a woman of fifty-something, she had a remarkable body. Her breasts were small and firm, her stomach flat and her legs in fine shape. Nicole guessed that she had never had children and that she probably did yoga or worked out. As she did neither, Nicole decided that if she looked half as good at Kaija's age it would be a bloody miracle.

The second time in the sauna was also preceded by a cold shower but this time Nicole took care to get as cold as possible. It was a sensible precaution, for when she re-entered the sauna it felt nowhere near as hot. Feeling much more comfortable, Nicole stretched out on the top bench. She hadn't realised she had been so tense until every muscle in her body gave in to the heat and left her with no option but to relax. It felt… she searched for the word… therapeutic.

After a time Kaija took the *vasta*, placed it on the stones and ladled some water over it. The steam was hot, but somehow more bearable. The steam also carried with it a sweet smell.

'*Koivu* oil, from the silver birch leaves. It is very good for the skin; an astringent like witch hazel,' Kaija explained. 'Now, would you like me to beat you or would you rather do it yourself?'

That, Nicole thought, is possibly the weirdest question I've ever been asked. However, she nodded her head. 'You had better, I wouldn't know how.'

It was exhilarating. The sensation was not one of pain, but of pleasure with an edge to it. Kaija skilfully beat her legs, arms, breasts and stomach, but never too hard.

'Now you,' she said and handed the *vasta* to Nicole.

'If you're sure…' she began, but the woman turned towards her and smiled.

'You'll be fine.'

'I've never beaten anyone before,' she joked nervously.

Kaija looked at her tenderly. 'Well, there's a first time for everything.'

Finally, Kaija pronounced herself satisfied and, taking the *vasta*, told Nicole to lie down on her stomach and then commenced beating her quite gently; moving from her legs up to her back and arms. Lying down was cooler and Nicole found herself almost trancing with the pleasure. It was delicious. Her skin tingled and though she was now getting a little too hot, she wanted it to go on.

After a couple of minutes Kaija laid the *vasta* down and with strong experienced fingers, massaged her scalp. 'Enough for the moment,' she said. 'All done. Time for another beer.'

By the third trip into the sauna, Nicole was thoroughly enjoying the heat and the company. Nicole had expected the sauna to be bearable, maybe even enjoyable, but what she had not expected was the sense of euphoria. Her whole body felt alive and the external warmth had shifted to inside. It was probably endorphins, she mused, but decided against further analysis. It was enough that she was glowing. The intimacy she felt with another woman was an added bonus; something she hadn't experienced in years, if ever. It made everything easy between them, so when Kaija handed her the shampoo, it seemed totally natural they should wash and rinse each other's hair and all the time chatting like old friends.

Still dressed only in the bathrobes, they went back upstairs and fell naturally in step with the supper preparations. As the salmon steaks cooked and Nicole made a salad, Kaija opened a bottle of white wine and poured them each a glass.

After dinner Kaija took Nicole to her study and ensconced her in an old leather club chair while she went to make coffee. Nicole sat there, trying to savour the moment. The study was gorgeous, but she couldn't see herself being able to afford a similar oak desk and leather club chairs. They were stunning, but she preferred the clean lines of the Finnish furniture in the lounge room. The furnishing and lighting in the study were all 1930s Art Deco. Genuine too, she guessed. Kaija has an eye for detail, Nicole noted; even the photographs and pictures on the walls had Deco style frames. The only exception was an odd-looking certificate in a cheap modern frame that was hung above the desk.

Nicole stood up to take a closer look. It was one of those joke certificates made to look like a genuine diploma. She couldn't understand the Finnish, but in bold letters at the bottom was a sentence in English.

With much appreciation from the Mary Hevonen Society.

Below it was a photograph of a group of students surrounding a statue of a naked woman. They appeared to be tossing their caps in the air; a graduation ceremony, maybe?

Then Nicole saw something that caused the euphoria from the sauna to vanish in an instant. It was as though a window had been opened and a blast of chill arctic air had filled the room.

Kaija looked at the object of Nicole's attention, sensing that something was wrong. 'That is just a joke that some of my students sent me after their graduation. The beautiful statue is *Havis Amanda*. It's the most famous of Vallgren's Parisian Art Nouveau works.'

Nicole had no interest in the statue. 'What's the Mary Hevonen Society?' she asked, unable to drag her eyes away from the photograph.

'That's another joke. It's not really "Mary Hevonen"; not two words at all. It's a play on *merihevonen*. A *hevonen* is a horse and *meri* is the Finnish word for sea.'

'Seahorse?'

'Yes, it was their little joke because the Seahorse was their favourite pub.'

'And the woman at the side watching?'

Kaija leaned over and lifted the certificate from the wall. 'This one?' She pointed to a young woman with long blonde hair who was looking directly into the camera.

'Yes, who is she?'

'Auli Saarinen; bright girl.' Kaija shrugged, 'I've no idea what became of her.'

Nicole took the certificate and sat down. She examined it in disbelief. She was correct, she knew it, no doubt at all. She took a deep breath and steadied the rush of emotions. 'That's her. That's the woman in the boat, the woman on the recording, the woman who called herself Aino. That's the woman we've been looking for.'

Kaija looked at her in disbelief. 'You're certain?'

'Yes, unless she has an identical twin. Her hair is longer, but I have stared at that face so many times. No, I'm certain. And the thing about the seahorse...'

'Just a moment,' Kaija said and went over to the desk and began to hunt through the drawers. 'Here,' she said, 'this is a better photograph. Is that her?'

The picture showed a group of young men and women posing on a stony beach outside a small wooden hut set in a forest landscape. The log hut had a chimney from which a plume of smoke was rising. Nicole realised it must be a sauna, which explained why the group was unclothed except for a couple of men with towels wrapped around their waists. The girl was at the centre this time, crouched, naked, smiling, her attention caught not focused on the camera, but on a good-looking older man to her right.

'Absolutely no doubt, that's our Aino,' Nicole said, with a sudden sense of relief. 'How old is the photo?'

Kaija thought for a moment. 'It was mid-summer in nineteen ninety-six. Auli's parents had a summer cottage and sauna on

Pikkususisaari, an island somewhere near Punkaharju. I remember that the cottage was very small, so most of us had tents.'

'You were there?'

Kaija laughed. 'Well, someone had to take the photos.'

Nicole's mind went off on another tangent. 'And the *hevonen* thing, the…'

'Seahorse?'

'The police doctor who examined her said she had a small seahorse tattoo on the nape of her neck.'

'A few of them had that tattoo; it was sort of a mascot for those who frequented the Seahorse.'

'Oh my god,' Nicole said softly to herself.

Kaija fetched Nicole's coffee and handed it to her then sat on the arm of the chair. 'Here, drink this. Then I'll get us something a little stronger as a nightcap.'

Nicole didn't know what to say, or what to think. There were too many questions and she had no idea where to start. Then it came to her; not a question, but a statement of something she knew was true.

'She studied Old Finnish, didn't she?' she asked, knowing that she was right.

'Yes. Old Finnish and Kalevala were her forte. Auli was very good. As good as Sirkka, maybe better.'

'Did you recognise her voice on the file?'

Kaija thought for a moment. 'No. Maybe I would now, but it never occurred to me that it was the voice of someone I taught.' She hesitated then added. 'Poor girl, I do hope she is still alive.'

'Okay,' Nicole said, more to herself than to Kaija, 'What to do?' But her confusion was such that she couldn't think straight. So she stopped trying to make sense of anything and sipped her coffee. Normally she avoided coffee after about three in the afternoon, but right now it was perfect. Everything was. She felt a warm rush of affection for the woman perched beside her and, reaching out, put her hand on her arm. 'Thank you, thank you for everything.'

'*Eipä kestä*! It's nothing, just our usual Finnish hospitality.'

'If that's true you must have extremely happy tourists,' Nicole laughed.

'I hope so. Now, I think we need that drink.'

'And I need to get my notebook and write down the name of everyone in the photograph.'

Kaija looked puzzled. 'Why?'

'Because tomorrow I am going to give a lesson on information sharing to a certain Finnish investigator.'

'Pentti Toivonen? He seemed rather nice…' Kaija began.

'He looks like a bloody owl,' Nicole laughed. 'Don't worry. I'll be gentle with him.'

Kaija returned from the kitchen with an ice-cold bottle of vodka and two shot glasses. 'Time for a Finnish lesson,' she announced, as she filled the glasses.

'I'm up for anything,' Nicole grinned.

'I certainly hope so.' Kaija handed her a glass. 'First of all, the vodka is the delightfully named *Koskenkorva* and you need to say –'

'Koss-what?'

'*Koskenkorva* means "ear of the rapids". Very poetic, don't you think?'

'If you say so, professor.' Nicole realised she was giggling like a schoolgirl.

'Pay attention! And the second thing you have to learn is *kippis*.'

'Excuse me!'

'*Kippis*. It means cheers.'

'Seriously? It sounds kind of…'

'Yes, so my English-speaking friends seem to delight in telling me.' She raised her glass. '*Kippis,* darling Nicole.'

'*Kippis,* darling Kaija,' Nicole whispered, 'and thank you again.'

'Enough. No more thank you.' Kaija grinned, then adopted a tone of mock severity. 'You are my guest tonight, young lady, and you will do exactly as you are told.'

Nicole drained her glass and held it out for a second. 'Yes, Ma'am.'

'Good,' Kaija said and refilled their glasses. 'Now, get your notebook and write down those names. Then I am afraid I will have to send you to bed.'

Nicole pulled Kaija to her and, closing her eyes, kissed her. It went on for some time. Then, as she felt a hand exploring her breasts, she paused, but only long enough to mumble that the names could wait until morning.

Helsinki woke to bright clear morning, which had looked perfect to Mitchell as he surveyed it from his hotel room. What was not so fine was the cold that assaulted his face and hands when he ventured out into the street. He started out along the pavement and then paused to look at a sign above a pharmacy. It was ten minutes after eight. He checked his own watch and confirmed that the sign was accurate. The sign then told him the bad news. It was minus two Celsius. He had known it would be cold, but minus two was too much, or rather too little. He did an abrupt U-turn and returned to his room, where he added another layer of clothing and cursed the fact he had neither gloves nor scarf.

By eight-thirty he was better dressed and in position with a clear view of the entrance to Kaija Rantaniemi's apartment building. There were an increasing number of pedestrians making their way to work, but nobody took the slightest bit of notice of the man standing in the doorway. They hurried by, heads down, eyes on the ice-slicked pavement, their warm breath weaving tiny vapour trails in their wake.

Fifteen freezing minutes passed before Mitchell saw the woman with the unpronounceable name emerge from the building. Wrapped in a long coat, hat, scarf and gloves, she was far better prepared for the weather. She checked the traffic and walked briskly towards Fredrikinkatu. Mitchell, glad to be moving, followed and watched as she made her way to a tram stop and after a couple of minutes boarded a tram heading for the city. It was a perfect scenario. He needed no more than thirty minutes to wipe her computer and he would be out of the building.

To his great relief the building was warm and by the time the lift reached the top floor Mitchell had unbuttoned his coat. Opening the door to the apartment was simple, and although there was a code box on the wall, the woman had not bothered to set the alarm. It concerned him as it could mean she was intending to return reasonably soon. His other worry, that the woman only used a laptop and had taken it with her, was allayed by the sight of a desktop computer in the first room off the entrance lobby. Hallelujah, he thought, and whistling softly, dug into his pocket for the USB. As he did so, he felt his mobile vibrating in the inside pocket of his jacket. He placed the USB on the desk and dug out his phone.

'Yes? Of course, everything is fine. I fixed the first problem last night.' He listened for a moment, nodding his head. 'Thanks. Yes, I'm cleaning up the second problem as we speak,' Mitchell said and again listened intently. 'Thank you, Quentin, you're very kind.' He stopped suddenly and switched the phone to his other ear. 'Jesus! In Finland? Do you want me to curtail her holiday…?' As he listened his face relaxed into a wide smile. 'Very satisfactory indeed, and by tomorrow I should be done. Thanks.'

He switched off the phone and shoved it back in his inside pocket. Then everything went wrong.

There was no warning and no noise. Suddenly his head was jerked backwards and he felt the edge of a knife at his throat.

'And how is Mister Grammaticus, Chris?'

The voice was quiet, the tone warm and friendly. It was a voice he recognised.

He said nothing, his mind desperately searching for an explanation of how things could have become so totally fucked up so quickly.

She jerked him backwards, forcing him down into office chair, then ripped the telephone wire from its socket, bent his arms back and tied them to the back of the chair.

'Well, Chris, you do have a problem with sex, don't you? Fancy imagining that you could break into this apartment and rape me.' She swung the chair round and he found himself face-to-face with a barefoot and near naked Nicole Parry.

'For christsake, Parry, you know I didn't fucking well break in…' but he stopped. Nicole Parry might as well have been naked. The only thing she was wearing, a white bathrobe, was undone at the front.

She searched in the desk drawers and found a roll of braided wire for hanging paintings. 'Perfect.' She tied his ankles to the chair and then removed his shoes.

'Imagine how emotional I'll be when I describe what you did to me over the last half hour.' She stood in front of him and removed her robe.

'Nicole please...'

'I think you should start working on your confession, don't you?' She took the knife and slashed the robe several times before putting it back on. This time she did it up. 'And we had better have some trouser action, don't you think?' Nicole unbuckled his belt, tugged part of his shirt free and then unzipped his fly. 'That should be enough. Now I have to make a phone call.' She leaned over and took the phone from his pocket. Then she picked up the USB. 'I think I'll give this to the local police as well.'

'Nicole. I'm doing my job, just like you. For fuck's sake, we're on the same side, aren't we?'

'Oh, are we?' Nicole picked up her bag from the club chair and rifled through it, searching for a card. She found it but then had to go back into the bag for her glasses. 'By the way, Mister Mitchell, whose holiday was it you were offering to curtail?' She put on her glasses, pushed the bridge firmly up her nose and dialled the number. 'I gave you a chance to work with me and you blew it. Sorry, but I don't do second chances.'

'Just listen. We have to talk about this...' Mitchell began, but it was too late.

'Is that Inspector Toivonen?' Nicole mouthed a silent kiss at Mitchell. 'I'm sorry to disturb you so early, Inspector, but someone just broke in and attempted to rape me. No, I'm not at the old apartment. I am at a friend's place. No, I don't actually know... wait a moment and I'll get the address. There's someone here who knows it...'

Chapter Nine

Heimo Harkimo's morning had been perfect up until 9:15. At 7:30 he had started the day with ten laps of the pool. At 8:30 he was comfortably ensconced in his office with a thermos of coffee and his wife's *pulla*.

Just before nine, Pentti dropped in to report that the safe house would be free of its guest by the end of the day. Heimo gestured for him to sit, poured him a coffee and pushed a plate of *pulla* towards him.

'If I ate every *pulla* she baked, I would look like one,' he sighed. 'And every night she asks how I enjoyed them. You know, eating *pulla* should be a pleasure not a duty.' He leaned back in his chair, pleased that Pentti had taken up the *pulla* challenge. 'So,' he said, changing the subject, 'is *she* going back to England?'

Pentti had his mouth full of *pulla*. He nodded.

'Good. Then clean up the place and return the keys.'

'Of course.'

'She still believes you to be police?'

Pentti was about to reply when his phone rang. 'Just a moment,' he said and excused himself.

Harkimo watched his friend as he left the office. He was a fine officer who, like himself, was underutilised. In the darker times of the year, when he was given to introspection, Heimo had mused more than once that it was a pity they were Finns. Almost anywhere else he could think of, their work would have been far more interesting. But Finland was cursed with decency. People even drove within the speed limit, and drink driving was virtually unheard of. The ordinary police had more exciting times with petty crime than SUPO had in years.

Heimo had no doubt that a terrorist incident could be dealt with; his doubt was that one would ever happen. Not that he wished that upon the country, but sometimes as he watched television shows featuring Mossad, the CIA or MI6, he wondered how he would fare in such a world. Even when watching some Swedish and Danish crime series on TV, he felt a pang of jealousy. Then again, he thought as he dutifully dunked another piece of his wife's *pulla* in his coffee, there was much to be said for a quiet, well-ordered life. He made a mental note to arrange an ice-fishing trip as soon as the lakes froze. Maybe they had already. The warm winter they had been experiencing was worse than a really cold one. At least in the cold you knew what you were dealing with, and you could trust the ice. A weekend in a cabin with a good sauna, big fish and decent vodka, was something other security services could probably only dream of. No, it was worse than that, they wouldn't even understand such a weekend.

There was no sign of Pentti returning, so Heimo pushed the remaining *pulla* out of reach and turned his attention to his in-tray. There was, as usual, a pile of immigrant vetting reports and minutes from the latest European conference on international terrorism. His morning, while no longer perfect, was normal – until 9.15, when his phone rang.

'Harkimo.'

'Heimo Harkimo?'

'Yes, who is this?'

'You probably don't remember me, but we met at the Club de Berne meeting last year in Switzerland. Quentin Grammaticus.'

'Of course, Mister Grammaticus, we were on the Counter Terrorist Group working party on border protection.'

'Exactly. A productive meeting, as I remember.'

It took Harkimo a couple of seconds to place Grammaticus. If his memory was correct, the Englishman was a senior operations officer who had sat like a grey ghost at the back of the meetings, contributing little, but from time to time leaning forward and offering whispered advice to one of the British terrorism experts. They had struck up a half-hearted conversation over coffee during one of the breaks and he recalled the man as good-looking, in his late forties, tall, willowy and pallid like someone who avoids the sun. The kind of person, he joked to himself, who is cast as an extra in a vampire crowd scene. Mostly he had found the man unreadable. Most probably he was British SIS or MI6 or whatever they called it these days. There must be a file on him somewhere.

'So how can I help you Mister Grammaticus?'

'Please, call me Quentin.'

'Quentin…'

'We are a little concerned about a British police officer who is supposed to be on holiday in Finland. A bit of family trouble at home, I'm afraid and, well, you know how it is, a friend of a friend thought I might be able to assist in getting a message to her to return as soon as possible.'

'Mister Grammaticus, as I am sure you are aware, this is not the usual channel for such an enquiry.'

'Of course. I understand protocol and all that. Still, it was worth a try. However, if you or the police do bump into a Nicole Parry, we would appreciate you letting us know.'

'I can assure you we do not make a habit of bumping into people. I am sorry I can't help you,' he said brusquely and hung up the phone.

Strange call, he thought. Why would British Intelligence be anxious to find Parry? Surely they had sanctioned her visit, or were at least aware that she had come to Finland to assist Pentti Toivonen in the matter of the murder of Matti Salomäki. It felt as if something was going on of which he was unaware. It was not a comfortable feeling.

For a while Heimo Harkimo sat slumped in his chair, gazing at his desk like a chess player contemplating a move. Eventually he took a sticky-note and wrote 'Ice fishing trip?' on it, then poured more coffee from his flask, turned on his computer and went searching for everything they knew about Quentin Grammaticus.

When Sirkka Mikkonen switched on her computer she shook her head in disbelief. The full screen slow motion video of a penis entering a vagina lacked any artistic value. Then the text formed,

133

letter by letter, leaving her in no doubt that her computer had just been 'fucked by Bulgaria's Heavy Metal Hackers'.

'Anna!' she called, but then remembered that her secretary had called in sick.

She dialled security and while she waited for them to arrive, she opened the cupboard and took out her backup hard drive. Thankfully she was in the habit of saving everything once a week.

Later, she accompanied the security guards to their office and watched the CCTV footage beginning from the time she had left the office the previous evening. There was no problem identifying a man entering the department and then, twenty minutes later leaving with Anna. The cameras had also recorded his return and subsequent exit. Unfortunately, the man had kept his head down the entire time and there was not a single frame that showed his face.

Sirkka went back to her office. The Bulgarian Hackers' image was still moving inexorably in and out. 'Well fuck you too,' she said quietly. She took a photo of the screen with her phone and then rebooted her computer from the backup drive.

While the computer was restoring her files, she phoned her secretary at home, but could get no sense out of her. She had never imagined that Anna was a heavy drinker, but the previous night must have been some party, for she claimed to have no memory of it at all.

The computer was still uploading files and displaying an annoying progress bar that was creeping along like a snail on Valium, so Sirkka decided to abandon work for the morning. She needed to get out and somehow expunge the hackers' image from her head. She rang Kaija, who was doing some consultancy work at the Finnish Literary Society Archives, and after apologising for disturbing her, insisted they meet for lunch.

'Somewhere I can have a stiff drink,' she added.

He had given the order and if everything went as planned, late in the afternoon, four members of the Vyborg motorcycle-touring club would cross into Finland at the Svetogorsk-Imatra border. They would book into a country hotel. The following day they might well go ice fishing or hunting; just tourists, enjoying the winter countryside.

Andrei Zaikov was a cautious man. If he had been less so he might have joined those who accumulated wealth quickly after the collapse of the old regime. They disgusted him and would one day pay for the manner in which they had corrupted Russia. Yet he was not without ambition and his networks, built slowly and carefully, had been designed not for a quick fix but for the long haul. In these fluid times power was a better asset than a bank account in Switzerland or several apartments in London or New York. That he had not achieved that power yet was, he assured himself, only a matter of time and a certain amount of good fortune.

Back in Vyborg he had fallen victim to internal FSB politics and sidelined, demoted, sent to shuffle papers in the London embassy. It had been the lowest point in his career. Then, seemingly out of nowhere, he was sent on a training course in Moscow. Except that it wasn't. He had been picked up from the airport and taken to a rather rundown *dacha* outside the city. There had been three men in the room where he was questioned. Two who did all of the talking and one who remained in the shadows, simply observing. When the third man, seemingly bored, went to the window and lit a cigarette, Zaikov got a glimpse of his face. He was tall, well-built and with a beard that reminded him of the old photographs of Trotsky. It was not an image that gave any comfort.

Eventually the strangers were satisfied, and offered him a chance to do something so bold and so startling that at first he thought it a trap. But, he had reasoned, there was no reason to trap him as he could fall no further, and he agreed to play the game. They provided him with contacts in Saint Petersburg, Vyborg, Helsinki and Moscow, and the encryption keys and phone codes he would need. They also gave him access to a generous source of funds. In return he kept working at the embassy and performed his few duties meticulously. Most days he could complete his tasks by midday and spent the rest of his time familiarising himself with London, solving sudoku puzzles or simply waiting.

At first, he heard nothing from the men from Moscow and began to think that their enterprise had been abandoned. But then the coded messages began and he did exactly as instructed and made contact with the British and Americans, who he was told, would assist him when needed. He was, he realised, the conduit between those who chose to remain in the shadows and those who were to be manipulated. His cooperation with the British and Americans would pay dividends, he had no doubt; but to ensure that outcome he knew better than to rely on them as friends. He trusted them no more than he trusted his superiors in the embassy, which is to say, not at all. At the embassy he kept a very low profile. When his superiors noticed him at all it was to make jokes about his addiction to sudoku. Mostly he was unnoticed.

His meeting with Grammaticus had been unsettling. The Englishman's self-confidence was irritating and his assurance that he had matters in hand had been too glib. Zaikov decided that he needed additional men on the ground, so before returning to his desk in the embassy, he had sent a text message to his associates in Vyborg suggesting they send four of their 'best boys' on a short holiday in Finland.

In the evening he would meet with the American. They were a nation of opportunists and as such he understood his contact far better than he understood Grammaticus. The meeting would take the same form as usual. A chance meeting in a pub, a glass or two of something to drink and an exchange of information. The CIA man would express his impatience at progress and Andrei would assure him that in the few weeks that remained, the final pieces would be in place. It was a dance they performed every month, the same steps and the same old tune. Except this time, he could offer the information about the British detective woman and the man from Finnish Intelligence. The American would not like that. The Finns were not in the loop, not in the food chain. They were superfluous and if they became annoying, Andrei had no doubt the Americans would agree with his preferred option: disposing of them. If that were the case then his motorcycle-riding associates would end their vacation and meet up with his watcher in Helsinki.

Pentti Toivonen stood still and observed the scene in front of him with a look of horror on his face and then swore quietly. '*Perkele, saatana, helvetti*!' He took a deep breath and turned to her. 'Nicole, what the fuck have you done?'

Nicole, unperturbed, smiled demurely. 'Oh, how rude of me, I forgot that you haven't met Chris Mitchell.' She walked over to Mitchell and lifted up his chin. 'Nice smile now, Christopher. This is Inspector Toivonen. Remember? I told you all about him. He's the nice man who is going to arrest you for attempted rape.'

'Nicole, for christsake...' Mitchell began and then gave up.

'*Voi vittu*!' Pentti swore again and then muttered, 'You had better have a good explanation.'

Nicole smiled sweetly. 'Pentti, he's a present for you.'

'What?'

'It's my way of thanking you for your kind hospitality.'

'Nicole!' Pentti snapped. 'Stop playing games! You can't do something like this kind of thing in this country ...'

'Oh, shut up and listen,' Nicole snapped back. 'Mitchell is MI6 or SIS whatever they call them these days. He works for Grammaticus. I was in bed when I heard him come in. I grabbed a knife from the kitchen and stopped him, as he was about to steal something from the computer. End of story.'

'Steal what? And whose computer? Yours?'

'This apartment belongs to Kaija, the woman we met with yesterday. Remember? She is the expert on your national poem or whatever. Sirkka sent Kaija a copy of the interview with the woman you think killed your friend Matti.'

Pentti looked dumbfounded.

She sighed. 'For God's sake! Pentti, turn on the computer and I will bet you anything you like that the MP3 file is there.'

'Is that what you were doing, Mister Mitchell?' Pentti asked.

Mitchell said nothing.

'He was going to download it onto this.' Nicole handed the USB to him. 'I suggest you get your tech boys to see if there is anything interesting on it.'

'Come with me,' Pentti ordered and strode off into the kitchen. Nicole glanced at Mitchell to make certain he was still secured, then followed.

'Now, you had better explain.'

'I thought I just did,' Nicole said. 'That man is involved in this case up to his friggin' neck. He was at Long Crendon when my friend Tom Myers was killed and he has admitted to me that Grammaticus had him break into my office at Hammersmith station and remove files and evidence about the woman in the boat. He says they have been ordered to shut down any attempt to investigate anything to do with the disappearance of the woman.' She was relieved to see that by the look on his face, Pentti was now taking her seriously.

'But this place, this apartment? You say it belongs to Kaija Rantaniemi?'

Nicole nodded.

'Then what are you doing here...' he looked her up and down, '...dressed like that?'

'Kaija was showing me how to bind a *vasta*, then we had a sauna and then... well, I had a sleepover,' she said, then added archly, 'It was more fun than being stuck at your sister's apartment.'

'Binding a *vasta*?' Pentti leaned on the bench, took his glasses off and rubbed his eyes. 'What a fucking mess. What the hell am I supposed to do now?'

'We had better get Mitchell out of here before Kaija returns. Oh, and I hope you can fix her phone. I accidentally pulled the wire out.' She looked down at herself. 'Oh, and I will have to go shopping for a new robe. This one seems to have sustained some battle damage.'

Pentti pushed himself up from the bench and looked at her coldly. 'We are going to take that man over to the safe house. Then get yourself on the first available flight out of Finland. I don't care where to. Then I will figure out how to deal with this mess.'

Nicole snorted derisively. 'Oh, really, Mister Owl? I'm sorry, but there's something rotten in the state of Finland and I intend to get to the bottom of it. Now, you can either help or get out of the way.' She didn't wait for a reply. 'I'm going to get dressed. I suggest you fix the phone and keep an eye on our would-be rapist.'

Leaving him alone with Mitchell while she dressed turned out to be a sensible strategy, because by the time she returned Pentti's anger had dissipated, although his manner remained stiff. He nodded at her. 'I have convinced Mister Mitchell that he should come around the corner to my sister's apartment.'

'Really?'

'Yes. And then we will leave him some time to contemplate his future, while you and I discuss your travel plans.'

'I hardly think there's much to discuss...'

'And then I will return and see if Mister Mitchell has decided to assist us or face a charge of assault with intent to rape.' Pentti paused and, allowing himself a hint of a smile, pointed to the telephone. 'I am happy to report it appears to be in working order.'

As if to confirm his statement, the phone rang.

Nicole looked at him and then at the phone. 'How the hell did you do that?' She picked it up. 'Hello? Oh, hello Kaija, I was just about to walk out... what?' She listened for a moment. 'Okay. Don't worry, I'll find it.' She put the phone down gently and turned to Mitchell. 'Nice work, Mister Mitchell, and Sirkka says thanks for the computer image and says you look like a star on the CCTV footage as well.'

Mitchell shrugged. 'I have no idea what you're talking about.'

'Never mind.' She turned to Pentti. 'I suggest you tell your tech boys to be careful with the USB. Apparently it has a rather nasty programme on it that was used to wipe Sirkka Mikkonen's computer last night.'

'Would you like to explain?' It was only mid-morning, but Pentti sounded tired.

'Later. I'll give you a hand to get Mister Mitchell nice and secure in your sister's place and then I am afraid I have a lunch.' She smiled politely. 'I'm sorry, it's girls only.'

The man who had been tailing Pentti Toivonen could hardly believe his luck. He watched in amazement as the Finn emerged with the English policewoman; two birds with one stone. Or three, if you counted the man they were bundling into Toivonen's car. He managed to get some good shots, and then put his camera on the car seat and followed at a safe distance until they vanished into an apartment on Fredrikinkatu. It was an interesting scenario and though he had no idea who their seemingly unwilling companion was, he had no doubt what his instructions would be. He sent a text message and, settling back in his seat, lit a cigarette and relaxed.

After a time, the woman emerged. There had been no response to his text, and, having no backup, he had no choice but to let her go. No doubt she would be back.

When the answer came it was as he had expected. Some friends from Vyborg were on their way to give him a hand with the cleaning. It would make for an interesting evening. Then, with any luck, he could catch a flight home first thing in the morning. In the meantime, he had work to do downloading the photographs and sending them off.

She had no problems finding the Ravintola Konstan Möljä. Nicole had decided that the central area of Helsinki was a manageable size, and a relatively easy place for a pedestrian to navigate around. She walked from Fredrikinkatu to Hietalahdenkatu in under fifteen minutes, slipping on an icy street once and only having to ask for help twice. The biggest problem was that when forced to ask directions, the street names were an almost insurmountable pronunciation problem. The locals, however, took shortcuts and she was happy that Fredrikinkatu was frequently shortened to 'Freda' – very sensible. In the case of Hietalahdenkatu, she avoided attempting to get her tongue around it. Happily, her friendly informants all knew the Konstan Möljä.

Kaija and Sirkka were seated at a table by the window and as Nicole entered they waved her over to join them. The restaurant looked as if it had been around for a while and had an obvious maritime theme, with lots of dark wooden planking and a fishing net hung from the ceiling. There were also one or two oddities, such as a mean looking hatchet on the wall above the window. Nicole hoped it was securely fastened.

'Hi Kaija. Sirkka, sorry to hear about your computer problem. Is it okay?'

Sirkka handed her phone to Nicole. 'See for yourself.'

Nicole took one look at the image and rolled her eyes. 'Very tasteful, I don't think. Still, it must have been a shock.'

'I was more angry than shocked, but I am lucky I had everything backed up.'

'She's taking medicine for the shock and I'm keeping her company,' Kaija chipped in, indicating their glasses of red wine. 'I'll order you one and then we can decide what to eat.'

Kaija patted the chair beside her. 'Sit and tell us about your morning. Hopefully it was a little less eventful.'

When Nicole finished recounting the morning's events, the two women stared at her as though she was crazy. Eventually Sirkka broke the silence.

'How can you be so calm?'

Nicole chuckled. 'You think I'm calm? I haven't a clue what I'm mixed up in. And, frankly, neither does my Finnish police friend. But calm is not how I would describe myself at the moment.' She had been careful to keep her description of events at the level of cops and crooks. Somehow, she didn't think anyone needed to know about Mister Owl's real job.

'He seemed nice enough,' Sirkka said and signalled the waiter. 'I'm hungry.' She peered disappointedly into her empty glass. 'I think we should also get a bottle.' Then added, lamely, by way of excuse, 'Well, it is cheaper that way.'

After the meal, Kaija poured them the last of the wine then raised her glass. 'Here's to your mystery,' she said, then added, 'soon may it be solved.'

'Thanks,' Nicole said, though she held out no hope of a speedy resolution. 'It would help,' she said cautiously, 'if I had some idea of what I was dealing with.'

'You need a plan,' Sirkka said.

'What I need, is to convince Pentti that he should work with me.'

Kaija looked thoughtful. 'You have Auli Saarinen's name.'

Nicole grinned. 'And he doesn't.'

'Auli Saarinen, the *wunderkind*?'

'One of the *wunderkinder*,' Kaija corrected gently, 'Yes. She was in a photograph at my place and Nicole recognised her.'

'And I have the names and a strong link between them and the people I suspect he is investigating,' Nicole turned to Sirkka. 'Why did you call her *wunderkind*?'

Sirkka laughed. 'Auli was the most prodigious Kalevala reciter I have ever come across. Right, Kaija?'

'Absolutely. She was one of only two people I know who memorised the entire work.'

Nicole frowned. 'Sorry, but why would someone do that? I mean, it sounds a bit obsessive. Like someone memorising the Koran.'

Kaija shook her head. 'No, it was just a game of... what do you call it, one-upmanship?'

'Yes, one-upmanship is good.'

'I was a couple of years younger,' Sirkka said, 'but I often went and watched Auli and her friends at their Kalevala evenings.'

'Kalevala evenings?'

'It was a competition with two contestants reciting alternate lines. When someone made a mistake, they were replaced, and at the end of the evening the winner was the one who had the most correct lines.'

It didn't sound to Nicole like a fun night out, but she kept the thought to herself.

'Auli and her friend Kullervo were the judges. They weren't allowed to compete because they both knew every line,' Kaija explained. 'And there was more to it. Each time someone made a mistake he or she had to buy a round of vodka, so it got crazier the longer it went on. People loved it.'

The addition of vodka into the mix did make it sound a little more interesting, Nicole thought. 'Well, they certainly don't do poetry slams like that in England.' She drained her glass and checked the time. 'I had better go and see if I can convince Pentti to keep me on.'

As she was putting her coat on, Kaija came and wrapped an arm around her shoulder. 'I have an idea of how you can persuade Inspector Toivonen.'

As Nicole listened her smile broadened. 'Nice one, Kaija. I'll tell him eight-thirty.'

'Perfect. And I'll meet you there at eight.'

For a long time, he sat with his head in his hands, unable to think. The feeling of nausea came and went and then returned again. Each time he tried to concentrate he was overwhelmed by a tsunami of emotions. Chief among them was betrayal. Somehow, things had gone dreadfully wrong. The simple had become complex, the straightforward was bent out of shape and he could see no way forward.

Gradually the confusion and nausea subsided, leaving him numb and cold, chilled to the bone. It was a feeling he never believed existed until this moment. The right thing to do was to make the phone call and let those above him decide the course of action. However, he was lucid enough to know that such a course of action would see him stripped of everything he had fought so hard for. Yet he could think of no way of salvaging anything from the crisis he found himself enmeshed in.

He looked again at the photographs on his desk, examining them for anything that might indicate they were somehow fakes, or that he was seeing things wrongly. But no matter how he looked at them, he still saw the same thing – DI Parry and the Finnish SUPO Inspector, Toivonen, supporting Chris Mitchell between them. There had been no explanation, just a simple text: *this just came from Helsinki.*

Eventually he decided that his only option was to wait and seek clarification. He sent an innocuous reply to Andrei Zaikov. Had anyone intercepted it, they would have thought it a harmless declining of a dinner engagement. Zaikov, however, would know Grammaticus was demanding an urgent meeting.

The answer to the awkward question of what to do with the man tied to the chair was not immediately apparent. Normally he would have alerted Heimo Harkimo and then brought the man in for questioning. Having told Heimo that he no longer needed the safe house and that the Englishwoman was returning to London, he was loath to mention anything quite yet.

That the man was supposedly British Intelligence complicated the matter. But on the other hand, he could be handed directly to the police for breaking and entering and even attempted rape. The bloody Parry woman had insisted she would press charges if Pentti even considered letting him go. However, he was not inclined to let the police have him. That this was connected with the woman and her associates he suspected of money laundering was obvious. How it was connected was less so.

'I think we should continue our little chat,' Pentti said eventually, and removed the gag Nicole had improvised earlier. He hadn't examined it before but now saw it was a pair of his sister's panties that he had brought over with his sister's other clothes.

Mitchell took a deep breath and shook his head. 'I've told you. I work for British Intelligence and it is your duty to inform them that you are holding me illegally.'

'Please, Mister Mitchell, you can say that as many times as you like, but it does not excuse the fact that you have broken laws here in Finland; laws that we take very seriously.'

Mitchell shrugged. 'Like you, I was just doing my job.'

Pentti went to the kitchen and filled a glass of water. 'I'm in no hurry, you just tell me when you are ready to talk.' He took a long drink and sighed with satisfaction.

After a few minutes he returned to the kitchen and tipped the remainder of the water out and rinsed the glass. Then he sat and waited.

After a time, he tried again. 'You know, I would be happy to overlook the legal problems. But you would need to give me something.'

'There's nothing to give.'

The man was stubborn, Pentti acknowledged; but then, he had few options, and in a similar circumstance he would probably have adopted the same strategy. 'There's always something to give. For example, if you cooperate, then I could possibly inform your Mister Grammaticus that you have been working with us.'

'And how exactly would you do that?'

Pentti pulled his chair closer and leaned forward in a gesture of mutual confidentiality. 'I need to know what you're after. Maybe I can help and give you some information. For example, does Grammaticus know the Russians are involved?' It was a wild shot, based on nothing but the possible link between the gun that had killed Salomäki and the FSB.

Mitchell snorted. 'See, that's your problem. I don't even know what anyone is involved in, let alone the fucking Russians.'

'Then how did you know about the files on Sirkka Mikkonen's computer?'

'I don't know anything about that.'

'Then why were you in Kaija Rantaniemi's apartment?'

'That's simple. I was meeting DI Parry.'

'That's a long way from the story she tells.'

'The bitch is a pathological liar. She's been suspended from duty and is wanted for questioning in England in connection with the killing of a gay man in Oxford.'

'Really?' Pentti pushed his chair back and stood up. 'I'm sorry we can't work together. You obviously don't need my help. I will phone the police and get them to collect you. Then I'll phone Grammaticus and inform him that you have been arrested and refused to cooperate on a case of mutual interest.' He picked up his mobile phone from the coffee table and flipped it open.

'Hang on.' Mitchell looked rattled. 'If I tell you what I know, do I have your word you'll say we were working together?'

'That's what I said,' Pentti replied, but didn't close the phone.

'Look, I have already told DI Parry this.'

'Tell me.'

'I honestly have no idea of the entire story.'

'Just what you know will be a start.'

'Something was being hatched between us, the Americans and the Russians. Then this woman turns up in a boat in the Thames. We think it was a message.'

'To whom?'

'We have no idea. But when she disappeared, alarm bells went off and my guess is that everyone involved is panicked by what she said in an interview with a British policeman.'

'Which was?' Pentti asked casually.

'That this Sampo thing has been stolen.'

'I'm sorry, what was that?'

'This Sampo has been stolen.'

Pentti nodded. 'Right. Just to be certain we are talking about the same thing. What do you understand this Sampo to be?'

'That's the problem. You see that's where things get a bit hazy. It's apparently a mythical object.'

Pentti closed his phone. 'Then you understand why I would have more than a little trouble passing this gem of yours on to my superiors.' He walked over and before Mitchell could react, stuffed his sister's underwear back in his mouth.

He was sitting trying to make sense of what Mitchell had said when there was a knock on the door. He went over and stood carefully to one side.

'Yes?'

'Nicole.'

He punched the code into the keypad and opened the door.

'Any progress?' she asked as she came in. She was carrying a shopping bag.

Pentti pulled a wry face. 'Only if the fact that the Sampo has been stolen is news to you.'

'Nah, old news.'

He laughed. 'And before I forget it, the correct quote is "something is rotten in the state of Denmark" and my name is "Toivonen", not "owl".'

'*An unweeded garden of things rank and gross in nature*, right? You are touchy!' She smiled warmly. 'Anyway, I have news for you.'

'Yes?'

'I haven't a clue what or where the Sampo is, but I am pretty certain I know who stole it.'

'I think I have had enough mystical shit for one night...' He looked at her and realised she wasn't joking. 'Are you serious?'

Nicole nodded in Mitchell's direction. 'Not in front of the children, dear.'

Pentti was confused. 'What?'

'It will keep. I have to go deliver this new bathrobe to my friend,' she said, indicating her shopping bag. Then she hunted through her pockets and produced a paper napkin and handed it to him. 'I'm taking you out to dinner. There's the address and everything written down, so you don't get lost. Try and be punctual. I hear that's a real virtue here. On the dot of eight-thirty.'

He peered at the napkin. 'But that's the *sikala*, the pigsty.'

'Oh, you are a class act, Mister Owl. Just be nice and don't call it that when you arrive.'

'But...'

'Later. I have a new bathrobe to deliver. Have a nice night, Christopher,' Nicole called over her shoulder and, picking up her shopping bag, gave them a wave before closing the door quietly behind her.

Chapter Ten

That almost everyone they met appeared to know Kaija, seemed to Nicole yet another example of how small Helsinki was. On their chill but brisk evening walk through the streets, four or five people greeted her warmly and nodded hello to Sirkka and Nicole. Although it was really cold, she enjoyed the walk, and the more she saw of the inner-city area the more she liked it. She imagined that everyone knowing everyone would make keeping things secret or private difficult but, she admitted to herself, that was an outsider's assumption. Maybe the Finns were not given to gossip in the way her neighbours in London were.

As they entered the restaurant, both the doorman and head waiter greeted Kaija like an old friend.

'Some clear soup to start, I imagine,' the doorman said discreetly, as he took their coats and scarves.

'Naturally,' Kaija nodded.

Nicole, aware that Pentti was not turning up for at least half an hour, was a little surprised. However, the idea of something warm was appealing. Though she had both coat and scarf, the chill night air had stung her face and now, in the warmth of the restaurant, she could feel it glowing.

'Welcome to the Seahorse,' Sirkka said, and shepherded her through the narrow door into the main dining area.

The longish room had large arched windows and fifteen or so tables on the left side, while on the right was a small bar and then five alcove or booth tables. The décor was not at all fancy. The simple wooden tables looked as though they came from a working-class café and the colour scheme was distinctly soviet era, with yellowy brown walls and an olive-green ceiling. The entire end wall was given over to a stylised painting of two black seahorses. Nicole wondered which had come first, the painting or the restaurant name.

The waiter guided them down the room to the last of the booths. The seats could easily have come from a nineteen-thirties railway carriage, Nicole thought; but the green upholstery was comfortable enough and the booth did give them a modest amount of privacy. The restaurant felt lived in and friendly, she decided as she slid in next to Kaija.

'Do you like it?' Sirkka asked, unable to read the expression on Nicole's face.

'Well, it's not what I expected.'

Kaija nodded. 'Like the set of an Aki Kaurismäki movie?'

'Sorry. I take it he's a Finnish actor?'

Sirkka laughed and the Finnish women rolled their eyes in mock horror.

'Really, girl, we are going to have to educate you,' Kaija said with mock severity.

'You've been doing a fair bit of that already,' Nicole said with what she hoped was an enigmatic smile.

The 'clear soup' that arrived was the not the warm broth Nicole had anticipated.

'Koskenkorva,' Sirkka explained as she raised her glass.

'The ear of the rapids.' Nicole hoped she had remembered it correctly.

Kaija's face lit up. 'Well done, *kippis!*'

'*Kippis*,' Nicole echoed and, following their example, downed the vodka. She pointed to the painting. 'I like the seahorses.'

'Done in the 1940s, but the restaurant goes back to 1934,' Sirkka explained. 'The place has lots of funny stories. The seahorse painting, for example. Nobody knows who did it. Some people say it was a student who didn't have any money so he painted it to pay his bill; others say that someone broke in one night and did it. Anyway, it's become quite famous and so has the restaurant.'

Kaija gestured around the crowded room. 'You can see why I had to reserve a table.'

'Thank goodness you did. You know, Pentti called it a pigsty. I don't get it. It certainly isn't that bad.'

Sirkka chuckled. 'That's *sikala* in Finnish but he didn't mean a pigsty but *the* pigsty. It's what a lot of people call it, but in an affectionate way.'

How calling a place a pigsty could be interpreted as affectionate escaped her. What surprised Nicole as she gazed around the room was that so many of the people were dining or drinking alone. At the nearest table an elderly man was reading a book with one hand while picking at some meatballs with a fork in his other. Near one of the arched windows sat a middle-aged woman, a small bright figure in an eye-catching dress of multi-coloured patchwork. At the rear of the room a group of students had joined three tables together underneath the seahorse painting, and by the look of the clutter of glasses, they had been there for some time.

Sirkka saw where she was looking. 'That's where the Mary Hevonen Society used to sit,' she said. 'And there's a photo of them on the wall somewhere.'

'Just up there.' Kaija pointed to the wall above them. 'That's why I especially reserved this table. I'd say there was more understanding of Kalevala in that one photo then half of Helsinki these days.'

Nicole stood and leaned over Kaija to look at the photograph. It showed seven young people, five men and two women. One of the women was Auli Saarinen.

'Why are they sitting like that?' They had two small tables between which two of the young men were seated, facing each other, each grasping their companion's wrists.

'Traditional singing,' Kaija replied. 'They hold each other's wrists and sway backwards and forwards to the rhythm of the lines. It's the way Kalevala was always sung.'

'I didn't realise that they sung it.'

Sirkka shook her head. 'Not really singing, more like chanting, each giving the next line.'

Kaija reached across the table and took Sirkka's wrists. 'Like this.'

'*Mieleni minun tekevi...*' Sirkka smiled as she rocked back.

'*aivoni ajattelevi...*' Kaija responded.

'*lähteäni laulamahan...*'

'*saa'ani sanelemahan...*'

'*sukuvirttä suoltamahan...*'

'… *lajivirttä laulamahan.*'[1]

Kaija released their grip. 'Like so!'

At the nearby table, the man who had been reading put down his book and applauded quietly. From the booth next to them a man who had stood to see who was performing, also clapped. '*Niin sitä pitää, hienoa!*'

'Just like the old days,' Kaija said wistfully.

'I'm not sure that this is a good idea.' Pentti did nothing to hide his reluctance.

He had arrived punctually and immediately seemed concerned by the presence of the other woman. For their part, having consumed a couple of vodkas, Nicole, Kaija and Sirkka were relaxed and happy.

'Sure it's a good idea,' Nicole said and gestured to a passing waitress. 'Our friend would like a Kosken-something, a vodka.'

'Coming up,' the waitress replied in unaccented English.

'So how is our guest?' Nicole asked.

Pentti, obviously uncomfortable discussing anything in public, looked around the room then leaned forward and spoke quietly. 'He is resting comfortably. Now, can you explain what the hell we are doing here?'

'Certainly, but not until you have had at least two vodkas and we've ordered some food.'

The menu was short on choices, but her Baltic herring turned out to be delicious. Nicole tasted some of Kaija's meatballs and thought they were pretty good as well and said so.

'Like home cooking,' Kaija said.

When they had finished eating, Pentti placed his knife and fork neatly together, edged his plate a little away from himself and prepared to leave. 'That was good. But now I have work to

---

1   *I am driven by my longing,*
    And my understanding urges
    That I should commence my singing;
    And begin my recitation.
    I will sing the people's legends,
    And the ballads of the nation.

do. And Nicole, it really is time for you to make arrangements to get back to England.'

'That hardly seems appropriate,' Kaija said, 'especially as she seems to have almost solved your case for you.'

'And caught the man who broke into my office and deleted all the files on my computer,' Sirkka added.

Pentti looked only mildly surprised by their support for Nicole. He was also annoyed that the women had obviously discussed things that he would have preferred be kept discreet. 'What Nicole has done has been helpful, but the case is a murder investigation involving a Finnish victim and a Finnish suspect. And I would suggest it is far from being solved.'

'Inspector,' Nicole favoured him with the sweetest smile she could conjure up. 'I think you should just listen for a moment. Firstly, I am not about to return to England –'

'There is no question of you staying,' Pentti interjected bluntly.

'As I said, listen –'

'What you don't understand is that I am going to have a very big problem explaining to my superiors what has gone on in the last twenty-four hours.'

Nicole shrugged. 'Then tell them something they want to hear.'

'Oh yes, such as?'

'If you kept quiet for a minute, you might learn something,' Kaija said sternly, in a voice Nicole imagined she would once have used on students who got on her wrong side. She looked at Pentti, who seemed extremely uncomfortable and irritated by the whole situation. She decided that they had baited him long enough and the time had come to hook him and reel him in. She took out her glasses and notebook.

'The woman you have been looking for is Auli Saarinen.'

Pentti looked startled. 'What?'

'Auli Ritva Saarinen was born in 1975 in...' she peered at the name, unable to pronounce it.

'Lappeenranta,' Sirkka interjected.

'She went to Helsinki University from 1994 until 1997,' Nicole continued, confident that she now had Pentti's rapt attention. 'She studied ancient literary Finnish and did a thesis that involved something to do with...' she paused and looked at Kaija. 'Sorry, you'll have to help me here...'

'Auli did her work on comparative variants and regional differences.'

'*Anteeksi, en ymmärrä,*' Pentti said, 'she did her thesis on what?'

'A great number of poems in our oral tradition have the same story told in slightly different ways. These are called variants. Auli looked at the variants to see if there were linguistic differences occurring in different regions and if these differences had a regional cultural significance or were merely linguistic ornamentation.'

'Right.' Pentti's dismissive expression showed clearly that he was underwhelmed by the information.

Nicole continued. 'Back then Auli was a member of a social club at the university and I suspect that its members are the people you have been investigating.'

Pentti held his hand up to stop her. He now looked alarmed. 'The names of the people and details of the investigation are not public information, Nicole.'

Nicole's glasses had slipped down her nose and she pushed them back up. 'Oh, Inspector, I would never dream of compromising your precious security by naming your suspects, even if I knew them. How could I? You certainly haven't shared that information with me.' She said it with all the innocence she could muster. 'However, I don't think there is any problem in my telling you the names of a rather odd little poetry lovers' club known as the Mary Hevonen Society.' She paused and peered over her glasses at him and then down at her notes. 'The eight members were six men and two women. The men: Antti Tervola, Tapio Hiltunen, Niilo Yli-Taipalus, Toivo Salo, Viljo Sepponen, and Kullervo Remsu known as Cal. The women were Anja Kujola and Auli Saarinen. My apology if I pronounced most of them wrongly.'

'Bravo!' Kaija, who had been coaching her, was impressed. 'Very good.'

For his part, Pentti just sat there, staring at her as if she had done something unspeakable. Nicole couldn't have cared less what he thought and knowing she had hit the mark with the names, pressed home her advantage. 'Now, this may not be the way you conduct an investigation in Finland, but I suggest that instead of spending all your time untangling money trails, you try looking for where the money has gone. I am sure your wonderful police could also do property and share searches as well. I will bet you a bottle of that, whatever it's called, vodka –'

'Koskenkorva,' Sirkka chipped in helpfully.

'Yes, that – I'll bet you a bottle of vodka that you find a link.'

'And I suppose you know where to find this Saarinen woman?' Pentti's face had become expressionless but his tone was deeply sarcastic.

'I have a bloody good idea where to start looking.'

'*Voi jumalauta*,' Pentti swore quietly, shaking his head in disbelief. 'I don't suppose it's worth saying that you've done enough and we will take it from here? No, I can see not.' He took his glasses off and gave his eyes a vigorous rub as though trying to eradicate the remnants of some nightmare. 'So where would you look?'

Hooked, Nicole thought gleefully; I have him. She turned to Kaija, who was obviously enjoying every moment of the tussle between the two of them. 'Kaija, can I have the photo for a moment, please?'

'Certainly, detective.' She produced a photograph from her bag. 'If it please the court, I would like to submit exhibit number one.'

Nicole took it and slid it over the table. 'This fun holiday snap was taken in nineteen ninety-six, at a cottage belonging to Auli Saarinen's parents. I'm sure you have the means to check if they still own it. It is on an island in a lake…'

Kaija anticipated Nicole's hesitation with the pronunciation. 'Pikkususisaari, near Punkaharju,' she said helpfully.

Pentti put his glasses back on and examined the photograph. 'And that's her?' He pointed to the blonde-haired woman.

'I have no doubt at all,' Nicole said. 'But just to be absolutely clear… Sirkka, exhibit number two please.'

Sirkka chortled, 'Yes, your honour.' She stood up and gently removed the framed photograph from the wall above their table.

Pentti spent time looking at it and then conceded, 'I think you're right. It certainly looks like the same woman. But there are only seven people in the photograph.'

Nicole nodded. 'The eighth is taking the photo. Remsu, if I'm not mistaken.'

Defeated, Pentti handed the photograph back. He allowed himself a slight smile. 'Okay, you're a damn good detective. But I'm under orders to make sure you leave the country. I don't suppose you have an idea of how I deal with my boss?'

She laughed. 'Simple. I go on the run and you tell your boss you're chasing me down. Of course, because we're on a limited budget, we'll go in the same car. Along the way we'll find Auli Saarinen and get her to confess everything. Meanwhile, your backroom boys and girls can trace where the money is going and by the time we come back with Saarinen, you'll be able to arrest the lot.' She shrugged nonchalantly. 'I mean, how easy is that?'

'I suppose you have an answer for everything?'

'Yes, and if not, I make it up. Now, are you going to order another vodka and congratulate the three of us or do I have to do it for you?'

The only light in the room came through the window to make yellow stripes on the ceiling from the streetlights down below. There were few noises; the rumble of a tram, an occasional car, and distant African drumming that stopped and started. Someone practising, he thought. The gag in his mouth made swallowing difficult and when he did manage to draw breath, it rasped in his now dry throat. His tongue felt swollen. One of his legs seemed to be numb and the rope tying him to the chair was too tight. Yet his main preoccupation was not his own discomfort, bad as it was, but what he would tell Grammaticus. There seemed no combination of words, of excuses, that would make the man understand.

One thing was certain, that bitch Parry would pay and pay dearly. Humiliation at the hands of that woman was one thing; having his good career ruined was another. Grammaticus had been oblique when discussing her future, but none of the scenarios he envisaged had anything oblique about them. She would have an accident. A tragic loss of a good officer, they would say. Committing suicide?

He liked that idea. She filled her pockets with stones before diving into the Helsinki harbour? Yes, it was a possibility. It played. She was depressed at the direction her career had gone. Her personal life was a mess. Suicide would seem an appropriate choice. The major impediment was his present predicament. The numbness in his legs was spreading and he could feel the first pangs of hunger gnawing away at his guts.

He came to a decision. When Parry and the Finnish policeman returned, he would say whatever they wanted to hear. It was obvious that they could not hold him indefinitely and he would play along and bide his time until he was released. After dealing with the police bitch, he would return to England having completed his task of getting rid of the MP3 files. It was half true, but Grammaticus would have no way of finding that out.

In his report he would paint a damning picture of Finnish non-cooperation. His righteous indignation would save the day. Yes, that was the way to play it. He felt a sudden elation at having seen a way through the mess he was in. If the gag had not been in his mouth he might have smiled.

He didn't have to wait long as a few minutes later there came the sound of someone at the door. A wave of relief swept over him at the realisation that his imprisonment would be at an end. But there appeared to be a problem with the lock and he waited an interminable time before the door swung open to reveal a man who, even in the gloom, he could see was not either Parry or the Finn.

The stranger who entered had his face obscured by a balaclava. He put down a small bag and without any pretence at skill, ripped the alarm system from the wall and tossed it on the floor.

The man looked him up and down and then said something in what Mitchell took to be Russian.

He tried to cry out, but with the gag in his mouth, all that emerged was a strangled sound. Then, to his relief, the man pulled the gag out of his mouth.

'And who are you?' The man's accent was thick and definitely Slavic.

'Christopher Mitchell,' he spluttered.

'You are CIA, no?'

'No!' He took a deep lungful of air. 'No, I'm British and being held illegally.'

The man laughed then, to his dismay, stuffed the gag back in his mouth. This is not happening, Mitchell told himself. The door was still open and at any moment Parry would come through the door. It didn't happen.

From his bag, the Russian took out a phone, wandered over to the window and peered down into Fredrikinkatu as he dialled. The ensuing conversation was definitely Russian and it was very short. The man returned the phone to his pocket then bent over and took a pistol from his bag. As he straightened up Mitchell was horrified to see him screwing a silencer into the end of the barrel.

Mitchell panicked. He tried again to call out. He tried desperately to get his legs to propel him anywhere, to get away. It was impossible and too late. The man advanced towards him, put his hand under Mitchell's chin, held his face up and looked him straight in the eye. Then he smiled. It's a joke, Mitchell thought; he's just trying to scare me.

'Goodbye, British,' the man said, and put the barrel up against Mitchell's temple and pulled the trigger.

Afterwards the man unscrewed the silencer and stood for a moment watching until the quivering subsided and the body became still and limp. Once he was sure that there was no more movement, he took out his phone and sent a text to the cleaning crew. Then, as he waited for them to arrive, he took an object from his bag and after some consideration laid it on the floor beside a growing pool of Mitchell's blood.

The morning arrived with a surprise – sunshine. The forecast had been for more drizzle and a top of seven degrees. According to the BBC it was already nine and going higher. Unnatural, Quentin decided; global warming had a lot to answer for. Thankfully, climate was not one of his department's concerns. He walked to the window and confirmed that the unseasonably good weather actually extended beyond the confines of the BBC studios and into the real world. It was not always the case.

The last forty-eight hours had been disturbing. Some kind of convergence of the unpleasant had occurred. Was it perhaps, a manifestation of Murphy's Law? He dismissed the thought as utter nonsense. Weary from lack of sleep, he returned to his desk and ran his eye over the latest status report from their little sister, MI5. It did not make happy reading. Judges had not only quashed the deportation of another radical Islamist cleric but also ruled that he be released from Long Lartin high security prison. And in Bradford one of their surveillance teams had lost track of a couple suspected of purchasing bomb-making materials, after one surveillance car was clamped and the other ran out of fuel. Fucking idiots. He read the report again just to confirm that there was no SIS involvement. Satisfied, Quentin flicked to his own report. His team in Northern Ireland following a Latvian arms dealer had stumbled on a new republican terror alliance styling itself as yet another new IRA. Well, he thought bleakly, at least they hadn't stuffed things up.

From Chris Mitchell there was nothing but silence. His scheduled contact time had come and gone hours before. Sloppy, Quentin concluded, and made a note to give the man a dressing-down when he returned. He retrieved the photographs Andrei Zaikov had forwarded him. What the hell was the man doing with Parry and a SUPO officer? He shuddered to think about it. The only possible explanation he could come up with was that Mitchell was drunk and being assisted by the other two. Still, he knew how strictly Grammaticus insisted that his agents adhered to the contact schedule.

Finally, there was the question of Zaikov himself. Since he had sent him a meeting demand the previous evening, there had been silence. Given his present frame of mind he labelled the silence as ominous. The Russian had mentioned a rendezvous with his CIA contact and since then – nothing. He could, of course, meet with the American. It was not his preferred option. Right from the operation's inception there had been an understanding that the 'troika', as Zaikov playfully called it, kept as much fresh air between themselves as possible. He had already met the Russian once this week, to do more could jeopardise… what? He sighed. God knows what he should do. Meeting with the American cousins was always trying but it was an option. There was something about the supercilious condescension he encountered that was irritating in the extreme. And their 'troika' partner, Sam Gordon – even if that was his real name – had a master's degree in arrogance.

The red phone on his desk rang. There was only one person who called this phone and she never did so for a social chat. He stood, straightened his back, took a deep breath and calmed himself before picking up.

'Yes, Ma'am?'

'I hear disturbing whispers from a certain northerly country.'

How the hell was C hearing anything that didn't come through him? He decided to bluff it out.

'And an annoying silence from our man on the ground as well.'

'Our transatlantic cousins suggest that disinfection may be needed.'

'Yes, Ma'am.'

'Nothing must disturb the preparations. I mean nothing.'

'And the English policewoman?'

There was a silence for a moment before she spoke again. Finally, she said, 'I agree with our cousins.'

'If it is necessary to bring our northern friends on board?'

'If they can locate and repatriate her, then yes. However, they must not even suspect that another game is in play. Do I make myself understood?'

'Clearly, Ma'am. And if the northern friends are reluctant, shall I send a specialist in sanitation?'

This time the silence was longer.

'Grammaticus, that is a question I did not hear and therefore I remain silent on that matter,' she said, and hung up.

He cursed himself for having asked the question, but *qui tacet consentire videtur* was answer enough. He opened his drawer and took out a bottle of single malt. He decided he would wait until evening before ringing the Finns. At the end of the day Harkimo would be tired, had probably already had a drink or two and hopefully would be vulnerable to his suggestions. In the meantime, he needed a little fortification and time to work out exactly what needed to be said. It would be so much easier if he could just tell the Finn to order someone to kill Parry. In a perfect world the conversation would be: 'Can you kill her for us, or should I send someone?' He sipped the scotch; sadly, it was not a perfect world.

'*Voi vittu!*' Pentti swore, grabbing Nicole and pushing her away from the door.

'What the fuck?'

'Shut up,' he hissed. 'The door... look.' He brought a finger to his lips, gesturing her to remain silent, then pointed to the slightly open door. 'Someone has been here.'

Nicole nodded and pressed back against the wall.

'Wait,' he whispered and, checking that she understood, pushed the door gently open and stepped in.

Nicole heard the click of the lights going on and then Pentti swearing again.

He returned to the corridor and beckoned her. He looked shaken. 'He's gone. Come.' He led the way back into the apartment. There was no need for an explanation of what had occurred; the smashed security box, the upturned chair and the pool of blood all told the story.

Nicole knelt down beside the pool of congealed blood. 'The same people,' she said quietly.

'The same?'

She picked up the bound birch leaves. 'See, a *vasta*.'

'*Vihta*,' he corrected. 'We call them *vihta*.'

'No, you're wrong,' she said and pointed to the braided birch twigs that held it together. 'This is a *vasta*, from the east. The method of binding is different. This is the same as the one we found in England.'

Nicole stood and made room for Pentti as he knelt and examined it for himself. Then he stood slowly and with a look of puzzlement turned to her. 'You're right. But how the hell did you know that? Most Finns couldn't pick the difference.'

'I'm not most Finns. I'm a quick learner and I have always believed that it is the smallest details that turn out to be the most important.'

Pentti walked over to the window and peered down at the street. After a time, he turned back.

'I think it is time for me to set the record straight with my boss.'

'And stop trying to find where the money is coming from and get someone to search where it's going.'

'One thing at a time,' Pentti said, 'because, in an hour from now, I may be out of a job. I think I have broken every rule there is and probably a few that will now be brought in.'

Nicole shook her head. 'Fine, you do what you have to do. But just make sure your boss understands that I am part of this now and need to be fully briefed. I would prefer that to be a rule you don't break.'

Pentti laughed dryly. 'I am beginning to think I couldn't get rid of you even if I tried.'

Chapter Eleven

'So let me sum this up. You teamed up with a British policewoman who is under suspension. You kidnapped a British MI6 agent and tied him up in what was supposed to be a secure safe house. Now you are telling me he is probably dead? And, to add a touch of the macabre, there was a *vasta* left in a pool of blood?'

Pentti nodded glumly. 'That is about it.'

Heimo Harkimo slumped back in his chair and massaged his neck. 'At this time of night I am usually tucked up in bed listening to my wife snoring. Instead, I am in my office and trying to work out what the fuck to do with you.' He sighed and rocked forward. 'Pentti, an hour ago I had a call from a highly placed MI6 officer who informs me that your Parry woman is a major problem and must be sent home as soon as possible.'

'With all due respect, I disagree.'

'And you base that on what? This Parry's bizarre story of a naked woman in a boat who you say was probably the same woman who murdered Salomäki? And some peculiar ritual involving a *vasta*?'

'Yes, sir,' Pentti replied, despite knowing how unconvincing it must sound.

Harkimo snorted. 'Of course, I forgot to include the small detail of the Sampo being stolen.' He shook his head. 'Can you understand that if I was asked to explain this to the Security Committee and told them that I sanctioned your continued involvement on those grounds, I would be sacked on the spot and possibly recommended for psychiatric treatment. *Jumalauta*! The Sampo is missing! Someone kidnapped the tooth fairy!'

'I understand that it sounds crazy –'

'Sounds? Pentti, it *is* crazy.'

Harkimo lapsed into silence. On the desk he saw the sticky note he had written himself about ice fishing. He screwed it up and tossed it in the bin.

Pentti tried desperately to think of something he could say but he knew there was nothing. Heimo Harkimo was right; any sane person would distance themselves from such absurdities as quickly as possible. Yet… yet nothing.

After a time Harkimo stood up, stretched, then sat again. 'I will tell you what I shall do.'

'Sir?'

'You will pick up this woman first thing in the morning and continue the investigation.'

'What –?' It was not what he had anticipated.

'Just shut up and listen. As far as I am concerned you are off the grid. I have no knowledge of what you are doing, understand?' He handed Pentti a piece of paper. 'You will call this number every day and report on your fishing trip. No names. If you locate the Saarinen woman, then report catching a salmon.'

'Sir.'

'If MI6 asks, I will say you are tracking the policewoman down. You have a week to convince me this insanity has some basis. In the meantime, I will follow up your suggested action on the money trail. But let me make this absolutely clear. I want no more fanciful stories about the Sampo. I want no bodies or *vastas*. Either you find something substantial or I am closing you down. Understand? And before you ask, I am doing this because anything this crazy might just be true, because nobody sane would make up shit like this.'

Before leaving Helsinki Pentti had changed cars and his clothes. The man who picked her up in the newish Saab still looked somewhat like an owl, but one dressed as a lumberjack. Under his checked fleece Pentti wore a tartan shirt, and around his neck a thick woollen scarf. His fashion masterstroke was a peculiar hat with long flaps over each ear. All that was missing were an axe and chainsaw, she thought. Mind you, she probably looked just as rural. On seeing the way she had emerged from the bathroom earlier, Kaija had handed her a woollen hat, mittens and quilted jacket. 'It will be colder where you're going,' she said, by way of explanation.

Nicole looked Pentti up and down. 'So that is an undercover disguise?' she joked, but the man didn't respond.

The weather had cleared and they drove in silence under a pastel blue sky. On either side of the road the forest still glistened with snow and frost and in the more open country, beside the wetlands and small lakes, the glare from the snow was so bright she wished she had a pair of sunglasses.

When, after a couple of hours, they stopped for petrol, Nicole stepped from the car to stand in the sunshine and stretch her legs. Yet there was no warmth in the sun and the cold so intense she quickly returned to the car. The landscape might be stunningly beautiful, she decided, but she preferred to view it through the windscreen of a warm car, rather than with the cold biting at her face and ears and rasping in her throat.

Eventually Pentti's lack of conversation became too much. Nicole leaned over, turned on the radio and searched for some music. Amidst a number of talk shows, she found what sounded like mediocre Argentinian tango music played on an accordion.

'*Humppa*,' he grunted. 'It's very popular in Finland.'

She switched it off.

'So,' she said as brightly as she could, 'What's the plan?'

'Mikkeli and lunch.'

She waited, but he simply kept driving. It didn't sound like much of a plan.

'And Mikkeli – this is a place or a person?'

'A place.'

God help me, she thought, if he weren't driving I would hit him. Even his driving was annoying. The road was superb, yet he drove the Saab in cruise control with the speed set well below any conceivable limit.

'You're not much of a talker, are you, Pentti? So tell me what you think about while you are driving.'

He glanced at her as though she had said something peculiar. 'I was thinking about what to eat for lunch.'

Mikkeli turned out to be a pleasant enough town. Pentti drove straight through and then down to a harbour on what Nicole at first took to be the sea, until Pentti took out a map and pointed at a large body of water. 'It's called Saimaa.'

It was huge. Around the shoreline the water was frozen, but further out she could still see patches of water. You could iceskate forever, she thought, finding the notion appealing. Maybe in another life, she admonished herself. Right now, skating was not on the agenda, even if the entire lake had been frozen.

They stopped at a red-painted wooden building with a sign that simply announced it was a *ravintola;* a restaurant, Pentti translated. For her part Nicole didn't give a damn what the Finnish word was as long as it meant food. She was suddenly ravenous.

Nicole ordered a beer, wild mushroom soup and reindeer stew. The elderly waitress, who was about as good a conversationalist as Pentti, grunted and looked at him, waiting for his order.

'I'll have the same.'

Then, after the beer arrived and they waited for the soup, Pentti suddenly found his tongue.

'We go tonight to the Herttua Hotel just past Kerimäki. We will book in as Tapani and Angela Koskinen. We live in Fredrikinkatu. I sell insurance. We are having a short holiday while you recover.'

'And I am recovering from what? Boredom, lack of conversation? And do I work, or am I a dutiful little wife?'

If Pentti comprehended her underlying tone, he gave no indication.

'You don't work because you have had a – I am not certain of the correct term in English – a *psykologinen ongelma*. A psychological problem?'

'Great. That sounds just like me. And have you been really clever and got an excuse for why I don't speak Finnish?'

He looked at her as if she was indeed crazy. 'I think the fact that you are English and are called Angela is probably enough.'

'So we are married.'

'For ten years. It is an easy number for you to remember.'

'So kind,' she muttered. She leaned over the table and clinked her beer glass against his. 'You know, Mister Lumberjack Owl, you are so clever you could be a spy.'

He was unfazed. 'And you maybe need to practise being… what did you call it, a dutiful little wife? Now, repeat everything about us.'

Nicole, deciding that the only way through this was to play along, bowed her head demurely. 'Yes, Tapani, whatever you say, Mister Koskinen.'

He winced. 'I think you should also call me *kulta*.'

'Why should I do that?'

'Because it means "darling".'

Back in the car, Nicole, entranced by the changing scenery, was quite happy that Pentti had resumed his silence. There were now many more lakes; and the forest, a mixture of pine, spruce and birch, seemed denser. At times they drove through areas of peat and swamp where tall grasses, poking through the snow and untouched by the sun, still held on to the previous night's frost.

As they moved further north there was far greater evidence of heavy snowfall than had been the case around Helsinki. Here the fields were buried, the trees bent under the white weight, and some of the smaller lakes were completely frozen, their surfaces dusted with snow; icing sugar on glass, she thought. Nicole found herself mesmerised by the lakes, not only the profusion of them, but that each had its own beauty. Some were dotted with small islands, others stretched away into the distance, and from time to time, she glimpsed a distant lakeshore cottage with a plume of blue wood-smoke drifting up into the afternoon air.

After a stop in Savonlinna for coffee, Pentti announced that it was time for them to start to address each other as Tapani and Angela.

'Fine by me, Taps,' Nicole growled.

Pentti looked at her, stone-faced. 'Tapani. And from now on wear this.'

She looked at the object in his hand. 'That's a wedding ring?'

'I believe it is customary,' he grunted, and started the car.

It was dusk by the time they reached the Hotel Herttua. The sight of an old army tank and several artillery guns pointing out towards the frozen lake in front of the hotel was not the warmest welcome she could imagine. However, the woman behind the reception desk greeted them in a friendly manner, and on learning that Mrs Koskinen was English, insisted on practising her language skills.

'I am sure you will be happiness here,' she said with a smile. 'And how long have you been married?'

'Ten glorious years,' Nicole said icily.

'Then may the Hotel Herttua be your second honeymoon.'

'Yes, the first was so long ago I don't remember it,' Nicole said and smiled at Pentti. 'Isn't that right, *kulta*?'

Pentti gave her a look that was as far from romantic as she could imagine.

'So why don't we order a bottle of champagne and have a cosy dinner, darling?' Nicole continued.

'Do you know what *Herttua* means in Finnish?' the receptionist beamed, obviously bursting to tell her.

'No. I am sorry my Finnish does not go much past the three "k's": *Koskenkorva, kippis* and *kiitos*.'

'Angela!' Pentti snapped. 'We should get our bag to the room get ready for dinner.'

'*Herttua* means, "duke", and tonight I am sure you will be a princess.'

'I think the term is duchess,' Nicole responded with the soft-est smile she could muster. 'But my duke is right, we should get changed for dinner.'

'And the champagne?'

'Maybe with dinner later,' Pentti mumbled and, picking up the bag, herded Nicole down the corridor. When they were out of earshot he glared at her. 'That was the most undisciplined performance –'

'Oh, all day in the car, not one attempt at a conversation, and now we are here you can't fucking shut up?'

He looked genuinely hurt. 'Angela...'

'Just open the fucking door... *kulta*.'

The room was perfect for a second honeymoon. That is, if perfection was described as narrow twin beds in a room from a soviet-era holiday camp for workers who had achieved the ten-year target for pallid paint production.

'Oh, be still my beating heart,' Nicole groaned. She tossed her coat, mittens and scarf on a chair and opened the curtains. 'Beautiful. Tell me Mister Duke, sir – those long snow-filled ditches between us and the lake...?'

'Historical trenches from the war.'

'Ah, my sort of hotel,' she sighed. She walked to the door and read the welcome message. In Finnish, Swedish, Russian and English it informed her that dinner was at six-thirty, that the sauna was open until seven, and that the fall-out shelter was accessed from a stairwell beside the pool.

'That's comforting. They have a fall-out shelter.'

'Every building in urban areas of Finland used to have a bomb shelter,' Pentti said with sudden enthusiasm, as if she had raised one of his favourite topics. 'But they are unusual in rural locations. In the last few years, the Ministry of the Interior have cut the numbers back a lot.'

'Fascinating.'

'It saves a lot of money...' Then he realised she was not really interested. 'I am going to have a walk,' he said abruptly. 'I will see you at dinner.'

He didn't invite her along, so she shrugged and, as he shut the door behind him, heaved a sigh of relief and lay down on the bed. To her surprise it was remarkably comfortable.

She had not intended to sleep but when she awoke it was after eight. Christ, she thought, I've missed dinner. She heaved herself off the bed and glanced in the mirror. She looked a wreck but decided that the Hotel Herttua probably didn't have some rule about personal grooming and, still groggy from sleep, picked up the room key and went in search of Pentti.

She found him propped up at the bar with a half-empty bottle of Koskenkorva, and to her surprise an ashtray full of cigarette butts.

'Drink, *kulta*.'

It sounded like an order, so she pulled up a barstool and waited while the receptionist, who obviously doubled as barmaid, slid a shot glass in front of her.

'I was just saying to Tuula, how good it is to hear such silence.'

So, they were already on first name basis. His speech was slurred and his usually erect posture slumped as he leant on the bar.

'She says that at this time of year it is so quiet you can hear the snowflakes as they bump into each other.' He let out a braying laugh. 'That's good, eh?'

The receptionist smiled a sheepish smile. 'It does get very quiet around here. But this year has been warm and some parts of the deeper lakes are still not frozen.'

Nicole realised that they must have been flirting before she interrupted.

'Snowflakes bumping? Very poetic, and so typical of Tapani to appreciate such a thing.' She drained the glass and pushed it forward for a refill. 'That's what I love about Tapani. Under that quiet exterior he is such a romantic. I remember when we first met, he said that having seen me was like seeing the moon's reflection disturbed by a raindrop in a pond and that after such an experience he was at the mercy of his heart.'

Pentti's expression hovered somewhere between awe and terror.

The barmaid's jaw dropped and she looked from one to the other with wonderment. 'What a wonderful couple. You are so lucky. I knew it the moment you came in. Such love is rare.'

For a moment Nicole thought she was going to cry. 'And when it comes to sex, he is such a man,' she said, and took Pentti's arm. 'Come, *kulta*, time to eat before we head back to bed.'

They stumbled through to the restaurant, where they sat at their table looking out into the night. Around them the trees were visible in the light spilling from the hotel. A few metres away she could just make out a tunnel entrance to one of the bunkers in the trenches.

'The moon's reflection disturbed by a raindrop in a pond? How the hell did you come up with that?' Pentti asked. He appeared to be totally sober.

'I read it or something like it once.'

He laughed quietly. 'Very good.'

She snorted.

'No,' he insisted, 'that was seriously good.'

'And all that vodka?'

He laughed and slipped the scarf from his neck. 'Old trick.' He pointed to a damp corner of fabric. 'It is very absorbent and you get your scarf dry-cleaned at the same time.'

'Waste of good vodka.'

He shook his head. 'No. My new best friend, Tuula, knows everything that goes on around here. Auli Saarinen is living in her family's old cottage on Pikkususisaari.' He paused and looked over her shoulder. 'Incoming. Here she comes again.'

Tuula came to the table and offered them the menu and wine list.

'I think you will find the slices of *kalakukko* delicious, but if you don't want fish we have some genuine Tampere *mustamakkara* with lingonberry jam and mashed potato.'

Pentti, instantly drunk again, laughed and deferred to Nicole. 'You choose, *kulta*.'

'Too easy,' she giggled. 'I'll have the first and Tapani will have the second.'

She looked up and watched as Tuula dutifully wrote the order down.

'And…' Tuula looked hopefully at Nicole.

'Of course, dear, we would love a bottle of champagne. After all, this is not just ten years of marriage; this *is* our wedding anniversary.'

Tuula gasped and covered her mouth with her hand. 'Oh, this is wonderful.'

Two minutes later, she returned accompanied by a rotund and florid individual who, if his uniform was any indication, was the chef. They placed glasses on the table and produced a bottle of champagne.

'This is a gift of the hotel.' Tuula clapped her hands and the chef popped the cork and filled the glasses.

Pentti lurched to his feet, raised his glass and bellowed, '*Kippis!*'

The ten or so other diners scattered around the room got to their feet, raised a variety of beverages and in ragged unison called out, '*Na zdarov'e!*'

'All Russians,' Pentti said quietly as they waited for the food.

'Is that important?'

Pentti grinned. 'Wasn't it you, professor, who said that it was the little things that were important?'

Nicole took one look at the blood sausage on Pentti's plate and was immediately grateful she had ordered the *kalakukko*, a rye pastry shell containing the most delicious fish she had tasted. She poured the accompanying dill sauce over everything and, mimicking Pentti's apparent inebriation, loudly declared it the apex of Finnish cuisine.

Their exit from the restaurant was the high point of the evening's theatricality. Pentti rose unsteadily, came around the table and assisted Nicole to her feet. Then he planted a kiss on her cheek. The Russians cheered. Hearing the commotion, the chef popped his head around the door of the kitchen and applauded.

'Have a wonderful night,' Tuula called out with a hint of envy.

Arms around each other for support, they swayed their way through the door, and after a full circumnavigation of the reception desk, found the corridor and eventually their room.

'Keep making a bit of noise,' Pentti whispered as he shut and bolted the door.

Nicole didn't really see the point but, laughing loudly, took off her boots and threw them in the direction of the nearest wall. Pentti switched the television on, turned the volume up and then sat on the edge of the bed nearest the window.

'Why all the spy stuff?' Nicole asked quietly.

'While I was in the bar I had a call from my boss. They checked the CCTV footage around the safe house and Kaija's apartment building. There was a man watching Kaija's. I think he had been tailing Chris Mitchell. And later there were some motorbikes outside the safe house. They had Russian plates.'

'FSB?'

'They are not that careless. If it was anything, it was freelance. The number plates will be traced. And we should have some results from the money trail by tomorrow evening.'

'And tomorrow during the day?'

Pentti stood and pulled the curtain to the side, then peered out into the dark. 'Tomorrow looks like a perfect day for a picnic.'

'Where did you have in mind?'

'Pikkususisaari.'

Nicole nodded. 'That would be right. But, just once, can we go somewhere I can pronounce?'

'Pikkususisaari. Little Wolf Island.'

'Fine. Sounds perfect for a picnic.' She yawned. 'Okay, enough. I need some sleep.'

They left the television on for a little longer then turned it and the lights off. In the dark she heard Pentti whispering something.

'What?'

'Happy wedding anniversary, Angela.'

'You too, *kulta*,' she whispered back and drifted off to sleep with a smile on her face.

In the middle of the night she awoke with the sick feeling that she had somehow missed something. She sat up in bed and looked across at Pentti, who was sleeping soundly. A chill ran through her. Pentti had said earlier that the Russians must have been tailing Chris Mitchell. That made no sense. She could think of no reason why they would have any interest in him, let alone know where to find him. They certainly would not have been interested in her either. That only left Pentti. The more she thought about it, the more it made sense. He had been investigating a money trail in which a substantial amount of cash was flowing from Russia, suspected a Russian weapon had been used in the murder of Matti Salomäki, and would certainly be known to the Russians as a SUPO operative. Yes, little things were important, but these were not little things. This was a potential disaster. What if they had been followed since Helsinki? Not once had she checked for a tail, and neither had she seen the stolid, dependable Pentti glancing in the rear-view mirror. And now they were in an isolated hotel in which the only other guests all appeared to be Russians.

Her paranoia was justified, she decided as she slipped out of bed and padded over to the door to check that Pentti had indeed bolted it. Satisfied that they were as secure as they could be, she returned to bed. It took her a long time to get back to sleep. When she did, she slept fitfully.

Breakfast at the Hotel Herttua looked pretty ordinary, she thought; a buffet of cold cuts of processed meat and two types of porridge.

She hadn't even known that porridge came in varieties. Her choice of porridge turned out to be not at all like the lumpy endurance test she had endured at boarding school. It was delicious. Before Pentti joined her, she was already on her second helping. She dolloped yogurt on top and then some kind of purple-coloured wild berries, and mixed the whole lurid mess with fresh cream.

'Ah, you are becoming more Finnish by the minute,' he said quietly as he leaned over and gave her an impeccably polite kiss on the cheek; the kind that couples exchanged modestly to hide the fact they had had a night of unbridled passion. Nicole hoped that the bleary-eyed and hung-over Russians appreciated the authenticity. It was, she conceded, rather pleasant.

'This mess is Finnish?'

He nodded curtly, 'Porridge, *viili*-yogurt and *mustikka*? Very Finnish.'

Outside, the world that greeted them was white and breathtakingly cold. A light dusting of snow had fallen during the night and now covered the cars and car park. Far out in the lake plumes of mist curled slowly above the small remaining areas of still unfrozen water. Everything else was white. Around the shoreline tree trunks rose as though floating out of a mist that cloaked the forest floor.

If Pentti took any notice of the picturesque scene, he gave no indication. Head down, face wrapped in his scarf, he strode ahead of her.

Nicole rather wished she had a camera. 'It's beautiful,' she muttered to herself and set out after him, intending to raise the concerns that had worried her in the night.

'Come,' Pentti held the car door open for her.

'Wait.' There was something wrong. She pointed to a clear set of footprints in the snow beside the car. 'We seem to have attracted some attention.'

Pentti nodded, unwrapped his scarf and tossed it into the car. 'Then we had better vanish.'

'And how do you propose we do that?'

To her surprise, Pentti laughed. 'Carefully.'

As they drove away from the hotel, Pentti turned on the GPS display and punched in their current location. For a man proposing to vanish, he drove remarkably sedately, half his attention on the road and the other half on the GPS.

'I take it you have an idea...'

'Just a moment,' Pentti said. He glanced in the rear vision mirror. 'Yes, as long as the map is accurate.' He turned off the main road and onto what looked like little more than a forestry track but which a sign indicated was a scenic lookout. Once they were under the cover of the trees he slowed down. 'There should be two roads to our right and then a T-junction.'

'And?'

'Just keep an eye out for them. We need to take the second right turn before the junction.'

'Yes, boss,' she said.

'I prefer "*kulta*".'

'*Kulta* status must be earned.'

The second road to the right took them up a winding rise to a large parking area from which the road continued down from the crest of the hill. Judging by the picnic tables, rubbish bins and a toilet block, it was obviously a popular spot. On a clear day, Nicole imagined there was probably a decent view.

As soon as they stopped, Pentti turned the engine off and grabbed his scarf, then got out and walked to a small viewing area. A sign indicated that lighting fires was prohibited and that the current fire danger was low. Well, Nicole thought cheerfully, that is one less thing to worry about. She climbed from the car and, bracing herself against the chill breeze, crunched her way across the snow to where Pentti was staring out into the clouds and mist.

'Nice view,' she said. 'So are you going to tell me what the master plan is?'

Pentti didn't seem to have heard her.

Eventually he patted her arm and pointed, not into the distance, but down into the forest below. 'See? That's the main road and over to the left you can see the forestry track we came up. If they had been following us, they would be on the main road and we could see them if they turned off.'

'Clever. And no tracks in the forest because the latest snow hasn't reached the ground and covered the road?'

'Exactly.'

'I know that this is me being picky, but who exactly are these people who might be following us?'

Pentti shrugged. 'No idea.'

'Well, that's reassuring.'

'But two of them are on Harley Davidsons with Russian number-plates and a third is in a dark green Land Rover with Helsinki registration. They arrived reasonably early this morning and didn't check into the hotel. They all got into the Land Rover to keep warm.'

She looked at him to see if he was joking. Apparently, he was not.

'So how do you know all this if, as I recall, you were asleep until about ten minutes before breakfast?'

He gave her a look that she was becoming accustomed to; as though she had once again redefined stupidity. 'Because they were not here when we arrived last night and the fact that they had left tyre marks in the snow means they came after it stopped snowing. I came out before going to breakfast and found that there were cigarette butts outside the Land Rover on both sides. I spoke to the receptionist who reports that a Russian "gentleman", as she called him, claimed to be a friend of ours and asked how long we were booked in for.'

'Impressive. I forgive you for being late for breakfast,' she said. 'And how long *did* we check in for?'

'I checked us in for three nights, so nobody should suspect we are leaving today.'

'Clever. But, why didn't they follow us immediately when we left the hotel just now? There was nobody on our tail.'

'Because they think they know where we are going.'

Nicole looked at him, perplexed. 'How?'

Pentti laughed. 'Because I told reception that we were driving to the Russian border and were expecting our Russian friends to join us for a picnic.'

'So, the Russian border, that's where we are going.'

Pentti shook his head. 'No.'

'You really like keeping things close to your chest.'

Pentti didn't respond and returned his attention to the road below. 'Just wait and watch. They shouldn't be long.'

It annoyed her that he was so matter-of-fact. Not even a hint of smugness. It was as though he expected her to think things through in the same way he did. But he was right. A couple of minutes later they saw the motorbikes and Land Rover following the main road.

'At least two of them have Russian passports, so they will eventually discover that we did not cross over,' Pentti said, and turned back to the car. 'Come, we can go now.'

They remained on the main road for another twenty minutes or so, then turned off onto a secondary road. Eventually it petered out and they crawled along a winding dirt track to a stand of silver birch beside a lake. Nicole had no way of telling whether the lake was large or small, as five or so metres from the shoreline the mist blotted everything out.

Pentti parked the car beneath the trees and pointed to the left. 'If the maps are accurate, the island should be in that direction.' He wrapped his scarf around his face and headed off.

'A small technical point,' Nicole said, when she caught up with him. 'If it is an island, doesn't that mean we will need a boat?'

He stopped and turned to her. 'Technically, yes. But a boat is not much use on the ice.' He strode on, leaving a vapour trail from his breath like smoke over his shoulder.

Leaving the birch forest, they came to an expanse of frozen swampland. A track of logs and planks had been constructed over the marshiest areas and was, she surmised, intended to make the walk relatively easy once it thawed in spring. Now, however, the snow-covered planks were slippery and made walking tricky. The only advantage to the fresh snow was that, apart from Pentti's footprints, she could tell that nobody else had walked along this way in the last twenty-four hours.

When they came through a bank of tall sedges, Pentti stopped and pointed at some poles sunk into the swamp. The shallow water around the poles was frozen solid.

'For tying your boat to.'

'In spring we would need a boat,' she said.

'No, even then we could walk.'

And then she saw it. A snow-covered board walkway ran from the shore out through long swamp grass to where it disappeared in the mist. Nicole turned and looked back the way they had come, but it too had been swallowed up and her world had been reduced to a circle surrounded by fog. She was going to ask Pentti if he was certain that the boardwalk led to Pikkususisaari. But he had gone.

She stood there for a moment, cursing him under her breath. Stepping onto the boardwalk, she was relieved to find it was solidly built and, because of the ice, not even slightly springy beneath her feet. Being encircled, trapped in a bubble of mist was disorienting. It felt like being inside a computer game in which the entire world was insubstantial and the only way out was to follow the boardwalk without having any sense of direction. Somewhere ahead of her was Pentti, so she started to follow him. It was then she heard the first scream.

Chapter Twelve

Why was it that Americans insisted on meeting in bars? Was it written in some CIA handbook that bars were safer than open ground, or a crowded public space? And then there was that thing about drinks. Sam Gordon, like every company man he had met with over the years, always had a glass of that red label rubbish in hand. Was Johnny Walker a CIA sponsor? Or was it a product placement deal, on the off-chance that they might be captured on some security camera? The notion amused him.

As he entered the Indigo Bar, he paused to let his eyes adjust to the gloom. There were only a dozen or so clients, all trendy, well-dressed, with expensive handbags and Italian shoes. At the bar, glass in hand, was Gordon, his attention focused on the barmaid's ample bosom. He didn't stand a chance. The American looked old and wrinkled, his fake tan strangely orange in the artificial light. Quentin also noted the security camera behind the bar. It probably covered the entire bar, so the question of a more discreet seat at one of the tables was superfluous.

Gordon nodded at him as he pulled up a barstool. 'Buy you a drink?'

Quentin looked at his watch. 'The sun is well and truly over the yardarm, as they say.' He caught the barmaid's eye and pried her free of a couple of male admirers at the end of the bar. 'A single malt, please. Talisker if you have it, no ice, no water.'

The barmaid didn't look old enough to be working in a bar, let alone know what a single malt was. Her other attributes probably got her the job. She smiled and surprised him. 'Of course. Talisker, sir.'

'Who exactly says that?' Gordon asked, his face and tone a question mark.

'What?'

'The sun over yardarm crap.'

Quentin wondered how many drinks Sam had already consumed. 'English people, Sam. English people.'

They waited until his drink arrived and the barmaid had moved back to where her admirers waited. Two men, married he surmised, and mesmerised by cleavage. Quentin checked around the rest of the bar. There was nobody of interest. Pretty damn good description of metrosexuals really, he thought.

'Tell me, who is queering the pitch?' Quentin asked quietly.

Gordon swung around on his stool. 'For christsake, speak fucking English.'

'I was under the delusion that I was. However, to put it in the simplistic parlance of your countrymen, who is screwing us?'

'Ruskies? Finns? Take your pick.'

'Really? You think the Russians? I thought you and Zaikov were the best of pals and had a very productive meeting.'

Gordon took a sip of his drink then placed his glass carefully on the bar. 'Is that what he said?'

Quentin gave a non-committal shrug. He hadn't a clue what they had talked about, but it seemed worth the punt. 'I guess the question is, are we still on track?'

'We have some time until February twenty-eighth.'

Yes, time for a lot more things to go wrong. But he didn't say it. It annoyed him that the Americans were so eager to push him and Zaikov to do all the hard work, and he had no doubt that if things went wrong Gordon would be miles away with clean hands and an innocent smile. However, if the operation were a success Sam Gordon would be at the front and centre, claiming the glory. He stared gloomily into his drink. 'You are still enamoured with Zaikov?'

'What's not to love? He's got eyes and ears on the ground, a direct line to the heart of the Russian military and the level of discontent within the FSB, and best of all we don't have to pay him. On top of that he has generously offered to do any sanitation work.'

'Yes, he does seem rather keen. I suspect he's intending to move on to bigger things and this operation is just a steppingstone. Still, it does seem a little peculiar that his masters, whoever they are, sought to include us in their little game.'

Gordon seemed to have lost interest. He checked his watch and then signalled for another round. 'You'll have one.'

It sounded to Quentin like a statement of fact rather than a polite offer. 'Don't mind if I do.'

'You know, Quentin, I have a theory about why these particular Ruskies are so keen to get into bed with us.'

'I'm all ears,' Quentin said, adopting his 'I'm fascinated' face. The drinks were coming, so he held up his hand for a pause.

The drinks were duly delivered and the underage waitress went off to flirt at the other end of the bar. He nodded. 'Please continue.'

Gordon leaned forward and whispered, 'It's the Arabs.'

'Right. The Arabs…' Now he was certain the man was drunk.

'They had their Arab Spring, and now the discontented Russians want one of their own.'

'A Russian Spring? I understood that they only just got democracy.' Quentin hoped his incredulity was masked by his expression of sincere interest.

'Right on! That's the point. They screwed up democracy. Oligarchs stole the family jewels and took them to London, Geneva, the Bahamas… fuck knows where… and the peasants are still peasants. The army can't get paid and the FSB, who thought they were in the winners' circle with the President being one of their alumni, are not much better off. So they figure that if those towel-heads can have a fucking spring, then why not the Army and the FSB?'

'Why not indeed?'

'Exactly. They have their Russian Spring starting February twenty-eighth, and when they depose the Tsar they have us all prepped and ready to run on to the field whirling pom-poms, flashing our tits and asses.'

'I'm afraid we Brits don't do cheerleading, but I catch your drift. So why are our wise masters signing up for this?'

Gordon drained his glass. 'First, they don't trust a Russian president who gathers more and more power to himself; and second, they didn't have to sign up. If these crazy fuckers make it work, then we will quietly applaud the new Tsar and the new regime will owe us. If it fails, well, we knew diddly-squat.'

Curiouser and curiouser, Quentin thought. Not so much because of the simplistic analysis, but because he never imagined himself in a conversation in which the word 'diddly-squat' made an appearance. He raised his glass. 'Well then, here's to the Russian Spring,' he said quietly.

It occurred to him that there were at least three ways to interpret Gordon's Russian Spring theory. Top of the list was that Sam Gordon was drunk. Or, secondly, Sam Gordon took him for a complete idiot who would grasp at any pearl dropped from the CIA. The third possibility was the least likely: Sam Gordon was right. On balance he decided it most probable that Sam Gordon was feeding him the company line, in which case he was a touch cleverer than Quentin gave him credit for.

Sam clinked his glass against his.

'By the way, your Brit policewoman is still nosing around. I thought you were going to shut her down.'

'The Finns are cooperating on that score.'

'You think? Zaikov says she's working *with* them.'

'Nonsense. I have a top source in SUPO who has her on his radar.' It wasn't completely true. But then, who in this bar was telling the truth about anything?

Gordon shrugged. 'Well, I suggest you talk to him again and find out why they are travelling around near the Russian border and passing themselves off as a married couple.'

It annoyed Quentin that the American had this habit of dropping his little gems in as casually as if they were worthless. Obviously, he had picked this up from Zaikov, a man who was supposedly working with both of them, not just the American. That annoyed him even more.

'I'll make enquiries,' Quentin said. 'In any case I have someone in play who can tidy up any loose ends.' He took a mouthful of the Talisker and swilled it around his mouth. It worried him that they were losing control of the game. The Americans didn't have eyes on the ground, as far as he could tell. Not that he trusted Sam Gordon on that score. The bastards could be playing a different game, though he doubted it. The long game was still in play and while that was the case, the Americans were along for the ride.

But the Russians? He trusted Zaikov only so far, and that wasn't very far at all.

'Talking of loose ends,' Gordon said casually and slid his phone to him.

It was not a good photograph, but the image on the screen was not intended to win awards. Its shock value was enough. The close-up of Chris Mitchell's head showed the entry point of the bullet and he was thankful it didn't show the exit. He steeled himself, determined to show no emotion.

'Courtesy of Zaikov, I take it?'

Gordon took the phone back and looked admiringly at the photograph. 'Neat job. He says that they found him in a SUPO safe house in Helsinki, tied to a chair. It was the safe house where Parry was shacking up with the Finn.'

Quentin took another drink. He knew he should get out of the bar and back to his office. He needed thinking time.

'This was your man, right?'

'A good man,' Quentin said with all the solemnity he could muster.

Of course the man was an idiot, Quentin thought as he climbed in the taxi. How hard could it have been to arrange an accident for a female cop in a foreign country? Sadly, that was a question that would never be asked. In the end it would come down to the blame game, and as he was running the operation, he was directly in the firing line. The complication was that the message from on high had been unambiguous – this operation didn't exist. Yet Mitchell was dead, and somehow he had to be accounted for. Quentin wondered where that left him. *A fronte praecipitium a tergo lupi* – between a precipice and a wolf – seemed to sum it up.

At first it was a single piercing scream that cut through the air. Then it changed to a keening, a disembodied sound borne on the fog. For a disconcerting moment Nicole felt as though the sound surrounded her small universe – a boardwalk in a bubble of mist.

As she hurried forward the sound changed again; no longer simply sound, but words chanted into the air and though she couldn't understand them, she recognised the metre that Kaija and Sirkka had sung across the table in the Seahorse. Somewhere ahead of her a woman was reciting lines from the Kalevala and she had no doubt who the woman was.

Nicole was about to call out to Pentti, when she saw him. The curtain of mist parted and he was standing where the boardwalk ended; on a stony beach in front of a cottage on the edge of a birch grove. She moved forward, ready to reprimand him for striding on ahead, when he turned and held up his hand for her to stop.

'There,' he said quietly, moving towards her and pointing out into the mist to his right.

For a moment she couldn't see anything, but as he came up beside her, she saw a woman standing on the end of a short wooden jetty that jutted out into the frozen lake. Despite the intense cold, the woman had bare feet and was dressed in what was either a nightdress or a plain cotton shift. Her long blonde hair fell in a tangle down her back.

'Is that Auli?'

Pentti nodded. 'I assume so. She screamed when she saw me, then ignored me completely and walked down the jetty. For a moment I thought she was going to jump onto the ice but then she stopped and started chanting.'

Nicole stared at the woman. 'She's not well. We had better get her inside before she freezes.'

Pentti took a step back and indicated that she should lead the way. 'You try. I don't want to start her screaming again.'

'Yes, I can see how you would have that effect,' Nicole muttered as she moved past him to a small ramp that led to the jetty. 'Hello, Auli.'

The woman ignored her and continued to chant into the mist.

Nicole turned back to Pentti. 'Do you understand what she's saying?'

He shrugged. 'It's the Kalevala, so it's old Finnish. Maybe something about her heart being hurt and that she is a miserable girl who would be better off dead and free from the sorrows and torment of her mind.'

'Cheerful. We need Kaija here to translate.'

'I think she is *mielisairas* – mentally ill.'

'Oh, really?' she responded with barely concealed sarcasm and turned back to the jetty. 'Listen, Auli, I know you speak English…'

For a moment the woman ceased her chanting and then turned to face her.

Pentti stepped up beside her. 'She's saying it is time for her to die and something about the fact that her mother, father, sister and brother would not cry if she died, if she drowned and sank deep in black mud.'

'She's more likely to freeze to death,' Nicole said, 'And I'm not about to let that happen.' She stepped onto the jetty. 'Auli, I'm coming to help you.'

It wasn't clear if the woman understood or if she felt a vibration in the jetty as Nicole walked towards her; but she turned and raised both arms, pointing at Nicole and spitting out words as if casting a spell.

'She just cursed you,' Pentti said, stating the obvious. 'Tuoni, the god of Tuonela – the underworld – has no words for you. Death does not share power and you will never leave here, not even to crawl to your own country.'

'Nice.'

The women turned away again and Nicole, thinking that she was going to throw herself onto the ice, walked quickly down the jetty and, reaching out her hand, touched her on the arm. 'Auli, I'm a friend,' she said gently. 'Come with me, let's go inside and get warm.'

There was no response, so she took the woman's arm and sensing no resistance, turned her around.

'Auli, I'm a friend,' Nicole repeated. She took a step back. The woman who now faced her was as pale as anyone Nicole had ever seen; and more than that she was absent, vacant, her eyes open but glazed and lifeless, as though she were dead. Like a zombie, Nicole thought, drained of life and blood and feelings. That the woman was ill was obvious; her eyes were ringed by deep circles and her skin was dry, with flecks of dead skin like peeling plaster. Now that she had stopped chanting her mouth hung open. Her lips were blue from the cold.

'Come,' Nicole said and led her back along the jetty.

Auli didn't resist. When she stepped onto the beach, she turned her head towards Pentti, regarding him as one might regard an inanimate object.

Pentti smiled. '*Nimeni on Pentti ja tämä on Nicole.* I'm Pentti and this is Nicole.'

Auli looked at him blankly and then turned her head and looked at Nicole with the same expressionless gaze.

'I am Aino,' she said quietly, 'and I am dead.'

Heimo Harkimo had gone through back channels, called in favours and broken every rule in the book, but by morning he had copies of bank statements from accounts of Antti Tervola, Tapio Hiltunen, Niilo Yli-Taipalus, Toivo Salo, Viljo Sepponen, Auli Saarinen and Anja Kujola. The only exception was Kullervo Remsu, who apparently was a foreigner and had no Finnish account.

After coffee and one of his wife's *pulla*, he put a sign on his door. *Ei Saa häiritä* – Do not disturb.

Under normal circumstances he would have handed the pile of statements to one of his officers to deal with, but given the probable illegality of what he was doing he set about examining the accounts himself. At first glance there seemed nothing irregular in any of them, so he poured himself another coffee and after arranging the accounts alphabetically, started with Tapio Hiltunen.

Hiltunen was the CEO of a large enterprise that specialised in paper and cardboard products with three factories, one in Helsinki, one in Tampere and the third in Imatra. Heimo put the company files to one side and turned to the man's personal account with Sampo Bank. It revealed nothing but page after page of everyday transactions; school fees for two children, regular car and mortgage repayments, donations to an African missionary hospital and a museum renovation fund. There was also a monthly sum to some-one Heimo assumed was an ex-wife. The man appeared to live modestly, and if he was involved in money laundering, it certainly was not through this account. A note attached to the file informed him that Hiltunen owned an apartment in Helsinki and a summer cottage at Pyynikki, near Tampere; all normal, nothing unusual.

He pushed the Hiltunen file to one side and turned to Anja Kujola. As a sculptor, the woman's name was familiar. She had received some media attention a few years earlier with an exhibition of massive sculptures based on motifs from the Karelian region. With one exception the exhibition had received excellent reviews and apparently sold well. The criticism by another sculptor that her work was derivative and 'the illegitimate offspring of a union between Soviet Realism and Finnish Romanticism' was dismissed as sour grapes. Despite her success, Kujola appeared to have little money and did not own a house or apartment. According to the attached notes she rented a studio in the Eastern Helsinki suburb of Kontula.

Heimo turned back to her accounts and went through them carefully. Some foreigner must appreciate her art, he mused, noting a regular payment from a Canadian bank. But nothing spectacu-lar; enough to live on and certainly nothing remotely like money laundering.

Then he saw it; a regular payment that exactly matched the sum she received from abroad. It would have seemed innocuous had it not been that it was a donation to a museum renovation fund. He checked the account number and, as he suspected, it matched the account that Hiltunen also contributed to. It's the little things, Heimo thought; and little things, like small keys, open large doors.

It only took him a few minutes to scan the other files and discover that every one of them contributed to the same fund. Yet the sums involved were small and certainly wouldn't have warranted scrutiny on an individual basis. But collectively it was a link between them and amounted to a sizable sum. Now all he had to do was discover the name of the museum whose account was being so generously supported on a regular basis.

Sam had left his meeting with Grammaticus with a nagging feeling that the Brit had lost control of whatever was happening in Finland. His first thought had been to signal Andrei to simply clean things up. But Grammaticus had insinuated that the Russian was not playing the same game. He decided a little precautionary examination might be in order. Having been instructed to stay at arm's length from Langley, he decided against ringing his controller. Instead, he went to the embassy and put in a secure call to a close friend whose security clearance was sufficient to allow him access to everything there was to know about Zaikov.

It was several hours before the information came through, and when it did, the alarm bells started ringing. According to his contact the file was so well-buried that he had begun to doubt that it even existed. However, he found it deep in what was jokingly referred to as the CSA – the Cold Soul's Archive – reserved for those who were deemed to be of no further use or importance. According to the file, Andrei Zaikov no longer worked for the FSB but the reasons for his dismissal almost two years previously were unclear. He had been station chief in Vyborg. It was hardly a stellar posting. His subsequent appointment as an assistant in the Visa and Immigration Office at the London embassy had been only secured, it was rumoured, because of family connections. In the CIA's view he had been pushed down and sideways, and they now classified him as an unimportant minor functionary.

Sam was stunned. What was most concerning was that nothing in the file had been disclosed to him during his briefing. That raised interesting questions about the source of his controller's intelligence information. No, Sam rephrased the thought, his 'so-called' intelligence information. Why had he been sold Zaikov as a rolled gold FSB asset when the man was a Cold Soul? His experience so far with Zaikov indicated the opposite. The man had the connections with the Russian Intelligence Service and obviously had his own people on the ground in Finland. Was the Cold Soul file window dressing, a red herring? And if so, why? The other option was that everything he was involved in was a sham, staged to distract from an entirely separate operation. Maybe he was being used as a fool, or bait, or both. It also galled him that Grammaticus had been right about Zaikov. There was only one thing worse than a Brit, and that was a smug one.

He turned his mind back to his initial briefing on the operation. No mention had been made of Zaikov's past; in fact, he recalled being clearly told that the man was FSB. Again he went over the possible explanations. Either it was a massive stuff-up by his superiors, or he had been deliberately kept in the dark. Normally he would have opted for the stuff-up, but there had been nothing normal about the entire operation, and a stuff-up of this magnitude seemed inconceivable. 'A watching brief' had been the phrase. There had been a direction to keep a discreet distance between himself and Grammaticus. The description of what was in play had been vague. 'Certain parties are receiving funds for a possible move to undermine the Russian President. We would prefer this was not disrupted.' 'This is not an official operation; it does not exist,' he was told, and no records were to be kept.

Sam considered contacting Grammaticus, but then thought better of it. First, he needed to know more. For almost a year they and the Brits had been in bed with someone they thought was FSB. It was time to switch the light on and see who had their head on the other pillow. Someone always got screwed in these situations and he was determined that it was not going to be him. In fact, if there was any screwing to be done, he intended to do it.

The door was so small and low that Pentti had to duck to enter, and once inside he found the wooden ceiling beams only just above his head. Entering the cottage was like entering a liminal zone. It was also a step back in time. The windows were all shuttered against the cold, the daylight and the outside world.

'Like a doll's house,' he muttered.

There was no electricity and the only illumination, from two kerosene lanterns, cast a pallid yellowish glow. Thankfully a large old-fashioned wood stove provided what Nicole's father would have called a 'toasty' atmosphere.

She guided Auli into a wicker chair. 'Let me get you something warm,' she said. The woman sat in the chair hunched towards the fire, off in another world, gazing at the firebox. She made no response.

The main room was barely furnished with a small wooden table, a couple more chairs and a tattered sofa covered in equally worn cushions. At the back of the room an alcove contained a rudimentary kitchen with a sink, a single gas ring and a large supplies cupboard.

'A heap of tinned food and packets of crispbread and some biscuits,' Pentti reported. 'It's pretty basic. There's instant coffee, milk powder and some sugar. Do you want a cup?'

'Why not? You make it sound so attractive,' she quipped, as she took one of the lanterns and went through the only other doorway. Despite the warmth of the cottage, she was still feeling chilled. A coffee of any kind would be welcome.

The bedroom was even more basic and contained only two bunk beds, one of which was made up. On the floor at the end of the bunk sat an open suitcase with what she assumed were the woman's clothes spilling from it. She opened a door at the end of the room and discovered a rudimentary bathroom with a toilet, hand basin and a small cabinet. She shut the door and, taking a blanket from the bed, returned to the living room.

'Five-star accommodation,' she told Pentti as she crossed to where Auli sat, still lost in her own world. Placing the blanket over her shoulders, Nicole knelt by her knee and tucked the blanket in around her. 'Auli, would you like some coffee?'

Turning her head, Auli looked at her as if seeing her for the first time.

'Do you like coffee?'

Auli didn't respond.

'Listen, Auli, outside you spoke English. What did you mean when you said you were dead?'

There was a flicker of comprehension in the woman's eyes. Then she raised her hand and ran her fingers through her tangled hair. She turned her gaze back to the fire and spoke very softly.

'I'm sorry, I don't understand what you are saying.'

'She's saying that her mind is often gloomy or misty, like that of a child. Something like that.'

Nicole chuckled. 'You're more of a Kalevala scholar than I first thought.'

'It was drummed into us at school. Not all of it, just the *kaunis* Kalevala; the "beautiful" Kalevala, the bits deemed suitable for *lapsen mieli* – a child's mind. The other thing is that some of the old Finnish words are standard Finnish, like *lapsen mieli*.'

'But what she is saying all comes from Kalevala?'

Pentti nodded. 'I can only guess, but I would say so.' He turned his attention back to the battered kettle he had placed on the gas ring. It was beginning to make encouraging murmuring sounds.

'I was just thinking of the Kalevala game that Sirkka mentioned…'

'Yes?'

'Do you actually remember any of the lines?'

'Maybe a few.'

Nicole smiled. 'Then say them to her.'

Pentti looked taken aback and suddenly shy. 'What? You mean recite my schoolboy Kalevala to her?'

'It's worth a try. We have to get through to her somehow.'

Pentti snorted. 'It will be a very short conversation.'

'Well, unless you have another idea.'

'Okay, but wait until the coffee is ready,' he said.

To their relief Auli accepted the coffee, clasping it with both hands, warming her fingers. Pentti pulled up a chair and sat beside her while Nicole perched on the sofa. He hesitated for a moment and then, after taking a sip of his drink, recited:

> '*Mieleni minun tekevi,*
> *aivoni ajattelevi*
> *lähteäni laulamahan,*
> *saa'ani sanelemahan,*
> *sukuvirttä suoltamahan,*

lajivirttä laulamahan.
Sanat suussani sulavat,
puhe'et putoelevat,
kielelleni kerkiävät,
hampahilleni hajoovat.'[2]

Auli's only response was to turn her head slightly in his direction. Well, Nicole thought, it was worth a try. 'It was impressive, even if it didn't work.'

'You have no idea how boring it was. That's why I find it hard to understand people devoting their lives to studying it.'

'Like Shakespeare? Yet it is somehow important.'

'You mean as cultural heritage?'

'I think you find depth in things when you turn your full attention...' she began, but stopped, aware of a change in Auli. She had straightened her back and was looking directly at Pentti. 'Auli?'

There was a hint of a smile on her face as she whispered, '*Veli kulta.*'

'*Kulta?*' Did she just call you "darling"?'

'Dearest brother,' Pentti said and held a finger to his lips, indicating she should keep quiet. '*Veli kulta... niin on.*'

For the first time since they had met, the woman's face looked alive. Her eyes sparkled as she reached over and grasped Pentti's arm and peered expectantly into his eyes.

He shrugged. '*En muista.* I don't remember any more.'

For a few minutes the three of them sat sipping their coffee. The only sound was the crackle and spark of the fire. Then, as though

---

2   *I am driven by my longing,*
    And my understanding urges
    That I should commence my singing;
    And begin my recitation.
    I will sing the people's legends,
    And the ballads of the nation.
    To my mouth the words are flowing,
    And the words are gently falling,
    Quickly as my tongue can shape them,
    And between my teeth emerging.

reanimated, Auli got up and went outside. Pentti and Nicole exchanged glances and Nicole rose, intending to follow her, but as she did, Auli returned with an armful of firewood, a blast of cold air and a flurry of snowflakes accompanying her through the door.

'*En muista myöskään,*' she said as she laid the wood down beside the fire. 'I don't remember anything.' Crouching down, she opened the glass fire door, fed the fire with a couple of pieces of wood, and then shut the door again.

'You remember the Kalevala,' Nicole said. 'You remember it very well.'

Auli stared into the fire, watching the sparks. 'It's all I have.' She lapsed into silence again and then sighed and returned to her seat.

Pentti took a photograph from his pocket. 'This is a man named Matti Salomäki. Do you remember him?'

Her face remained blank. 'Is this the man who wanted to steal the Sampo?'

'Do you remember him? You met him in Helsinki on a ferry to Savonlinna.'

'*Oisko täältä Sampo saatu, otettu omin lupinsa?*'

'Did he steal the Sampo?' Pentti shook his head. 'No, he didn't steal the Sampo. He was a policeman and someone killed him.'

Nicole drained the last of her coffee and after taking her mug to the kitchen alcove, pulled up a chair and sat beside Pentti. 'Auli, why did you tell us your name was Aino?'

Auli looked at her as if she was a child asking a stupid question. 'Because I was the only one and they killed me.'

'The only what?'

'I knew about the Sampo. I tried to warn them what would happen.'

'How did they kill you?'

'I don't remember.'

'But you're not dead,' Nicole said gently. 'You are alive and you will remember everything eventually.' She hesitated. 'Do you remember being in a boat?'

A look of surprise crossed her face but then she frowned. 'Aino. Aino is dead. *Kunne tyttösi katosi, minne sai sisarueni?* Kullervo says that. He knows she is dead. He knows my sister Aino is dead.'

Patiently, Nicole tried again. 'You were in a boat. There was a *vasta* beside you. We think someone had tried to kill you. You don't remember this?'

'Aino becomes a salmon and now everyone is trying to catch the salmon.'

Pentti leaned forward. 'Auli, who is Kullervo?'

Auli turned sharply and glared at him. 'You were a bad student. Kullervo is Kalervo's son, the boy with blue socks, the old man's son. His sister is lost forever.' She shook her head sadly. 'You must read thirty-five, two hundred and forty-five to three seventy-two. She is gone to death from shame because of Kullervo.'

'I'm sorry,' Pentti said.

Nicole grinned. 'You have homework, *kulta*.'

'No. I'm sorry for whatever has been done to her, but we're wasting our time. She's lost in some inner Karelian reality that has nothing to do with the real world. I'm sorry for her, but even if she came to trial for the murder of Matti Salomäki, there is no way she would be convicted.' He got to his feet. 'We are wasting our time. We should go.'

'No.' Nicole shook her head. 'She knows more.'

'More rubbish.'

Nicole ignored him and reaching out and took Auli's empty mug. 'Tell me about the Sampo.'

For a moment Auli didn't react, then she got to her feet. 'It was beautiful. The lid was so beautiful. We made it and then it was stolen.'

'Stolen? Who stole it?'

But Auli didn't seem to hear. Her eyes glazed over and after a moment she stood up. 'I am going to sleep now,' she said, wrapping the blanket around her shoulders, and went through to the bunkroom.

Pentti stared at the fire. 'Well, that was productive.'

'So, what did we learn?'

'Learn? I think the morning's lesson is that when there is no answer it is best not to ask the question. Now can we leave?'

Nicole glanced at her watch. 'God, it is still morning. You could lose track of time in this gloom.'

'Nicole, please. I have to go make a check-in call to my boss.'

'Can't you do it from here? I would rather not leave Auli now we have found her.'

'There is no phone signal.'

'Then go find one!' she snapped.

'Nicole –'

'You go. Make your precious call and I'll stay and keep an eye on her. You can drive up to the highway. There's sure to be a signal from there.'

Pentti looked at her for a moment and decided that he had little chance of changing her mind. 'But as soon as I get back, we are returning to Helsinki,' he said. And then added sarcastically, 'Is that okay with you, boss?'

'*Kulta*, is fine.'

'*Kyllä rakkaani.*'

'Did you just call me a cold raccoon?'

Pentti snorted. 'You may never know the answer to that question either.'

Part Three

Me nousemme kostona Kullervon

We shall rise in vengeance like that of Kullervo's

– Jääkärimarssi (Heikki Nurmio)

Chapter Thirteen

When the coded message arrived, Andrei Zaikov didn't panic. Neither did he hesitate. Knowing that the day would come when he would have to make a speedy exit from London, his preparations had been meticulous; his small bag was packed and his passports ready.

His section head paid only cursory attention to the application for compassionate leave. The poor bastard's mother was dying. Shit happened. There was no need to get an immediate replacement. Zaikov had always been a seat-filler who played Sudoku and made no effort to enhance his position. He signed the necessary papers and shoved them across the desk.

'I hope you get home in time.'

'Thank you,' Zaikov said and scooped up the travel authorisation and airline ticket.

The elapsed time between receiving the warning and walking out of the embassy, carrying only his single piece of hand luggage, was less than three hours. Unfortunately, the journey he was embarking on would take considerably longer.

Landing at Moscow's Sheremetyevo airport five hours later, he cleared immigration without a problem. His contact was waiting and, taking the envelope containing Zaikov's passport and travel documents, handed him a new SIM card and left without a word.

After lingering over a coffee long enough to reassure himself that he wasn't under observation, he made his way to terminal E, and using another passport, checked in to his flight to Tallinn with Estonian Air. While he waited for the flight he replaced his old SIM card, but decided against using his own phone, going instead to a pay phone to ring one of his Moscow contacts.

'You can kill him now,' was all he said.

It was not until he felt the aircraft lift into the air that he allowed himself to totally relax, and when the hostess came around, he ordered straight vodka. An overnight in Tallinn lay ahead and then a short flight to Helsinki. By the time he arrived in Finland, he would be on the final passport as Andrei Markovich Belov and his old life would be gone forever. Andrei Zaikov would be dead, the victim of a senseless attack in a Moscow back street.

It annoyed him that arranging his own death had cost him considerably more than he normally paid for someone else to die. The man in Moscow claimed it was inflation. Andrei considered it extortion. However, when the time came he knew exactly how he would deal with scum like that. The man and his mafia colleagues would be squashed like the vermin they were. The new Russia would have no place for them. Neither would there be a place for the oligarchs who had bled the system dry. And his former FSB colleagues, those bastards who had undermined his career, they would receive special treatment. Their ultimate fate would be the same as that intended for their former colleague, the President. It was a pleasant prospect, Andrei mused, and ordered himself another vodka. To a pure Russia, he toasted silently.

Outside the cottage the morning mist had evaporated, giving him a clear view out across the lake. It was far larger than he had imagined, the far shore just a blur in the distance. Even though the day was now clear and sunny, the cold was intense. It was probably fifteen degrees below zero, he estimated, and certainly there was no prospect of it warming up. Pentti glanced back at the cottage. At least Nicole would be safe and warm until he returned. He checked his watch. It was now just after midday and his next scheduled call to Heimo was not for an hour, so he had plenty of time. Pulling the flaps of his hat down over his ears, he set out along the boardwalk, treading carefully in the fresh covering of snow.

His earlier suspicion that Auli Saarinen had murdered Matti Salomäki had been replaced by uncertainty. The woman was obviously unbalanced, but he doubted she could kill someone in cold blood. Her entire demeanour was that of a victim, not a perpetrator. Yet the more he mulled over her story, the less sense it made. How had she ended up in London, and who had attempted to kill her? And then, if it were the same individuals, why had they not simply finished her off in the hospital?

Then there was this bizarre Kalevalan motif confusing the whole issue. None of it made sense. Certainly, the people involved with Auli Saarinen back in her university days appeared to have an above average understanding of the epic. Then again, so did thousands of Finns. In the modern context it made absolutely no sense. What was it that Auli had said about the Sampo? *'It was beautiful. We made it and then it was stolen.'* And there had been something about the lid being pretty. She had sounded so matter of fact, as if the damn thing was real. These days Sampo was the name of a bank, not a mythological object or metaphysical construct. *Jumalauta*, he swore to himself. Entertaining the notion of a stolen Sampo was insane. The woman's ability to recall entire verses from the Kalevala and to use them as a means of communicating might be considered a skill by some. But an arcane one, and in the light of a murder investigation that had now claimed two lives and possibly the attempted murder of Auli, expertise in the national epic was simply a distraction.

Yet the nagging questions and doubts refused to go away. It had surprised him that it had been Nicole who brought up the question of the Sampo. He had not the faintest idea what had prompted her to do that, but he had to admit she was a remarkable policewoman. Difficult, at times impossibly rude and dismissive, but she possessed great instincts and must have had a reason for bringing the Sampo into the conversation. Not that it had gotten them very far. Pentti suspected she was as tenacious as a *Karjalankarhukoira*, a Karelian bear dog with the scent of a bear in its nostrils. *Sisu*, that was the word. If the English had more women like her they would have had a word for it as well. He made a mental note to explain *sisu* to her, not that it really translated into English; maybe something like totally focused bloody-mindedness.

He came to the end of the boardwalk and walked along the path to the stand of silver birch where he had parked the car. As he approached the now frost-coated car, he heard a sound from in the trees.

'Good afternoon, Mister Toivonen.' The man spoke English, but the accent was unmistakably Russian.

Pentti turned around slowly.

The man stepped from the trees and gestured towards a black Mercedes parked just beyond Pentti's car. 'Please get in the back seat. Tesak is going to take you for a little ride.' He spoke politely but with an authority that suggested he would not take a refusal lightly.

Pentti looked him up and down. He was a tallish individual, his grey hair topped by an old-fashioned Astrakhan hat. He appeared well-dressed, wrapped against the cold in an expensive looking three-quarter length woollen coat. His smart black leather shoes were highly polished. Pentti decided that the man was not suitably dressed for a struggle. Which, given the calm confidence of the man's tone, was worrying.

'I'm sorry,' Pentti said evenly, 'but I have a prior engagement.'

It was the last thing he said for a while. He neither heard nor saw the man behind him. For a fraction of a second, he was conscious of a blow and then unconscious.

'Your other engagements have been cancelled,' the man said as he walked over and looked down to where Pentti lay in the snow amidst stalks of grass rimmed and stiff with frost. He turned to the biker who had felled the Finn. 'On second thoughts, Tesak, put him in the trunk. I believe that's traditional on these occasions.'

His attempts to contact Zaikov failed. It was as though the normal channels of communication had gone dead or, more disconcerting, been compromised. After two days of silence Quentin momentarily considered telephoning another contact in the Russian Embassy, but immediately dismissed the idea as compromising both his own and Zaikov's security. Yet it was imperative he found out the circumstances of Mitchell's death. And Parry? Hopefully she was dead as well. If not, he would have to devise a new strategy.

Whatever game was being played, he no longer knew the rules. The instruction to cooperate with Zaikov had been clear, and he had done that. The Russian had asked little of him, and if Sam Gordon was to be believed, the Americans were also on a watching brief. But watching what? More like garbage collectors, he though bitterly, cleaning up Zaikov's mess. If indeed it was Zaikov's.

The absurd staging of a photo of a dead girl had gone wrong right from the start with the boat running aground on a mudflat. Whoever was responsible for managing the incident hadn't even killed her and she had ended up in hospital. Another complication. Even then things would have been fine if it had not been for an over-zealous policeman who had insisted on interviewing the semi-comatose woman. But despite the stuff-ups, he had done his part. He had orchestrated the removal from the hospital and subsequent delivery of the semi-conscious woman to Zaikov's men without any trouble. It should have ended there, yet there was a ridiculous panic over the police interview and the fact that the barely alive woman spoke another language; in what insane scenario did that have anything to do with anything? Hopefully she was well and truly dead now.

You are supporting Zaikov, he had been told, as the political aspirations of his associates may well be advantageous in the long run. What was that supposed to mean? I need a cup of tea, he decided, and was about to get his assistant to fetch one when his telephone rang. It was Sam Gordon.

'I suggest you read page eight of the *Komsomolskaya Pravda*,' the American said tersely and hung up.

Quentin put the phone down. *Komsomolskaya Pravda*? Why not the *Zimbabwe Times*, or *Azerbaijan Daily*? He had no idea what the American was playing at, but decided to humour him, so he rang the Russian section and asked for the paper.

'The digital version is available online,' he was told in a tone that suggested he was a Luddite.

'Fuck you too,' he said quietly after he hung up. He dialled his assistant and ordered a cup of Russian Caravan with a slice of lemon.

As his tea arrived, a message from the Russian section popped up on his screen with the URL for the online newspaper.

Although he could understand a small amount of spoken Russian, he couldn't read a word, so was thankful that his computer, seemingly cognisant of his linguistic shortcomings, offered him an instant translation. Page eight, Gordon had said. There were no page numbers on the digital version, and having no idea of what he was supposed to be looking for, Quentin sipped his tea and, starting at the front page, worked his way slowly through the stories. He hadn't been following recent developments in Russia, so it made interesting reading.

The Russian President received plenty of positive coverage of his instructions to the Federal Security Service to create a national system of protection against hacking threats. In the decree the President tasked the FSB to protect 'information systems, and information and telecommunications network in the territory of Russia, in the diplomatic and consular missions abroad.' Good luck, Quentin muttered. Ironically, the following story explained that the next generation of Moscow's children would learn from electronic textbooks and graduate with advanced computer skills – producing a whole new generation of hackers.

After reading stories of migrants from Kyrgyzstan being convicted for attacks on Muscovites, and an op-ed article calling for harsher immigration policies, Quentin decided that, with its stridently nationalistic tone, the *Komsomolskaya Pravda* had taken an editorial turn to the right since its establishment back in the 1920s by the 13th Congress of the Russian Communist Party. There were no 'Russia for the Russians' headlines, but the paper's underlying slant was obvious.

He switched to a tab labelled 'incidents' and found himself immersed in story after story of murders, assaults and terrorist incidents. It was fascinating to remind himself how unsettled the country had become in recent years. Yet, despite the internal troubles, there appeared to be little overt censorship of the news.

The trial in the Sverdlovsk Regional Court of the Urals 'rebels' who had been preparing an armed rebellion, intending to seize power in Russia, was covered in great detail. Not the sort of thing that would happen here, he thought thankfully.

He turned his attention to the next story and realised why he had been having trouble getting in touch with Zaikov. The man had left Britain and if the paper was to be believed, he was dead. According to the report, he had been shot and so badly mutilated that he was only identified by a passport and travel documents found in his jacket. A police spokesman was quoted as saying that the victim had put up a brave but futile struggle. The police suspected robbery was the motive, but had not discounted other possibilities as Zaikov was a former high-ranking member of the FSB. The phrase 'former member of the FSB' jumped out at him.

Quentin pushed his half-finished cup of tea away. He took a glass and a bottle of scotch from his drawer, poured himself a decent shot, and reread the story. Realising there was nothing more to be gleaned, he did a quick search of other online papers from Moscow, but it seemed that the *Komsomolskaya Pravda* was the only daily to cover the incident.

He had always been wary of the Russian, but he wouldn't wish an end like that on anyone. He walked to the window and looking out into the night, raised his glass. '*Dulce et decorum est pro patria mori,*' he intoned solemnly, but somehow he doubted that Zaikov had died for his country.

Nicole awoke to find Auli crouched down, adding wood to the fire.

'I fell asleep,' she yawned.

Auli continued poking the fire and chanting softly.

'I know you can translate that,' Nicole said as she stood and stretched. She remembered watching the fire and then dozing off, but had no idea of how long she had slept. Maybe she had needed it, but at the moment all she felt was groggy and disorientated.

'The young girl stokes the fire, rocks the fire to brightness, tends it with her fingers.'

'Fine. Just be careful you don't burn yourself.'

'But then she drops it.'

Nicole smiled. 'Best be careful then.'

'Tukela on tuletta olla,
vaiva suuri valkeatta,
ikävä inehmisien,
ikävä itsen Ukonki.'

Auli closed the gate and turned to Nicole, frowning as she pondered the translation. 'It is gloomy, hard, and tedious to be lightless, to be fireless. It is lonely for the people, lonely even for God.'

'Then we had better keep it going. I wouldn't want God to be lonely. Now, if you will excuse me, I must go to the bathroom.'

Auli put a hand on her arm, stopping her from moving away. 'Do you have a name?'

'I'm Nicole. My friend Pentti told you that before.'

Auli looked confused. 'Where is this Pentti?'

Nicole looked at her watch. It was just after three in the afternoon. 'That is a very good question.' She gently lifted Auli's hand from her arm. 'But now I really must go to the loo.'

As she was washing her hands in the ice-cold water, she glanced in the mirror of the cabinet above the small basin. My hair is a fright, she thought, and looked around for a brush or comb. She opened the cabinet and found an old-fashioned bone-handled brush. It was worn, but she decided it would serve the purpose. Before brushing her hair, she examined the bottles of pills on the shelves. There were five of them, their labels unfortunately in Finnish. Taking a piece of toilet paper, she placed one of each kind of pill on it, wrapped it and popped it in her pocket.

'What are all the pills for?' she asked as she came back to the fire.

Auli looked blank. 'Pills?'

'Medicine.'

'Medicine to make me remember.'

'Do you remember to take them?'

'One pill from every bottle every morning,' she recited. 'That is easy to remember.'

Nicole nodded. 'Did your doctor tell you that?'

'Doctor? Kullervo gives me the pills.'

'Kullervo? Who is he?'

'You did not go to school?'

'Yes.'

'Then you did not study well. Kullervo is the one who will avenge the murder and the tears. He wishes to grow quickly stronger and to repay his father's death and the tears of his mother. You must read it. It is all there. Thirty-one, seventy-seven to one hundred and ten.'

'Of course.' Nicole grinned. 'Just as soon as I get back to the real world...' She stopped as a sudden thought struck her. Or, as she playfully put it, her little men, her filing clerks, came back with a reminder. She searched her pockets, and to her relief found the scrap of paper Pentti had given her back in Helsinki. She looked at it and then showed it to Auli. 'These numbers, they are not a phone number, are they?'

'Of course not! Zero, one, seven is poem seventeen. *Seitsemästoista runo*. And five, two, three and five, two, six, are the line numbers.'

'So, do you know that verse?'

Auli looked at her with unbridled contempt. 'I think you are a very stupid person.'

'You would not be the first to think that,' Nicole said. It was dawning on her that Auli's bluntness reminded her most of herself. Not the madness of course; at least, not yet.

'*Ei sanat salahan joua eikä luottehet lovehen;*
mahti ei joua maan rakohon, vaikka mahtajat menevät.'

'And what does that mean?'

'Even though the powerful people have gone, the magic is still ready. Words shall not be hidden, nor spells buried; might shall not sink underground, though the mighty go.'

Nicole thought for a moment. It didn't appear to make any sense, but then, nothing about this woman did. Maybe she needed to stop thinking in logical terms. But what other way was there? 'Is it important, Auli?'

The woman's face was screwed in concentration. 'It was... I think. I told someone once that it is *not* true.'

'What is not true?'

'Might shall not sink underground.' Auli shook her head as though to clear it. 'It has. It has sunk underground. It is beneath the memories.'

They didn't speak again for a few minutes. Auli sat with her head in her hands. Occasionally she tugged at her hair as though administering pain in order to focus on whatever thoughts were troubling her. Poor woman, she really is twisted up in her own fantasy world. Nicole stood, moved behind her and began to gently massage her neck. Auli didn't resist and after a time Nicole felt her relax. For the first time she managed to get a good view of the seahorse tattoo on Auli's neck. It was, she decided, quite attractive.

'That felt nice,' Auli said softly, tears running down her cheeks.

'I'll make some more coffee,' Nicole said, mustering all the brightness she could manage. 'I think we could both do with a cup. Let's hope Pentti gets back soon, I am absolutely famished.'

It was as if the fog was lifting. Slowly he felt himself surfacing. His eyes opened but vision was hazy, his head pounding with an intense migraine. He shut his eyes and forced himself to concentrate. He remembered walking towards the car. He remembered the well-dressed man addressing him – after that, nothing. The pain in his head was not about to recede anytime soon, so with his eyes still closed he concentrated on the rest of his body. He was lying in a foetal position on a hard, cold surface, his hands tied in front of him and his feet tightly bound at the ankles. The air around him was warm. Inside, he told himself, I am in a room with some kind of heater. He drifted back into the mist, thankful of the respite from the throbbing in his skull.

Later, when he surfaced again, he could smell cigarette smoke. Somewhere nearby a man was speaking, but he couldn't hear well enough to distinguish individual words. He opened his eyes for a couple of seconds and took a mental snapshot. The room was small, a storeroom maybe, or a garage. A single low wattage light bulb was fixed to the low ceiling, and despite lacking a lightshade it did little to dispel the gloom. The floor was painted concrete. Over near a door were a sleeping bag, a blanket and pillow. Two men were seated on cheap plastic chairs. One of them was smoking. The other man had a bottle of something. In a corner was the source of the warmth, a small bar radiator. He glanced back at the men. One had a pistol on his knee and the other had placed his on the floor beside his chair. They both had silencers or flash suppressors attached. The weapons were a long way from where Pentti lay.

His thoughts were scrambled but he remembered the man saying someone called Tesak would take him for a ride. They were Russians – Tesak, means 'machete' in Russian. It was not a comforting thought.

After a time, the blinding pain in his head became a dull ache. He had passed out again, or slept, and woken to the noise of a door opening and the scrape of a chair being pushed back. He looked around the room. The two men were standing at a half-opened door having a discussion with whoever was outside. The other men were out of sight but Pentti could see a hallway or landing and what looked like a stairwell banister. So it was not a garage, but an empty room in a house or apartment; and wherever it was, it was not on the ground floor.

While the men were involved in their conversation, he turned his attention to his restraints. Plastic tie-locks had been fastened so tightly around his wrists that they dug into his skin. His ankles were similarly bound, but didn't hurt in the way his wrists did. Ignoring the pain, he attempted to move his hands, but they were tied too tightly for anything more than minimal movement. Freeing himself did not appear to be an option.

Before he could investigate further, the door swung fully open and a man stepped into the room.

'So, Mister Finnish spy, you are awake.'

Pentti recognised the expensive coat and highly polished shoes.

'You will be pleased to know that we have decided to keep you alive until we have disposed of the woman.' The man paused, waiting for Pentti to respond.

Which woman, Pentti thought, Auli or Nicole? He said nothing.

'There is someone who would like to talk with you. I suggest that you cooperate fully. Keeping you alive is of course not possible, but if you assist us, then we will make your death less painful.'

'Very generous,' Pentti grunted.

The man shrugged, went to the door and ushered in a short, thickset individual who looked around and then limped across the floor and squinted down at Pentti. The two guards stepped in to flank him, their pistols in their hands. The man nodded at them and they moved forward and dragged Pentti into a sitting position against the rear wall.

'My name is Belov, Mister Toivonen, and you have caused me considerable annoyance,' he said in heavily accented English. 'As has your British policewoman.'

'Policewoman?'

'Please, let us not play games. The sooner you tell me where she is, the sooner our business can be concluded.'

'And what business is that? Killing Finnish Intelligence officers like Matti Salomäki?'

If Belov was surprised by Pentti's accusation, he gave no indication.

'Salomäki was another annoyance.'

'He was my friend,' Pentti snapped, 'and was simply doing his job.'

Belov laughed. 'He had gotten too close to one of my tame Karelians, so we terminated him and then made an example of the woman; a message, if you like.'

'Except the woman didn't die,' Pentti said.

'A mistake that is shortly to be corrected. But the Saarinen woman served to send a warning to her misguided group.'

'Your tame Karelians? Is that why you leave a *vasta* beside a body?'

'Nice touch, isn't it? I'm told that it appeals to them, sort of like a signature. You see, they are romantic, deluded and naïve, but they channelled the funds we needed in the belief that we would further their Karelian cause, and of course we paid them a tiny percentage. For the moment we need them alive, at least for a little while longer.'

The man was over-confident and full of his own self-importance, Pentti decided. His Achilles' heel. Not that he was in any position to exploit it.

'Yes, we know about the money laundering. It is only a matter of time before those whose money it was are informed. I don't see them being too happy about the situation.'

'Mafia thieves, every one of them,' Belov snarled. 'They are not true Russians; they are the vermin who will be first to pay the price for what they have done to Russia. They are scum and will be cleaned away, they and their immigrant friends. Russia belongs to true Russians.'

Russia for the Russians, Pentti recognised the phrase. It was the slogan of the Russian far right. 'It's still a crime to launder money, no matter what its source,' Pentti said. To his surprise, Belov smiled at him.

'You really don't understand, do you? The skimming of money from international transfers was – how should I say – protected. What you and your toy spy service didn't see is that we have friends in the British and American governments who have been protecting our enterprise. And they will continue to do so, because should word of their complicity leak out, they would be severely embarrassed.'

Pentti sighed. 'Belov, I have never heard such nonsense. Why would the English and the Americans be party to theft and money laundering?'

Belov beamed. 'Because, my stupid little man, they distrust our President as much as true Russians do, but unlike us, are not in a position to do something about the situation. When we depose him and purify the country, the English and Americans will turn a blind eye because they will have a Russian government they can trust.'

'I said I have never heard such nonsense. Let me correct that. The word is insanity.'

'Then you are a fool,' Belov sneered. 'We are coming to a great moment in history. Sadly, you will not be around to appreciate it.'

Pentti shook his head. 'You're a lunatic.'

Belov signalled for a pistol from one of the guards. He limped over to Pentti and pressed the end of the silencer up against his temple. 'Mister Toivonen, where is the policewoman?'

Pentti realised that the quickest way to get killed was to tell him what he wanted to know. 'Get fucked, Belov.'

The man showed no emotion. 'Your choice,' he said quietly, and handing the pistol back to the taller of the two guards, nodded at him. 'Thank you, Tesak.'

Tesak needed no encouragement. He lashed out with a boot and kicked Pentti so hard that he crashed sideways and slid along the wall. Then the man walked over and kicked him again.

The pain in his ribs and leg was so intense that Pentti thought he was going to black out. But the Russian wasn't finished with him. He pulled Pentti to his feet and pushed him into the arms of his companion. The man gripped Pentti by the arms, and supporting his weight, turned him towards Tesak. The blow to his stomach that followed knocked the air out of him and the man let him fall to the floor. Tesak walked over to him, and was preparing to kick him again, when Belov signalled him to stop.

'A moment, please.' He took a phone from his jacket pocket and answered it. The conversation only lasted a few seconds. Then Belov came over to Pentti.

'The things a phone call can change, no? I am pleased to say that I don't need your assistance in finding the English policewoman. Apparently, she is having a lakeside holiday. Let's hope she doesn't fall through the ice.'

Pentti wanted to tell him to get fucked again, but was doubled up with cramps and still struggling to get his breath.

'A friend tells me that I will find her with the Saarinen woman, and she is a lot easier to locate. After which I will have no further use for you. However, in the meantime you will remain as a little insurance.'

Belov turned, and without a word to the others, limped from the room.

The man with the shiny shoes came over and looked down at Pentti and addressed him casually as though discussing the weather. 'I did suggest you assist. I'm sorry, but I think an easy death is no longer an option. I will have great pleasure in letting Tesak and Vlad play with you. In the meantime, I suggest you get some rest. Dying can be a very tiring business.' He nodded at the guards and left the room.

Gradually Pentti's breathing came back to normal but the pain in his ribs and leg refused to subside. His mind was racing, trying to process what Belov, in his arrogance, had disclosed. But first he had to free himself, because all the analysis in the world was worth nothing if the information died with him. The guards? One was Tesak, the taller one. The other more thickset, bull-necked one was Vlad. Every bit of information was important. Think, he ordered himself, make an inventory of what you know. But the pain in his ribs and leg engulfed him to the point where thinking became impossible.

The shorter man, Vlad, seemed reasonably relaxed as he checked that the door was securely locked, lit a cigarette and sat down. The other man, Tesak, was more nervous and paced the floor for a few minutes before going to the window and peering out in the street.

It was night time, Pentti realised. Christ, he thought, I must have been unconscious for hours. Tesak continued to stare out the window, then, muttering something over his shoulder to Vlad, he took a long swig from the bottle. Vlad swore at him and getting to his feet, grabbed the bottle and drained it. For a while both men lapsed into a sullen silence.

It dawned on Pentti that he had no idea where he was. From the Punkaharju region it would have only been a short trip to the Russian border. The thought that he was in Russia was not pleasant. Even if he did manage to get free and overpower two armed men, he faced the prospect of a decidedly hostile environment.

He concentrated on the sounds around him. From far away he heard a muffled bass sound. Someone was playing music. There were cars in the street. Moderate traffic indicated that they were near a main road. Then, to his relief, he heard a familiar sound – the rattle of a tram. Either he was in a Russian city that had tramways or, as his instincts now told him, he was in Helsinki. Hopefully it was the latter. It occurred to him that that amount of traffic and the fact that the trams were still running meant it was probably early evening. From memory the last trams ran until sometime after one.

A couple of minutes later the distinctive sound of a Finnish police siren confirmed his location. Unfortunately, it raced along the street below, oblivious to his fate.

Despite the pain in his chest and leg from the beating, and in his wrists from the ties cutting into his circulation, he dozed off again. When he awoke to the sound of the two men arguing, his migraine had reduced to a headache and the pain in his body had become tolerable. Tesak and Vlad were having a heated discussion about the need for food and more vodka. Both men sounded very inebriated and neither seemed inclined towards going out in search of supplies.

Eventually Tesak pocketed some money and grudgingly left the room. Pentti knew it was probably the best chance he was going to get.

'Vlad, may I have some water?' he croaked.

The man frowned at Pentti's use of his name, but he picked up his pistol and walked over to him, and checked the ties on Pentti's wrists and ankles. Then he returned to his chair, took a small bottle of water from a backpack and rolled it across the room.

'Thank you,' Pentti said. He had nearly said '*spasibo*', but stopped himself; aware that it was better his captors did not know he understood Russian.

It was a struggle to unscrew the top, but with the Russian watching closely, he managed; and using both hands, he raised the bottle to his lips and drank, feeling the sweet relief.

Having quenched his thirst, he offered the bottle back to the man, who reached out and took it, then picked up the top from the floor and screwed it in place.

'Water is good,' Vlad said, his words slurred from the alcohol. 'But vodka is better.'

'I agree,' Pentti said, forcing a smile. 'Hopefully your friend can get some more.'

'Tesak can get what he wants,' the man snorted. 'The question is, will he bring it back before he drinks it?'

'He is a true Russian.'

Vlad nodded. 'But an animal when he has a drink.'

'We Finns are like that,' Pentti offered, desperate to keep the man engaged.

'Ah, but we could defeat you at drinking, every time,' the man laughed.

'True,' Pentti conceded. 'But we last longer in the sauna.'

'You are a crazy people. I saw that someone dies in the sauna.'

'It happens. Maybe that is not a bad way to die.'

The Russian appeared to be thinking about that. He took out his cigarettes and lit one.

'May I have one?' Pentti asked.

'Why not? A last cigarette is a tradition.'

Even though he was drunk, the man took no chances. He lit the cigarette, and standing at arm's length, carefully handed it to Pentti.

'Thank you.'

'They say they can kill you,' Vlad chortled.

'Yes, but very slowly.'

Pentti had never smoked, but he took a drag on the cigarette, getting the ash red-hot but without actually inhaling.

Another police car wailed along the street below and the Russian went to the window. 'It is snowing again,' he said and stared out into the night. 'It will be colder at home in Piter. Already the river will be frozen.'

With the man's attention elsewhere, Pentti turned the cigarette in his fingers and pressed it gently against the plastic tie on his wrist. There was an instant smell of burning plastic, so he took another puff and blew the smoke towards the back of the room. Thankfully the Russian was engrossed in the view from the window and didn't appear to notice.

'You say the river in St Petersburg will be frozen. I hear it is a beautiful city in winter.'

'Winter is shit,' the man said morosely. 'Summer is better. After the beginning of June is best. That's the time of the *beliye nochi*.'

'What's that?' Pentti asked, feigning ignorance. He had been in St Petersburg twice during the time of the 'white nights', when the sun hardly dipped beneath the horizon. It had been a good time, but he preferred to spend *Juhannus* – midsummer – in Finland. He had often spent the night drinking around a bonfire with Heimo and his friends at his summer cottage.

'The day lasts all night and everyone has a big party. And there is no fucking snow.'

The man seemed obsessed with snow, so Pentti dropped talking about St Petersburg. 'Is it snowing hard outside?' he asked.

Vlad squinted up at the sky and then down at the road. 'Big snow. The streets are already white. It'll be deep by morning, if it keeps up,' he said morosely. 'I liked snow as a child. Each winter I looked forward to it and when the first snow came I would run outside and try to get the big goose-feather flakes to land on my tongue.' He sighed. 'Then when I grew up, I hated the fucking shit.' He fell silent, but continued to stare out the window.

Pentti made another attempt at burning the plastic tie and again blew away the smoke. Using all his strength, he tried to force his wrists apart; but although there seemed to be some movement, he was still bound. The cigarette was getting shorter and no matter how he contorted his fingers, it would soon be too short for him to push onto the plastic restraint. He puffed on the cigarette and tried again. Then, putting the cigarette carefully on the ground, he tried to pull his wrists apart. There was no give. He needed extra leverage and so in one last act of desperation, he pushed his hands between his legs and, gripping the fabric of his trousers with as much strength as he could, he forced his legs slowly apart. The plastic dug into his wrists so painfully he could barely stand it, but then, to his enormous relief, he felt the plastic pull apart.

'Why did you start hating the snow?' he asked as nonchalantly as he could.

'Why?' The Russian shrugged, but kept his attention on the street below. 'Because snow is no longer something to play in. It's just a dead weight to be shovelled from your door. And after a thaw it refreezes and... it's shit. Nice and white in the beginning of winter, then black and... you know. Then it becomes sludge.'

'Sounds just like my life,' Pentti said. He picked up the cigarette and pressed it down on the tie around his ankles. With his hands free he was able to apply the heat more easily and within seconds he was free.

'Everyone's life,' Vlad said. 'You start playful. You end up as sludge.'

Pentti flexed his wrists gently, getting the circulation flowing again. He rotated his ankles and quietly stretched his legs. He glanced at the pistol lying on the floor beneath the chair. But he dismissed the idea of making a dive for it. He had no idea of the make of the weapon or if it was loaded. The chair was too light to inflict any damage. What I have, he acknowledged, is only the element of surprise.

Then an idea occurred to him.

'Your mate Tesak is taking his time,' he said.

Vlad glanced around at him. 'The bastard is probably sitting in a warm pub drinking my money.'

'Or down in the street sharing the booze with the whores.'

'There are whores here?'

'Everywhere!' Pentti laughed. 'And thirsty ones at that, especially in these temperatures. They need more than a big Russian to keep them warm.'

The man thought about that for a minute and then, freeing the catches on the double-glazed window, swung it open. The blast of air and flurry of snowflakes that blew into the room felt as if they had come directly from Siberia.

'I'll kill the cunt,' the Russian swore and leaned out to get a better view down in the street.

Pentti didn't hesitate. He knew he would only get this one chance, so he sprang up and hurled himself at the man, striking him so hard with his shoulder that he propelled him through the window. The man went so easily that Pentti nearly followed him, but he just managed to grasp the window frame in time to save himself. Vlad had no such luck. He screamed and for a second it looked as if he would keep his balance, but then he fell forward. His arms flailed behind him as he tried to get a grip on the window, the ledge, on anything. Then he was gone, tumbling through the

217

air. If it had been a movie, Pentti thought, he would have been hanging on a ledge, his fingers slowly losing their grip. Thankfully life was sometimes far more straightforward. He poked his head out and saw the man sprawled in the snow three storeys below. He didn't move.

Realising that Tesak might return at any moment, Pentti shut the window and picked up the pistol. It was a Makarov PB – *Pistolet Besshumnyi* – a pistol with a silencer. He checked the magazine. All eight rounds were present. Not his favourite weapon, but under the circumstances it could be a lifesaver if he ran into Tesak.

With a body on the street and the other Russian about to return, he knew he had little time. He grabbed a blanket and wrapped it around his shoulders and over his head. Now, with any luck, he would look like some homeless alcoholic. He hurried onto the landing and shut the door behind him.

Beside him was the metal gate of an ancient lift, but he decided the stairs would be faster. Despite the pain in his legs, he took the stairs two at a time. At the lobby he paused and cautiously approached the door. All he could see through the glass was the snow drifting down.

He pushed the door open and, wrapping his head in the blanket, went out onto the street and crossed the tram tracks. Behind him a tram was coming up the road but the snow was falling too heavily to see the number. The area felt familiar but he couldn't immediately locate himself. He hurried on a few metres when, to his dismay, he saw Tesak crouched beside Vlad's body on the pavement. Apparently, the man was still alive and appeared to be talking to Tesak. On the ground beside them were a pizza box and a bottle of vodka.

Pentti turned in the opposite direction, hoping that the man's attention would remain on his injured companion. Fifty metres or so ahead there appeared to be cars coming out of a corner, so he headed back across the road, moving as fast as he could so as not to attract attention. But as he reached the other side of the road, the Russian looked up and saw him. For a fraction of a second, he looked astonished; then, realising it was Pentti, he struggled to his feet, fumbled for his pistol and set out after him. The ground was treacherously slippery with snow and the man fell, giving Pentti a few more precious seconds.

Pentti was thirty or forty metres in front of the Russian, but he knew that despite traffic on the street the man wouldn't hesitate to take a shot at him. He glanced around desperately, hoping that a police car would come by. Never when you need them, he thought bitterly. Ahead of him was a tram stop. The sign said Töölöntori. Now he knew exactly where he was. The Ma'amma Rosa restaurant was on the corner, and for a moment he considered taking refuge there. But he dismissed the notion as, given the Russian's drunken state, he couldn't take the risk of the Russian following him inside.

Ahead of him a cyclist gave up his attempt to make progress on the snow, dismounted and, trudging through the snow, walked his bike around the corner of Tykistönkatu.

Behind him Pentti heard the pop of the silenced pistol being fired. If it was the same type of pistol, Pentti thought, he had seven shots left.

'You are dead!' Tesak bellowed, and set out after him, scrambling over the barriers at the tram stop and only narrowly avoiding a motorist cautiously navigating through the snowy conditions.

For someone drunk, the man was remarkably fast, and Pentti realised that with his injured leg he couldn't outrun him.

He nearly fell on some ice as he rounded the corner into Tykistönkatu, but steadied himself and dashed past the cyclist. Knowing he was only seconds ahead of Tesak, Pentti made an instinctive decision and slid under one of the cars parked outside Ma'amma Rosa. He lay still for a moment and then, ignoring the pain in his severely bruised leg, rolled on his side, the pistol in his hand. He felt along the left side of the pistol's slide and disengaged the safety.

'Tvoyú mat!' Tesak swore as he rounded the corner and stopped on the pavement, breathing heavily and leaning against one of the trees beside the pavement.

The cyclist, alarmed at events, stopped and looked at the Russian holding a pistol. 'Is there a problem?' he asked in English.

'Did you see him, a man running? He stole something,' Tesak improvised.

The cyclist nodded and pointed. 'He went over there. He crossed the road and went to the right.'

'*Spasibo,*' Tesak grunted and set off in pursuit.

'My pleasure,' the cyclist said and then called out, 'Good luck!' Then he wheeled his bike over to a large black station wagon. 'You can probably come out now. He has gone down Töölönkatu,' he said softly.

Pentti rolled onto his back, slid out from under the car and staggered to his feet.

'I see you have a gun as well,' the cyclist said calmly. 'That is most unusual.'

'Thank you, that was courageous.' Pentti flicked the safety on, then unscrewed the secondary suppressor and slipped it into one pocket and the pistol into another. He held out his hand. 'Pentti, *keskusrikospoliisi.*'

The man extended a gloved hand. 'Markku, *sikariasiantuntija.*'

Pentti looked at him questioningly. 'A cigar expert?'

'It's a living,' the man grinned, then glanced nervously towards the end of the street. 'Hadn't we better get off the street before the mad Russian returns?'

'I need a phone. May I borrow yours?'

The man shook his head. 'I'm sorry, I don't have a mobile. But in my shop around the corner, there's a phone.'

'Thank you,' Pentti smiled.

Chapter Fourteen

Quentin looked at the red telephone as if it were malignant or an alien species. Not once since his elevation to Senior Operational Officer status had he used it to call C. It was a receptacle of calls, a receiver, designed for one-way traffic. When C rang, he always stood to answer it. Not at attention, but standing nevertheless. There had been times of crisis, of bombings, threats and outrages, when he had expected it to ring, times when his orders came from on high, calling him to action in the national interest. Those calls he welcomed and received with a sense of pride. Those calls empowered him. Lately, however, the calls had been enervating, debilitating.

Worse still was the ephemeral nature of the instructions that he received. Instructions that he was expected to decipher not by normal operational rules, but somehow intuitively; instructions for events that 'did not exist'. Sadly, the non-existent events had unravelled to the point where he felt the only course was disengagement. Zaikov was dead and therefore required no back-up. Mitchell was another unfortunate item of collateral damage. The policewoman's meddling probably no longer mattered. Whatever game had been in play was over and therefore whatever information she had gleaned was worthless. The policewoman was temporarily out of the picture, probably dead, but should she reappear he felt confident he could organise a suitable exit for her. That was it. An exit strategy – that would be his approach.

He picked up the red phone and dialled.

'Ma'am, I have unfortunate news about a certain Russian friend.'

The woman didn't interrupt him once, which in itself he found unnerving. When he finished with a flourish about tying loose ends, closing loopholes and such, there was a moment of silence.

'Ma'am?' The line was still open. He thought he heard another voice in the background. Was her hand over the mouthpiece and a muffled conversation taking place? Who is it she talks to? he wondered, not for the first time.

When she finally spoke, it was simply a list of instructions, delivered in a monotone.

'One. It is necessary that we take out a little insurance against any repercussions from this unfortunate affair about which the JIC remains unaware. Two. There is to be no further exchange with our American friends. Three. You will personally take charge of briefing our Finnish allies through your contact there. The loss of one of our agents while on holiday in their country is a suitable entrée. You will stress that he was on holiday, Grammaticus.'

'Yes, Ma'am. I believe I have his leave application on my desk.'

'I would expect so.'

'The other matter – that of the policewoman?'

'I leave that to your discretion, Quentin, discretion being the key word. Do I make myself clear?'

'Of course, understood. *Ars est celare artem*, Ma'am. The true art is in hiding the art.'

'Thank you, but I also went to school.'

'Of course, Ma'am,' he apologised and moved quickly on. 'And should the Americans request a meeting?'

'I believe you are unavailable,' C said bluntly and hung up.

Quentin replaced the telephone carefully and took a step back from his desk. That, he decided, went far better than he had expected. There had been no rebuke, no recriminations. The fact that the JIC – the Joint Intelligence Committee – was oblivious to the operation was puzzling and raised the question of who, other than C and her whispering wraiths, knew about it. It was no longer such a great concern. It is ended, he thought, the whole damn mess. It still irked him that he had no clear picture of what the entire affair had been about. It was like a bad dream in which the wraiths had given him one part of a jigsaw puzzle – a blank piece.

When Pentti didn't return within a couple of hours, Nicole allayed her growing concern by trying to convince herself that the nearest shop was probably a considerable drive away and that he would soon return loaded with supplies. However, by mid-afternoon she had abandoned the notion he was shopping. Several times she went to the door and stood staring towards the boardwalk, hoping to see him striding towards the cottage. On each occasion the cold drove her back inside. The morning mist had gone, and though it was becoming overcast again it seemed there was no more snow on the way.

If Pentti had run into trouble with the Russians, then there was no telling how long he would be. It was like being stuck in some absurd reality TV show where she was expected to survive on her wits. Fat chance. There was a fishing rod in a cupboard beside the door, but she knew that she lacked the skill and patience to embark on a fishing expedition.

For her part, Auli remained staring into the fire, rousing herself from time to time to fetch wood or poke at the embers.

Eventually, when her own hunger prompted her, Nicole asked Auli if she needed something to eat. But the woman shook her head.

'I am going to lie down,' she replied and went to the bunkroom.

Great, Nicole thought. Maybe I should just take some tablets and hibernate.

She sat for a while until pangs of hunger reminded her it was a very long time since she had eaten. Pentti had found coffee and tea in the kitchen and mentioned something about tinned food. She went and opened every cupboard and drawer. To her relief she discovered a cupboard under the sink that was stocked with tinned and dried food. The dried chanterelle mushrooms looked as though they would be easy to prepare, and would probably go well with one of the tins of what was described as 'export quality open fire cooked salmon in water'. Even she could open a tin and soak some mushrooms. There were also, she found, cans of perch

223

and vendace. Nothing spectacular. Or so she thought, until she unearthed some tins of lime and pepper tuna and tikka masala flavoured smoked clams in oil. The clams sounded like a cultural and culinary clash in which her tastebuds might come off second best. In the end she fished out the chanterelles and the salmon.

After putting a handful of dried mushrooms on to soak, she went to the bunkroom to ask Auli if she would prefer one of the other kinds of fish. There was no sign of her. Suddenly concerned, she went to the cottage door. It was beginning to get dark, the cold had intensified and small snowflakes were drifting down. She returned inside and put on her coat, then closed the fire door and went outside.

There was no sign of Auli on the jetty so she hurried down the beach and onto the boardwalk.

'Auli!' she called, but there was no reply.

She walked the entire length of the boardwalk until she came to the grove of silver birch. There was no sign of Auli, but what she saw filled her with dismay. Pentti's car was sitting exactly where he had parked it. Worse still, she could just make out tracks in the snow of a car and what looked like motorbikes.

She ran over to Pentti's car and put her hand on the bonnet. The car had obviously not been used in hours, the metal so cold her fingers nearly froze to the surface.

'Fuck!' she screamed in frustration. For a moment she stood there feeling absolutely lost and impotent. No phone. She tried the car door. It was locked. She considered trying to break into the car and hot-wiring it, if that was indeed possible with a Saab, but knew she couldn't abandon Auli. 'Fuck!' she screamed again, then turned and retraced her steps.

Back in the cottage there was still no sign of Auli so Nicole lit a lantern, stoked the fire and, feeling utterly defeated, opened the fire door and sat watching the flames. Pentti, the bastard, had better be dead, she thought darkly; or shackled to a fucking wall, because no other bloody excuse is going to pass muster. It was then she heard the click of the door latch.

'About fucking time,' she snarled as she turned her face towards the door. But it wasn't Pentti.

'It's ready,' Auli said, her glowing face wreathed in a smile.
'What? What is ready?'
'The sauna, I have heated the sauna.'

Heimo Harkimo looked worn out. The skin on his face and neck was slack and drooping and there were dark bags under his eyes. What was he, Pentti tried to remember, sixty-five? That was his age at his last birthday but he looked considerably older now. What hair he had left was in a state of rebellion, escaping in tufts from underneath a small leather beret. When he sat and unbuttoned his coat, Pentti saw that he was wearing track pants. He had obviously just climbed out of the comfort of his bed and thrown his clothes on. He was also in a bad mood; a man who detested surprises suddenly confronted by one.

When he arrived at the Töölön Sikarikauppa, the proprietor, Markku, had quickly ushered him through an unmarked door next to the shop.

'This is our smoking salon,' Markku explained. 'I will bring you coffee.'

Heimo had not been impressed, but waited until the man was out of the room before voicing his displeasure. 'This is not a secure location,' he growled as he took the Russian pistol from Pentti. 'I'll keep this.'

'Heimo, listen, I have been tied up while two Russian thugs tried to turn me into *confiture*… into jam. I have injured one, hopefully terminally; and the other, a psychopath who goes by the charming nickname of "machete", has been chasing me through the streets and taking shots at me with a Makarov. I was not about to stand in a tram queue or wait on the street for a taxi.'

Heimo looked at him as if he were the psychopath. 'And the man in there?' he asked, pointing towards a back room where the shop owner had gone to brew the coffee. 'Who the fuck is he?'

'He's a cigar expert who probably saved my life. He certainly put his own at risk by pointing this Tesak in the wrong direction.'

'And the car? What have you done with that?'

'It's parked near Pikkususisaari. The keys should be on top of the front right tyre, unless the Russians have taken it.'

'Pikkususisaari?'

'It's an island near Punkaharju, where we found the Saarinen women. Nicole is taking care of her.'

'Taking care of her?' Heimo frowned. 'You surely didn't think it was necessary –'

'No, not like that. I mean looking after her in the sense of keeping her safe.'

Heimo looked relieved and was about to say something, but he stopped as the shop owner returned with a tray of coffee and biscuits.

Markku had taken off his outdoor gear and was wearing a plain brown woollen waistcoat over a bold paisley shirt. It had been years since Pentti had seen anyone wearing paisley and getting away with it. His small woollen cap matched his waistcoat, and with black-rimmed spectacles and a friendly grin, he looked vaguely like a large version of a pagan *Joulupukki*. And, true to form, he was carrying presents.

'Here, two espressos and some rather ancient *piparkakut* left over from Christmas. I am not sure which one, but they were in a tin.'

The ginger biscuits looked fine to Pentti. At the moment he would have eaten flavoured cardboard. 'Thanks, Markku. You're a gentleman.'

'And I dissolved a couple of aspirin in water for you. If that doesn't work, I probably have something stronger next door.'

'I might take you up on that,' Pentti said, 'but I'll see how I go with the aspirin first.'

'Thanks for the coffee,' Heimo said and loaded a teaspoon of sugar into his cup. 'You have an interesting occupation.'

Markku smiled. 'An eclectic bunch of enthusiasts keep me in business. I sell the cigars in the shop next door and once a week we have a gathering in here to enjoy them. A cigar club, I suppose.'

'I will keep it in mind,' Heimo said, 'I am partial to a cigar on occasions, but only if my wife is visiting relatives. She disapproves.'

'I am certain that your wife is not about to interrupt your conversation, so maybe you will enjoy this.' He fished in the inside pocket of his waistcoat and produced a cigar. 'A Montecristo Havana, Open Series Regatta. There is a double guillotine cutter and matches on the table.'

'Montecristo? Really, you are too kind,' Heimo murmured with undisguised relish as he took the cigar.

'My pleasure,' Markku nodded. 'Now, I'll leave you. I only came in tonight to do my stocktake. I'll be next door if you need anything.'

After they were left alone, Heimo clipped the cigar, removed the ring wrapper and lit it. 'Nice chap,' he said. 'Now, start at the beginning and don't miss anything out.'

When Pentti had finished recounting the events of the last two days, Heimo sat and thought for a while. Then he put the stub of the cigar in an ashtray and pushing himself out of his chair, got up and walked over and examined the sofa.

'Do you need to go to hospital?'

'I am extremely bruised, but I don't think anything is broken.'

'Then here is what we will do. You will stay here tonight –'

'No!' Pentti protested. 'I need a car and a new phone and I need to go and get Nicole and Auli before those goons find them.'

Heimo shook his head. 'You listen to me, Pentti. It is after midnight, it is snowing heavily, and you are in no condition to drive. I will find you some food and you will get some sleep –'

'Heimo, I can't do that.'

'You have no option. It is an order, Toivonen.'

'But…'

'By morning I will have found you a car and you can drive up to Punkaharju. In the meantime, I will begin putting pressure on some of the so-called tame Karelians. If the incident with the Saarinen women in London was a supposed warning, I want to know what it was they were being warned about and why.'

'And the Russians?'

Heimo thought for a moment. 'We will tread carefully. The last thing we want to do is create an international incident with our neighbours. So I'll talk to our Russian contacts about this Belov.

I am also concerned about the implication that the British and Americans are playing games in our patch without consulting us. I will do some digging around. Now, what else do you need, other than food and sleep?'

'I will need a weapon,' Pentti said.

'I will get you your TRG-42,' Heimo said without hesitation, 'and a USP Compact to slip in your pocket.'

'Fine.'

'But Pentti, no hunting, understand? You need some mopping up, then call me and I will make it happen. I can call on the *Karhu* team to lend us a few of the *Karhukopla*. Your priority is to get those women back here. Is that clear?'

Pentti's adrenaline levels were receding and he suddenly felt so tired he would agree to anything. 'Absolutely,' he said. While he felt he deserved a shot at extracting a little revenge, protocol dictated that the *Karhukopla*, the 'Beagle Boys', were the right people for almost any situation. And there was a personal connection; the crack squad were from his old counter-terrorism unit, the Karhu team. Against them, people like Belov and Tesak wouldn't stand a chance.

'Then it's settled. You stay here and I will go round up some food.'

'But what about, Markku, the owner?'

Heimo shrugged, 'I will have a chat with him about national security and the availability of a blanket for you. I'm sure he's the type that will understand.'

'And?'

'In the morning I'll have a car delivered.' Heimo buttoned his coat. 'Don't even think about putting your head out the door.'

'Yes, sir.' Pentti would have laughed but his ribs still hurt, even after the aspirin.

Sam Gordon felt as if the oxygen had been turned off. His Russian contact had left the country and got himself killed and Grammaticus, with whom he was supposedly working in tandem, had fallen off the radar; no calls, no messages, nothing.

To make matters worse he had been summoned to a meeting in the embassy at an ungodly hour of the morning. He tossed back a shot of bourbon, grabbed his jacket and in a foul mood and bleary-eyed, took a taxi to 24 Grosvenor Square.

His mood was not improved by being ushered into a secure room and told to wait.

The woman who came in twenty minutes later didn't bother introducing herself; neither did she say whom she represented. It could be anyone, he thought, the CIA, State Department, bloody Department of Fisheries for all he knew. She was dressed in a smart full-length coat and scarf, but carried no bag or document case. Sam guessed that she had just come off a flight from Washington.

There were no social niceties, no offer of coffee or apology for the lateness of the hour. For a moment she stood before him, appraising him. He said nothing but waited patiently for her to take a seat. She didn't. Instead, she launched straight into reciting a litany of stuff-ups, all of which she implied were his responsibility. She obviously knew the situation better than he did, with everything in her head, no file, and no notes on an iPad or smartphone.

'And Zaikov leaving the country? You had no indication this was going to occur?'

'No.'

'Did the British agent know and not tell you?'

He thought it undiplomatic to remind her that the SIS did not refer to themselves as 'agents', but 'officers'. Instead, he shrugged. 'I have no way of knowing. But I guess not.'

She raised an eyebrow and looked at him disapprovingly.

'You are not employed to guess. I suggest you leave that to the analysts.' She didn't wait for a response but moved on to the next topic. 'Your call to Zimmerman requesting background on Zaikov was irresponsible.'

'Given my position, I hardly think so,' Sam protested.

'It was irresponsible because it breached your standing orders. Irresponsible because it may well have alerted someone to the fact we had an interest in him. Irresponsible because it may well have precipitated his flight and ultimately his death.' She hardly paused for breath. 'Your brief was to assist him, not endanger him, and certainly not to request more information than you had been cleared for. There was a reason for Zaikov's file being buried. It was not supposed to be accessed. Zimmerman has been suspended pending an enquiry.'

'That is grossly unfair,' Sam exploded. 'I was misinformed or misled, right from the beginning, and Zimmerman was simply following a request from me.'

'A request you were not authorised to make, to gain access to information you were not cleared to see. I suggest you avoid outbursts that could be interpreted as insubordination.'

What he wanted to say was 'go fuck yourself', but what he said was, 'I hear you.'

'Good.' She gave him a half smile.

The bitch is human, he thought.

'What is the status of the policewoman, Detective Inspector Nicole Parry?'

'Unknown. Probably dead.'

'I asked for status, not another of your guesses.'

'Okay, unknown.'

'Status of Toivonen, the SUPO agent?'

'Unknown.'

'And the other British agent, Mitchell...'

'Operational Officer Mitchell is dead.'

'Killed by?'

'Unknown.' He had wanted to say 'incompetence'.

She paused, glanced around the room and, to Sam's relief, finally sat.

'Agent Gordon, the ratio of "unknowns" to "knowns" is unsatisfactory.'

Sam decided against making a quip about Donald Rumsfeld and his 'unknown unknowns'. What he really wanted was a stiff drink, a cigarette and a bed, preferably occupied by the young waitress from the Indigo Bar.

When the woman spoke again it was more softly, as though sitting had taken away the imperative to interrogate. Or maybe, he thought, she was simply tired and suffering from jet lag.

She glanced at her watch. 'Do you know where Quentin Grammaticus is at the moment?'

There was something in her tone that suggested she already knew the answer to the question.

'If he has any sense, he's tucked up in bed.'

'He's at Heathrow waiting to board the first flight to Helsinki. We have a concern that the British may be going soft on their support for Zaikov and –'

'But Zaikov's dead,' Sam interjected.

'His network and their aspirations did not die with him,' the woman snapped. 'You would do well to remember that. We are making every effort to contact his people, and when we do they will be asked to make direct contact with you.' She reached into her coat pocket and pulled out a SIM card and a small white card with a number printed on it. 'They will phone you on this number.'

Sam took the SIM card and pocketed it. He glanced at the number on the card.

'Where the fuck is country code 358? The UK number should start with 44.'

'It's Finland. Now listen. We have information that Grammaticus has a scheduled meeting with Heimo Harkimo, a senior man, a SUPO veteran. If it transpires that the meeting goes ahead it might indicate that the English have decided to cut a deal and inform the Finns. In that case Grammaticus is to be impeded in any way you see fit. I hope I make myself absolutely clear.'

'And this is authorised?'

'Agent Gordon, none of what you are involved in is authorised. The Government of the United States has no knowledge of you or your actions. However, there are three highly qualified specialists on their way to Helsinki to assist you, should you need it. They are travelling as a delegation of pulp and paper mill executives and will be staying at the Hotel Kämp. I understand they will have specialist equipment available.'

Sam was stunned. There had been no suggestion of direct action in all the hours of briefings he had undergone before leaving the States. Mind you, they had lied to him about Zaikov.

'Is that clear?'

Sam simply nodded.

The woman got to her feet and shook his hand. 'Good luck, Agent Gordon.' She said sweetly. 'And remember, you fuck up and you're fucked. We don't fucking know you.'

Then she left.

Highly qualified specialists, the woman had said. She meant a hit team. Fucking jargon. Specialist equipment? What was that code for? Machine pistols, sniper rifles, grenades, fucking rocket launchers? For christsake, a hit team, for use against the Brits, the Russians or the fucking Finns? For the first time in years, he thought that retirement was a sensible decision.

'Wait for me. I'll be five minutes,' he told the taxi driver.

Sam alighted and stood for a minute with his face up into the rain. Above him, the light on his apartment had been switched off. The young waitress was probably sound asleep, or she had given up waiting and gone home. What was it that Kinky Freedman used to say? *Fuck 'em and feed 'em fruit loops.* That summed up how he felt about everything and everyone.

Inside the apartment he poured a very large glass of bourbon, but he left his coat on. With his drink in hand, he checked the bedroom. The girl was there. Asleep. But he didn't have time to indulge or regret. The taxi was waiting and he needed to pack.

Nicole closed the cottage door behind her and hurried to catch up with Auli who, in an uncharacteristically buoyant mood, was almost skipping along the forest path, swinging the kerosene lantern by her side. Her mood changes, Nicole had realised, were wild and unpredictable. Still, she preferred the up times.

The path took them around behind the cottage, over a small rise and out onto a half-moon shaped bay. There in front of them, with smoke emerging from a chimney, was the log sauna that she had seen in the photograph back at the Seahorse pub in Helsinki.

'Come,' Auli called gleefully and raced ahead to the door of a small annex, pulling off her clothes as she ran.

By the time Nicole entered the annex, Auli was naked and busy filling a sauna bucket from a tub of water.

'We keep water here, otherwise it is all frozen,' she explained. Then her face dropped. 'I am sorry. I have forgotten your name.'

'Nicole.'

'That is a good name!' she exclaimed. 'Now, please get ready to come in together so we do not escape the heat.'

'So that the heat does not escape,' Nicole corrected gently and started undressing.

'That's what I said.'

'Of course it was. I'm sorry.'

Auli smiled. 'You cannot help being stupid about sauna. *Olet ulkomaalainen...* you are a foreign person.'

'I am indeed a complete foreigner. But I have been in the sauna with your professor.'

Auli looked perplexed. 'My professor? I am not a student.'

'You were once, in Helsinki. Sirkka was your professor.'

'Sirkka? I don't remember.'

Nicole folded her clothes together and looked for towels. There were none.

Auli glanced around, searching for what Nicole was looking for.

'Oh, I am sorry. There is no *vasta*. It is the wrong time of year and I hate frozen ones.'

'I'll be fine,' Nicole grinned. 'Lead the way.'

Auli placed the lantern on the floor in the far corner. It was dim, but in the soft light, Nicole saw that sauna was a far cry from the modern electric sauna she had enjoyed in Helsinki. There was no stove, as such, but a neatly piled heap of stones, radiating heat. The wooden walls and ceiling were black from decades of smoke, and the benches worn smooth with soap, water and time. But the biggest difference was the smell. It was delicious, and the atmosphere was softer than in the electric sauna. It was also considerably cooler.

'This is perfect,' she said.

'Many people find the *savusauna*, the smoke sauna, too much work, too long to heat and too much soot. But the *löyly* is the best,' Auli said. 'The atmosphere is best, the steam softer.' To demonstrate she took a copper scoop and threw some water on the pile of stones. 'See?'

'Indeed,' Nicole said and settled onto the top bench beside Auli.

The lower temperature in the *savusauna* allowed them to stay in longer than she had in Helsinki. When they emerged, Auli grabbed her hand and ran through the snow, across the beach and onto the ice. 'The lake is waiting! I cut a big hole!' she cried, spinning round then splashing down on her back into a circle of water.

She is so like a child at times, Nicole thought, and then her bare feet reached the ice and her playful thoughts came to an abrupt halt. It was so cold it felt like her feet were on fire. This is not a good idea, she thought as she tried to tiptoe to the edge of the hole. There should be a sign: this way for heart attacks or death from exposure.

Nevertheless, she lowered herself into the water. It was extremely cold, but felt warmer than the air temperature. 'Enough!' she screamed after a few seconds, and slithered up onto the ice like a beached seal, then clambered, slipping and sliding, to her feet. The lake water had been freezing, but the feeling as she emerged was exhilarating. Her body was glowing, and although the air temperature was below zero, the two of them sat on the pebbled beach, their bodies steaming as they threw stones into the neatly cut hole in the ice.

Now we are both children, Nicole thought. The small snowflakes falling on her skin felt like frozen kisses. It amazed her that somewhere so remote and so cold could feel so good. She followed Auli's example and stretched out on the snow-dusted pebbles, gasping at the cold on her back. Overhead, clouds scudded across a moon that was sailing up the sky amidst a ceiling of stars. There were no large storm clouds and it seemed to Nicole that the snowflakes seemed to be coming out of nowhere. She was about to ask Auli about it when the woman reached out and touched her arm.

'Look,' Auli whispered pointing away to the sky in the north. '*Revontulet.*'

Nicole craned her head and gasped. 'Northern lights, *aurora borealis*,' she said, realising she was also whispering. The shimmering curtains of light – purples, yellows and greens – radiated out and then shifted, moving like the frailest gossamer in a breeze. Yet she was aware of their immense power and that filled her with a sense of awe. It was like nothing she had ever seen before. Soft pulses of light rose and fell in slow-motion waves of luminescence, drifting, arching, evaporating and then reforming. She had always understood the word 'breathtaking' to be a metaphor, she thought, as she reminded herself to breathe.

'*Revontulet*,' Auli repeated, 'it means "fox fire" in your language.' Then, gazing into the distance, she recited.

'*Portit Pohjolan näkyvi,*
Paistavi pahat veräjät,
Kannet kirjo kiimottavat
Miehen syöjästä kylästä,
Urohon upottajasta.'

'Is that from the Kalevala?' Nicole asked.

Auli shook her head. 'It's just an old poem about the northern lights that talks of the evil gates of the north, of Pohjola.'

They fell silent, but didn't take their eyes off the awe-inspiring display in the sky. A perfect curtain had formed, its immense folds fringed in green, changing to blood red as they reached high into the outer reaches of the atmosphere.

'The sky is bleeding veils of death,' Auli said quietly. 'We should go back to sauna.'

Nicole nodded. She felt suddenly frightened. Not by what Auli had said, but a sudden awareness of her own frailty, naked on a beach of snow-covered pebbles, miles from anything she knew or was familiar with. For all its awesome beauty, the sheer power of the aurora left her feeling tiny, hopeless and, she realised, very cold.

Back in the warmth of the sauna she cheered up, distracted by the pleasure of having her hair washed and rinsed for her. She did the same for Auli, and following her example, scrubbed her with a rough mitt and some strong-smelling tar soap.

After they were both rinsed off they sat in silence, letting the heat seep deeply into them. In stark contrast to the fear she had felt on the beach, Nicole found herself in a state of gentle bliss. She turned to Auli and was about to tell her what she was experiencing, when she saw a glint of tears running down the woman's cheeks.

'Auli?' Nicole reached out and put her arms around her, drawing her close. Auli, her voice trembling, started to chant.

'Kalevala,' Nicole murmured, knowing instinctively that this time she was correct.

Auli rewarded her with a faint smile and, wiping the tears away, translated.

'When I cannot dare to weep, When I cannot weep among the people, I will weep in the sauna. Weep in the sauna secretly, Submerging the bench and loft rafters in troubled tears.'

In her arms Auli was shivering, but not from the cold.

Eventually, when their hair was dry, they dressed, picked up the lantern and made their way back towards the cottage. As they reached a broader part of the path, Auli stepped alongside Nicole and took her hand.

'Thank you,' she said.

Nicole was about to reply when she heard a sound. She pulled Auli to a halt and peered out into the lake and then ahead.

'Auli,' she said quietly. 'There's someone coming to the cottage.'

Chapter Fifteen

His first instinct was to shoot Tesak on the spot. But his initially incandescent rage had turned to a simmering heat, and with Vlad in hospital, Tesak was going to be needed, as there were others he wanted dead, and soon.

'Which hospital?'

'Meilahti.'

'And the police?'

'I hear that they will interview him when the sedatives they have given him wear off, probably in the morning,' Tesak said. 'They also say he may never walk again.'

'He won't,' Zaikov said flatly, 'and you will make certain of it.'

'When?'

'Now. Take a couple of the boys to make sure the nursing staff are not a problem.'

After Tesak had gone, Zaikov poured a drink and, cursing the squalid apartment, the snow and the incompetence of his men, pulled his chair up to the window and watched the snow; white flakes in a gun-metal grey sky. He needed thinking time to sort out the disasters of the last twenty-four hours.

He drank slowly, nursing his glass, letting his mood settle. Watching the snow was therapeutic and after a few minutes he was ready to turn his attention to analysing the situation. The injuries to Vlad and his imminent death were a minor inconvenience compared to the threat posed by Pentti Toivonen. The man knew far too much to be allowed to live. But the problem of finding him seemed insurmountable in the present circumstances, so he put the issue to one side and turned his attention to the women.

They were a nuisance, but not critical, unless Toivonen had managed to communicate with them. He rated that as less than probable, but nevertheless something not to be totally ignored.

Of the two, it was the policewoman who worried him most. She had been a constant irritant from the moment she poked her fucking nose into a file that should not have existed. The Saarinen woman was no threat to anyone. Even if she stopped taking the drug regimen the Karelian had her on, it would be weeks before she recovered, and even then it was doubtful that she would regain much of her memory. Bitch should have died before. Next time there would be no last-minute reprieve. She and her would-be Karelian colleagues had been marked expendable from the beginning.

He got up to pour himself another drink when the thought struck him that this might be the time to call on his American contacts. They were not in a position to decline his demands, but the question was rather whether they were in a position to assist. He had no idea what assets Gordon had at his disposal, but it was probable he could call on some backup.

Then another thought occurred to him. If, as the Karelian had suggested, Saarinen and Parry were still in the Punkaharju region, then that is where Pentti Toivonen would go. A welcoming party might solve several problems at once. Toivonen, Parry and Saarinen – three birds with one stone. Or, most likely, if his marksmen were as good as they claimed to be, three birds with three shots.

He looked at his watch. It was time for the morning's scheduled call. He picked up his phone and dialled his St Petersburg contact.

'Resting peacefully,' he said.

He supposed that someone with a sense of humour had chosen the phrase. 'Thank the Lord,' the formal response came back. Followed by a request for him to take down a phone number.

'Your Uncle has a new number,' the man said and hung up.

So maybe the Americans did not need a lot of persuasion, especially if they were handing out their phone numbers like whores in a bar.

He walked over to the kitchen and refilled his glass, then took out his phone and sent a text message to his Uncle Sam.

Old friend wants to meet

With the two-hour time difference, it was still early morning in the UK and he didn't expect a reply for a while. In any case, the man was not an early riser. Yet by the time he had walked back to his chair and lit a cigarette, the phone beeped. The message was even more of a surprise than the speed of the reply.

Bar Hotel Kamp 1330

He was in Helsinki? That seemed almost too good to be true. Zaikov had anticipated having to put some pressure on Sam Gordon. He had not expected him to be a mind reader, especially as he would have no idea who exactly the message was from. Choosing a bar as the meeting place was typical of Sam Gordon; it was either sensible tradecraft so he could keep an eye on who was coming and going or, more likely, so he could get a drink. Whatever the case, the one thing he knew he had in his favour was the element of surprise. The last person Sam Gordon would be expecting was a dead man.

The man carrying the flashlight switched it off as the women approached. As they got closer Nicole could see by the light of the lantern she was carrying, that he was leaning casually against the cottage door, smiling.

'Hello, Aino,' he said softly.

Auli immediately let go of Nicole's hand and ran to meet him. He stepped forward to greet her and, sweeping her up in a huge hug, lifted her off her feet.

Nicole, unsure of what was happening, stood back. The man was tall, over six feet she estimated, and well built. He was, she thought, extremely handsome. His face was as pale as Auli's but the skin was healthier. With his fine features and high cheekbones, a full head of straight blonde hair and a slightly androgynous look, she imagined a modelling agency would have paid good money to have him on their books.

The man put Auli down, but didn't let go of her. He looked over her shoulder at Nicole.

'And you must be Nicole.'

'Yes.'

His face broke into a broad grin. 'It's a pleasure to meet you at last. Pentti told me I would find you both here. I'm Cal, by the way.'

The accent was American. No, she corrected, Canadian. Nicole stepped forward, held the lantern up and looked him up and down.

'Where's Pentti?' she asked bluntly.

'Still in Helsinki, unfortunately. Something important came up and they called him back.' He released Auli and opened the door. 'Come in. It's not good for you to stand around in the cold after a sauna. I've put wood on the fire and made some coffee.'

Nicole didn't budge. 'How did Pentti get in touch with you? There's no telephone signal here.'

Cal ushered Auli inside and then turned back. 'Nicole, relax. I live on the other side of the lake. And we have very good reception there.' He turned on his heel and went in, leaving the door open for her.

Nicole stood there for a moment and then realising she had no other option, followed him inside and shut the door.

Auli was seated in her usual chair in front of the fire, but now she was turned towards the man, her face glowing and animated as they locked wrists. He rocked her in time as he chanted softly. She had no idea what they were saying but had no doubt the two of them were reciting the Kalevala.

After a time, Cal released Auli's wrists and applauded. '*Erittäin hyvä*, fabulous!'

'Charming,' Nicole muttered, crossing to the table. She picked up a cup of coffee and handed it to Auli. 'Here, drink this.'

Auli took the coffee and smiled. 'I think I beat him.'

'It's a game,' Cal said. 'We played it at university. Except this is a variation or what we call an inversion. I quote something from the Kalevala and Aino has to respond with a quotation that not only makes sense, but comes from some part of the text that precedes my quote. There's nobody else that can do it except us.'

There was a hint of arrogance in his voice that irritated Nicole.

'Yes, I know about your Kalevala games at the Seahorse. Kaija told me how clever you both were.'

He peered at her, puzzled. 'Kaija?'

'Kaija Rantaniemi.'

'Really?' He narrowed his eyes and stared at her. 'Well, you have certainly been doing your homework.'

The warmth had gone out of his voice and Auli, realising something had changed, leaned forward and grabbed his arm, seeking reassurance. He brushed it off. 'Not now, *kultaseni*.'

Nicole, sensing she was also right about something else, pressed on. 'And by the way, Mister Remsu, her name is Auli.'

That stunned him. But instead of responding, he crossed to the table, added some sugar to his coffee, and taking his mug, went and looked out the window. After a time, he went through to the bathroom.

Seizing the opportunity, Nicole went quickly over to Auli, crouched down and grasped her hands. 'Listen, Auli, do you really trust this man?'

Auli looked confused. 'Kullervo is my brother,' she said and freed her hands.

'And I look after her,' Cal said quietly.

Nicole started, and turned around to find him standing at the bedroom door with the bottles of Auli's pills in his hands.

'And just for your information, she likes being called Aino.'

'What is it you're playing at, Remsu?'

He stared at her coldly. 'I am looking after you. Now get your coat on. We are going.'

'We are not going anywhere. Pentti will be coming back here looking for us.'

To her surprise he laughed. 'Your faith in him is commendable. However, I'm sorry to tell you Pentti is not coming.' He looked at his watch. 'In fact, he's probably dead by now.'

'You're lying –'

'Just shut the fuck up and get your coat.'

Despite her shock at his claim that Pentti was dead, she walked over and sat in the chair beside Auli. 'We are staying,' she said flatly. She expected him to get angry, but instead he brushed past her and went to Auli.

'*Mennään nyt, kultaseni*.'

Auli got to her feet obediently, then tugged at Nicole's sleeve. 'We have to go now.'

Nicole shook her head. 'I'm sorry, but I don't trust this man and I'm not –' She stopped. Cal had pocketed the bottle of pills and was standing with a pistol in his hand pointing directly at her.

'We are going. Get your coat, or you'll freeze to death.' To make certain she understood, he cocked the pistol.

An armed man was not someone she was going to argue with, and reluctantly she got to her feet. 'And where the hell are we going?'

He shrugged. 'Somewhere safer and warmer than here.' He turned to Auli. 'We are going for a ride on my sleigh, *kulta*, and I know how much you enjoy that. Now get dressed up as warmly as you can, we have a long ride in front of us.'

Auli needed no encouragement and looked positively radiant at the prospect.

As they walked out of the cottage and down the beach, Nicole had her first experience of real panic. They walked not towards the boardwalk, but down onto the ice. He is going to take us far out into the lake and shoot us, she thought. The northern lights had vanished and what had started as a magical night of sauna and stars and aurora had suddenly become an empty black space in which she saw nothing but her own demise. And Pentti? The man had said he was probably dead already. What did *already* mean? It had a ring of inevitability about it. No, she swore to herself, the man is lying, and Pentti isn't dead and I am going to stay alive. She repeated the thought, but somehow it failed to convince her.

They must have walked for five minutes, long enough for her to begin wondering if he knew where he was going, or indeed if he had any destination in mind. Then, by the light of his torch she saw that he was following his own footprints on the snow-covered ice. It seemed they were going in a straight line. Maybe we are to walk right across the lake, or just to the centre. She had a mental flash of the hole in the ice near the sauna. You could slide a body under the ice and it would vanish until spring. Or be eaten by fish with no trace remaining. Stop it, she rebuked herself. Concentrate on where you're going. Remember everything. But there seemed nothing to remember, just the night and the seemingly endless trudging over the snow-covered ice.

Eventually Cal stopped and Nicole saw the reason for their long walk. The man was standing by a snowmobile. Not wanting to alert them, he had stopped far out on the lake and walked to the cottage. The machine had a sledge hitched on behind, and Auli, obviously familiar with it, climbed onto the sledge without hesitation. Nicole stood her ground, her eyes firmly on the pistol in his hand.

'Where are you taking us?'

Cal didn't bother replying. He flashed his torchlight over the sledge and gestured to her to follow Auli's example.

'No thanks, I'll walk. I need the exercise.'

'Get in!' he snapped at her.

You can't outrun a bullet, she told herself, and in any case, the falling snow was lighter now and certainly not enough to provide cover. Even if he had not had a weapon, she knew there was no way of escaping in the dark without a flashlight. Freezing to death on the ice was not on her agenda, she decided, and neither was abandoning Auli – so she clambered aboard.

From the snowmobile's seat Cal took a visored helmet and gloves and prepared to put them on. 'There are blankets. Use them,' he ordered brusquely. 'Or freeze.'

Thankfully there were small cushioned seats in the sledge and sitting was not as uncomfortable as it looked. There was also Auli, who, the moment Nicole sat down, wrapped her arms around her and pulled the blankets over them both.

She's like a child, Nicole thought as the machine roared into life and picked up speed over the ice. And Christ! I feel like her fucking mother.

'It's all written,' Auli shouted to be heard above the noise of the snowmobile.

'What? What's written?'

'Everything.' Auli laughed. 'It's in the Kalevala. *Tule korjahan, korea, maan valio, matkoihini!*'

'Auli, you keep forgetting I don't understand a word.'

'Of course you do. It is what Kullervo says.'

'And what the hell is that, exactly?' Nicole asked, wondering why she bothered to keep up a shouted conversation with a woman who was obviously unstable, or drugged out of her mind.

'That's what Kullervo says,' Auli repeated. 'Come into my sleigh, my fine woman, the country's loveliest maiden, journey with me.'

'Great. Really great!' Nicole yelled, forgiving herself for the lie. If she never heard another word from this fucking Kalevala, it would be too bloody soon.

The most important thing was to figure out what the hell was going on. Why had this Cal, this Kullervo Remsu, come to get them? And what the fuck did he know about Pentti? Bloody Pentti! Why was she concerned about him? He was okay, she grudgingly admitted to herself. Okay, in an owlish kind of way. He was so Finnish, whatever that meant. And Auli? Why had she become so protective of Auli? Her job was to find out... what? Christ, she thought, I'm losing it.

Then something happened that stopped her thinking about anything. The snowmobile stopped, the engine was switched off, and she was suddenly aware of a profound silence. Then, from in front of them she heard Cal's voice.

'Look,' he said, in an almost reverential tone.

Nicole sat up, and freed the blanket from around her face. It was bitterly cold. The snow had stopped and there, from horizon to horizon, was a sudden burst of brilliance. The aurora had returned – this time not in the green and reds that had predominated earlier, but a massive display of shimmering white ribbons that pulsed across the sky with such power that she was incapable of thought.

Beside her Auli had her face tilted towards the heavens with a look of ecstasy.

As they watched, a ring of pure white formed high above them and from it the lights radiated out, reaching down in curtains that folded in on themselves time and time again.

It astounded her. She was transfixed by the power of something so far above her head, and beyond her comprehension, that it eclipsed the fear and hopelessness her predicament demanded.

As the snowmobile engine coughed then spluttered into life again, she felt strangely detached. She snuggled closer to Auli and swore to herself that somehow she would survive whatever lay ahead. 'We'll be fine,' she said, too quietly for anyone to hear.

Tiredness and the motion of the snowmobile over the ice was just beginning to lull her to sleep when the roar of the engine diminished and she felt them slow down. Sitting up, she popped her head out from under the blanket and looked around. Apart from a few small clouds, the sky had cleared and above her the stars burned brightly against the black backdrop of the night. There was no moon, but ahead of them she could clearly see the shoreline of the lake, a dark line of trees stretching away both left and right. There was no sign of habitation, no lights or buildings, just seemingly endless forest.

For another couple of minutes Cal cruised along the shoreline. Eventually he turned into an inlet and drove into a wooden shed, where he parked beside two other snowmobiles.

Cal cut the engine, removed his helmet and, producing the pistol again, gestured with it for Nicole to get out. Auli, seemingly unfazed by the weapon, simply followed.

'Come,' Cal ordered after he had padlocked the shed door. 'We have a way to go. Just follow the path.'

Nicole looked into the trees, until she saw a break between two large spruces. It was narrow, but despite the lack of moonlight, there was enough illumination from the surrounding whiteness for her to follow it with ease. It surprised her that the visibility was so good and that Cal had not bothered to turn his flashlight on. The path that meandered through the trees looked well used, but she could not imagine for what reason. From wherever it started, it just led to the lake. Maybe fishermen, she thought.

They had walked for about ten minutes when Cal called for them to stop. 'Sorry,' he apologised, and before Nicole had time to react, he had pulled a hood over her head. 'Put your hand on Aino's shoulder; she knows the way.'

'Her name is Auli,' Nicole spluttered, her voice muffled by the fabric. It felt like a pillowcase, she thought, but what the hell is it that he doesn't want me to see?

Fortunately, the path was relatively flat and the snow beneath her feet firm and not too deep.

'Not far,' Cal grunted, from just behind her.

Auli remained silent but slowed her pace so that Nicole didn't stumble.

'Okay, wait a moment.'

She heard the snow crunch beneath his feet as he walked away from them. Inside the hood it was difficult to hear much other than her own breathing, but she could make out Cal having a conversation with someone. He had summoned someone, she realised, as she heard several pairs of feet walking over the snow towards her. Someone took a firm hold of her left arm and then another took hold of her on the other side.

'There are steps,' Cal warned, and then added gently, 'Aino, you come beside me.'

Seven steps, Nicole counted, broad ones. Even the little things are important, she told herself, though why the number of steps or their size should matter was beyond her. Ahead of her, she heard a door being unlocked. A metal door? It opened almost silently, no creaking hinges. Beneath her feet the surface was no longer snow, but hard. Non-slip, she decided, and tested it by trying to skid her feet across what felt like concrete.

'Careful!' Cal barked, thinking she had stumbled.

Behind them she heard the door being shut and locked. By the sound of feet on the surface and a slight echo, she figured they were in a large room. Here the air was far warmer and with so many layers of clothing on she found it unpleasantly so.

'Nice place you have here,' she said, infusing her words with as much sarcasm as the hood would allow.

Cal didn't respond to her, but said something to the men supporting her and they ushered her in a slow arc to the left and then, turning her, took her to the right. Nicole realised he was attempting to disorient her – foolish really, as she had no idea where she was in the first place.

They entered a smaller space and after a few seconds she heard a door shut and then a vaguely familiar hum. An elevator, she thought, and her guess was immediately confirmed as she felt the downward motion.

After leaving the elevator there was again a slight echo as they walked along what felt like a corridor. She counted thirty paces before they turned through a doorway. Somewhere to her left she could hear voices, people chatting in a casual manner. The few words she did hear, she recognised as Finnish. They moved into another space and the voices faded. Behind her she heard a door slide shut. Then another door right in front of her was opened and the men released her arms and gave her a gentle shove, propelling her forward. At the same time the hood was taken from her head and she found herself in a room that could best be described as a cell with a shower and toilet cubicle. A single bed and a wash-basin with a single tap were the only furnishings. She turned and found Cal standing at the door. He no longer held a pistol, but a quick glance at the two men standing behind him confirmed her suspicion that he no longer needed one.

'Where are we?'

'Beneath the memories,' Auli whispered.

Cal smiled. 'The headquarters of the Real Free Karelia Movement, and it's from here...' he paused and switched to Finnish, '*me nousemme kostona Kullervon.*'[3]

Nicole looked at him as if he was totally insane. 'The what?'

But he gave a dismissive wave of his hand. 'Another time, if I decide to keep you alive that long.'

Nicole found that rather than being intimidated, she felt angry and decided to goad him. 'Well, that's friendly. Now why are you even bothering to keep me alive at all?'

'Insurance. Simply insurance.'

'You really are crazy, Mister Remsu, if you think you can kidnap a British policewoman and not have someone come and find me. And when they do, you won't be packed off back to Canada, or wherever it is you come from. You'll be spending years in a Finnish prison.'

Cal laughed. 'Come and find you? You really have no idea where you are, do you? They could comb every metre of Finland and nobody would ever find you. You see, this place doesn't exist.'

---

3   *We shall rise in vengeance like that of Kullervo's.*

'Doesn't exist…' she began, but he turned and left the room. As he did so, one of the men outside stepped forward and shut the door. The next thing she heard was the sound of the door being locked and bolted. It wasn't soundproof and she could clearly hear a conversation between the men. Unfortunately, it was in Finnish. Then she heard Cal's voice speaking in English.

'Come on, Aino. Time to make you comfortable.'

Heimo Harkimo was as good as his word and by six in the morning Pentti was handed the keys to an almost new dark blue Ford Mondeo. He signed the forms and waited until the fresh-faced delivery driver wandered off through the snow in search of a cab.

As soon as the man was gone Pentti went straight to the boot and checked that Harkimo hadn't reneged on his promise of his rifle. A familiar padded carry-bag was there. It was old and slightly grubby, unmistakably his. Beside it, neatly folded, was a white full-body snowsuit. Harkimo gets extra points for that, he thought, mentally thanking the man. He unzipped the rifle bag. His TRG-42 was there, as were two ten-round magazines of .338 Lapua Magnum cartridges. He took out a smaller bag containing the Zeiss sight that was specially calibrated for him to use without his glasses. He quickly attached it, slotted in a magazine and, after putting the rifle and spare mag back in the carry bag, placed it within easy reach on the back seat.

Inside the car he opened the glove box. The USP Compact and two magazines were wrapped in a piece of cloth. The promised mobile phone was also there. He switched it on and again, slightly surprised by Heimo's thoroughness, found it had only one stored number – Heimo's mobile. Pentti put the phone on the passenger seat and glanced around the car's interior. Given the equipment inside, it had obviously been requisitioned from the police. The specialised GPS and mobile tracking system were brand new and the detachable 'mag-mount' blue light still had clear-plastic protective film around it. Somewhere in Helsinki an officer was going to be missing his vehicle. The light was a good idea, he thought, and peeled off the film. It was still snowing heavily and he didn't relish the three-hundred-and-fifty-kilometre drive that lay ahead, but he was not going to stop or slow down for anyone. He attached the light to the roof, located the siren switch and set off.

The traffic was still light and with only minimal use of the siren and light, he was soon on the outskirts of the city, making his way via the E75 to Route 5. The Mondeo was not a car he had driven before but he found it easy and, if not for the circumstances and reduced visibility because of the snow, he would have added 'a pleasure' to drive. The naturally weighted steering made driving effortless and the brakes were firm and easy to modulate. Even though he drove hard, he didn't have a single moment on the slippery, snow-covered roads when he felt he was pushing too hard. Several times his mind drifted into contemplating everything that the Russian, Belov, had divulged; but each time he forced himself back into concentrating on the driving. If he didn't get to Punkaharju in time, then everything else was of secondary importance.

He only stopped once, with a quick detour into Lahti for a takeaway toasted sandwich and strong black coffee. Though the snow was still falling, it was lighter now and visibility was good. Once back on the highway he turned on the light and siren and put his foot down.

Under normal circumstances and in good conditions, he might have made the trip in around four hours. He checked his watch as he turned off the road onto the track that led to Pikkususisaari: three hours and thirty-five minutes. He had intended to follow the path directly to the beginning of the boardwalk. But then he saw tracks in the snow. Sometime in the previous hour or so another vehicle had driven along the road. He couldn't be certain of the time, but any longer than that and the tracks would have been snowed over.

He slowed right down. According to the GPS there was another small side-road off to the right. He found it and after a hundred metres or so backed off the road and parked out of sight. Hopefully his own car tracks would soon be obscured, but not willing to take the risk, he snapped off a branch of spruce and dusted snow over them. It was not a good job and certainly would not stand up to any close inspection, but to a casual observer it might just escape notice. He removed the blue light, broke off a couple more branches, and placed them over the bonnet and roof of the car.

Finally, he pulled on the camouflage snowsuit and took the rifle out and left the bag on the back seat. Before locking the car, he removed the small pistol from the glove box, slotted a magazine in and pocketed the other. Then he carefully placed the car keys on the front right tyre and set off, cutting through the forest, following a moose path in a slow arc to the left.

When he came to the Pikkususisaari road, he checked the car tracks more carefully. It was a large vehicle and had driven very slowly down the road. A four-wheel drive; possibly a Land Rover, he surmised, but whatever it was it would easily have carried four to six people.

He followed the road, stopping every few minutes to listen, but the forest around him remained silent. The weather was changing and the snow, which earlier had been lighter, was now much heavier. When he finally caught a glimpse of the lake, it was wreathed in slowly swirling curtains of mist. The temperature had dropped again and he was grateful to Heimo for the snowsuit that afforded warmth as well as camouflage.

A few hundred metres on, he stopped. He was still around a kilometre from the boardwalk and yet, for some reason the vehicle had turned right down a rough track. It made no sense, unless they were being ultra-cautious and doing what he had done, parking well away from the cottage and making their approach on foot. The Pikkususisaari road continued on down a slight incline to the left but there were no tracks of car, man or animal.

He hesitated for a moment before deciding that the best course of action was to follow the tracks. If the occupants had left someone guarding the car, then it was best to neutralise them before moving on towards the cottage.

The tyre tracks continued up a slight rise to a flat area overlooking the tree-lined lakeshore. There, parked in the open, was a grey Nissan Pathfinder. It was unguarded. To his surprise there were only two sets of footprints in the snow. Whoever they were, they had climbed out of the vehicle, retrieved something from the back of the car and then headed down a small path towards the lake. The car was local. According to a bumper sticker it had been purchased from *Savonautokeskus* – a car company in Savonlinna.

Pentti slipped into the forest and, crouching down, used the trees for cover as he moved very slowly towards the top of the rise. He stopped and surveyed the available positions. Then, down on his stomach, he crawled to a spot between two snow-covered boulders. He flipped out the stock and removing his glasses, adjusted the sight.

His position was perfect and despite the falling snow, it was only a few seconds before he saw two individuals some five or six hundred metres below at the edge of the ice. He tweaked the range finder. They were easy targets; head shots. He held his breath and focused in on them one at a time and then took his finger from the trigger and flicked on the safety-catch.

One appeared to be a boy about twelve years of age. The other looked like his father. If they were of any danger to anything it was to fish. Out on the ice he made out two holes and folding chairs. Beside one of the holes an auger and ice-saw were lying on a burlap sack. Above each hole they had rigged their fishing gear. A ribbon of blue wood-smoke drifted up from where the boy was in the process of coaxing a fire into life. Pentti wondered if they would ever realise how close they had come to being shot. Had the snow been heavier and his view less clear… Folding the rifle stock, he dismissed the thought and slid backwards into the forest.

By the time he reached the edge of the silver birch grove where the Saab was parked, the visibility had deteriorated. Heavy snow was falling, and to make matters worse, the previously light breeze had become a strong wind from the north. He peered through the swirling snow until he located the car. It was completely covered in snow. Using the rifle sight, he panned over the surrounding area looking for footprints. There were none, so he shouldered the rifle, stepped onto the road and, despite the injury to his leg, jogged down to the car.

Again, he stopped, crouching behind the Saab, checking the forest edge and as far out onto the ice as he could given the poor visibility. Nowhere did he see any sign of anyone, hostile or otherwise. Still, he waited for another couple of minutes and then set off towards the boardwalk leading to Pikkususisaari.

Finding the path turned out to be a problem as the snowfall in the last few hours had covered it completely.

He paused, weighing up his choices. Following what he thought to be the direction of the boardwalk was the shortest route to the cottage, but it would leave him exposed. Going the longer route, scouting the forest perimeter, seemed more sensible. Under the trees the snow was not as deep and he could travel faster. He would also have the advantage of reasonable cover.

The forest route was not as straightforward as he had anticipated and it took him thirty minutes of scrambling over fallen trees and ducking under snow-laden branches before he caught a glimpse of what he assumed to be the island about fifty metres to his right. From what he could make out, the island had no beach on this side, but rather a steep bank, a metre or so high and along which snowdrifts were forming.

He crouched down and watched. There was no sign of movement. However, the clear ice between him and the island provided no cover and crossing it would leave visible footprints. The advantage was that it would hopefully bring him to the rear of the cottage, and from memory the only windows it had faced out onto the lake.

Pentti decided that he had no option but to cross the open ice. But still he waited, watching not the island now, but the weather. The wind had increased and the driving snow had reduced visibility even further. It was on the verge of being a whiteout – perfect for providing cover, but almost impossible for seeing any opposition, let alone getting a clear shot.

When he moved, he bent over in a crouch and ran as fast as he could across the open area. Reaching the island, he flopped down into a snowdrift and caught his breath.

Again, he waited, listening, but he heard nothing but the moaning of the wind through the trees. He scrambled up the bank then moved cautiously through a thick forest of mixed trees – mainly spruce and birch – stopping every few metres to take his bearings.

If his instincts were right, he told himself, the cottage should be ahead and slightly to his right. Under the trees he was protected from the worst of the wind and visibility was restricted not so much by snow, but thick undergrowth. He moved on again, through an area of large boulders and older trees with roots sprawling between the rocks, in their search for soil.

When he finally caught a glimpse of a log structure he halted again, puzzled. It was not the cottage.

'*Vittu Saatana!*' he swore, cursing his own lack of preparedness. There might be several small islands here. He had only taken a cursory glance at a map some days back. Given the weather conditions and the roundabout route he had taken, he could conceivably be on the wrong island.

He moved cautiously forward until he was pressed up against the side of the building, then, peering around the corner he realised it was not a cottage at all, but a small sauna – a *savusauna*. Maybe he was in the right place. Of course, the cottage had a sauna and he had seen the photographs of it back in Helsinki. He strode to the front of the sauna and checked it was empty. Through the flurries of snow he could make out the short beach and what looked like a hole in the ice. It had frozen over, but only recently. 'Sometimes you can be particularly stupid,' he muttered out loud.

The path from the sauna to the cottage was easy to find and his spirits lifted as he could see the traces of footprints. Two sets. So the women had had a sauna; that was a good sign.

He cautioned himself against relaxing and, stepping off the path, made his way between the trees running parallel to the path.

He had only gone a few metres when he heard a noise. He stopped and slid to the ground. He could see nothing, but then he heard it again; a male voice, shouting. He couldn't make out the words, but after a moment another far clearer voice replied. The speaker was Russian and he sounded impatient and uncomfortably close.

Pentti, glanced around and seeing a couple of tree stumps, rolled to them and slithered in behind. Again, the more distant voice called out. This time the response was slightly further away. At least two men, Pentti thought, and eased the rifle's safety catch off.

For almost a minute he heard nothing but the wind. It had picked up considerably, tearing at the trees above him. The thought that flashed through his mind, of a branch snapping off or even an entire tree falling, was not a comforting notion. He had heard of it happening. What was it the foresters called them, widow makers? Concentrate, he castigated himself, and moved forward again.

Coming over a slight rise, he found himself about a hundred metres from the cottage and, slightly to his left, there was a momentary glimpse out to the lake. Then he could see nothing as a flurry of snow obliterated the view.

Pentti decided that this was as far as he needed to come for the moment and he sank into the snow behind some small bushes. He took off his glasses and using the scope tracked across his field of fire. If the men were there, they were safely behind a curtain of snow that was blowing almost horizontally across the lake whipping up more snow off the ice as it went. He swung around and focused on the cottage. The door was open.

Pentti extended his arm and swept an arc of snow from in front of him and patted it down as hard as he could to compact it, then extended the rifle stock and adjusted his position until he felt comfortable. The cleared arc gave him maybe twenty to thirty degrees of movement, just enough to cover the beach and lake foreshore if the present whiteout conditions lifted. It didn't give him a direct shot towards the cottage, but he was not about to take a chance if Auli and Nicole were inside.

For a moment the wind dropped slightly and somewhere a man took advantage of the respite in the noise to call out. The voice that responded was closer and directly in front of him on the lake.

Pentti's biggest problem was the impossibility of determining the range. The snow was coming in waves and even when it was at its lightest, he had nothing in front of him to judge distance by. Then he saw a movement out on the ice. A man was walking on an angle out onto the lake. Pentti had him in his sights for only a moment before he was gone behind the snow. What he did see was alarming. Even with limited vision there was no mistaking the Heckler & Koch UMP the man was carrying.

Pentti shifted his position slightly to the left and tried to estimate where the man was going. It didn't make any sense his going out on the lake, unless they had decided to approach from that direction. Yet there had been no footprints or vehicle tracks on the road in.

For a moment the wind died down a little and though the snow was still falling heavily he had a vision for a reasonable distance out onto the lake. The man had stopped and was gesticulating to someone. It was less than four hundred metres. Pentti adjusted for the wind, and hoping that the conditions held for a few more seconds, pulled the rifle firmly into his shoulder. He took a deep breath and then began to exhale. He stopped his breathing and with the man squarely in his sight, touched the trigger. The wind was picking up again and he hesitated, wondering if he should correct for it, but the distance didn't warrant it, he decided. The man was still standing, but the snow blowing around him began to obscure him again. Okay, Pentti thought, and pulled the trigger. Out on the ice the man spun and then crashed to the ice where he vanished beneath the billows of snow blowing along the lake's surface.

'*Paska!*' Pentti swore, realising that it had not been a clean shot and that by the way he fell the man had been hit in the shoulder.

There was silence for a moment before the wind gusted through the trees. He lay still, safe in the knowledge that whoever the men were, they would have no idea where the shot came from. Their logical response would be to panic.

Then he heard a sound he hadn't anticipated and he knew without doubt how the men had approached the cottage. From out on the ice came the throaty roar of first one and then a second snowmobile. The men wasted no time and within seconds he heard them accelerate away from the island. Then a third one started up and set out after the others; three snowmobiles, each capable of carrying two men. His instinct was that there had been only three men, but he waited until the sound had faded away before rising.

He walked directly out on the ice until he came to the spot where the man had fallen. Already the windblown snow was obscuring the tracks, but the bloodstain on the ice was clear. He stepped carefully around it and examined the snow. The man had risen and walked a few paces before falling again. Other tracks joined his and it looked as if two companions had half carried or dragged him to a snowmobile. Maybe there were four men, Pentti reasoned, three drivers and one passenger? And, worryingly, two places available for… whom? Two women? It was a disturbing thought. But nowhere in the snow had he seen the extra footprints that Auli and Nicole would have made.

He walked a wide circle until he had established the fact that there were tracks from three snowmobiles. A few bloodspots beside one set of tracks showed him that the man had been taken aboard.

The wind had abated slightly and looking back he could see the island and the cottage. But he fought against the urge to check it immediately. If he left it much longer, the sets of footprints in the snow would disappear and it was important to know exactly what the men had been doing. So instead of going directly back to the cottage, he retraced the footprints of the men. One had waited with the snowmobiles; he had smoked two cigarettes and crushed an empty packet and dropped it in the snow. There were three other sets of tracks. One had gone to the right of the cottage and taken up a position at the far end of the beach, one had advanced directly and the third, the one who had been wounded, had walked as far as the beginning of the boardwalk before returning to the point where he had been shot. Satisfied there was little else he could learn, Pentti made his way toward the open door of cottage.

There were signs of fresh snow having been tramped inside, but the cottage was empty and the fire cold. The place felt not just vacant, but abandoned. A dolls' house bereft of dolls, Pentti thought. He checked carefully for any trace of what had happened. That they had eaten was clear, evidenced by empty tins and two plates, unwashed in the sink. There were also three used coffee cups. There was no sign of a struggle and the bunkroom and bathroom had been left just as they were.

Then he saw something pushed to the back of the small table; a screwed-up piece of paper. He opened it carefully and found five pills, each one of which was different. He wrapped them again and put them in his pocket so they could be analysed once he returned to Helsinki. He nearly missed the other slip of paper, mistaking it for rubbish. He picked up the torn off piece of envelope and recognised it as the same piece he had used to write down the Kuopio telephone number he had handed to Nicole. He turned it over. On the back Nicole had written: *Show to Sirkka.*

There was nothing else he could do so he closed the cottage door and set out for the boardwalk. Now all that mattered was that he got back to Helsinki as fast as possible. He ignored the snowed-in Saab; there was no way he could get it started, not now, probably not until spring. Hopefully Heimo would understand.

When he reached the car, he stowed the rifle and headed for Kerimäki. Helsinki was four hours away, but if he didn't get some food and warmth into himself soon, he was going to be a danger to other drivers.

In Kerimäki he stopped long enough to wolf down a bowl of stew followed by a strong coffee. Preoccupied with his concerns about the two women, he hardly tasted the food, but he was feeling considerably better by the time he returned to the car. He turned on the light and siren and unlike the previous trip, he didn't turn them off until he was back in Helsinki.

Chapter Sixteen

Heimo Harkimo returned from a gruelling meeting with the Intelligence Committee to the news that Quentin Grammaticus had arrived at the airport and was being taken directly to his hotel. It was expected that he would be arriving at SUPO HQ in an hour and a half. The timing suited Heimo, who needed time to mull over the meeting he had just attended.

What had irked him most about Intelligence Committee was its amorphous nature. Everyone represented their own interests and those interests centred on shifting the attention and, more importantly, the responsibility, away from themselves. The agendas of the military, the police, the Prime Minister's Department, Foreign Affairs and the rest of them had nothing in common. To make matters worse, in the present situation nobody knew exactly what they were dealing with. The one point of agreement was that being left in the dark suited nobody's agenda and that it was potentially serious. Everything had been off the record and no decisions had been made. However, Heimo was left in no doubt that there were several perceived problems and that SUPO was to 'sort them out'. And turn water into wine, he thought bitterly.

He checked his phone and found three new calls from Toivonen. There was also a brief text message informing him that Pentti was on his way back to Helsinki and needed an urgent meeting. He checked his watch and decided he had time for a brisk stroll and some thinking time. Also, enough time to pick up a Danish pastry, for himself, not Grammaticus. He was welcome to his wife's *pulla*.

It was a long time since he had seen a man wearing a camel hair coat and cravat and he fervently hoped it would be a while before he saw another. Heimo stood and looked through the one-way glass at the Englishman removing the coat and hanging it on the coat rack, then peeling off his gloves, carefully pulling each of the fingers straight, before tucking the gloves in one of the coat pockets. A neat man, meticulous, Heimo thought. A tidy mind as well, most probably. He would need it, if the intelligence about him was accurate.

During the last hour he had reread the file on Grammaticus and knew, despite the man's eccentric dress sense, that he was not to be underestimated. There was not a lot of detail about his early background. His university qualifications were mentioned, as was his stint as a ministerial advisor in Foreign Affairs. After his secondment to the SIS twelve years ago, the information became even sparser. His attendance at various security-related conferences was merely a shortlist of dates and places with the annotation that he was registered simply as an advisor.

According to the Finnish records, Quentin Grammaticus was most likely a senior officer in the Special Operations Department. Another source, whose identity had been deleted, claimed he was involved in the running of the unit known as 'The Increment', an outfit supposedly responsible for deniable operations on foreign soil. A dissenting note remarked that there was no confirmed intelligence on the existence of such a unit.

Shadows chasing shadows, Heimo thought as he watched Grammaticus settle into a comfortable armchair. What kind of shadow are you? he wondered. Well, he was about to find out, and picking up a folder, he stepped into the room.

'Good to see you, Heimo.' The Englishman rose to meet him, crossing the floor and firmly shaking his hand.

'Quentin, welcome to Helsinki. It's a pleasure to see you again, though sadly under less than perfect circumstances.' He gestured to Grammaticus to resume his seat. 'So, how was your flight?'

'Pleasant enough,' Quentin said, 'And the hotel is top rate, thank you.'

'Our pleasure, I assure you,' Heimo beamed. 'I have ordered tea, but if you prefer coffee…'

'Tea is fine, thank you.'

'Good. Then let's get down to work.' Heimo took a seat beside the coffee table and placed the file on the table. 'I have a preliminary report on the events involving your colleague, Christopher

Mitchell. Unfortunately, it is in Finnish, but I have requested a translation which you will have as soon as it is completed.'

'Too kind,' Quentin murmured.

'I promise you we are doing everything in our power to discover the circumstances surrounding the incident in order that you can provide that information to his family and colleagues.'

Quentin nodded gravely. 'Much appreciated and I assure you that Her Majesty's government will cooperate in whatever way we can.'

'A most unfortunate affair,' Heimo murmured and added softly, as if to himself, 'for all concerned.'

It was, Quentin thought, like opening moves in a chess match played, not in order to win the game, but to discover what each move revealed about the opponent. Quentin had harboured concerns about the meeting with Harkimo, but even in the first few minutes he recognised he was facing a professional, someone who knew how the game was played.

'For all concerned,' he echoed. 'Mitchell was a good man, and it grieves me he should have had an accident while on holiday in your country. I know how much he was looking forward to it.'

There was a quiet knock on the door.

'*Sisään!*' Heimo barked, getting to his feet, then held the door open for a young man carrying a tray of tea, coffee and cakes. The sight of the food was a welcome one as he had nothing on the flight and had not had time for an early lunch at the hotel.

As soon as the man had left the room Heimo moved to the door and locked it. 'There are some discussions best not interrupted,' he said. He gestured to the *pulla*. 'Please help yourself.'

'I could not agree more,' Quentin said. 'And thank you, I must say they look particularly appetising.'

'In regard to the young English policewoman...'

'Nicole Parry.'

'Yes. Following your request, we made some enquiries.'

Quentin took a sip of his tea. 'Much appreciated.'

'Can you tell me anything about the official status of this woman's investigations?'

Quentin placed his cup down gently. Careful, he warned himself, take this very slowly. 'My understanding, Heimo, is that whatever she is involved in is not official, and certainly Her Majesty's government has not sanctioned her actions. To do so without going through the normal liaison channels with your government would be a breach of protocol that we would not condone.'

If Heimo believed any of that he gave no indication. Instead, he poured himself some more coffee before continuing.

'Would it be possible she is acting on instructions from within your police service that your government is unaware of?'

Quentin smiled. 'I can assure you the answer is most definitely not. DI Parry is officially on holiday and facing suspension and disciplinary action on her return.'

'Holidaying in Finland seems unseasonably popular at the moment and sadly, as in the case of Mister Mitchell, it appears not to be free of hazards.'

'It would indeed be tragic if Parry were to also have an accident,' Quentin said evenly. 'Although she does not make friends easily, and from all reports she is a rather difficult character.'

Heimo nodded, 'So I have heard.' He paused and for a moment sat thinking. It was time to do some trading, but he was reluctant to embark down that route until he had a clearer idea of just how cooperative Grammaticus was willing, or authorised, to be. He decided to nudge things along.

'I have also heard that there are others following her endeavours with some interest.'

Quentin brushed some crumbs from his knees and sat back. This was no longer chess, he decided, but poker; and it was time to raise the stakes.

'Yes, our boys and girls also report interest from your closest neighbour. From what I understand, our American friends report that they hold the same view.'

Heimo raised an eyebrow. 'Americans? Now that is interesting. I wonder what it is that has captured their attention.'

'The same thing that attracted DI Parry; a certain woman in a boat.'

Heimo laughed. 'That is such a fascinating story, but one wonders why our Russian neighbours would be interested.'

Quentin shrugged. 'Self-interest maybe? There have been whispers of unrest amongst the faithful and of course this concerns Her Majesty's government and our American cousins.'

'As it should concern all of us,' Heimo said pointedly.

Quentin sat up and looked the Finn straight in the eye. 'The very point of my coming to see you.'

'Then I shall listen with interest to what you have to say.' Heimo gestured towards the teapot. 'But first let me get you a fresh pot. Or is it time for something a little stronger?'

Quentin smiled. 'A splendid suggestion.'

Heimo nodded and was getting to his feet, when his phone rang. 'One minute. Please.'

He walked to the window, and had a short conversation then closed his phone and turned back. 'Something of interest has turned up. Come, we will postpone the drink just for a moment.'

He unlocked and opened the door and gestured for Quentin to follow.

From the corridor they took the lift down to the next floor and, with Heimo leading the way, went through the building until they came to a door with a security keypad. Heimo punched in a code and pushed the door open.

'Just one moment, please,' he said and went in, closing the door behind him.

He was back a few seconds later. 'Just making sure there is no sensitive material,' he joked. 'Please.' He shepherded Quentin into the dim light of a control room manned by half a dozen operators seated in front of an array of CCTV monitors. 'Through to the next room,' Heimo said and crossing behind the operators opened another door, and held it for Quentin.

The room had a single large monitor on the wall. In front of it were a table and four chairs. 'One of our briefing rooms,' Heimo explained and then added apologetically, 'Certainly not up to the high-tech standards you are used to, I am sure, but with our budget it's a miracle we have one at all. Please take a seat.' He picked up a remote from the desk and was about to turn the monitor on when his phone rang again.

'Modern communications can be annoying,' he grumbled, but took the call, stepping away and speaking quietly in Finnish.

Quentin took a seat and waited. Both the control room and this briefing room seemed state of the art. He had no way of assessing the systems and computer power of the place, but his intuition was that Harkimo had been overly modest in saying they were not up to British standards. Even the chair he was sitting in was better quality than those in his own office. Certainly, his department's budget didn't run to what looked like designer furniture.

'I have a colleague joining us,' Heimo said as he closed his phone and took a seat. 'Hopefully he can brief you on the latest developments.'

Quentin nodded. 'I must say how much I appreciate your helpfulness. It certainly beats that which we receive from our so-called American friends.'

'Yes, sadly our experience is the same. Information tends to be a one-way street, despite the agreements we have in place. And we have concerns about their methods.'

Quentin laughed dryly. 'I'm afraid that the days of the gentleman spy are long gone. If indeed they ever existed.'

'I have a soft spot for Mister Smiley,' Heimo said, 'but I'm not so fond of James Bond. I am afraid our lives are far less glamorous. I get the sense somehow that the Americans prefer Bond.'

'I can assure you, Heimo, that many in Britain feel the same way. There are those who feel that the CIA has gone too far in the direction of a paramilitary organisation.'

Heimo nodded. 'Yes, their reliance on drones and Special Forces to eliminate American adversaries overseas is troubling, to say the least.'

'Questionable practices that are best kept at arm's length. And it raises the issue of just how closely our services can work together if we have different codes of practice.'

Heimo heaved a sigh. 'But where would we be without the Americans to lead the way? After all, they do have access to so much information.'

And not always accurate information, Quentin was about to say, before there was a quiet knock at the door. Heimo rose and opened it.

'Mister Grammaticus, let me please introduce one of our finest officers, Pentti Toivonen.'

The man who walked in didn't look the slightest bit like a spook. To Quentin, he looked like a lumberjack. Nevertheless, he stood and extended his hand. 'Pleased to meet you, Toivonen.'

'My pleasure, and please call me Pentti.'

Heimo hovered for a minute then indicated that they should sit. 'We'll talk in a while, Pentti, but first I think you should see this as well.'

He pressed a button on the remote and sat down again.

The screen flickered to life and showed what was obviously footage taken from a security camera.

'Vantaa airport, three days ago,' he explained. 'We had an alert on a passport.' He paused as several passengers passed in front of the camera. Then he froze the frame. 'This man.'

The man looked to be in his middle-fifties, his face lined and with heavily hooded eyes that seemed cast in a permanent squint.

'That's Belov,' Pentti said. 'Absolutely no question.'

Heimo shrugged. 'And that's what his passport claimed. Yet, I have a problem. You see, his Russian passport appears to be genuine. But when we checked, it transpired that Andrei Markovich Belov was born in the village of Zimlenki, in the Vekshmaiski district of the Kuibyshev region. According to the records he was drafted with the rank of private into the two hundred and seventy-second rifle regiment, one hundred and twenty-third rifle division in nineteen thirty-nine. Unfortunately, he was killed on February the second, nineteen forty.'

'Well, whoever it is, he is the same man that was in the apartment with Tesak and Vladimir,' Pentti said.

'Which reminds me. You won't have heard, but I'm afraid Vladimir died,' Heimo said.

Pentti was visibly shocked. He had pushed the man and so, under Finnish law, SUPO officer or not, he was culpable. At the least it would mean an inquiry. 'What? When?'

'The same night he accidentally fell from a window.'

'*Jumalauta!*' Pentti swore, took off his glasses and rubbed vigorously at his eyes.

'He had his throat slit in the hospital.'

There was silence for a moment as Pentti grappled with the notion.

'Poor bastard.'

Quentin gave a polite cough. 'Did he have a limp?' he asked quietly.

Both men turned to look at him.

'A limp... who?' Heimo asked, momentarily confused.

Quentin pointed to the screen. 'Your Russian friend, Mister Belov.'

Bewildered, Pentti looked at the Englishman. 'Yes, he had a pronounced limp in his left leg. But how do you know that?'

'Because I know him and I'm guessing he is behind whatever it is you are investigating. His name is not Belov. He's an ex-FSB officer by the name of Andrei Zaikov. According to the *Komsomolskaya Pravda*, his badly mutilated body was discovered in a backstreet of Moscow a few days ago,' he paused and allowed himself a smile, 'which just goes to show you shouldn't believe everything you read in the newspapers.'

There was silence for a moment and then Heimo beamed.

'I'll organise something to drink, and after I have had a chat with Toivonen, I think you had better be briefed on what it is we both seem to be dealing with.'

'That,' Quentin said, 'sounds splendid.'

Four hours before the meeting in the bar in the Hotel Kämp, Sam Gordon arrived at the hotel and enquired at reception about the American pulp and paper delegation who had checked in the previous evening. He was politely asked to wait. The receptionist made a phone call and then signalled to him.

'Room 215, sir. They are expecting you.'

The man who greeted him at the door looked like he had come direct from central casting. Cast, not as a pulp and paper executive, but as US Special Forces. One hundred and eighty centimetres plus, and a body that looked like it had pumped more iron than a battalion of weightlifters. Dressed in T-shirt and jeans and with a jarhead haircut, the man took Sam's hand and crushed it in his. 'Bradley Armstrong, sir. And you would be Mister Smith?'

Sam was not in the mood to play games. It was too early in the morning, the weather would freeze the balls of a statue, and he would rather be anywhere else but Helsinki. 'Whatever,' he grunted. 'Call me Sam.'

As he went to enter the room his cell phone vibrated in his pocket.

'One minute,' he said to Armstrong and pulled out the phone. The message was as short as it was enigmatic.

Delivery tomorrow kulkuri poika

The delivery part he understood – weapons and ammunition – but what the fuck was *kulkuri poika*? He pocketed the phone and turned his attention back to the tall American. 'Okay, Brad, let's go.'

'Yes, sir,' Armstrong replied. 'Come and meet the boys.'

The 'boys', Wesley Green and Zach Sulkin, could not have been more different. Green was African-American, and dressed in a flash business suit that would not have been out of place on a Wall Street banker. Sulkin, on the other hand, was young, overweight, looked like a computer nerd and was dressed in clothes that probably came from some downtown charity. He looked nothing remotely like Special Forces or a pulp and paper expert. With the headset for his iPod permanently plugged in his ears, he looked like an overgrown teenager.

Once the introductions were over, Sam got down to business. 'Expertise?'

Sulkin raised his hand like a kid in school. 'Coms, computers, explosives and anything electrical.'

Sam looked sceptical. 'Really?'

'Sir, I have advanced special demolitions skills, surreptitious entry, and advanced special ops coms training. I can speak Russian, sir.'

'Okay, okay.' Sam turned to Green.

'Ex-Seal, sir,' the man shrugged, as if that explained everything, 'and I speak MSA.'

'What the fuck is MSA, Green?'

'Modern Standard Arabic, sir.'

'Like we are going to need that,' Sam snorted derisively.

'I rate as a sniper.'

'Good. That's a skill I can use.' Sam turned to Armstrong. 'So what do you bring to the table?'

'Ex-Marine, sir. Close combat instructor. Arabic and French.'

Sam looked at him. 'That's it?'

'One tour in Iraq and two in Kabul, Afghanistan.'

'I know where Kabul is,' Sam said quietly. 'Right, so you are my muscle.'

'Can you brief us on the mission, sir?' Green asked.

'At this time there is no mission. That may change depending on the meeting I'm about to have. I want you to get dressed in the nearest thing you have to ordinary clothes and by twelve-thirty get down to the hotel bar.'

'My kind of mission,' Sulkin chuckled.

Sam ignored him. 'Find yourself a magazine or newspaper and go to separate tables. Sulkin, take the seat at the far end of the bar. Green to the left of the door and Armstrong to the right.'

'Coms?' Sulkin asked.

Sam turned and glared at him. 'Listen, it's a small bar and the last thing we want is three spooks with earpieces whispering into their sleeves. This is not a fucking movie.' He turned back to the others. 'I have a meeting with a contact that I have never eyeballed. I have to guess he knows what the hell I look like, but just in case he mistakes one of you for me, then politely decline any offer of a drink or a chat. Understood?'

'Sir,' came the reply – in triplicate.

'If and when this individual shows, I'm expecting him to brief me on the situation. Until then, I am just as much in the dark as you.'

'What about weapons, sir?' Armstrong asked. 'We were told they would be made available here.'

'Tomorrow. I'm expecting more delivery instructions.'

'So today for this meeting, we should improvise?'

There was something in the way he said 'improvise' that conjured up images of kitchen knives and piano wire. 'Negative on that; this is not some third world burg where we can go garrotte a few natives. These guys are supposed to be our friends, right?'

'Right, sir.'

'I'm told our armoury will be delivered tomorrow. However, today there is a very good chance he may bring some muscle. Just note it, do nothing.'

'So,' Sulkin asked, 'what exactly are we doing in the bar?'

'Drinking coffee, having a beer, reading a newspaper. You are eyes on the ground. I want to know about anyone following my contact. I want to know if the contact has backup. But this is strictly hands-off. You watch and report later. If you have a real problem then text me on this number.' He handed over a slip of paper. 'Put it in your phones on speed dial. Right?'

'Texting? How fucking high-tech,' Sulkin muttered, not quite quietly enough.

'You have a problem with that?' Sam snarled.

'No, sir,' Sulkin raised his palms in a gesture of surrender. 'No problem, sir.'

Pentti had argued against taking any backup, but Heimo had insisted that two of the *Karhukopla* – the Beagle boys – from the Karhu Team would add a certain frisson to his visit and he ended up in the back of a van with two silent men in flak jackets, cradling H&K MP5s on their laps, and with H&K USPs holstered on their belts. They were both big men, solidly built, hard men, yet they moved with a certain economy and grace that belied their ability to kill without resorting to their weapons. Pentti had known Jukka and Eero for some years and liked them both, but their presence on this occasion seemed like gross overkill. It appeared even more so when they arrived at the Kontula Arts Centre.

'Just an exploratory visit,' Heimo had instructed. 'Let her know we have eyes on her. See if you can't rattle her a little. You never know, you might get lucky.'

Pentti had queried the choice of Anja Kujola, but Heimo had insisted that she should be first. 'After all, she is a woman and as such was probably closer to Auli Saarinen than most of the others.'

'And if she doesn't want to talk to me?'

'Then bring her in and we'll have a more persuasive chat.'

The Arts Centre building had started life as some kind of factory in the 1960s, but now housed a café and exhibition space at street level and a number of studios and workshops on the top three floors.

There was no back entrance, so they had no choice but to enter through a door in full view of the café patrons. The sight of three men, two of them armed, their faces hidden beneath black balaclavas, was less than subtle and brought half a dozen people out onto the pavement.

Ignoring the jeers from a couple of inebriated students, they entered the building, locking the street door behind them, and climbed a bare concrete staircase to the second floor.

There was only a single door on the right of the landing. To the left the stairs continued up to the next level. Pentti signalled for the two men to stand to one side, then knocked and waited. From the other side of the door he could hear music and guessed it was so loud that his rapping on the door could not be heard. After waiting a moment, he knocked again, this time much louder.

Seeing there was no response, Eero gestured for Pentti to get out of the way so he could break down the door. Pentti shook his head.

There was a single old-fashioned carved wooden doorknob, with a few traces of green paint worn smooth by years of use. There was no keyhole, so he grasped the doorknob and turned it. The door swung open into a space that appeared to take up the entire floor. Dust motes drifted in spears of light from small windows high in the walls, that however provided little general illumination. What had once been a factory was now mostly empty space and what looked like a living area and workroom at the far end. Half a dozen large pillars reached to the roof above and, from what Pentti could make out in the gloom, the walls were covered in graffiti art.

The music was playing at full volume; the Butthole Surfers' *Pepper*, booming out from two amp stacks. At the centre of the empty floor, a tall woman on rollerblades was waving a long silky scarf and dancing like Isadora Duncan on speed. Dressed in a full-body, day-glow yellow leotard and rainbow leg warmers, she had her back to the door, head down and, engrossed in the music, hadn't seen them. She twirled on, oblivious, her shoulder-length blonde hair tied back in a ponytail, flicking from side to side as she skated.

Despite her odd outfit, Pentti recognised her immediately from the photograph in the file that Heimo had compiled – Anja Kujola, thirty-nine years of age, divorced, no children.

Some will die in hot pursuit and fiery auto crashes.

He knew the lyrics by heart, but even if he hadn't liked the song, bursting in with a couple of Heckler & Koch sub-machine guns was taking musical criticism to unnecessary heights, he decided. However, though amused by the music and the sight of the woman off in her own world, Pentti grinned at the men and indicated that they should step into the room.

Some will die in hot pursuit while sifting through my ashes.

As the men fell in beside him, Pentti gestured to them to lower their weapons.

Some will fall in love with life and drink it from a fountain.

The woman circled at speed and as she turned at the far end of the room she glanced up, saw them, and dragging her right foot behind her, came to an abrupt stop.

That is pouring like an avalanche coming down the mountain.

For a moment she stared at them and then, draping the scarf around her neck, skated over to her workspace and turned off the music. Pushing hard against the workbench, she propelled herself forward and rolled towards them.

'What the fuck do you think you're doing?' She seemed more angered than scared at the sight of the armed men.

Pentti walked forward into the centre of the room. 'You are Anja Kujola?'

She ignored his question. 'Who are you?' she demanded as she skated in a circle around him. She stopped and pointed to the armed men. 'And, more to the point, who the fuck are they?'

Pentti held up a police ID. 'Pentti Toivonen, *Keskusrikospoliisi*.'

'Well, you are obviously in the wrong place, so please close the door behind you as you leave,' she said and, her eyes fixed on him, began circling him in a wide arc.

Pentti swivelled around, watching her. 'I want to talk to you about money laundering.'

'As I said, you're in the wrong place. I certainly don't have enough money to get anything laundered.'

'You make a substantial donation every month to a museum foundation.'

She circled again and then came to a stop in front of him. 'The Karelian Memorial Museum Fund, is that what you're talking about? Since when has philanthropy become a crime?'

'Since the money was not yours.'

'It was sent to me to donate to the museum.'

'From the James Street branch of the Northern Lights Credit Union in Thunder Bay, Canada?'

She shrugged. 'I suppose so. I've never bothered to check.'

'Who is it that so generously gives you money?'

She looked at him coldly. 'I don't think it is any of your business.'

Pentti laughed. 'That's exactly what Cal said you would say.' It was pure bluff, but the expression on her face showed that he had hit home.

'Cal said what?'

'That you would probably try to wriggle out of it and deny everything.'

'Bullshit. Remsu is full of bullshit and so are you. Now piss off.' She did a neat pirouette on the toe of her rollerblades and skated off towards her workspace.

Pentti signalled to Eero and Jukka to stay put, and followed her.

'Tell me about this man, Remsu.'

'What's to tell? His parents were evacuated from Karelia not once but twice. His father died from wounds he got in the war. He's a brilliant man, but too full of himself.'

'Brilliant? How?'

'He knows the Kalevala backwards and is apparently an extraordinarily good computer programmer.'

'But you don't like him?'

'He's okay…'

'But?' Pentti sensed he was only getting half of the story.

'I never like the way he treated Auli.'

'In what way?'

Anja took a deep breath and then exhaled slowly. 'Look, it's none of my business, but they have been lovers for years and while she is totally in love with him, he treats her like a convenience.' She paused and held up her hands. 'As I said, not my business.'

Pentti stepped around some piles of modelling clay. 'This is where you work?'

'When I'm not being intruded on,' she retorted.

Anja had set up the space partly as a workshop and partly living area. A half-completed metal and wire sculpture sat at the centre of a pool of light. Pentti had no idea what it was intended to eventually look like but at the moment it had the appearance of a road accident. Around it were scattered the tools of her art: some expensive welding gear, gas bottles, a blowtorch, wire cutters and a solid wooden workbench. The bench was covered in piles of sketch paper, brushes and sets of metalworking tools. To one side of the bench were a large painter's easel, a heap of painting paraphernalia, oil paints and boxes of acrylic spray tins. A pile of paintings, canvas stretched over pine frames, was stacked against a concrete pillar. Behind the space was her open-plan living area, a wardrobe, bed, a table, a couple of chairs, a DVD player and small flat screen TV. Apart from the welding gear there was little sign of opulence. There was a door in the wall. A bathroom, he surmised, and walked over to check.

'Do you mind if I have a look around?' he asked, and without waiting for a reply, opened the door. It was a bathroom.

'Only if you have a search warrant,' Anja responded frostily, 'otherwise fuck off and take your black dogs with you.'

'You're determined to be friendly, aren't you?' Pentti grinned. Turning, he called out, 'Jukka, the warrant please.'

Jukka nodded and crossed the floor, taking the warrant from a pocket in his flak jacket. He held it out to her.

She shook her head and waved him away, but he stayed put. 'Okay, okay, so you have a warrant.' Anja slid back into a chair and held up her hands in mock defeat. 'You have your dogs well trained,' she said with a hint of a smile. 'Do they bite?'

Pentti decided she was relaxing just a bit too much and adjusted his tone. 'Show me your tattoo,' he snapped.

'What?'

'Your tattoo, the seahorse.' It was another bluff, but one he felt confident about.

'Who says I have a tattoo?' she said angrily. 'Anyway, that is definitely none of your business.'

Pentti moved closer and stood directly over her. 'Miss Kujola, you don't seem to appreciate that you're in real trouble. Money laundering is a very serious offence, as is being part of a criminal conspiracy. Now, you can either show me the tattoo or we can go downtown and I will get an officer to strip search you.'

The woman looked stunned and sat up straight in her chair. 'You really are a bastard, aren't you?'

'I've been called worse.' He turned to Jukka. 'You'll note that Miss Kujola is refusing to cooperate. I think we may have to bring her along.'

The man nodded and stepped up beside her. 'Yes, sir.'

'On the back of my neck,' Anja said quietly.

'Speak up!' Pentti ordered.

'The tattoo, it's on the back of my neck.' She pulled her ponytail out of the way. 'See.'

Pentti glanced at it. It was exactly the same seahorse tattoo as the one he had seen on Auli Saarinen. 'Thank you. Nice tat.'

He watched as the woman sank back into her chair and glared at him. Pentti turned away and moving over to the workbench, made a show of carefully inspecting everything including the piece she was working on. 'You make a lot of money from this... stuff?'

'I make a living. Grants mostly,' she shrugged. The fire had gone out of her and she sounded meek and vulnerable.

'Yes, I suppose the government needs to support people like you with our taxes.'

He paused beside the pile of framed paintings and flicked through them. Then he stopped and carefully pulled one free and held it up. 'And this, Miss Kujola, how do you explain this?'

The painting was obviously a work in progress, but even in its rough form its subject was clearly discernible – the body of a naked woman in a boat, a *vasta* by her side.

'Just something I'm working on.' Anja turned her face away. 'It's nothing.'

Pentti brought it over and held it in front of her. 'On the contrary, it is most interesting. Tell me about it.'

'I said it was nothing!' she spat. 'Now leave it alone.'

Pentti didn't budge. 'It's an interesting motif. Is that the correct word, a motif?'

'*Jumalauta*!' Anja swore angrily. 'Have you got some sort of religious problem with nude women? It's just a study based on the Kalevala.'

Pentti nodded sympathetically. 'It's Aino, right? And, just for the record I have no problem with naked women... as long as they're alive.'

For a second the woman shivered and then, taking a deep breath, pulled herself together. 'Yes, it's Aino. So what?'

Pentti frowned. 'I'm sorry, but it's not my field of expertise so correct me if I'm wrong, but didn't Aino drown herself, or something? I don't recall there being a boat.'

'And what is your field of expertise, apart from coming into people's private space and intimidating them?'

'I hardly think discussing Aino and the Kalevala constitutes intimidation,' he said lightly. 'If that were true I would be arresting academics.' He paused and leaned the painting against the table leg in front of her. 'So, in your mind, Aino didn't drown?'

'She was drowned and then I put her in a boat. It's called art,' she said slowly, as if speaking to a child, her voice loaded with sarcasm. 'I don't see it as a big deal. If you really want to know, I am doing it as an homage to Akseli Gallen-Kallela.'

'Ah, really, an homage?' Pentti sighed, 'Gallen-Kallela is a bit too romantic for my taste. I never had much time for him or Järnefelt, Edelfelt and Pekka Halonen. There's that portrait woman, what was her name? Yes, Helene Schjerfbeck. Nice, but not my style. Mind you, I do have a print of Hugo Simberg's *Wounded Angel*... but then, doesn't every Finn?'

Anja looked at him in disbelief. 'You know something about art?'

'Only what they taught me in the Police Academy,' he smiled benignly. 'But I remember what Halonen said about art. "Art should not jar the nerves like sandpaper – it should produce a feeling of peace." And I'm afraid your work jars.'

'I beg your pardon?'

'Now, tell me where you got the inspiration for that sketch.'

'I told you that –' Anja began.

'Don't lie anymore. I'm tired of the lies.'

'I'm not –'

'You are lying. That is not Aino.' He picked up the painting again and held it directly in front of her face. 'That, Miss Kujola, is a crime scene. The woman is Auli Saarinen, and I suggest only someone who committed the crime would be able to reproduce it in such detail.' He turned to Jukka. 'We're taking this with us,' he said, and handed him the painting.

'There is something...' Anja got carefully to her feet and skated over to the wooden bench. From under a pile of papers she produced a foolscap envelope. She turned and handed it to Pentti.

'I received this.'

Pentti opened the envelope and slid a photograph out. Mounted on cardboard and bordered by a heavy black frame like a funeral photograph, was a close-up of Auli Saarinen unconscious in the boat on the Thames.

'Who sent this to you?'

'There was no message with it. It was slid under my door one night and I found it the next morning.'

'But why would someone send this to you?'

Anja looked pale and frightened. 'I think it was a warning.'

Pentti looked up from the photograph and stared at her. 'A warning about what?'

'That I should keep quiet about the Sampo.'

'The Sampo?'

She looked up and matched his gaze. 'My statue of the forging of the Sampo – I donated it to the museum. Then it was stolen.'

Pentti looked bemused. 'Why is that something to keep quiet about?'

'One night, before they sent me the photograph, Auli rang me. She sounded really stoned, or drunk, which wasn't like her at all. She said they were going to kill someone and that they would destroy the Sampo.'

Pentti slid the photograph back into the envelope, handed it to Jukka then turned back to Anja. 'Who are they?' he asked gently, 'and who are they going to kill?'

'They have killed *her*.' Anja paused, swallowed hard, struggling to regain control of her emotions. 'The night she phoned me she sounded really frightened but when I tried to talk to her, she hung up and I never heard from her again. Then about a week later the photograph arrived.' She looked at him beseechingly. 'It's true, honestly true.' She sat again and buried her face in her hands. 'Poor Auli, she was my friend and the painting was going to be my tribute to her. But I got scared and never finished it.'

'This Sampo sculpture, why would someone steal it?'

Anja looked up. 'Maybe for the metal, who knows? The real question is *how* did they steal it?'

'What do you mean?'

She got to her feet. 'Come and see.' She led him over to a corner of the warehouse and pulled some old bed sheets off a large object. 'That, Mister Policeman, is Ilmarinen forging the Sampo'.

The figure of the ancient smith was only slightly smaller than life-size. At his feet was a large anvil on which sat an object resembling a large box with a decorated lid.

'Just a moment,' Pentti looked confused. 'I thought you said it was stolen.'

That produced a smile. 'So you don't know everything about art.'

'Certainly not about sculpture.'

'The finished sculpture was stolen. This,' she explained, 'is the clay sculpture from which I cast the final work using the old fashioned *cire perdue* or lost-wax technique.'

'You make a wax mould, then enclose it in…'

'It is put into ceramic slurry,' she explained. 'Then, when that dries, I melt out the wax through small wax tubes. Then pour in the bronze. It's slightly more complicated…'

Pentti nodded. 'I get the picture.' He looked up at the sculpture. 'Somehow I imagined something far smaller.'

'That's my point. How did someone steal it? It would be extremely heavy to move.'

'There's something missing.'

'Yes, Ilmarinen's hammer, it's around here somewhere. I cast it separately and when I finished, I had a place to slot it through his hands to keep it stable.' Anja tossed the sheets back over the sculpture and turned to Pentti. 'You know, Auli was here with me the day we took it to the foundry to be cast. She was so excited that I was giving it to the museum.'

Pentti went to her and put his hand on her arm. 'I'm sorry, Miss Kujola, but you do need to come with us and make a statement.'

Anja took a deep breath and turned towards the door. There were tears rolling down her cheeks. 'Poor Auli,' she repeated softly to herself.

'I suggest you take your skates off,' Pentti said gently.

Chapter Seventeen

Nicole was unable to sleep as her brain wrestled with an overload of incomplete fragments of information. She had knocked on the door, demanding to be let out, and then, getting no response, had gone to bed. After tossing and turning, she gave up, pulled on her clothes and, with a blanket wrapped around her shoulders, sat hunched on the bed. What she needed more than anything was a notebook and pen to make a list of what she actually knew and another of what she needed to know.

The problem with compiling a mental list was that things got lost. The little men in her head who filed her information seemed incapable of keeping up with the spinning of her mind. Facts, she told herself sternly, from the start.

She was in Finland. It seemed like forever. London, Hammersmith station, her unrenovated house – they all belonged in a different time, almost a different universe. Tom. Tom was dead. No, she castigated herself, stick to the present. Finland. A lake. They had crossed, she guessed, from west to east. The island was Pikkususisaari? She said it out loud. It sounded right. Okay. The man was Kullervo Remsu, known as Cal, and he was one of Kaija's former students. He was a member of the Mary Hevonen Society. He was the only non-Finn. Canadian? Was that it? Very good looking, she mused, a bit like… the architect in London, but his name had gone. For christsake, concentrate!

Snowmobile. How long had they travelled? Had they really gone straight across the lake, or over and then up or down the shoreline? Pointless, she told herself. You don't know how long it was and you certainly have no idea of the speed. Dead end.

Auli was a member of the Mary Hevonen Society. Why had she nearly died in London? Why did Cal insist on calling her Aino? Where was she now? Her mind is all fucked up. Drugs, definitely the drugs, but what were they and why? No question that Cal is keeping her taking them. Again, why? Her mind skipped. What had any of this to do with money laundering? Pentti's friend, shot? Why? Where was Pentti? Had he really told Cal where she was? It didn't seem likely. What had Cal said? 'If he's not dead already.' None of it made sense.

Fragments. Like trying to see your reflection in a shattered mirror. Maybe that was what Auli felt too, as she struggled to remember things. But she remembers the Kalevala. Alzheimer's disease? Not that she has it, but didn't people who have it remember old memories while losing the present? Then there was the Sampo. God knows what that is about.

Fragments. She was underground. She had entered a building and gone down in an elevator. What was it Auli had muttered about the might being underground, beneath the memories? Was that what she had said? Her mind skipped again. She was imprisoned. There were people here. Men. She couldn't recall hearing a female voice. Cal was armed with a pistol. She had no idea what type. It didn't matter; a pistol was a pistol. The aurora. That had been beautiful but almost terrifying. The Real Karelian Freedom Movement, is that what he had said? Was that like the Real IRA? What was the *vasta* all about? Little things, she reminded herself, it's the little things that are important.

But there were too many little things, too many questions.

Nicole realised she was getting nowhere and lay down again. Sleep, she told herself, you need sleep.

She had no idea how long she slept, or only dozed, but she became aware of sounds. People were talking close by. It sounded as if it came not from directly outside, but from a room next to hers. The voices became louder and she could make out the sound of a man and a woman but there were other noises she couldn't distinguish.

She draped herself in the blanket and went to the door, pressing her ear against it. For a moment she listened then, startled by what she heard, pulled back from the door. He was making love to her. The sounds were mostly from him, talking in a coaxing tone, emitting a growl like an animal. Auli was quieter, but every now and then Nicole heard her calling out something in Finnish.

Nicole went back to bed and curled up, wanting to bury her head beneath the pillow and escape the sounds. But she didn't and, giving in to a voyeuristic impulse, strained to listen. Whether it was lovemaking or just fucking wasn't clear. Whichever it was, it seemed to go on for a long time. Then there was silence for a while, followed by a door being shut and the unmistakable sound of a bolt being slid into place. There were footsteps and then, slightly further away, another door, a sliding door, closing.

Nicole listened for a little while longer but heard nothing. Eventually she went to sleep.

When she awoke, feeling groggy and disoriented, Nicole had no idea if it was day or night. She located a light switch and turned on the single overhead light. According to her watch it was seven o'clock. Morning, she guessed. The notion of having a shower crossed her mind, but she dismissed it. There was no way of locking her door from the inside and the thought of Cal or one of the other men walking in was disturbing.

For a while she sat on the bed, trying to order her thoughts, but she was hungry so she went to the door and banged on it. There was no response.

Half an hour later she heard the bolt being retracted and the door unlocked. It swung open and a man stepped in and placed a tray covered with a tea towel on the end of her bed. Another man, armed with a pistol, remained at the door.

'It's okay, I'm too hungry to attack you,' she quipped.

Neither of the men responded. After glancing around the room, they backed out of the door and shut it. This time she heard no bolt. She resisted going to the door and seeing if it would open; instead, driven by hunger, she took the tea towel off the tray.

The breakfast was exactly what she needed. Two soft-boiled eggs, some toast and jam and a pot of hot, milky coffee.

When she had finished eating and had a second cup of coffee, she washed her face and having no comb, ran her fingers through her hair. Now, she thought, let's try the door.

To her surprise it swung open. For a moment she expected one of the armed men to step in and shut it, but as that didn't eventuate, she cautiously stepped into the doorway and looked around at a tastefully furnished lounge area. There were several chairs and small coffee tables and four or five beautiful Finnish hand-knotted *ryijy* rugs scattered on a Norwegian Rose Fauske marble floor. She recognised it as the same marble as her bench top in London. To one side of the room was a large framed photograph of a very small and dilapidated wooden church set in a rural landscape.

'It's the Chapel of St Barbara at Kokkoilain Karelia,' Cal said. He was seated at the centre of a small but comfortable lounge area, relaxing in an armchair. A coffee cup and a newspaper were on a coffee table in front of him and he had obviously been waiting for her to emerge.

'Good morning, princess,' he said. He gestured to another chair. 'You should have brought your coffee.'

She found his friendliness off-putting. 'I've had enough,' she mumbled.

'I've been waiting to show you around.'

'Really? How nice,' she said flatly, her attention on the newspaper. She couldn't read the Finnish, but she could tell from the date that it was the morning's edition. So they were near a city or town. It's the little things.

He got to his feet. 'Come, I'll show you the nerve centre.'

She didn't get up. 'Where is Auli?'

He shrugged. 'Sleeping, probably.'

'Is she okay?'

'Well, that depends on your definition of okay.'

She scowled at him. 'Mine certainly doesn't include having someone screw me while I'm under the influence of drugs.'

'Oh dear,' he said with mock sincerity. 'Did we keep you awake? She has such a voracious appetite which I do my humble best to satisfy.' He paused and leered at her. 'Actually, I think I do pretty well. It's such a pity she can't remember it in the morning.'

'You know you'll never get away with this.'

That seemed to amuse him immensely. 'And you intend to die stopping me?' He gave a dry laugh and gestured for her to follow him. 'That's enough of the fun and games. Come.'

He opened the sliding door and led the way across a corridor to a high-tech security door. With a single handle and an access dial, it looked like the door to a bank vault. 'Solid steel, class five, armoury door,' he said with a hint of pride.

Boys' toys, Nicole thought. 'And what do you keep in there?'

He was concentrating on the combination and didn't respond. The door swung outward and he ushered her through. What she saw took her breath away.

The room the entered was a large circular control room that looked like something out of a futuristic sci-fi movie. Three men and a woman were seated in front of a bank of computer screens and to one side two men were keeping an eye on a series of monitors showing security camera images of the perimeter of the building.

'State of the art computing power and a few tasty innovations,' he said proudly. 'Information is power and we have it in spades.'

He's right about information being power, Nicole thought and if pride was his Achilles' heel then she needed to keep him talking. Every bit of information she could glean was important. She just hoped she had the opportunity to use it.

'Innovations? It just looks like a control room and a few computers.'

'Well, there you would be wrong,' he said smugly, and taking her by the arm he took her to a window into a side room. 'See? Chip stacking.'

'What the hell is that?' she asked.

'Around ninety-eight per cent of the energy in data centre computing is used for moving data, which only leaves two per cent to do the actual computations. So what we've done is chip stacking.' He had lost her completely but hadn't noticed, which suited Nicole, who had switched her attention to the images on the security monitors. Her hope that she would get a glimpse of the exterior of the building and maybe some clue as to where it was, came to nothing; all she could see was snow-covered forest.

She turned back to Cal who was still in full flight, extolling the virtues of the technology at his command.

'Mounting 3D chips vertically reduces the percentage lost to moving data because the data no longer travels 10 centimetres, but less than a millimetre. You can imagine the savings.' He pointed into the room. 'Those are the stacks. The problem is that they generate a huge amount of heat and it took us a while to solve the heat dissipation problem. And we are still looking at phase-change memory and at thermophotovoltaics. In the meantime, the excess heat is used to heat this entire building.'

'Sure,' she said and then in an attempt to keep him talking, added, 'it's fascinating. But must have cost a lot.'

Cal laughed. 'Millions. But that's the beauty of the system. You see, it generates more money than we can ever hope to spend.'

'What?' she asked, suddenly genuinely interested.

'We skim a minute percentage off international money transfers. Mostly out of Russian banks. The individual amounts are so small that they go unnoticed and even if they are, each amount is marked as a European Credit Transfer Facilitation Fee.'

'You're stealing money, Cal, and everyone who does that is eventually caught.'

He laughed. 'Not when we have an agreement with the British and Americans to turn a blind eye.'

Nicole stared at him, trying to ascertain if he was being serious. 'Why would they do that?'

'Because they want our little project to succeed.'

'What little project is that, then?'

He looked at her for a moment, deliberating the risk of saying more. Then his face relaxed into a smile. 'It's a pity you won't live to see it.'

'See what?'

He gestured at the control room. 'This is not an operations centre, this. This is history being made. Sadly, I do not totally trust my Russian friends, so I am keeping you as a little insurance.'

He's a megalomaniac, she decided. 'Sure, for which you will end up dead or in prison.'

The smile dropped from his face. 'You're not listening, are you? I just said that we have backing from the Americans and from your government. In just a few days from now everything changes. We won't need any of this anymore.'

'What changes?'

'We are financing the next Russian revolution and in return, Finland will get Karelia back.'

He truly believes this? He's a psycho, she thought. 'Cal, let me tell you one thing.'

'Yes?'

'You are totally insane.'

If she expected him to react angrily, she was disappointed. He smiled benignly.

'After the twenty-eighth, nobody will think that. Particularly not you, because my parting gift will be a one-way trip to Tuoni's kingdom, to Manala.'

'Never heard of them,' she snorted, 'and I don't think I have the correct visas. So tell me about the twenty-eighth.'

'It's the day the Russian President dies, and I have organised it so you will die at the same instant. I'm sure he will make a pleasant travelling companion on your way to hell.'

As he had expected, the American was already in the bar. His own advance team had warned him that Sam Gordon had back-up – three men at least – and they were all in the bar pretending to fit in. By the description he had been given, at least two of them were ex-military and the third was probably their technical support. It was a standard configuration and to be expected. What was unexpected and mildly disappointing was that Gordon had felt the need to use them at all. It was amateur and smacked of distrust. No matter how hard they tried, ex-soldiers did not make good agents. Hopefully their other skills could be put to good use.

Zaikov stepped through the door and stood for a moment, amused at the look of horror and surprise on Sam Gordon's face. Then he walked over, pulled up a chair and sat down.

'Nice to see you, Sam,' he said quietly.

Sam took a deep breath, composed himself and smiled. 'You do a very poor imitation of being dead.'

'Hopefully others are convinced,' Zaikov said. 'Oh, and by the way, it's Belov now, at least for a while. Andrei Belov.'

Sam shrugged. 'Whatever. Our people bought the story. We were all very sad, of course.'

'Touching.'

'I take it you have a reason for killing yourself off?'

'I decided my former employers might be a little upset over my vanishing. It is easier this way. In ten days' time, after the twenty-eighth, I will resume being Zaikov.'

Sam nodded. 'I have often thought of doing the same; disappearing, that is. It would make life so much simpler.'

Zaikov leaned forward and lowered his voice. 'Don't disappear just yet, Mister Gordon; we have work to do in the next few days. After that, should you want to change your lifestyle, I can assure you my partners can be very generous.'

'Too kind,' Sam muttered. 'Now, what is it you need from me?'

Zaikov glanced around. 'Your men probably have skills we can use. We have a very troublesome SUPO agent and a British policewoman who continue to cause annoyance.'

'And their being neutralised would what...?'

'Would make me very happy.'

'Then, if the circumstances are conducive, I will make my men available.' There was also the question of Grammaticus, but he decided against mentioning it.

Zaikov reached into his pocket and took out a brochure. 'This is the Karelian Memorial Museum.' He handed it over. 'The building, the quaintly named *Kalevala House*, is where the policewoman is being held at the moment. I think that the SUPO agent, Pentti Toivonen, will probably try to reach her there.'

Sam peered at the brochure, turned it over and examined the small map on the back. 'It's completely surrounded by forest?'

'Completely. Access is by a rural road to the front of the building and there is also a path through the forest from the lake.'

Sam nodded. 'Okay, sounds easy.'

'No. It is not so easy. You see, the building has both visual and thermal security. I also suspect that it has highly armed and well-trained men protecting the place.'

Sam looked puzzled. 'Why? What's in this museum that requires that sort of security?'

'It is at the centre of the entire operation. They have computers skimming the funds for us.'

Sam sat forward. 'So that is why we are protecting you? Money laundering?'

Zaikov laughed. 'The project needed massive funds and this was the simplest way. And, of course, we have your backing for the project itself.'

'You want to engineer regime change in Russia, right?'

'And to do that we need a system to disrupt electronic communications in Russia for a couple of days from the twenty-eighth, and their computers have that in hand.'

'And the people in this museum, they can do that?'

'Believe me, if anyone can they can,' Zaikov said and waved his hand dismissively. 'Now, one more small detail.'

'Yes?'

'After this is over, we don't intend that its computer capabilities continue to function. We shall destroy the museum and dispose of the Canadian man, Remsu, who runs it.' Zaikov took two small photographs from his pocket and slid them across the table. 'The first man is Pentti Toivonen, the other is Kullervo Remsu. Show them to your men, because if we get lucky we can take them both out along with the policewoman. Toivonen is a threat and Remsu… well, let's say, he is no longer of use to us.'

Sam studied the photo. 'What's the Canadian involved in this for? Just the money?'

Zaikov laughed. 'He is an idiotic idealist who was stupid enough to believe us when we said that when our people take control of Russia, we will give Karelia back to Finland. I am afraid he is going to be disappointed. He'll be happier dead, I think.'

'One more thing. What the hell was that text message about *kulkuripoika?*'

'Ah yes! My Finnish friends thought it was a good joke. They tell me it's a song from the nineteen seventies by Tapio Rautavaara.'

'And what the fuck has that got to do with anything?'

'The title translates as… I'm not sure what you Americans call them these days but maybe "bums" or "hobos". A *kulkuripoika* is a hobo boy.'

'Stop stuffing around, Zaikov.'

'Just follow the instructions and you'll find it's the name of the place where the weapons for your team are waiting.'

'And what exactly is happening on the twenty-eighth?'

'Oh, didn't you know? It's Kalevala Day and to celebrate we have a little surprise in store.'

They questioned Anja Kujola for three hours and then, convinced she had told them everything she knew, informed her she was free to return to her studio. Quentin, who had been allowed to observe the interview from behind the one-way glass, agreed with Pentti and Heimo that there was no reason to keep her but, like them, he was unsure of where her information left them. He also agreed with Heimo's directive that she was not to be informed that Auli was still alive. There was only a small chance she would have communicated it to anyone else, but that was a risk they were not prepared to take.

'So where do you intend to concentrate now?' Quentin asked as they filed into a meeting room to have coffee.

'For a start, I think we can forget about the theft of the sculpture. It's interesting, but hardly worth following at this stage,' Heimo said. He handed a file to Pentti. 'On another subject, the lab report on the pills. A lot of complex chemical names that all lead to amnesia, unconsciousness or death, depending on the dosage. Long-term use could cause permanent memory loss.'

Pentti glanced at the file. 'Yes, it was what I suspected.'

'And the telephone number?' Heimo asked.

'I rang Sirkka Mikkonen, and Nicole was right; it was not a telephone number, but a reference to some lines in the Kalevala. I wrote them down.' He took out a notebook and flicked through it. 'Here. *Even though the powerful people have gone, the magic is still ready. Words shall not be hidden, nor spells buried; might shall not sink underground, though the mighty go.*' Pentti closed the notebook and looked up. 'Not exactly useful stuff.'

'So why did Auli Saarinen give what looked like a telephone number to Matti Salomäki just before he was killed?'

'Sorry Heimo, I have no idea. Maybe it was something silly like his asking for her telephone number and she decided to play her Kalevala game with him.' He shrugged. 'Who knows?'

'Okay, we'll leave that. Now, what about the other members of this university club?' Heimo asked. 'Should we pull them in one at a time?'

Pentti sipped his coffee and mulled over it for a moment before responding. 'It would probably be useful. They are all channelling funds to the museum, so we could confront them with the money laundering issue and see how they react. I would also bet that they have all received a copy of the photograph of Auli Saarinen in the boat.'

Heimo nodded. 'Our investigations into them turned up another interesting coincidence.'

'Yes?'

'At one time they have all been part of the Free Karelia Movement. In fact, they were all paid-up members of *Karjalan Liitto* until four years ago when they resigned en masse. And it was then that they first started funding the museum.'

'What is this *Karjalan...* organisation?' Quentin asked.

Pentti turned to him. 'I can explain more later, but for now, just think of them as a group of refugees from Karelia who actively support the return of the ceded territories to Finland.'

'You don't want to question them yourself?' Heimo asked.

Pentti shook his head. 'No. At the moment our priority should be finding Parry and Saarinen. And for that, I think the museum and its director require a visit.'

Heimo held up his hand to stop him. 'Well, there we have another problem. I requested the architect's blueprints for the museum and it appears they have been removed. I'm having it followed up, but don't hold much hope.'

'What about the architect – surely he has copies?' Pentti said.

'He died three years ago.' Heimo said, then added, 'Natural causes. Heart attack. His estate may have the plans, but it could take weeks and we don't have that much time.'

'So? We go in blind?' Pentti muttered.

'I'm afraid so. And there is another matter that may or may not be related, but given the timing and for your own security, I feel we had better look at.'

'Which is?'

'We had a security alert yesterday on four individuals coming through Vantaa airport. Americans.' He placed some photographs on the table. 'Two of them look like military types; the third... well, we're not sure about him, but they came in on the same flight.'

'Not very sensible,' Quentin grunted.

Heimo held up a fourth photograph. 'And this last one is, I understand, known to you.' He placed the photograph on the top of the others. 'He came in on a flight the day before.'

'Well, well, look who's coming to dinner.'

Pentti, who had been pacing restlessly, stopped and sat down again. 'I believe you know this man as Mister Gordon? He was travelling on a passport in the name of...' He glanced down at his notes. 'Benjamin Prentiss.'

Quentin nodded. 'What is it the Americans say? We go way back.'

Heimo smiled. 'So I understand.'

'Really? And how did you come across that little gem?'

'We are a small country, Quentin, and by nature a rather shy people, but we compensate by having a certain skill in watching and listening.'

It was Quentin's turn to smile. '*Credo quia absurdum est.*'

Heimo didn't miss a beat. '*Crede quod habes, et habes.*'

'And Zaikov?' Quentin asked. 'Surely we need to locate him.'

Heimo smiled. 'We may have done that already.'

Quentin, mildly surprised, was impressed. 'That is splendid news.'

'Not completely good news.'

'But you know where he is?'

Heimo shook his head. 'We know where he *was*. The Americans had a meeting with Belov this afternoon at the Hotel Kämp.'

'Zaikov,' Quentin interjected. 'And did you arrest them?'

Heimo shook his head. 'No, we made a decision to let them go.'

'But that's madness!' Quentin spluttered. 'Why on earth didn't you grab him while you had the chance?'

'Because more can be gained by following them and finding out what they're up to.'

'Them?'

'Like Gordon, Zaikov has his foot soldiers with him, four men at least. We have the number of the vehicle they hired and it is only a matter of time before we locate it.'

'Well, obviously it's your call, but...' Quentin held his hands up in supplication. 'Gordon is no fool and neither is Zaikov. They'll know they're being set up.'

Pentti nodded. 'I imagine they're counting on it. Zaikov and presumably Gordon know that we intend stopping them, or at the very least making public what we know. If Parry is alive, she would be a complication they don't need. I think that Belov... Zaikov's hit list, will include both of us.'

'And we would hate to disappoint him,' Heimo said. 'So, Pentti, I think your instinct to visit the museum is right. My bet is that the Americans and the Russians are both heading towards Punkaharju and probably have DI Parry dangling as bait. I want you to get to this Remsu and as soon as you find out what they're up to, let me know and I'll alert the Russian government.'

Quentin looked bewildered. 'But we'll be walking into a trap.'

'Exactly, except that we know it is one, so can take counter-measures.' Heimo scooped up the photographs and retrieved the file on the drugs from Pentti. 'And just to make sure, I am sending Eero and Jukka along as support.'

They have a hell of a lot more autonomy than I do, Quentin thought. There were no apparent phone calls seeking authorisation, no dark lady sequestered in a secret office issuing commands. He made a mental note to study the SUPO model when he returned to Britain. That is, if I return, he thought darkly. He turned to Heimo. 'Where is this place?'

'Punkaharju? It's where the Karelian Memorial Museum is located,' Heimo explained. 'It's also very close to the Russian border, and we must be careful not to disturb our neighbour.'

'I would appreciate permission to accompany Pentti.'

Heimo and Pentti exchanged glances.

'Tell me, Quentin,' Heimo asked softly, 'why are you really here?'

'It's complicated…' Quentin hesitated, unsure of how much to reveal. 'The American…'

'Gordon,' Heimo interjected helpfully.

'Gordon. He and I were tasked with protecting Zaikov's back while he was in the UK. Making sure he didn't inadvertently draw attention to himself while he went about pursuing his interests. My understanding of the nature of those interests was limited, but it appears to be the case that Her Majesty's Government and the Americans had sympathy with Zaikov's long-term goal of effecting a political change in Russia. However, as things have developed, we now have a somewhat more jaundiced view and have become reluctant to continue. If I may be blunt, we are protecting our national interest by untangling ourselves from whatever is going on. If, as seems certain, the Americans still have faith in Zaikov, then Sam Gordon becomes a problem to be dealt with.'

Heimo looked at him quizzically. 'And who exactly is this Zaikov?'

'He was sold to us as a former high-ranking FSB officer. He was head of station in Vyborg, but was dismissed or demoted because he became too close to some radical Karelian nationalist groups. He now claims to have strong connections to disaffected elements within the FSB and military.'

'Disaffected with?' Pentti asked.

'Disaffected with the Russian President. Along with the Americans, we have been concerned at his hunger to concentrate power in his own hands. But we have little faith in Zaikov's machinations solving that problem.'

'And Gordon?' Heimo asked. 'Should he remain a problem, would you be willing to solve the situation?'

Quentin didn't hesitate. 'Were I not in your jurisdiction, most certainly.'

Heimo nodded. 'Of course, under our law, I'm not able to provide you with the means to do such a thing. However, should the circumstance arise and you are left with no choice, then finding a spare Heckler and Koch would probably not be difficult.' He paused and looked Quentin directly in the eye. 'I hope you remember how to use one?'

'Absolutely,' Quentin said as convincingly as he could, while at the same time hoping it was true. It had been over eighteen months since his last firearms refresher course in which he had not been a shining example of marksmanship. But an H & K was more about noise and shock value than accuracy. He decided he would cope.

'Then, Quentin, if you understand we will do nothing to antagonise our neighbour, I think accompanying Pentti is a splendid show of inter-agency cooperation.'

'Splendid,' Quentin echoed and looked over at Pentti, who had taken off his glasses and was rubbing his eyes. It appeared he was less than happy with the proposal. 'I'm sure we'll get along famously.'

Pentti replaced his glasses and peered at Quentin. 'But can you ski?'

'I did a bit of Nordic skiing at Oxford. I was in the Inter-varsity biathlon team. Never a champion, alas, but I came third one year.'

Pentti had managed five hours of sleep. He needed a lot more, and Heimo, who had summoned him for an early morning meeting ahead of his departure for Punkaharju, looked as if he hadn't slept at all.

'The rumblings of Russian instability have caused more than a little concern. I have spent most of the night being grilled by representatives of the Cabinet Committee on Security, the Minister of the Interior's special advisors, the Security Secretariat and God knows who else.'

'Why? Do they know something we don't?' Pentti asked, eyeing Heimo's thermos flask and wondering if it contained coffee.

'Reports from our sources talk of potential unrest in a number of strategic locations including Kubinka air base. We are also picking up an increase in encrypted traffic between Chekhov-Sharapovo, Chaadayevka near Penza, Voronovo in Moscow, and a facility at Lipetsk.'

Pentti was not convinced. 'Heimo, it could be anything. The Russian military might be running exercises.'

Heimo frowned. 'Of course, but our Interior Ministry people are questioning if there is a connection between events there and the arrival in Helsinki of what looks like an American hit team.'

'And you said what?'

'That we have our eyes on the Americans and are confident we can contain them.' He paused and reached for his thermos. 'That satisfied nobody.'

'And Zaikov? You informed them about his arrival on a false passport?'

'It was odd. They knew about Zaikov and, while acknowledging he was a serious threat, they were particularly concerned that nothing happens to him.'

'I don't understand?' Pentti frowned.

'Well, understand this,' Heimo snapped. 'I was left under no illusion that taking him out would create a diplomatic incident with our neighbours. Watch and report was the order. I repeat, an order. You may question this Remsu, but for the moment do nothing more.'

Taken aback by Heimo's vehement tone, Pentti simply nodded.

Heimo unscrewed the lid of his thermos. 'Coffee?'

'Thank you,' Pentti said. 'Oh, and did you find the map I needed?'

Heimo grinned. 'I have a copy. The archivist in the cartography section thought I was insane wanting something so old.' He reached down beside his chair and retrieved a cardboard tube. 'There you are, a souvenir of the Continuation War.'

'You didn't tell anyone why you wanted it, I hope.'

'Trust me, Pentti, the archivist just thinks I'm a history buff. It's not supposed to leave the premises, but I'm sure you'll look after it.'

Pentti laughed. 'I'll put our British friend in charge of it and if it gets damaged we can blame him.'

Heimo produced two cups and was about to pour the coffee when one of his telephones rang. He picked it up, listened, grunted his thanks and hung up.

'If it is a military exercise, it's a serious one. The Strategic Rocket Forces at Kuntsevo in Moscow have just been put on alert.'

The courier left the new American Innovation Centre in Helsinki's Kaivopuisto district and made his way to the central railway station. As instructed, he went to the left luggage hall, selected a locker, put four euro in the slot and placed a small yellow envelope in the locker. After checking it was secure, he took out his phone and sent a text message containing the number.

The weather had cleared so he strolled down to the Toripojat at the Kauppatori, put the locker key on the table and ordered a coffee and *possumunkki*.

'Excuse me.'

He looked up at the man who had addressed him in English.

'Yes?'

'Did I leave my key here?'

'This one?'

'Thanks. That's a relief. I thought I'd lost it.' The man smiled. 'Sorry about interrupting your breakfast.'

'Not a problem.' He handed the man the key and turned his attention back to his coffee and pastry.

The white landscape reminded him of winter in Vermont – pretty to look at and shitty to be in. Although it was picturesque when viewed through the car windscreen, the prospect of getting out and walking in it was less appealing. He wouldn't have minded a decent conversation, but Sulkin was locked into his iPod and apart from annoying bursts of tuneless humming, was silent. Green was sound asleep. Sam stared grumpily at the countryside for a while and then, relaxed with Armstrong's careful driving, shut his eyes and dosed off.

Just before Imatra they turned off the highway on to Asematie and stopped at the Hotelli Kulkuripoika. It took Sam a moment to make the connection. Then he understood. This was the '*kulkuri poika*' of the text message.

'Hallelujah, welcome to the hobo boy hotel,' he murmured to himself and clambered out of the car. 'This is it, boys. Home for the night and as you can see, in luxurious accommodation.'

The hotel looked like a brick shoebox, but he had stayed in worse. By the expression on the faces of Armstrong and Green, they were deeply unimpressed. Sulkin didn't seem to care. He shrugged and continued nodding his head in time to whatever was playing on his iPod.

Their rooms were not ready for them and wouldn't be for at least another two hours.

'Check-out is not until twelve,' the receptionist explained. 'And then we must make up the rooms.'

Sam Gordon looked at his watch and declared ten-thirty in the morning to be exactly the right time for lunch and a beer. Nobody disagreed.

After lunch he took the yellow envelope from his pocket, ripped it open and fished out a set of car keys. He walked casually across the snow outside the hotel to the end of the car park and pressed the unlock button on the key holder. A set of lights on a white Toyota Hiace blinked.

'Thank Christ,' he muttered to himself. He went to the van, slid the side door open and, after checking that nobody was observing him, flipped a tarpaulin off some boxes. Everything was there; the weapons, ammunition, the snowsuits and what looked like too many wooden boxes of plastic explosive. He opened one and examined the contents. It was not the semtex or C-4 he was used to, but labelled 'PENO' and came in 200-gram cartridges wrapped in silver paper. It would certainly do the job. He opened another unmarked box and found a variety of timers and detonators.

'Perfect,' he said quietly and replaced the tarpaulin and locked the door. As he walked back to the hotel entrance, he felt a rush of adrenaline. In the morning they would link up with Zaikov's Russians. It was almost party time.

Having studied the maps carefully, Pentti drove them to an abandoned logging camp a kilometre north of the museum. It had taken longer than expected to leave Helsinki, a delay caused by needing to provide suitable clothing for the ill-prepared Englishman. For his part, Quentin did his best to blend in and though feeling like an over-dressed snow-bunny, didn't complain. When they arrived at the logging camp he was grateful for the clothing, as it was colder than anything he had ever experienced.

'Minus twenty-six Celsius,' Pentti told him in a manner he found far too cheerful.

Quentin did the conversion in his head. 'Minus nine point six Fahrenheit? There ought to be a law against having to work in such temperatures,' he grumbled.

The two Karhu Team men, Eero and Jukka, scouted the camp and reported back that it was secure and that one of the old cabins was habitable, with a stove and some bunks. 'There are no mattresses,' Jukka added.

'We won't be sleeping tonight,' Pentti said. 'But I suggest we get a fire happening and see if we can get some rest now.'

With the stove going and despite the quality of the food, that Quentin took to be instant soup rations, they were surprisingly comfortable. Eero and Jukka were obviously used to operating in such primitive conditions and within minutes of eating had laid out their padded snowsuits on the bunks and fallen sleep. Pentti, like Quentin, found relaxing a little more difficult and sat on some wooden crates around the stove. He slid a map from a cardboard tube and began examining it.

'What's the map?' Quentin asked.

'The defensive positions built by the Finns during the Winter War and the Continuation War; old trenches, bunkers and so on. I thought it might be useful to know where they are in case we have to spend a night out in the real cold.'

'You mean colder than this? Christ, I hope not.'

'I have some Koskenkorva,' Pentti produced a small half-bottle. 'It's just the thing for circumstances like this.'

'It's vodka?'

'Finnish, and very good.'

Quentin took a sip and decided that good was a subjective judgment, but in the absence of Talisker or Laphroaig, it was better than another helping of the armed forces survival ration soup. He took a second sip and handed the bottle back to Pentti. 'In Helsinki you said you would explain the Karelian Freedom Movement.'

Pentti sipped the vodka. He opened the stove door, poked the fire and fed in some small twigs. 'We call it the *Karjala-kysymys* – the Karelian question, but in fact it refers not just to Finnish Karelia but includes Petsamo, parts of Salla and Kuusamo, and four islands in the Gulf of Finland, all of which were ceded to the then Soviet Union after the Winter War and the Continuation War. Finnish politicians tend to avoid the issue, but there are those in Karelian organisations and some right-wing groups like *Suomen Sisu* who want to regain sovereignty over Finnish Karelia and the other territories. There's no real chance of it happening because no significant political party openly supports the idea.'

'I'm sorry, but my knowledge of Finnish history is pretty damned rudimentary. Winter War? Continuation War?'

'Understandable,' Pentti laughed. 'My knowledge of the Tudors could be written down on a postage stamp.' He took another drink and handed the bottle over. 'The Soviets attacked in November nineteen thirty-nine in what the League of Nations deemed an illegal incursion. It started when a Soviet border post was shelled with, according to Soviet reports, the deaths and injuries of some border guards. Research conducted years later by Finnish and Russian historians concluded that the shelling was carried out from the Soviet side of the border by an NKVD unit with the express purpose of providing the Soviet Union with an excuse to invade.'

'A classic trick to create a *casus belli*.' Quentin sighed.

'Exactly,' Pentti agreed. 'You know, I grew up with this history. I know the stories, I've seen photographs, but I still can't imagine how it was for the soldiers fighting that war. You think it's cold today at minus twenty-five or six? In January nineteen forty the Karelian Isthmus experienced a record low temperature of minus forty-five degrees.'

'Jesus!'

'The war ended in March nineteen forty with the Moscow Peace Treaty. In the treaty the Soviets demanded the territories for security reasons, primarily to protect Leningrad, which was only forty kilometres from the Finnish border. There was no pressure on people to leave the ceded territories, but almost all did. The result was that four hundred and ten thousand Finnish Karelians were evacuated to Finland.'

Quentin shook his head in disbelief. 'That's a huge number.'

'About twelve per cent of Finland's total population at the time.' Pentti stared into the fire. 'It gets worse.'

'Really?'

'During the Continuation War two hundred and sixty thousand Finns returned to Karelia, only to be evacuated again in June nineteen forty-four.'

'It sounds like a nightmare.'

'It was,' Pentti said quietly. 'And I guess, for some people like Remsu, the wounds have never healed.'

'But surely he was too young...'

'His parents...' Pentti started. 'I don't know the whole story, but his father died and his mother... Maybe she killed herself? No, I don't remember. Anyway, for him and a lot of other Karelians the *Karjala-kysymys* has never been answered.'

They lapsed into silence for a few moments before Quentin stood up. 'I think I'll try and rest.'

'Good idea, Quentin,' Pentti said. 'I'll stoke the fire and then have a rest myself.'

'What time are we setting out?'

'As soon as it gets dark.'

Quentin gave a brittle laugh. 'Well, that's something to look forward to; a quiet stroll in the woods on a cool night and a visit to a museum.'

'That about sums it up,' Pentti smiled. 'Now get some rest, you'll need all your strength, particularly if we have to wrestle any Russian bears.'

Chapter Eighteen

She had lost track of time. In the bunker, as she thought of it, there was no day or night, and outside the control room area she hadn't seen a single wall clock. Nicole judged it to be morning when breakfast arrived and evening when she was given supper. Although no longer locked in her room, her access was restricted to the lounge area, and a small library. All other doors were locked with keypads and biometric security. There was no sign of Auli and, in what she took to have been the last twenty-four hours, no contact with Cal Remsu.

Nicole was sound asleep when her door was pushed open and the light was switched on. Someone shook her by the shoulders.

'Wake up, please.'

She opened her eyes to see a woman bending over her.

'Come please. It is Aino. Maybe she is dying.'

Nicole blinked, rubbed her eyes and sat up. The woman standing beside her bed was clearly distressed. She was young, a girl. Probably no more than late teens or early twenties, her long hair braided and wrapped around her head like photos she had seen of Ukrainian peasants.

'What? Where is Cal?' Nicole asked as she tried to fully wake herself. She stumbled out of bed and started pulling on her clothes.

'He's away,' the girl replied.

Nicole tucked her blouse in and did up her belt. 'Okay, take me to her.'

The girl nodded and led the way through the lounge to a security door. Nicole tried to see the sequence she punched in but she did it too quickly.

They followed a corridor that curved around to the right – we are circling the control room, Nicole surmised. At the next door on the left the girl again punched in some numbers but again too fast for Nicole to see, though it appeared to be a different combination. The sign on the door read: *Sairaala*.

'It's our infirmary,' the girl explained. 'Aino is in here.'

'Her real name is Auli,' Nicole said testily, and pushed past her.

Auli was lying on a state-of-the-art medical trolley, covered with a blanket. She looked dead. Her skin colour had a slight bluish tinge.

'Christ! What happened?'

'She had a seizure, or a fit or something, and fell over.'

Nicole bent over and put her face next to Auli's. 'She's still breathing.'

'Can you help her?'

'I'm a policewoman, not a bloody doctor. You should call a doctor.'

'I'm a nurse assistant, not a doctor. You have to do something.' The girl was wide-eyed, a look of panic on her face. 'We can't let anyone in. Surely you have first aid training.'

Nicole rounded on the girl. 'Now, listen to me. This woman needs proper medical care, not my rudimentary first aid.'

'But...' the girl began and then burst into tears.

Nicole took a deep breath. 'Okay, okay, calm down. What's your name?'

'Hillevi Virtanen.'

'Then, Hillevi Virtanen, show me your medical cupboard. I need syrup of ipecac and some hand washing soap. Liquid soap.'

The girl nodded and scurried into a side room. 'Come and look,' she called. 'I don't know about any syrup, but there's some liquid soap.'

'Then get it!' Nicole snapped and shouldered past her.

The cupboards in the small anteroom were stacked with medicines. Most of them seemed like antibiotics and a range of flu and painkillers. Then she saw them: two brand new bottles labelled '*Oksennusainetta*' with the words 'Syrup of ipecac' in parentheses.

'Bingo!' she exclaimed and took a bottle. Using an emetic was the only thing she could think of. If nothing else it would probably purge whatever was in her stomach, hopefully including the drugs she had been given. They were probably in her bloodstream as well, but given the circumstances, Nicole could see no other option.

'Hurry!' she yelled and hunted around for a spoon. She found a small one beside a tin of instant coffee.

'Liquid soap,' Hillevi said and held out a pump-bottle decorated with flowers.

'Perfect,' Nicole said and handed her the bottle of ipecac. 'I can't understand Finnish, so I need you to tell me exactly what it says about dosage.'

The girl squinted at the bottle. 'It says fifteen to thirty millilitres.'

'That's a couple of tablespoons,' Nicole looked at the teaspoon in her hand. 'Say, four of these.'

'Then it says she has to have water straight away, two hundred and forty millilitres of water. It says repeat if vomiting does not occur in thirty minutes.' She handed the bottle back. 'You are going to make her vomit?'

'With your help.' Nicole nodded. 'She may have swallowed some drugs and we need to make her throw up. Get a basin and then I'll need you to hold her head for me.'

Giving an emetic to an unconscious person was not something that had been covered in any of the first aid modules she had been required to attend. The police FASE or 'First Aid Skills Enhanced' probably came closest, but she had only ever done the course once and somehow failed to attend the mandatory annual refresher. Nicole looked at the unconscious woman on the trolley. Her breathing appeared to have improved, but there was no sign of her vomiting.

'How long has it been?'

'Eighteen minutes.'

'We may have to give her a second dose, or try a spoonful of liquid soap.'

'That would taste…'

'Dreadful. Yes, I know. But it is supposed to trigger vomiting.'

As if on cue, Auli twitched and gave a spluttering cough.

'Quickly! Get her head to one side over the bucket.'

Hillevi moved fast and managed to prop the bucket under Auli's chin just in time.

From the first explosive vomiting episode to the last of the dry retching took almost fifteen minutes, but at the end of it Auli had her eyes open and was breathing normally. Nicole noticed that her skin was no longer tinged blue but infused with uneven splotches of pink. It looked, she thought hopefully, like the skin of someone recovering.

Auli rolled her head to one side and looked Nicole directly in the face.

'Hello,' she said. 'Who are you?'

'You don't remember? I'm Nicole. We were on the island and had a sauna together.'

Auli's face showed no sign of recognition. 'Have I got the plague?' she asked, not as if she was terrified by the thought, but rather that she was curious.

Nicole laughed lightly. 'Auli, nobody has the plague. You seem to have fainted. It's nothing to worry about.' Nicole hoped her lie was not too transparent.

Auli didn't respond.

'Come,' Nicole said to Hillevi, 'we can't leave her here. Bring her to my room and we'll put her bed beside mine so I can monitor her.'

'I'm not sure...' Hillevi began.

'Listen. Do you want her to have another seizure? If she's with me I can keep an eye on her. I'm sure you don't want to be responsible for her death.'

'But...'

'Hillevi, I'm a police officer. Please just do as I ask. My friend Cal will be very grateful because, as you know, he cares a lot about Auli.'

Her bluff, mentioning Remsu's name, seemed to do the trick, and the young woman nodded mutely and wheeled the trolley towards the door.

'I'll just get some more drugs in case we have another episode,' Nicole said in what she liked to think of as her 'official' voice.

Back in her room, with Auli sleeping, Nicole despatched Hillevi to fetch a cup of tea. While the girl was away she stashed the packets of drugs under her mattress. She couldn't be certain, but they looked to be the ones Cal had been dosing Auli with and now, unless he had another stockpile, he would have no fresh drugs to give her. She had also taken a quantity of painkillers.

Later, she woke to find the cup of tea, duly delivered but untouched, cold on the table beside her bed. Again, she had no idea of the time – it could have been night or day, but beside her, on her trolley bed, Aino was lying on her side, looking at her and softly chanting lines from the Kalevala.

'You're awake,' Nicole said as she sat up and reached out her hand. Without hesitation Auli took it and held it firmly.

'I have become the plague,' she whispered. 'I am one of Louhi's children, sent from the foggy islands to slay the people of Kalevala, to spread disease.'

'No,' Nicole said firmly. 'It is just a bad dream. You've been ill and had a nightmare.'

Auli shook her head and began chanting again.

'Auli! Listen to me. You are not well. Try and relax.'

'It was prophecy. I am death's daughter and it is I who have sickened Väinölä's people, the descendants of Kalevala. I am killing them with an unknown disease. Everyone will die with even the floors beneath them rotting and their bed sheets all corrupted.'

'Auli! Stop it at once!' Nicole shouted. 'You are ill. This is just the sickness coming out.'

'Kill me!' Auli hissed. 'Kill me and destroy the Sampo or everyone will die.'

Nicole put out her hand and touched Auli's forehead. She was burning up with fever and Nicole could feel her trembling under her touch.

'Lie still, I'll get you some water.'

But Auli refused to let go of her hand. For a moment she stared at Nicole, her eyes wide, her pupils dilated. Her breathing was uneven, ragged gasps rasping in her throat. Her face was covered in sweat.

'I remember you,' she croaked.

Nicole pulled her hand free and swung her feet to the floor. She took her teacup, emptied it down the sink and filled it with water.

'Here, drink this.'

To her relief, Auli accepted the cup and holding it in trembling hands managed to take a sip.

'Wait,' Nicole said and rummaged through the packets of drugs under her mattress until she found some aspirin. She took two and dropped them in the remaining water in the cup. 'Now, drink that up; it will help you fight the fever.'

'You're Nicole,' Auli whispered. 'I remember you.'

'I remember you too,' Nicole smiled. 'We're friends, remember?'

'Were you in time?'

'In time for what, Auli?'

'In time to find the Sampo.'

'The Sampo that was stolen?'

Auli nodded. 'Did you find it?'

Nicole shook her head. 'Not yet. We haven't found it yet.'

'You have to find it, or everyone will die.'

The turrets of Freda's Jugendstil buildings were covered with snow and, if the weather forecast was to be believed, there was more on the way. Fine for the tourists, Heimo thought as he stepped around a young Japanese couple taking photographs. He supposed they found it picturesque. It was not a good morning to be walking, but the notion of being stuck in the office had been depressing and he had ditched his wife's *pulla*, tugged on his woollen cap and headed out in search of a bacon and egg roll. It was not what his doctor would have recommended, but then he had never been one to follow medical advice.

As he turned from Fredrikinkatu into Lönnrotinkatu the first flurries of fresh snow drifted around him in an unpleasant reminder that winter still hadn't run its course. There were more tourists here, despite the weather. A tour group of Europeans, Germans, he guessed, had alighted from a bus and were crossing the road from the *Vanha kirkkopuisto* to Lönnrotsgatan. They gathered, huddled, in front of the statue of Elias Lönnrot.

'*Dies ist der berühmte Dichter Elias Lönnrot, die Kalevala zu-sammengestellt.*' The tour guide's tone came across as reverential even through the drifting flakes of snow. The tourist appeared more cold than interested.

Heimo stopped for a moment and gazed at the statue. It always looked the same. Covered white in winter with the snow and bird shit in the summer. Poor old Elias left out in the cold. There had been a time when every kid in school had the Kalevala forced down their throats. Not all of it, of course, just the 'nice' bits, the *kaunis* Kalevala. Nowadays, he thought bitterly, you'd be lucky to find one kid in ten who knew anything about it. Finland was no longer the land of the Kalevala, but rather, Nokia and *Angry Birds*. Still, at least it was the land of something.

He continued walking and turned right alongside the park and down Yrjönkatu, making a circuit that would lead him back to the *Suojelupoliisi* office in Ratakatu.

Heimo had always loved the Old Church Park, the *Vanha kirk-kopuisto*. With hundreds of victims from the plague buried beneath its trees and gardens, it was a constant reminder of his mortality. In summer he liked to escape from the endless meetings and sit on one of the benches and read the paper. It didn't happen very often, but was a great pleasure when it did. A paper. Good idea. He had more coffee at work and he would try to make an effort to relax with a bit of reading.

The day before had been a grind. Hour after hour they had interviewed the former members of the Mary Hevonen Society – a foolish name, but one that had somehow become attached to them. It had been unproductive. They had, as Pentti previously surmised, all received the photograph of the Saarinen woman apparently dead in the boat. They had all donated money to the museum, but apart from that had no apparent knowledge of what the hell was going on.

What was of more interest was a discovery by the financial investigation team of frequent large cash deposits made into the museum's bank account. The investigators had no idea of the source of the money but the consensus was that it had been smuggled across the frontier from Russia. Given that the countries shared over seven hundred kilometres of border, it would not have presented much of a problem to professional smugglers. The amounts were staggering but bore no relationship to the needs of the museum, whose actual budget appeared quite normal. What the money was intended for was an open question.

There had been only one communication from Pentti, informing him that they were preparing to confront Cal Remsu. Hopefully it would go well and within a few hours they would have a clear picture of what was going on.

Back in the office he poured himself some coffee from his thermos and settled back to read. He had only read a couple of pages of the *Helsingin Sanomat* when he came across a small news item reporting that the Russian President was to attend a Kalevala Day celebration in the Republic of Karelia. Surprisingly, his visit was not to the capital, Petrozavodsk, but to Vyborg, close to the Finnish border. Though this was unusual, it was of little more than passing interest. However, it was the next sentence that alarmed Heimo and literally sent shivers down his spine. According to the paper, the Russian President would be taking part in a half-marathon. As part of the festivities to commemorate Kalevala Day, at the end of the race he would unveil a statue of 'the forging of the Sampo'. The paper went on to note that the work was by Finnish artist Anja Kujola.

'*Jumalauta!*' Heimo swore and reached for the phone. 'I need an urgent meeting with the Prime Minister and the President,' he snapped. 'No, not tomorrow, now!'

After sleeping for an hour, Pentti stoked the fire, put some water on to boil and then went to the cabin door. Outside, the weather had changed completely. A bank of low cloud had closed in and though the temperature had risen slightly, thick snow was falling and the wind was picking up.

'*Sissin sää,*' Jukka muttered as the others joined Pentti at the door.

'What's that?' Quentin asked.

'Perfect weather for our little guerrilla operation,' Pentti grinned. 'Nobody is expecting us, and in this weather we can move quickly without being seen or heard.'

'Lovely,' Quentin said unconvincingly.

'And hopefully the conditions will hinder any thermal imaging security.'

'Have we an actual plan?'

Pentti laughed. 'We're just visiting a museum, not fighting an elite battalion.'

'Seriously.'

'The access road circles the building and has two car parks. The one at the front is for visitors and the rear one is for staff and delivery vehicles. We don't have a blueprint of the building, but it is safe to assume there are at least two entrances, one adjacent to each car park; there may be others. There is also a ski trail from the lake to the rear of the building. Our information says there's a hut on the lakeshore that's used for equipment storage, fishing gear and so on. We're going to try and locate the hut and the ski trail and approach the museum from that direction.'

'And when we get to the museum?'

'We do nothing hostile unless the situation demands it. The object of the exercise is to locate our primary target, the Canadian, Remsu. After that we'll try and find Nicole Parry and Auli Saarinen.'

'You know what they say in England about plans?'

'Probably the same as we do. No plan survives first contact.'

'That would be it,' Quentin said.

'First we have coffee,' Pentti said and led the way back inside. 'We had better have it now, because I doubt we'll be offered any if and when we get inside.'

'The canteen is probably closed anyway,' Eero joked. He took out a flask and laced each mug of hot, sweet, black coffee with a dash of vodka.

Jukka, Eero and Pentti spent a few minutes checking equipment and packing their small backpacks, while Quentin sat quietly, enjoying the coffee.

'You might like to help carry this,' Jukka said. His mouth curled in a broad grin and he handed Quentin a Heckler & Koch UMP45 and an extra magazine.

'Thanks.'

'Only use it on semi-automatic,' Pentti advised. 'The mags hold only twenty-five rounds, so you won't want to waste them.'

'I won't,' Quentin said, finding it hard to imagine himself firing the weapon at all.

Despite being unaccustomed to what Eero explained were Finnish Army forest skis, Quentin was thankful he had skis of any kind. Before setting out he had walked a few paces from the cabin to relieve himself and found himself floundering through thigh-deep snow. It was, he decided, not his idea of a holiday in a winter wonderland.

After leaving the cabin they headed into the forest with Jukka in the lead, picking an undulating path beneath snow-laden branches and around huge snow-capped boulders. Visibility was so poor that if it were not for the ski tracks in the snow, Quentin would have had difficulty following Pentti. Behind him, Eero glided silently along, content to bring up the rear.

After about thirty minutes they broke out of the forest and onto a snow-covered lake where Eero took over the lead and Jukka dropped to the back. Quentin had no idea of how far they still had to go, but despite the increased exposure to wind and falling snow, he found the flatness of the lake surface preferable to the forest. Back in London his fitness regime didn't include anything other than an occasional game of squash with a friend in the Foreign Office and he found himself acutely aware he was not in particularly good shape.

Out on the ice the snow, packed by the wind, was firmer and the going much easier. They increased their speed and covered more ground in the next ten minutes than they had in the previous thirty.

Eero stopped and pointed towards the forest edge to their left. Pentti and the others skied up alongside him.

'Is that the hut?' Eero asked.

'It has to be,' Pentti said. 'Let's check it out.' He turned to Jukka. 'You stay and cover us in case of trouble.'

Whatever activity there might have been around the hut in the past had been buried beneath subsequent falls of snow. But just to make certain, Eero skied around the hut.

'It's clear,' he announced.

'It's also locked,' Quentin added, indicating the padlock and chain.

'Not for long,' Pentti said and waved to Jukka to join them. 'Who has the can opener?'

Jukka shrugged off his backpack, unzipped it and took out a large bolt-cutter. In seconds he had cut the chain and swung the door open to let Pentti, who had produced a flashlight, in first.

In the centre of the hut were four snowmobiles, and strapped vertically against the walls were a couple of kayaks amidst an assortment of nets, rods and other fishing paraphernalia.

'I should have sent two of you to collect these before we set out; it would have saved that slog through the forest,' Pentti said, shining his light on an almost new Lynx Xtrim Commander.

Quentin felt buoyed by Pentti's description of their trip so far as a slog. 'We could use them on the way back,' he said hopefully.

'It comes under the heading of auto theft in this country,' Pentti said with mock severity. 'Still, that is an excellent idea. Jukka, you're the one who always claims to have misspent your youth. Can these things be started without a key?'

Jukka laughed dryly. 'In a heartbeat. It has electric and rewind starter. Not a problem.' He walked over to the wall and opened a small cupboard. 'Even less of a problem with the spare keys sitting here.'

Quentin shook his head. 'They left the keys? They wouldn't do that back home.'

'Finns are very law-abiding,' Pentti laughed. 'I mean, who would steal a snowmobile?'

'Hopefully us,' Quentin grinned.

'Good point.' Pentti pointed to a sledge and some boxes. 'Have a seat. Ten-minute break and then we move on.'

The others sat, but Pentti continued moving around the hut, examining the snowmobiles in the torchlight.

Eventually Jukka asked, 'What are you looking for?'

'This.' Pentti pointed to some frozen snow just in front of the passenger seat. 'See the dark splotches? That's blood. Russian blood. So, this is where they brought the man I wounded.'

Jukka took the flashlight, squatted down, and examined the splotches. 'I think you're right, which is worrying.'

Pentti nodded in agreement. 'Because that means the museum may well have some of those Russians protecting whatever they are doing there.'

'Charming,' Quentin growled. 'Who would have thought Finland was such an inviting place?'

After they had rested, Pentti gave them a final briefing. 'If the intelligence and the maps are accurate, then there's a ski trail from here to the museum. I estimate it should only take us five or six minutes. But we stop before the trail comes out into the rear car park. We'll get as close as we can using the forest as cover because if we have direct line of sight to the building, then we have to assume they can see us.'

'The weather is on our side,' Eero said, glancing out the door where the wind had increased and the snow was not so much falling as blowing horizontally.

'Let's pray it holds,' Pentti said. 'I'm not certain about thermal sensing, but let's assume they have it.'

'It's fucking useless in this weather,' Jukka said. 'You could run a moose up to their front door and it would hardly make an impression. Especially if it's covered in snow.'

'Let's hope so,' Pentti said. 'Now, when we get there we find a safe location to use as our rendezvous point if we run into trouble and get split up. Eero...'

'Yes?'

'When I give you the signal, I want you to do a circuit of the building looking for possible entry points and also any visible security.'

'Yes, sir.'

'If we find a way in, then Jukka, Eero, you stay outside while Quentin and I go chat with Remsu.'

'Surely it's better if one of us goes with you,' Jukka protested and then turned quickly to Grammaticus. 'No offence, sir.'

'None taken,' Quentin grunted.

'No,' Pentti said firmly. 'If this were a military installation then we wouldn't be doing this. We'd simply call in the Beagle Boys or the Karelia Brigade and overrun the place. But given the political sensitivities, I would rather approach Remsu on a more pragmatic and diplomatic level.'

Quentin held his hand up to attract attention. 'Excuse me for butting in, but are you suggesting that just you and I go in?'

'Exactly. You're a representative of Her Majesty's British Government. It adds a certain cachet.'

'And unarmed?' Quentin asked.

'Unarmed.'

Jukka was still concerned. 'Sir, with all due respect, Eero or I should come with you. Only one of us needs to remain outside.'

Pentti shook his head. 'The answer is no. Now prepare to move out.'

'Resting peacefully.'

'Praise the Lord.'

Their security ritual out of the way, Zaikov dictated the list of code numbers.

'Is that everything?' the man in St Petersburg asked.

'For the time being,' Zaikov replied. 'And at your end?'

'We are confident that spring will come early. It begins on the twenty-eighth, with the rising yellow sun.'

'That has been agreed?'

'Right across the country they are waiting for the news broadcast from Vyborg.'

'It will happen,' Zaikov said emphatically and ended the call, getting out of his chair. He went to the kitchen and took a bottle of vodka from the freezer. He deserved a drink, he decided. He filled a shot glass and raised it in a silent toast to Cal and his team of hackers.

Over the months they had laboured away and each task they completed became part of Zaikov's treasure trove of code numbers. Each code number represented a step towards the victory that those in Moscow dreamed of. No, he corrected the thought; each number was, in itself, a victory already won.

The computer systems of the strategic bases, the radar sites and command posts that the numbers represented had all been hacked and now contained a cyber bomb that lay dormant and would, at the designated time, be triggered, crash the system and render the facility inoperable. And if that did not create enough disruption, the second wave of attacks would be more public. The major government, banking and transport websites were poised to be brought down simultaneously by a number of different methods from massive DDOS – Distributed Denial of Service – attacks to DNS spoofing or DNS poisoning, that would send their links to a single homepage – that of the new regime. It had taken almost two years of preparation but now he was confident that the cyber-attack would be devastating.

On the other hand, the 'rising yellow sun' was brilliant in its non-technological simplicity. In the first few hours of the uprising, there were concerns about how to identify troops supporting regime change and those still loyal to the President. The answer was as basic as it would be effective: single yellow armbands.

But the aspect of the entire affair that gave him most pleasure was the reference to 'the news from Vyborg'. In just eight days' time, on the twenty-eighth of February, the signal that would trigger subsequent events would be a live television broadcast. He poured himself another glass. Now, he mused, all he had to do was keep everything on track.

The fever took her again and she floated, hovering between the two opposing worlds. Between summer and winter. Fragments of summer filtered, golden, lay like a thin filling in winter's ice cold, snow-white wedding cake. She remembered summer back then, her back against warm Helsinki bricks, her eyes closed, savouring the taste of summer with its long Bulevardi nights and beer. And nights that didn't truly come but flowed from summer day to summer day with the after-midnight sunset-sunrise shadows washed clean and free with laughter and with vodka.

I should have saved those summers, she thought, caught their shadows, pressed them between the pages of my books and sheltered them from the wind that whispered winter.

But the book with all its wondrous poems was lost, its pages torn and blown like the leaves of autumn, soaked with rain, limpid, shapeless, the words washed away, dripping from the pages like inky tears. Years ago, it was. And yet… and yet she remembered the words. 'I am driven by my longing… *Sanat suussani sulavat, puhe'et putoelevat, kielelleni kerkiävät, hampahilleni hajoovat.* 'I remember the words unfreezing in my mouth and tumbling from my tongue. I was happy then, back then, in summer. And even in the pause of autumn, with its turned collars, kicked leaves and rain, she remembered smiles that, like the tumbling words, she had let flutter to the rain-slicked cobbles at his feet. Kullervo too, she remembered, back then so young, so full of words and poems and love. She searched memory for this love but saw only a china doll in shattered fragments on the floor. The image fades to black. It's gone. No wedding cake, no china bride, just another morning curtained away behind autumn clouds, waiting for the time when it will freeze.

Kullervo. She struggles to recall his face, his voice, and the smell of him in a bed that was far too small. Kullervo faded to black. The terror of his absence causes her to scream and in a brief moment of lucidity, she surfaces. Sees a face.

'Who are you?'

'Nicole, remember?'

She shuts her eyes. Kullervo is holding her. It is late autumn now. *Veli kulta, veikkoseni, kaunis kasvinkumppalini!*[4] She sees back then. Sees them rise, satiated, from the bed. Scrambling into

---

4   *Dearest friend, and much-loved brother,*
    Best beloved of all companions

clothes. They rise amidst the fall of leaves and snow and wind-creaked, rusted, summer hinges. *Lähe nyt kanssa laulamahan, saa kera sanelemahan yhtehen yhyttyämme, kahta'alta käytyämme!*[5] Rugged up with scarves and gloves and love, they feast on cold marble tables, cracked beneath the weight of waiting for each other. They walk, in country mud and orchards, in railway halls and market squares. Vodka drunk against the wind,behind Helsinki's Turkish tombs, they dance old dreams to sleep. Until they falter, out of step and breath and words, beneath the last birch branch with leaves in some neglected, bare and windswept park. *Harvoin yhtehen yhymme, saamme toinen toisihimme näillä raukoilla rajoilla, poloisilla Pohjan mailla.*[6]

'Auli, you must wake up!' the strange woman commands. 'There is something happening.'

Fever rolls like a wave.

'I am awake,' she says to ghosts from years before.

'They're waiting for us. Auli, please...'

'Winter is always waiting,' she says out loud. She knows this now and realises that she knew it way back then, in summer, when they first shook hands. She saw the future with its long snow ridges, frost and ice, and an island cottage on a lake with wind and hoods and fur and Kullervo. She saw the two of them in winter, frozen to each other, staying till the last, for warmth and not for friendship, for body heat and not for love.

'Make an effort, Auli. Please, you have to wake up.'

'They have the Sampo,' she says, her voice suddenly crisp. Then gone again, tumbling into the cold and dark where, out on the frozen lake, she sees herself, a brittle frosted china bride, her pieces

---

5   *Come and let us sing together,*
    Let us now begin our converse,
    Since at length we meet together,
    From two widely sundered regions.

6   *Rarely can we meet together,*
    Rarely one can meet the other,
    In these dismal Northern regions,
    In the dreary land of Pohja.

glued together, spinning slowly on this vast white wedding cake.

'Oh, for christsake!' Nicole says and slaps her.

They stopped just back from the edge of the forest. Unfortunately, the wind had dropped and only light snow was falling. Unless the weather changed again they would be without the cover of a heavy snowfall. However, as long as they remained in the forest they were safe from observation and had a clear view of their target.

Ahead of them, in a clearing, the museum lay like a squat black shadow surrounded by snow. Pentti stood for a moment watching, looking for signs of movement. He saw none. There were two floors; the bottom one was windowless and looked as though its massive black granite walls had grown from the ground, while above it, the second storey was a modernist fantasy, all angles, glass and huge metal beams. There were only a few lights on, but the impression that it was deserted was belied by the presence in the car park of a dozen cars and a large personnel transport van. All the vehicles were covered in a layer of snow and had obviously been there for several days. There were no fresh tracks that he could see.

Pentti signalled to Eero to begin his circuit of the building and then gestured to Jukka and Quentin to come to him.

'Damn bad timing; the place is shut,' Quentin joked, as he skied up alongside.

Pentti pointed to the cars. 'Given the number of cars, I would guess that there are more people inside than just a caretaker.'

Jukka nodded and did a quick calculation. 'The van can carry sixteen or seventeen and if we count four people per car, then we are looking at possibly fifty people.'

'A hell of a lot of people for a nightshift in a mere museum,' Quentin observed quietly.

'If only it were,' Pentti replied. 'But the numbers don't matter. What matters is that we get to Remsu, preferably without harming anyone.' He raised his TRG-42, adjusted the sights and panned slowly along the building.

317

'Four cameras. I would guess their fields of vision are intersecting, as the individual cameras appear to be static,' he reported. 'They look pretty standard, so are probably not equipped with thermal imaging.'

'No blind spots?' Jukka asked.

'Yes, and it's perfect.' Pentti lowered the rifle. 'The usual mistake.'

Quentin peered at the building, but although he could make out a couple of the cameras, he couldn't figure out what Pentti meant. 'What blind spot?'

'Directly beneath them, pressed against the wall of the building, none of the cameras would see you.'

'But getting to the wall...'

'Ah, that's the trick.' Pentti laughed.

Quentin was not convinced. 'But if we are going in unarmed and if, as you keep saying, you don't want casualties, why don't we bowl up to the front door and ring the bell?'

'The element of surprise gives us a psychological advantage. And I like surprises, as long as I'm the one delivering them.'

'*We* are the ones,' Quentin corrected, 'and as long as the response to our surprise doesn't come in the form of a bullet.'

'Interesting building,' Eero said, materialising by their side.

He's good, Quentin thought. He hadn't seen or heard the man returning.

'And?' Pentti asked.

'Static bullet cameras back and sides. I estimate by the spacing that each has a visual arc of about thirty-five degrees and blind spots beneath.'

'That's what we figured,' Pentti interrupted. 'Sorry, go on.'

'The front's a different story,' Eero continued. 'There are four high-end Mirasys video cameras controlling the perimeter in the front of the building and two in the car park looking back to the entrance. The car park ones scan one hundred and eighty degrees every fifty or sixty seconds. The steps up to the building fan out to about twelve metres at the base to five or so at the top. Seven steps. The doors are massive plate glass sheets and look like they are equipped with motion sensors that may well double as alarms.

Anyway, given the video surveillance, the front door is not visitor-friendly. Well, at least to our type of visitor.'

'Other entrances?'

'There's what looks like a regulation fire door to the left of the front steps. But it's sheet steel and would make gaining entry a very noisy affair.' He paused and pointed to their left. 'But opposite the end of the car park is a service entry beside two industrial size Gasum LNG tanks. It appears to be a double door and we could probably get in without waking the neighbours.'

'Gas tanks?'

'Yes, two of them.'

Pentti looked up at the weather and then at the building. 'If we were behind the tanks, would we be visible?'

Eero thought for a moment and then shook his head. 'No. We have to get there, but once beside the tanks we should be fine.'

'Then let's relocate,' Pentti said, and shouldering his rifle, signalled the others to follow.

From the forest edge to the LNG storage tanks, Pentti estimated was about twenty metres. He checked the weather again but there was little of the deterioration he had hoped for. If anything, the wind had dropped away and there was little hope the lightly falling snow would provide any worthwhile cover. 'Jukka, you first,' he said quietly. 'Take it nice and slow.'

Jukka nodded, took off his skis, pulled up his hood and after adjusting his pack, dropped down into the snow and began to inch his way forward. As he left the shelter of the trees he went flat on his stomach and burrowed as deeply as he could before sliding forward.

Every metre or so he stopped and lay still for thirty seconds. For Quentin it was like watching a man doing slow-motion breaststroke in the snow. Obviously it was a well-practised skill, and he thought bleakly, one I will be expected to emulate.

It took Jukka ten minutes to cover the distance. Once safely beside the gas cylinders, he signalled for the next man to follow.

'I'll go, then Quentin. Eero, stay in the trees and cover the exit after we go in.'

'Left out in the cold again,' Eero shrugged in mock indignation. Then he smiled. 'No problem, just bring me a hot chocolate if you find the canteen open.'

'You have my word.' Pentti sank down into the snow. 'Quentin, wait for my signal then do exactly as I do. There's no rush, and if you take your time we won't set off any sensors.'

'Understood,' Quentin said.

'You can leave your weapon with Eero, we won't be needing it on the way in.'

Pentti, staying in the track that Jukka had forced through the snow, crossed the open ground without a problem and on his signal, Quentin set out after him. To his surprise it was relatively easy, as the loose snow was now packed firm by the weight of the two men who had preceded him. For a moment, as he lay still, the image of his office back in London flashed into his mind. It seemed a long time ago and very far away. He had always loved the comfort and the status, but here, lying in the snow, God knows where in Finland, he felt a sudden sense of aliveness he hadn't experienced in a very long time. Time to move again, he told himself and started again to worm his way forward.

As he crawled in beside one of the tanks, Pentti grabbed Quentin's shoulder and assisted him to his feet.

'Well done,' he said, 'but we have a slight problem.'

'Which is?'

'Come and look.' He turned and stepped over the pipes leading from the gas tanks to the building. A few metres further on he stopped beside the door. 'See? No external opening device and the door looks like thick steel.'

Quentin nodded and turned his attention back to the tanks. 'I don't suppose you would be interested in the British way of doing things?'

There was something in his tone that caused Pentti to think he was toying with him. 'Come on, then. What's your solution?'

'*Aut viam inveniam aut faciam.* In other words, if there is not a way, invent one.' Quentin glanced at Pentti and Jukka who were staring at him with blank expressions. 'Listen,' he continued. 'If we can't get in to them then we have to get them to come out to us. The beauty of that is that in order to do so they will have to open the door.'

Pentti frowned. 'Are you seriously suggesting we knock?'

Quentin shook his head. 'Only metaphorically. I think you'll find that if we turn off the gas supply, they will have to come out to investigate.'

Jukka shook his head. 'Surely you need a key or an industrial size wrench in order to do that?'

'No, Quentin is right.' Pentti turned his attention to where the two gas cylinders fed into a single pipe. Above it, encrusted in ice and covered in fresh snow, were several pressure dials. They were not what he needed. 'There must be an emergency shut-down lever.' He took a step back and looked along the wall. 'The lever there, behind you, Jukka. What does it say?'

Jukka edged along the wall and peered at the small sign. *Hätäpysäytyspainike.* Emergency stop switch.

Pentti turned back to Quentin and clapped him on the back. 'Thank you. I can see this inter-service cooperation is paying off already. Okay, Jukka, when I give you a wave, switch the thing off and get in behind the tanks. We'll take the other side of the door and go down in the snow. If we get a chance, we'll just slip in. If not, then we'll need to disable whoever comes out. And for God's sake, if they come out with weapons, don't fire. Particularly near the gas tanks.'

Jukka grinned. 'You're no fun.'

'Exploding gas tanks are not our thing, okay? Now, brush some snow over our footprints and take cover.'

Once they were in position Pentti signalled to Jukka to turn the emergency lever then he ducked down in the snow beside Quentin. 'I've no idea what happens when you turn that off, but obviously anything using gas will stop working, and there may also be an alarm triggered by a drop in pressure.'

'Hopefully they'll send out a maintenance man and not a bunch of armed security guards,' Quentin said, suddenly wishing he had a weapon again. 'Anyway, my training has been more on the theoretical side of things, so I'll just follow your lead.'

'Fine. If I say move, don't hesitate and stick close behind me.'

They fell silent and waited.

Five minutes went by and Pentti was beginning to think that they needed another strategy. Around them the snow was falling again, although only lightly, and the wind had not picked up. He was about to get to his feet when he heard the noise of a bolt being slid back and light spilled out onto the snow as the door swung inwards. The two men who appeared were armed with nothing more than a torch and they didn't even bother to look around but went directly to the gas tanks and began scraping away at the frost and snow, in order to examine the pressure dials.

Pentti nudged Quentin and got to his feet. Sticking close to the wall, they edged their way towards the door and with the two maintenance men out of sight between the tanks, were able to slip into the building undetected.

The entrance lobby was deserted and they could see no sign of a security camera. Ahead of them was a corridor that went straight ahead to a set of swing doors and what presumably was the museum proper. On one side of the corridor was a storeroom and on the other a maintenance workshop. The storeroom was in darkness, but a light inside the workshop revealed a table scattered with dominoes. Pentti paused and glanced at a small TV next to the table, but it wasn't a video security display. Not unless there were several naked men and women nearby being observed having sex in a sauna.

'Whatever gets you through the night,' Quentin murmured.

'Quickly,' Pentti hissed. 'We have to find the stairs.'

They moved rapidly down the corridor, through the doors and found themselves at the rear of a massive marble floored entrance foyer. To their right was an elevator and to the left a sweep of broad wooden stairs leading to the top floor. The entire place was in darkness with the only illumination being emergency exit signs on the huge glass doors at the other side of the space.

'A camera,' Quentin said quietly, '… and another. Both bullet-style, on either side of the front door.'

'But not moving and not focused in this direction,' Quentin observed.

'Yes, but look up above the doors. That's a dome camera and there's no way of knowing where it's focused.' Pentti didn't hesitate. 'We can't afford to hang around if the maintenance men decide they have a security situation. We'll have a look around upstairs but stay in the shadows directly behind me.' He made for the stairs without waiting for an answer.

The top section of the museum was open-plan and at a glance they could see that it was deserted. There were, however, dome cameras at either end of the space. Fortunately, there were several rows of glass cabinets at right angles to the cameras which provided some protection, so they dropped to the floor beneath the closest ones.

They had no idea if they had been seen but after five minutes went by without any sign of a guard investigating, Pentti relaxed and glanced around at the display cases. 'Old wooden skis, some wooden drinking mugs, snowshoes, sauna buckets and other bits and pieces. It looks like this is the section for ancient Karelian history,' Pentti said quietly.

'That one's not so ancient,' Quentin said, pointing to a series of images in a glass case. 'Photographs of people being hung and shot.'

Pentti squinted at the exhibit and read the large caption above the photographs. '*Genocide in Soviet Karelia: nineteen thirty-seven and nineteen thirty-eight.*'

'Another gap in my history education,' Quentin said.

'Another bit of Stalin's madness.'

They lapsed into silence for a moment and then, after checking his watch, Pentti signalled that they were going to move. 'There's nothing up here. At least, nothing we need. There are cars outside, so the people must be somewhere.'

'Maybe a basement?'

'Possible,' Pentti conceded, but didn't sound convinced.

Returning to the ground floor, they skirted around the rear wall of the entrance hall, discovered an office, the canteen, toilets and exhibits that focused on the history of the evacuations after the Winter War and the Continuation War. But the nearest thing to other human beings were a couple of life-size models of Finnish soldiers crouched in a mock-up of a trench.

'There is the elevator,' Quentin said as they completed their circuit and stood pressed against the wall beside the double doors through which they had first entered. 'Or we could go watch the porn film with the maintenance men.'

Pentti frowned but realised that the Englishman was right. If part of the complex lay underground, and there were no stairs, then the elevator was their only option, 'Shit! We may as well have rung the front door bell.' He heaved a sigh and crossed the doors to the elevator. 'Okay, let's try.'

Quentin looked at the elevator's single button and swore quietly. 'Fuck! It only goes up.'

'It can't do,' Pentti said impatiently, and pressed the button.

It was at that point that he realised that any notion he had had of having the psychological advantage of surprise vanished. The door opened with a loud bell chime and the light from the elevator spilled out like a floodlight, illuminating the entire foyer.

'No point in hanging about,' he said and pushed Quentin into the lift in front of him.

Inside there were two buttons, the top one of which had a sign indicating it was for opening or closing the doors. The second button was apparently for starting the lift moving. Pentti pressed for the doors to close and as they did a green arrow on the bottom button offered them the option of going up.

'It makes no sense!' Pentti said.

'I think we should follow the instructions,' Quentin nodded in the direction of the elevator's rear wall. A small, framed notice, the top of which was fixed to the wall by a single large screw, had what he took to be detailed safety instructions in Swedish, Finnish and Russian and, in bold type, a telephone number to ring in emergencies.

'There's no mention of going down,' Pentti growled.

'No, but I suggest you look more closely.' He pointed to the wall beside the frame where several handprints had smeared the otherwise highly polished metal. 'Why would someone rest their hand there if not to do this…?' He pushed the frame and it pivoted on the single screw. Behind it was an unmarked, black button.

Pentti looked at him with admiration. 'How the fuck did you notice that?'

'*Minima maxima sunt;* the smallest things are most important.'

Pentti shook his head in disbelief. 'You know, that is exactly what Nicole Parry keeps telling me.'

'Must be true,' Quentin laughed nervously. 'So, are you going to press it or not?'

Pentti nodded, pressed the button and the elevator began to descend slowly and in almost complete silence until, after about ten seconds, it came to a stop. Both men braced themselves, unsure of what awaited them. The doors opened and they found themselves facing a tall, thickset man. Behind him stood two uniformed guards cradling sub-machine guns.

The man's face broke into a broad smile. 'Welcome to Kalevala House.' He stood examining their faces for a moment. 'You must be Toivonen and your companion is Mister Grammaticus from MI6. Gentlemen, I do wish you had let me know you were coming. The museum is so much more interesting with the lights on.'

Pentti and Quentin stepped out of the lift and the door shut silently behind them.

'Remsu, we've come to have a private discussion, nothing more. There's no need to have your goons here, so let's get rid of them and their weapons.' Pentti said.

Cal Remsu looked at him as if he had said something incomprehensible. 'I'm sorry. I'm not certain you understand your position. You have just intruded and are lucky you weren't shot.' He paused and the smile returned. 'But let's not quibble. Please, follow me. We have lots to discuss, and I'm sure you could use a drink.' He turned and began to walk away, expecting them to follow. Then he stopped and turned. 'By the way, my congratulations on finding the elevator button. You know, you're the first to do so. After we make ourselves comfortable, you must tell me how you did it.'

Chapter Nineteen

The meeting had taken place in what was probably the most secure location in the Parliament – the sauna. At the end of their discussions the Prime Minister leaned over and said quietly, 'This meeting never took place.' Then he turned to the other men. 'Gentleman, I think we have sweated long enough. Can I offer you a beer?'

Heimo Harkimo showered and dressed with the others, but declined the offer of beer. What lay ahead looked like being a long night and one for which a clear head was an absolute necessity.

His instructions were clear, but he had voiced serious concerns about the plausibility of what he now needed to explain to others. Things would have been much easier if he could precede his remarks with the phrase 'I have been instructed by the Finnish President and the Prime Minister to inform you…' That was not going to happen. The meeting had not taken place.

His instructions to not contact the Americans seemed like lunacy. Surely, if anyone could play a constructive role in defusing the situation it was the Americans? Apparently not. For he had been told firmly that under no circumstances was he to inform the Americans of anything.

His first call would have to be to the British. Okay, he told himself, let's get that done because everything else depends on their response. They would probably think him insane, he thought gloomily. He checked the time. It was eight twenty in the evening, London time. He picked up the secure phone, gave the numbers that the security protocols demanded and waited.

'Good evening, Mister Harkimo, I am informed you had an interesting sauna,' the woman said. 'I've been awaiting your call.'

So much for a meeting that never took place, Heimo thought. Someone had already contacted MI6.

'Thank you, Ma'am, and my apologies for the lateness of the hour.'

To his surprise he heard the woman laugh.

'Mister Harkimo, unfortunately our adversaries do not observe regular office hours, so neither, I suspect, do you or I.'

'True, Ma'am,' he replied and then, deciding that there was no point in procrastinating, plunged in and disclosed the main points of the sauna meeting.

When he had finished there was a pause before C responded.

'I appreciate your openness. As to your proposed course of action, I will need to discuss this with certain parties. May I get back to you in an hour, two at the latest?'

'That would be most helpful,' Heimo said.

'One other thing…'

'Yes Ma'am?'

'I am interested in the status of the British policewoman. I have been led to believe she has caused certain difficulties.'

Heimo didn't hesitate. 'Then let me assure you, with all due respect, your information is incorrect.'

'Really? I must say I am surprised by that.'

'On the contrary, I can say that without the woman's remarkable tenacity and professionalism, we would probably not have discovered the predicament we find ourselves in until far too late. It is thanks to this young woman we have a slim possibility of averting what could be a disaster,' he said, then added, 'a disaster for all of us.'

'Thank you, Mister Harkimo. I am grateful for the clarification about Detective Inspector Parry and will make sure suitable appreciation is shown when she returns.'

Heimo laughed. 'That is assuming we let her return – she is something of a valuable asset.'

'We will talk later, Mister Harkimo.'

And that, Heimo thought, was the easy part. The next call would be far more difficult and he held out little hope of even getting the call accepted, let alone convincing anyone that what he proposed was serious.

Cal Remsu stood with his hands on the back of the chair, and despite what should have been a tense situation, he appeared to be totally relaxed, even nonchalant. He had taken them through the corridors to the small lounge area and offered them a seat as if they were invited guests. The only sour note was the presence of two security guards who stationed themselves at the door cradling their weapons.

'I can't imagine what you thought you would achieve by breaking in here,' Cal said. 'But let's put that aside and relax. I'll organise a drink in a moment or two.'

Pentti, annoyed at the man's arrogance, was in no mood for small talk. 'I want to see Miss Saarinen and Detective Inspector Parry.'

Cal raised his eyebrows. 'And what makes you think they are here?'

'Because I am not a fool, Remsu. They were in the cottage on Pikkususisaari and when I returned to look for them I was attacked by some of your men. They escaped on a snowmobile. I have just seen the same snowmobile in the shed beside the lake.'

'You apparently wounded one of the men,' Cal said. 'That was unfriendly.'

'Let's drop the games. Kidnapping is a very serious –'

'Kidnapping?' Cal laughed. 'Believe me, you would end up looking like more of a fool than you are. They both came along voluntarily.'

'Then you won't mind me seeing them?'

'Auli Saarinen is unwell, and the British woman has been looking after her.'

Quentin sat forward in his chair. 'Listen, Mister Remsu, I am a representative of Her Majesty's Government in Great Britain and I demand to see Miss Parry.'

'You demand nothing!' Cal snapped. 'However, I shall let you see her.' He got to his feet and walked to the end of the room, where he took out his phone, punched in a number and had a brief conversation. 'Auli is asleep, but Nicole Parry will come along,' he said as he turned back.

'What is it you do here?' Pentti asked.

'I manage the museum.'

'And the money that has been flooding in?'

Cal sat and studied Pentti for a moment. 'So, it's the money.' He sounded disappointed. 'Why is it that people like you are always concerned about the money and never about the principles?'

'What principle would that be, Mister Remsu?' Quentin asked.

'Freedom, and self-determination.'

'For whom?' Pentti asked, even though he knew where the conversation was headed.

'For Karelia, for me, for my parents and hundreds of thousands like them.' He stood again, agitated, the anger spilling out of him. 'The treaty of Moscow after the Winter War and the Paris Treaty after the Continuation War were treaties of betrayal. We lost more in those treaties than we ever did in the wars. And since that time no Finnish Government has had the guts to stand up to the Russians and to hold them accountable for war crimes against civilians. My father watched his brother being shot. He saw his house and barn burn. He lingered for years after the war and eventually died of his wounds. My mother witnessed her family being shot and it destroyed her. After my father's death she hung herself. And I? I am an exile too. I found a home in Canada because nobody in Finland cared. But that has changed and, in the end, it is up to people to take the case of Karelia's freedom into our own hands.'

'Remsu, it's a dream. Nobody can turn back the pages of history, no matter what wrongs or injustices were done.'

To Pentti's surprise the man laughed.

'We are about to make that dream a reality.'

'You think?' Quentin scoffed.

'Not just think, Mister MI6. I know. We have spent years preparing and even if you wiped this place from the face of the earth, and me with it, there is nothing you can do now to stop events unfolding.'

'Stop what exactly?' Pentti asked.

But Cal had turned away as a young woman appeared at the door. He beckoned her in. 'Hillevi, we would like some coffee…' he paused and peered at Quentin, 'or would you prefer tea?'

Quentin, unsure if having a cosy chat over a cup of tea was the right way to go, glanced at Pentti, who shrugged and nodded. 'Tea, thank you,' Quentin said.

'Fetch my laptop, Hillevi, and then get the English woman to help you as I am sure she knows how to make tea the way our distinguished English guest likes. What about you, Toivonen? Coffee?'

'Yes,' Pentti said, then paused until the young women had departed before repeating his question. 'What exactly are we unable to stop, Remsu?'

'On February twenty-eighth the Russian President will be part of the Kalevala Day celebrations in Viipuri –'

'Vyborg,' Pentti interjected, 'It's called Vyborg these days.'

Unfazed, Cal continued, 'He is taking part in a relay race and then inaugurating a statue. The statue was a gift from us.'

'The forging of the Sampo, by Anja Kujola,' Pentti said.

'Exactly,' Cal beamed. 'I am glad you have been doing your homework.'

'The statue you told her was stolen.'

Cal shrugged. 'Unfortunately, Miss Kujola does not share our spirit of friendship with our Russian neighbours and would not have approved. Neither did Miss Saarinen, who became aware of the statue's role in precipitating future events.' He smiled. 'Sadly, she became very ill and now can't remember what she learned.'

'Let me take a wild guess,' Quentin said laconically. 'You plan to kill the President with an explosive inside the statue?'

'You British were always such clever spies. Yes, he slots in the hammer and the fun begins.' Cal said, and then glanced at the door. 'Ah! Refreshments have arrived.'

The young woman stepped aside to let Nicole enter carrying a tray of drinks, before crossing to Cal and handing him a laptop. He took it from her, opened it and turned it on. 'Thank you.' He dismissed the girl with a wave.

As Nicole placed the tray on the coffee table, she glanced up at Pentti and smiled. 'Hello, Mister Toivonen,' she said casually, as if there was nothing unusual in the circumstances.

Pentti found it hard to match her tone and failed completely at hiding the sparkle in his eyes. 'Miss Parry.' He gestured to Grammaticus. 'I'm not sure you two have met. Quentin Grammaticus, Nicole Parry.'

'I am something of an admirer of your work,' Quentin said and rose to shake her hand.

'Very kind,' she murmured demurely. 'And now, I'll play mother. The tea is for you, I would imagine.'

'Thank you.'

'And the rest of us having coffee?' She didn't wait for a reply, and taking the coffee pot, poured three cups and handed them around. 'This looks very cosy. So, what have you all been chatting about?'

'Take a seat,' Cal said. 'I was just telling them about our Kalevala Day surprise for the Russians.'

'A bold plan to blow up the Russian President, apparently,' Quentin said lightly, as though discussing the weather. Then added, 'By the way, thanks for the tea. Very nice.'

'Pleasure,' Nicole said. 'And did he tell you about bringing the internet in Russia down at the same time?'

'Most ambitious,' Quentin grinned.

'Not too difficult for a nation that brought the world Angry Birds,' Cal said.

'Angry birds? I'm afraid you've lost me.'

'It's a computer game,' Pentti explained.

'Right. Alas, not my forte,' Quentin said. 'But I am sure it is very clever.'

Pentti sipped his coffee and then put the cup back on the tray. 'Remsu, I don't understand why you are telling us all this. I can have you arrested and charged with enough offences to put you in prison for the rest of your life.'

To his surprise, Cal was nonplussed.

'Of course, you could. But here is the thing. You won't.'

'And why not?'

Cal took a small memory stick from his pocket and plugged it into the computer. 'Because of this.' He leaned over, pushed the tray to one side and put the computer on the coffee table. 'What you are about to see has been sent to major news organisations, governments, and social media sites on the internet. At present it is heavily encrypted and nobody can access it. If I don't log in every few hours and refresh it, the encryption key will be distributed. Trust me, you will not want that to happen. Watch.'

He pressed enter and then sat back in his chair, studying their faces with a smug grin.

The screen showed first a satellite image and then cross-faded into a map of Finland and Southern Russia. The title scrolled down the screen: *Seeking Regime Change in Russia*. After a moment the voice-over began. It was in English with Russian and French subtitles.

While the world watched the attempts of brave Russians to bring the country back to the people, out of the hands of the mafias and oligarchs, few people realised that this was not simply a people's movement. Behind the scenes other forces were at work. Key players were the American CIA, Great Britain's MI6 and the members of the British police force and SUPO, the Finnish Secret Security Agency, all of whom were working to effect regime change in Russia.

As each organisation was named, their logos were shown on the screen.

With the assistance, encouragement and backing of these organisations, billions of dollars were illegally siphoned from banks and into the hands of those planning the coup. But it is not just siphoning of money to be used for weapons and explosives that is as abhorrent as it is shocking, it is their active engagement in a plot to assassinate a head of state: the President of Russia.

The President's face was shown on the screen for just a moment before the scene cross-faded to London's Thames Embankment. Quentin squirmed, sensing what was coming and knowing with certainty how his career would be swiftly curtailed if the images were ever made public.

Who were these shadowy figures behind the plot? It can now be revealed that a senior British MI6 officer, Quentin Grammaticus, was a key player. He is seen here meeting with a man identified as a Russian agent. He is also captured on security camera footage at a sleazy club in London. The man he is seen talking with here is CIA Agent Samuel Gordon, another key player in the plot.

The footage in the Indigo Bar and that on the Embankment clearly identified Sam and Quentin. Zaikov had been more fortunate in having his back to the unknown photographer.

As time for the Russian coup came closer, so confident were the people involved that they were seen openly meeting in the Finnish capital, Helsinki...

The series of still photographs that followed showed Pentti and Quentin coming out of the SUPO building. Sam Gordon was captured on security camera footage in the foyer of the Hotel Kämp. The scene dissolved and still photographs showed Pentti and Nicole escorting Chris Mitchell out of Kaija's apartment.

Another person involved has been identified as a serving English policewoman, Detective Inspector Parry, seen here with a Finnish Secret Service agent Pentti Toivonen, escorting another MI6 officer, Christopher Mitchell, from an apartment in Helsinki. Only a matter of hours later he was found dead from a single, execution-style shot to the head.

Again the scene changed, this time to Punkaharju.

Toivonen and Parry were also filmed entering a hotel in rural Finland, in close proximity to the Russian border. According to the hotel records they booked into a single room under false names and claiming to be a married couple, Tapani and Angela Koskinen. Several observers described their behaviour as 'drunken'.

Cal, who suddenly appeared tired or bored, leaned over, shut the laptop and removed the memory stick. 'There's more like that, much more. But I'm sure you agree TV stations would kill to break a story like this. And we have ensured it will go viral on Vimeo and YouTube.' He tossed the memory stick to Pentti. 'I suggest you show this to your friends in high places.' He yawned, sat back with a smile and drained the last of his coffee.

For his part, Pentti felt sick to the stomach, knowing that the impact of such a story being made public would be disastrous – a political and diplomatic tsunami that would not simply wash away careers, but probably governments as well. He glanced at Quentin who, pale and stony-faced, was staring at his hands. He turned to Nicole, who for some inexplicable reason was smiling.

'Well?' he asked quietly.

'I think Mister Remsu and his small documentary make a good case for remaining quiet.'

Pentti, perplexed by her apparent acquiescence, shook his head. 'You're a nasty piece of work, Remsu,' he said.

Cal yawned again. 'I have been called worse. Now, I think you should be on your way.'

'Not without Auli,' Nicole said.

'She is of no account now and I have neither the time nor inclination to keep looking after her.' He signalled for his security guards to step aside. 'You can trust me. Keep out of my way and my little video will never be seen.'

Pentti got to his feet and gestured for the others to follow. 'Where's Auli?'

'I asked Hillevi to get her ready,' Nicole said. 'She's not very well. I think she'll recover but I'd like to get her to a doctor, just to make sure.'

'Hillevi?' Quentin asked.

'The young woman who came in with me,' Nicole explained.

'Excuse me if I don't show you out. I am sure you know the way,' Cal said. He stretched back in his chair and shut his eyes. He looked exhausted.

Pentti looked at him and turned to Nicole. He was about to speak, but she held a finger to her lips. 'Later,' she said quietly. 'Once we are out of here.'

Pentti took one look at Auli and realised that there was no way they were going to be taking her with them. She was in the grip of a fever and the words that came from her over and over, rasped from her throat. He leaned closer, trying to catch what she was saying.

'No surprises,' Pentti muttered and turned away from the bedside.

Nicole, distressed at the condition the woman was in, shouldered past him. 'What?'

'No surprises,' he repeated. 'It's stuff from Kalevala.'

Nicole turned on him angrily. 'You don't get it, do you? It may be the same old same old, but each time she has recited something from the Kalevala it has meant something. It's all she has left when she's in this condition.'

Pentti shrugged. 'Okay.'

'So what's she saying?'

Pentti, realising Nicole was right, smiled and returned to the bedside.

'She's asking *Jumala*, the old God, to grant her good luck so that she can die with honour in Finland's sweet land and in beautiful Karelia. I can't understand everything because she's mumbling and it's old Finnish, but it is something about guarding her from the whims of men and the crooked words of old hags and protection against water spirits.'

'And that's all in the Kalevala? Christ, it's one weird poem.'

'We can't take her outside in her condition,' Pentti said. 'What she really needs is a hospital.'

Nicole knew he was right. She leaned over and squeezed Auli's hand. 'Get better,' she whispered.

Auli moaned and they watched for a moment as trembling wracked her whole body.

'Poor woman,' Pentti said and turned towards the door. 'Come. We sort out this mess and then we'll find a way of helping her.'

As they were heading down the corridor to the service exit Pentti asked the question that had been nagging at him. 'What the hell was wrong with Remsu? He was just too relaxed, and in the end he looked as if he was going to fall asleep in the chair.'

'Some of his own medicine,' Nicole grinned. 'I put some of the pills he had been giving Auli in his coffee.'

Pentti thought it a bad idea and did nothing to hide his disapproval. 'Why on earth did you do that?'

'Because I could,' Nicole said, surprised by his anger.

'If he hadn't decided to let us go, we still would have had to deal with him and the guards. And what if you have poisoned

336

him? Remember what he said about logging on every few hours to stop the video being released.'

'Pentti. The man pisses me off, okay? And he treated Auli like shit!'

Pentti was far from convinced. 'Jesus, Nicole! There are far more important things at stake than settling a score for the sisterhood.'

'Oh, fuck off!' she snapped and strode ahead to walk with Grammaticus.

The Avangard stadium in Vyborg didn't appear to have changed much since it was first built back in the nineteen thirties. Zaikov glanced at the old photograph and then up at the reality in front of him. Like an oval racetrack around a sports field, he supposed, though it was hard to visualise with the entire place buried under snow. The snowploughs would take care of that before Kalevala Day. To his right was the grandstand for the dignitaries. The non-covered seating area, for those deemed to be of less importance, was on the other side of the ground and according to the information he had were simple concrete steps. There was no sign of them, as they still had to be cleared of a lot of snow. He shivered, handed the photo back to his aide and plunged his hands into his pockets. It was miserably cold and a mist and light snow obscured what he had come to inspect, the statue at the far end of the sports ground.

'The statue is already in place on the embankment just in front of the trees at the northern end, sir,' the aide said, and anticipating that Zaikov would not want to walk across the snow, opened the car door. Zaikov nodded curtly and got in.

It was little more than a football field, he thought, but it would serve the purpose. The grandstand probably seated several thousand. The car parks were at the southern end and the perimeter road was suitable for emergency vehicles. It was shoddy, but adequate.

They drove around the left-hand side of the field and stopped a short distance from the trees, and Zaikov found himself trudging through the knee-deep snow towards the freshly laid concrete apron that surrounded the statue. The entire thing was covered with a tarpaulin, which in turn was weighed down by fresh snow.

'Take it off,' he ordered.

His aide yelled back at the driver to give him a hand and the man reluctantly emerged from the warmth of the car, donned a coat and gloves and made his way up to the edge of the trees. The two of them struggled for a few minutes getting the snow off the tarpaulin and finally, the tarpaulin off the statue.

When they had finished, Zaikov looked at the statue of the Kalevalan hero Ilmarinen forging the Sampo. It was far larger than he had imagined and, he admitted reluctantly, a well-executed piece of art.

'There's something missing,' the aide said.

'A piece of the handle of Ilmarinen's hammer, it's to be the baton in the marathon,' the Zaikov explained. 'It's on display in the mayor's office until the day of the race. It's all been arranged. The athletes set out from in front of the statue of Väinämöinen in Monrepos Park with a local female runner carrying the hammer handle. When they arrive outside the stadium, the President will take the baton from the woman and complete the event by running one complete lap, and then when he gets to the statue, he slots the hammer into place.' He pointed up to the statue. 'See the rings formed by Ilmarinen's hands? The hammer handle slots between them.' And the hammer completes the electronic circuit that explodes the damned thing, he thought, but didn't say. He turned and looked through the mist and snow to where he could just make out the grandstand. They would be far enough away from the site of the explosion, he decided. Though one could never account for fragments flying through the air. Still, that was not his problem.

It was as they came out of the forest beside the hut that Pentti's phone rang. He struggled for a second, removed his gloves and then answered the call. For a moment he stood still, and then with a wave to the others indicated they should wait in the hut, skied a few metres further out onto the lake, and stopped.

Nicole, still smarting from Pentti's jibe about the sisterhood, looked at him for a few seconds. He could be such a pig, she thought, then turned and followed into the shelter of the hut.

Pentti listened for a moment before ending the connection. What Heimo was suggesting was unprecedented. If the call had come from anyone else, Pentti would have dismissed it as a hoax. But Heimo had been serious and what he had said was not an option, it was an order.

He skied quickly over to the hut and taking out his flashlight, shone it on the snowmobiles. 'Eero, we are requisitioning three of these. Check they have fuel and get them started. Jukka, you and Quentin go on one and Eero on the other. I want you to head back to the cabin and warm yourself up. But don't get too comfortable as we will be going back to Helsinki as soon as I return.'

'And me?' Nicole asked. She was slightly startled by the change in him. His usually gentle manner had vanished and he had become authoritarian in a way she hadn't seen before. She didn't like it.

'I've been instructed to take you with me.'

That would be right. Instructed. Not that he wanted me to go with him. Fuck him, she thought. 'Who has instructed you to take me, and where exactly?'

He spun around and shone the torch directly in her face. 'You are coming with me. That's an order. It's not my decision, if it was up to me you would be going with the others.'

'So? I don't get a say?'

But he had turned away and was shining the light so that Eero could check the fuel tanks. She pushed past him, found a storage box and sat on it.

Within ten minutes Eero had three of the snowmobiles outside the shed and running smoothly. Pentti beckoned Jukka over and handed him his rifle and spare clip. 'Look after these,' he said brusquely.

'How long will you be?'

'I have no idea. Get the fire going, but be prepared to move out as soon as we get back.' He picked up two helmets, turned to Nicole and handed her one. 'Put this on.'

'Yes, sir,' she said and pulled a face at him. He ignored her, strode over to the machine and mounted it. 'Come.'

Reluctantly, she climbed on behind him.

He didn't wait for the others to depart before setting off. 'Hold on tight,' he shouted above the noise of the engine. It was the last thing she felt like doing, but as he increased speed, she realised it was the only sensible thing to do and she gripped him around the waist and pressed her face against his back for protection from the wind.

They appeared to be heading out towards the middle of the lake and after about fifteen minutes she yelled out to him. 'Where are we going?' but he either didn't hear or was simply ignoring her. Fuck you too, she thought, but she didn't loosen her grip on him.

Then suddenly he stopped and let the motor idle. Swivelling around, he removed his helmet and gestured for her to do the same.

'Can you see that?' he pointed ahead of them.

'What?' She peered through the dark but couldn't see anything but the frozen lake and the forested shoreline.

'Directly ahead and then just to the right of us.'

There was something large and black on the ice. For a moment she thought it was just a rock, but then the breeze swirled the falling snow away and she saw that sitting a couple of hundred yards away was a helicopter.

'Christ!' she swore, 'what's that doing there?'

He craned his head around so that he could see her. 'It's a Russian military helicopter. Heimo rang and ordered me to bring you to meet a Russian investigator to explain what we know about Remsu, the money laundering and this supposed plot against the Russian President.'

'You could have told me all this back there,' Nicole said.

'I couldn't. I'm sorry, Nicole, but I was told not to even mention it to Grammaticus or my own men. And I didn't have time, I was told to get here as fast as possible.'

'Okay… okay, but why me?'

Pentti shrugged. 'I have no idea, but I guess we are about to find out.'

He put the snowmobile in gear and crawled forward at walking pace until they were abreast of the helicopter. Ahead of them a man jumped down from the craft and waved a torch at them, indicating that they should stop. As Pentti switched off the motor, three men armed with submachine guns came around from behind the helicopter and surrounded them.

'Get off, please,' barked the man with the torch.

They dismounted and he waved them to stand still. 'I am sorry, but I must search you.' He didn't wait for either of them to agree, but moved straight to Nicole and patted her down. 'Is okay,' he said and pushed her gently to one side. He repeated the search on Pentti and then stepped back. 'The machine will stay here. You will walk please.' He pointed into the dark. 'Follow footsteps.'

Nicole looked ahead and suddenly realised that they were just off the beach of Pikkususisaari.

'Home sweet home,' she said bleakly, wishing she was anywhere but here.

The distance was deceptive and it took them about five minutes to get from the helicopter to the beach in front of the cottage. As they approached it, two more men stepped out of the dark and they were subjected to another search. Neither of the men spoke, but when they were satisfied, they simply grunted and indicated they could proceed.

'Friendly types,' Nicole muttered.

'Russians,' Pentti responded lightly. 'Fucking Russians.'

At the door of the cottage, a man in uniform who was smoking a cigarette stepped forward to greet them. Pentti wasn't sure if he was a large man or his thick uniform coat provided all the bulk. He was tall, slightly plump-faced, with a moustache and small goatee beard and, to Pentti's surprise, he spoke in perfect English.

'I am Alexander Sedov. Thank you for agreeing to meet us and also I thank your government for its friendly cooperation in allowing us to meet on Finnish soil.'

Pentti took off his right-hand glove and shook Sedov's hand. 'Pentti Toivonen, and this is my colleague, Nicole Parry, from the UK.'

'A pleasure,' Sedov murmured and tossed his cigarette into the snow. 'Please, come in from the cold.'

The interior of the cottage was so warm that Pentti suspected that the Russians had been there for some time. Only one of the oil lamps had been lit and it cast very little light, but as Sedov ushered them towards the table, he could just make out that there were two other individuals sitting hunched beside the stove. It was impossible in the gloom to tell if they were armed or not, but he suspected so.

'Please sit,' Sedov said, 'as unfortunately we have only limited time.'

As instructed by Heimo, Pentti told the Russians everything he knew about Cal Remsu, Anja Kujola, Andrei Zaikov and Sam Gordon. From the questions they asked it appeared they already knew a great deal.

'And the video he threatens to release?'

Pentti handed the memory stick to Sedov.

'Do you mind if I copy this?'

'Not at all,' Pentti said.

Sedov rose and took it across to the two men hunched around the fire. One of them produced a laptop, plugged the stick in and began to download the file while Sedov returned to the table and turned to Nicole.

'Tell us what you can about the facility beneath this museum.'

Nicole described it as best she could.

Finally, Sedov pushed his chair back from the table and stood up, retrieved the memory stick and handed it back. 'So, you both agree that this Remsu believes he can carry out his intention to harm the Russian leader?'

'He believes it, and I am afraid I think he has the capability. How many dissident Russians will take part in his venture is not for me to speculate,' Pentti said.

Sedov thought for a moment then sat down again. 'What would you suggest is the best course of action?'

'He has to be stopped,' Nicole said, 'but his threat of releasing that video should be of great concern.'

'Agreed,' Sedov said.

Pentti nodded. 'The video is damaging, but no matter what is done about that, surely the first thing that needs to happen is for the explosive to be removed from the statue and for your President to cancel his appearance at this event in Vyborg, as I suspect they will have a contingency plan.'

'Others disagree,' Sedov said, and smiled.

'Who? Who disagrees?'

One of the men who had been sitting in the shadows beside the stove stood up and turned his face toward the light. Pentti was startled. For a second, he thought he was imagining things, but the man's features were so familiar. He was shorter than Pentti had imagined and his hairline had receded further than the official photographs revealed, but even in the shadows of the cottage there was no mistaking the face.

'I disagree,' the man said. 'I gave my word I would come to Vyborg, and so I shall.'

Pentti was startled. He had read reports that the Russian President spoke some English, but he had never expected to hear it himself.

'Mister President, my apologies,' Pentti said and got to his feet as Nicole scrambled to do the same.

'Sit, sit! And you too, Detective Parry.'

He walked over and shook hands. 'It's a pleasure to meet you both. I and my government commend you on your uncovering this nasty nest of intrigue.'

Nicole rather wished her colleagues back in England could hear those words. 'We are just doing our jobs, Mister President,' she said and remained standing.

The president ushered Sedov out of the way and took his seat. 'Please sit. I am afraid on the instructions of your superiors in consultation with me, your work is not quite finished. You see, I fully intend to go ahead with the celebrations in Vyborg. I *will* run the final lap of the relay and I *will* most certainly place this hammer, or whatever it is, in the statue. It will be televised and those who are stupid enough to think I will give in to terrorists will see they're wrong.'

'But the explosive in the statue…' Nicole began.

'Please, as Sedov says, we have little time. He will give you the number of my liaison officer, who will provide you with everything you need. Unfortunately, you only have eight days in which to accomplish a most difficult task.'

Pentti nodded. 'Then, Mister President, tell us clearly what it is you expect from us.'

The President exchanged a glance with Sedov then turned his attention back to Nicole and Pentti. 'I want you to manage the event so that it takes place exactly as these terrorists expect, but with one slight change. Only one change.'

'And what is that?' Nicole asked.

The Russian President smiled benignly at her. 'Miss Parry, I would prefer to skip the part where I get killed.'

After two hours they heard the sound of a snowmobile. Although they knew it was almost certainly Pentti and Nicole returning, Jukka was taking no chances. He tossed his weapon to Eero and signalled for him to stay inside, then picked up his own weapon and slipped out the door.

Two minutes later he heard the pitch of the engine change as the snowmobile slowed down and emerged from the forest. To his relief it was Pentti.

As soon as he was off the machine, Pentti took off his helmet and turned to Nicole. 'Go inside and warm up. I'll just be a minute.'

Jukka waved to him and then led Nicole towards the door.

As soon as they were safely inside and out of earshot, Pentti took out his phone, checked he had a signal, and dialled.

Heimo must have been awaiting the call, for he picked up on the first ring.

'Well?'

'I take it he has clearance for flying in and landing on one of your lakes?'

'Trust me, clearance came from the highest level.'

'Okay. Here's what he's asked us to do –'

'I know. I have just spoken to Sedov.'

'And?'

'Your orders remain the same: to do everything in your power to bring about a positive outcome.'

'Let me be clear,' Pentti said, aware that Heimo's phrasing had been carefully chosen. 'Is "a positive outcome" the same outcome that our visiting neighbour outlined?'

'Affirmative. You are to do whatever is necessary. And to include both Parry and Grammaticus.'

'Of course.' It would have been illogical not to, given how involved they had become. And Pentti suspected that he would need them in the next few days if they were to figure out how to carry out the kind of operation the Russian President had requested, if indeed it were possible.

'Pentti, there is also a slight complication with the Americans. I think we need to neutralise any chance of them disrupting things.'

'But you expressly said not to involve them.'

Heimo snorted. 'Neutralise is the word I used, that doesn't mean involve. Though if you need any of their expertise, I feel we should have it on hand.'

'Okay, okay.' Heimo was being uncharacteristically cryptic and Pentti wondered if the call was being monitored.

Heimo cleared his throat. 'I have sent Ilkka Heiskanen to meet you at the Imatra turn-off on to Asemäentie. I estimate you should be there in a couple of hours.'

'And what then?' Why send Heiskanen? Pentti wondered. The man was a specialist, not in siege situations, but in bomb disposal. No doubt there was a reason for Heimo's choice.

'The Americans are staying in the Hotelli Kulkuripoika. I suggest you wake them up and arrest them.'

'Arrest them? What for?'

'You will find that they are in possession of a set of keys to a white van. My understanding is that the van is filled with weapons and explosives. Which is why I've sent Ilkka. We don't want any nasty accidents with booby-traps and so on.' He paused then added. 'Is that sufficient?'

Pentti was astounded. 'How the hell is that going to play with the Americans?'

'I don't think that they will be too eager to say anything, not that they will have a chance to say much for the next few days,' Heimo said, pitching his voice at its most reassuring tone. 'It is my thinking that we take them out of circulation and persuade Gordon to play along. From what I hear about the Remsu video, he does appear to have a starring role.'

Pentti wasn't totally convinced. Anyone who could switch sides because the circumstances changed could easily do so again, given an opportunity. His view that the Americans were consummate opportunists had not changed over the years. So, if Gordon was to be brought into the loop, he would need to be constantly under observation; and given the short amount of time and the fact that they yet had to come up with a strategy, he wasn't sure they could afford to also have the task of monitoring Gordon and keeping him on a tight leash. However, he was cold and tired and there was a long night ahead.

'Whatever you think is best, Heimo,' he said. 'I'll be in contact once we have sorted the Americans.'

'Drive carefully,' Heimo said, 'I hear the roads are quite icy.'

On the journey south, Eero drove while Nicole, Quentin and Pentti began to go over every detail they knew about Remsu, Zaikov and the intended attack on Kalevala Day. What they knew was quite considerable; what was not clear to any of them was how to proceed.

'It's upside down,' Pentti yawned. 'Usually with this amount of information we would be going to arrest people. Instead we are supposed to make the bloody thing happen.'

'Without anyone getting killed,' Quentin added.

Nicole shook her head, 'No, that's not quite accurate. Without the Russian President getting killed. There was no caveat on any other collateral damage.'

It was one-thirty in the morning by the time they rendezvoused with Ilkka Heiskanen. He was half asleep and dozing in his car with the engine idling and the heater on.

'You took your time,' he growled as he got out, stretched and lit a cigarette.

'The roads were icy,' Pentti said. 'This is Quentin and Nicole.' He nodded his head in the direction of Jukka and Eero. 'And you know the Beagle Boys.'

'Yes. Hi Quentin… and Nicole.' He stretched out his hand.

'Pleased to meet you,' Nicole said in what her father had always called her 'refined' voice. The man didn't look like a soldier, or a security officer. He was thin, tall and wiry, built more like a dancer, Nicole thought. Yet the delicate looking fingers that emerged somewhat reluctantly from the warmth of his gloves gripped her hand like a vice.

Introductions over, Ilkka gestured at Pentti to gain his attention. 'You check the Americans out of the hotel, and then get this Gordon chap to open the van for me. I hate surprises.' He tossed his cigarette in the snow and slid back into the warmth of his car. 'Remember that. No surprises.'

'I don't imagine there will be one,' Quentin said. 'It's not Sam's style. He's not that devious.'

Ilkka peered at him. 'All the same…'

'Don't worry,' Pentti said reassuringly. 'We'll make sure Sam Gordon opens the van.'

The night manager, a girl of eighteen or nineteen, looked startled at the arrival of five men and a woman at the hotel door in the middle of the night. The girl looked half asleep, her hair was dishevelled and she had obviously just thrown a coat on over her nightdress. Nicole guessed she had been asleep on the job. No, she corrected herself, as she caught glimpse of a man hurriedly getting dressed in a room at the rear of the hotel office, maybe not actually sleeping.

'Police.' Pentti flashed an ID card at her. 'I need the room numbers of the Americans. And your spare keys.'

Flustered, the girl looked at him. 'But they're asleep.'

'They are checking out, so I suggest you get their account prepared.'

'I'm not sure that I'm allowed...' she began. Then she caught sight of the weapons that Eero and Jukka were holding and quickly handed over the keys.

Nicole stepped up to the reception desk. 'And if it's not too much trouble, we would like a photocopy of their registration and account.'

The girl simply nodded.

Keys in hand, Pentti signalled to the others to follow him up the stairs. At the top he checked the room numbers and held up two fingers, indicating that two of the Americans were sharing a room. He approached the first door and after checking that Nicole and Quentin were well back and that Eero and Jukka were ready, he slipped the key into the lock and gently turned it. Fortunately, the men had not attached the security chain, so Jukka and Eero were able to walk in unimpeded.

It was over in seconds. Armstrong and Green were taken completely by surprise and overpowered with nothing more than a few grunts of protest.

Once they had been secured, Pentti stepped into the room. 'Gag them as well,' Pentti said quietly, as he inspected the plastic slip-lock fasteners on their wrists. 'Then throw their coats around their shoulders.'

In the next room, Sulkin also proved to be no problem. He seemed vaguely surprised but meekly held his hands behind his back while they secured him.

'I won't give you any trouble...' he began.

'Gag,' Pentti said.

Sam Gordon's room was right at the end of the corridor and if the name on the door was any indication, he had upgraded himself. The sign read: *Lemminkäinen Suite.*

'I'll do this one,' Pentti whispered and handed the key to Jukka. He produced a pistol and waved at Quentin, Nicole to stand well back.

Sam Gordon had been more careful than the others and had slotted the security chain in place. He needn't have bothered because as Pentti slammed his shoulder against the door, the frame splintered and the door swung open.

Sam Gordon sat upright and as Jukka and Eero burst into the room he knew there was nothing he could do.

'Time to check out, Mister Gordon,' Pentti said as the men hauled him from the bed. He was naked.

'Just let me get dressed.'

'I think we'd all prefer that,' Pentti said curtly.

It had all happened so quickly and without the slightest bit of resistance. Then when confronted with the knowledge that Pentti had about the van, Sam produced the key and meekly opened it for Ilkka to inspect.

'All safe and secure,' was his verdict. He tossed the keys to Eero. 'Just don't have an accident, okay?'

'Hang on,' Pentti held up a hand. 'Let's transfer the explosives and weapons to the trunks of the cars and put our American guests in the rear of the van. Jukka, you travel with Eero, and Quentin, could you go with Ilkka – he desperately needs someone to keep him awake… and improve his English.'

The three-hour drive to Helsinki seemed much longer and although she dozed from time to time, Nicole was unable to fall properly sleep. Once they were in the city, Pentti dropped her off at the safe house with the assurance that it had been cleaned since Mitchell had been killed there. She was so tired she didn't care.

Chapter Twenty

It was ten in the morning when they assembled at SUPO headquarters. Unlike the others, who were still feeling groggy from too little sleep, Quentin had slept well and was impatient to get on with things. His early morning call to London had been brief and to the point. 'You stay until this is done' had been the command. He was about to explain that it was still unclear what, if anything, could be done, but the line had gone dead. 'Nice talking to you too, Ma'am,' he muttered to himself.

As they followed Quentin and Heimo along a hallway, Pentti stopped and put a package into Nicole's hand.

'What's this?' she asked, looking at the plain brown wrapping paper.

'Highly confidential research material.'

She looked at him. 'Research material?' He was straight-faced and appeared to be serious. She unpicked the sticky tape and pulled the paper away. 'It's a book?'

'Looks like a book, feels like a book, even has pages like a book? Probably it is a book,' he said sagely.

Nicole pulled a thick volume free of the paper. It was a copy of *The Kalevala*.

'It's in English,' Pentti said and then added, 'It's supposed to be a good translation.'

Nicole was touched and smiled broadly. 'It's huge, but I'll try and get through it before lunch.'

'There'll be a quiz,' Pentti joked.

'Thank you, that was very sweet of you,' she said, and meant it.

For a moment she thought she saw him blush, but he shrugged and strode off after Heimo.

At the end of the hallway an armed security officer stepped back to let them pass. 'Come,' Heimo said as he swiped a card, opened the door and ushered them in. 'While you were all sleeping, I've had this conference room set up as a war room for you. Computers, secure telephones including a direct line to Sedov. Hopefully there's everything you'll need.' He dug in his pocket and produced some swipe-cards and tossed them on the table. 'These will get you in and out.'

Nicole, bleary-eyed and not yet fully awake, tried to look appreciative. The comfortable chairs that had been shunted to the corners of the room looked inviting, but the large oval table with its array of computers struck her as intimidating rather than helpful. She wasn't sure why she found it so, but was immediately thankful that Pentti put it into words.

'There's a couple of things missing,' he said flatly.

Heimo raised an eyebrow, questioningly. 'Yes?'

'An idea of what the hell we should do.'

'Or even where to start,' Nicole added.

Heimo shrugged. 'You have seven days. I am confident you'll come up with something. I've pulled in Jukka, Eero and Ilkka for the duration, and we can get more muscle if that's what's needed. What else?'

'A coffee machine.'

Heimo grinned. 'I think the budget will be able to cope with that. I'll even donate my wife's freshly baked *pulla*.'

'I'm sure you will,' Pentti grinned.

'And a teapot and some tea,' Quentin said. 'I always think better with a nice cup of tea.'

Over the next couple of hours their desultory conversation consisted of little more than expressions of tiredness, separated by extended silences. After a time, Pentti and the others abandoned the seats around the table and relaxed in the comfortable armchairs at the corners of the room. At one point, Nicole could have sworn she heard Pentti snoring.

For a while she thumbed through the copy of *The Kalevala*, trying to see why so many people made such a fuss about it. Mostly it just looked like a lot of words about people with names that were impossible to pronounce. But she persisted, pushed her glasses back up her nose and, making random selections, read several of the poems.

Suddenly Pentti sat up. 'I have an idea!'

Quentin, who had also been dozing, opened one eye and looked at him. Nicole closed the book.

'I'll go organise us some food,' Pentti said and heaved himself out of his chair and left the room.

'The most constructive thing anyone has said so far,' Quentin yawned. 'And I think it's time for a cup of tea.'

Nicole got to her feet, placed the book on the table, and stretched. 'Cup of tea sounds good. I'll put the jug on.'

'So, how's the book?'

'On the large side, but some interesting stories.' She switched the jug on then sat at one of the computers and typed in a search query. 'Look at that. You search for *Kalevala* and there are over two million results.'

'Tell me about it. Back in London when this whole thing started to get weird, I asked Chris Mitchell to find out what the hell a Sampo was, and he said there were over twenty million results from a Google search.'

'That's a lot for something that nobody seems to be able to fully explain,' Nicole said and picked up the book again. 'Maybe if I keep reading, I'll find out.'

'What sort of stories are they?' Quentin asked.

'Well, I have only been browsing, but I came across what sounded like the first recorded road-rage incident with some young punk crashing into an old guy's sledge.'

'Typical,' Quentin laughed.

'And for his troubles the young guy got sunk in mud up to his neck by the old man,' Nicole said. 'Then there's a bizarre story about a mother sewing her dead and dismembered son back together. It's probably the first description ever of microsurgery. And some other randy old fellow whose wife dies and he makes a metal wife in his forge and then complains that she's cold in bed. I mean, that borders on bent.'

'Most peculiar,' Quentin said as he examined a packet of tea bags. 'Bloody postman's tea!' he exclaimed, holding up a bag. 'Why they don't outlaw these stupid little envelopes of tea dust and get the real thing, I'll never know. They're an insult to the word tea.' Despite his disapproval he made two cups of tea, added a splash of milk and handed one to Nicole.

'So, we have a statue that has to explode and nobody is to get killed, and a bloody revolution that is to go ahead? And we are supposed to make sure it happens.' He shook his head. 'Big question is why.'

'And why doesn't the Russian President simply destroy the statue and arrest the plotters?'

Quentin sipped his tea and thought about it for a moment. Then he looked over his cup at Nicole. 'You know, I think he wants the coup attempt to take place. This has very little to do with what might happen in Karelia. That's just the signal. What he is really interested in is what happens in the rest of Russia.'

She knew instinctively he was right. 'Of course! You close the Vyborg stadium thing down and you maybe catch some of the ring-leaders, but let it go ahead and you have a chance of catching a majority of the dissidents.'

'If they have planned it right, yes.'

'That's why he was insistent that everything goes ahead as the coup leaders intend...'

'And the television coverage of the Kalevala Day celebrations has to show the killing of the President as a signal for the coup to begin.'

They sat in silence for a moment, enjoying the unexpected sensation of clarity.

'So we are creating a television spectacle,' Nicole said, thinking it through as she spoke. 'Something that will fool those watching.'

'Non-reality TV,' Quentin laughed.

'What we need,' Nicole said slowly, knowing an idea was forming, 'is something like the story in *The Kalevala*.'

Quentin's brow furrowed. 'Sorry, lost me.'

'The Golden Bride. It's the story of the lonely man who made himself a metal wife.' She looked at him, but his expression was one of total incomprehension. 'We need a metal president...

Something that looks like the President...' But the train of thought petered out as she realised it was going nowhere.

Quentin laughed. 'I know that the President thinks he's an iron man and a golden boy, but yet another statue is not the answer.'

They lapsed into silence again.

Suddenly Nicole got quickly to her feet and turned to him. 'Oh my God! You are a bloody genius!'

'What?' Quentin, startled by her sudden outburst, looked totally confused.

'It's the Sampo. It's the bloody Sampo. Of course it is!' She grabbed the book from the table and ran her finger down the index. 'The Forging of the Sampo... poem number ten...' She flicked through the pages. 'Here! No, not Vaino-whatever. Here! Ilmarinen; the smith, the bloody blacksmith, he's the one that forged the Sampo and he's the same old man who made the golden wife.'

Quentin shook his head. 'While I am happy to see you so suddenly enthusiastic, would you mind stopping babbling for a moment and tell me what the hell you are on about?'

Nicole's eyes were shining with excitement. 'Don't you get it? We need another Sampo, one that doesn't explode. You said that another statue was not the answer, but it is. Christ! Why didn't I think of that earlier?'

'Because it's insane?' Quentin said. 'Because you are still so tired you're not thinking straight?'

'No! Listen! This is not a stupid idea at all. Just shut up and let me talk it through.'

It was like being hit by a tsunami, he thought, but he did as he was told and sat back and listened.

'Pizza,' Pentti announced enthusiastically – only to be ignored. Having trudged through the snow with the food, he had expected a somewhat warmer reception. He stood just inside the door and watched. Everyone appeared totally immersed in some task or other. Heimo, who was sitting at one end of the table having a phone conversation, glanced up, saw him and put his hand over the phone.

'Sit down,' he said and then returned to his conversation.

Grammaticus, huddled over a computer with Ilkka, looked in his direction and with a broad grin gave him a thumbs-up sign then returned to his conversation.

'Okay, so we need a flat tray truck *and* a crane?'

'The best trucks have their own crane,' Illka said.

'And a power cut – is that possible?' Nicole, at the far end of the table, was shouting down a phone. 'Power cut. You know, like no electricity. A disruption, understand? Yes, exactly!'

'Pizza,' Pentti repeated and slid the boxes onto the table.

Ilkka nodded appreciatively but then returned his attention to Grammaticus and the computer screen.

'Cable-ties? Maybe six or seven to be on the safe side.' Quentin asked. 'Is that right? Anyway, it's on the list now.'

'And a small mobile generator. We may have to work through the night, and a good light source is essential.' Ilkka said.

'Visas!' Nicole shouted. 'Yes. I'll let you know how many.' She hung up with a look of triumph on her face. 'God, that felt good! Everything is doable.'

Heimo also put his phone down and called to Nicole down the length of the table. 'That was Crawford.'

'I thought he was retiring,' Nicole said. 'What did he want?'

Heimo snorted. 'To tell you that he has decided not to retire.'

'Excellent,' Nicole said. 'He's a good man.'

'And to tell you he can't get you out of some disciplinary hearing. You are to be questioned by them in the morning.'

Nicole felt her stomach sink. 'Oh Christ! I thought that had been buried.'

'Don't worry. I told him that we were not available and that you are working with us on a highly complex case. I also told him that you are a credit to British policing and a shining example of inter-agency cooperation, and deserved a medal not a reprimand.'

'How the hell did he take that?'

Heimo grinned. 'He seemed to take great delight in it and promised to relay it word for word to the disciplinary committee. I told him the commendation came from the highest levels of two governments – ours and Russia's.'

Pentti took a seat and leaned forward. 'Anyone care to tell me what's going on?'

'Just a minute,' Nicole said and picked up her phone. 'Yes? Pool? Oh, right a journalists' pool. One TV feed. Fine. Any word on mobile phone coverage?' She listened for a moment before she hung up. 'Sorry, Pentti, what was it you said?'

Before he could answer, Heimo interjected. 'Thanks to some brilliant thinking by Nicole and Quentin, we have the beginnings of a possible solution; risky but possible. But, and I emphasise, *but*, it depends on you convincing Anja Kujola to help us.'

'Kujola? The sculptor?' Pentti was totally perplexed. 'Why her?'

'Hand me a slice of pizza, and I'll explain.'

For the next twenty minutes Pentti listened intently as Heimo, Quentin and Nicole briefed him on the idea. It was, he decided, fraught with danger, a high-wire act with no safety net. Every step depended on the step before, and each needed to be taken at precise moments. One slip and the act – and it was most definitely an act – would tumble to the ground. He pushed away the box with the last slice of pizza and rose from his chair. 'What you are suggesting is insane,' he said quietly. 'If we had weeks or even months to plan this, even then it is doubtful we could pull it all together, let alone make it work.'

'Pentti, we have a week,' Heimo grunted. 'And we have no other option. Either we do this or – or what? I don't hear you coming up with an alternative.'

Pentti walked to the window and stared out into another bleak winter's day. 'What you are suggesting we create and carry out in meticulous detail and timed down to the last second, is a television account of the assassination of a president.'

'But...' Nicole interjected, 'the President said he didn't want us to stop it.'

'Let me finish,' Pentti said. 'You are saying that we should film an assassination, but it is more than that. It is the signal for the start of a coup. If the coup fails and the dissidents are caught, we have interfered in another country's sovereign territory in order to assist its president get an even tighter grip on power. And the other possibility that nobody seems to care to contemplate. Where do we stand if the coup becomes unstoppable? We are all concerned by the possibility of Remsu's video becoming public. But if things go wrong, our film will make the damage that Remsu might make pale into insignificance. The political backlash would not be survivable.'

Nobody responded. In the silence that followed, Pentti turned away from the window and returned to the table. He sat, removed his glasses and rubbed at his eyes. Then he looked up and slowly replaced his glasses. 'That said,' he continued. 'I have no better idea. In fact, no idea at all. So, if you'll excuse me, I'll go and visit Anja Kujola.'

Zaikov followed the instructions to the letter. The weather for the next few days was not going to cause a problem, and with any luck there would be no need to bring in the snowploughs again. Cold and sunny was the long-range forecast; sunny, with a chance of explosions. He smiled at the thought.

The latest snow had been cleared from the access roads, the seating areas had been cleared, cleaned, checked and double-checked for explosive devices and finally every possible vantage point that might tempt a sniper had been evaluated and where possible rendered inaccessible – with one exception. My sniper, and mine alone, Zaikov mused, will have a perfect line of sight and no possibility of disturbance. Even if the detonation device were to fail, the President would make an easy target. As his sniper had said, even a blind fool could kill him from that distance.

Then he turned his attention to the problem of the media coverage. His informant was adamant that there was now to be only one television crew with two cameras. It was not the way he had envisaged it, but it did make them easier to handle. He inspected the area allocated to the media and requested that a cable be laid out and secured for the second camera. The cameraman wouldn't have any shelter if the weather turned nasty, but then he wasn't going to be out there for long. Next to the President, he would be the closest person to the statue and as such was certainly not going to survive the blast. He showed the technicians exactly where the camera cable was to be laid, and despite being cold and hungry he waited and watched as they carried out his instructions. Once they were done, he dismissed them with a stern reminder that security was paramount and they should talk to nobody about the preparations at the stadium. It irked Zaikov to have to lecture them. In the old days they would have done the work, and then been shot. In the old days such things were more straightforward.

He looked around, trying to see if there was anything he'd forgotten.

Satisfied that everything was in order, he phoned his contact in Saint Petersburg. 'It's done,' he said. 'All cleared and sealed off. Nobody in and nobody out from now on, unless we need to clear more snow away.' He terminated the call and signalled to his driver that he was ready to head back to the hotel for a sauna and some food.

He remembered hearing a phrase in an American film; he couldn't recall the name of it, but the line had stuck in his memory. At first it had been simply a few words, which in context, had entertained him. Now, suddenly, they haunted him. *Not on my watch.* The character, a CIA officer, had sworn that he would defeat some presidential assassination attempt with those words. Nobody is going to kill the President, *not on my watch.* They hadn't of course. The officer had almost been killed, but survived; and wounded and bleeding had somehow kept going long enough to drag the President from the line of fire. That's right, Sedov, remembered, the shot intended for the President had hit the CIA guy. Too damned good-looking to die. Too damned good-looking to have actually been a CIA officer. In America, if you were that good-looking you got to *play* at being a CIA officer, you didn't need to actually *be* one. Not that being good-looking was ever going to be his problem, Sedov thought. *Not on my watch.* Life imitating art didn't come close to describing the logistical nightmare he found himself entangled in. This border between fiction and reality was far too close, and one slip and the border could be breached. We are going to kill the President and we are going to save the President. He would rather have had neither scenario. But the make-believe and the real were so close together, and he had orders to proceed. He said it aloud. '*Not on my watch.*'

The phone rang. About time, he thought. The director of Ruskino Media, the film production company in Saint Petersburg, had said he would have an answer in an hour. It was now four hours.

'Sorry about the delay, but you know how it is, things got hectic around here. Anyway, the good news is that we can do it. We have a mobile production facility that we can make available –'

'That you *will* make available,' Sedov snapped.

The director ignored the tone of command. 'We have availability in late March and again in early –'

'Listen, and listen very carefully.' Sedov spoke very slowly and clearly. 'The mobile production facility and your best technical people are to be on the road to Vyborg no later than midnight.'

'Who the hell do you think you are?' the director exploded. 'We have a full schedule at the moment and we can't just turn things on and off because some jumped-up bureaucrat wants to throw his weight around. We have a massive crew working on a Danish Russian co-production at the moment and I'm sorry, but I can't afford to have actors and producers waiting around. It is simply not going to happen.'

Sedov waited for the man to finish venting before he spoke. 'No later than midnight is what I said. Now, if the production vehicle is not on the road by midnight, I will explain what happens. At one minute past twelve, Spetsnaz Group Alpha officers will forcibly remove the vehicles and the necessary technical staff, who will be dragged from their homes if need be. At the same time, you will be arrested. I hope I make myself clear? And it goes without saying that Ruskino Media will cease to exist by morning. Now, you have fifteen minutes to confirm the arrangement. You will call me back on the same number. Oh, and the jumped-up bureaucrat you are talking to is General Sedov of the FSB.' He hung up the phone and lit a cigarette.

Seven minutes later the phone rang. Apparently Ruskino Media's co-production with the Danes had been rescheduled to late March.

Sam Gordon was not a happy man. Separated from his colleagues and placed in a cell that redefined the lower end of 'Spartan', he had been afforded nothing but a bowl of porridge and some left over *pulla*.

Eventually, after twenty-four hours, the cell door was unlocked and Pentti entered. He waited until the door was locked again before speaking. Sam remained sitting on the bed.

'Mister Gordon, you are an embarrassment to your own government and an unfortunate and unnecessary complication for mine. Our Russian friends advise us that it would be best if you were to disappear completely. I'm sorry to say that there are those among my colleagues who also hold this view.'

'Fuck off, Toivonen,' Sam said. There was no tone of malevolence in his voice, but rather boredom, born from his belief that this was all a game.

Pentti shrugged. 'I don't think anyone has the idea of anything official, but the notion of icing you has appeal.'

'You've been watching too many American movies,' Sam snorted derisively. 'Nobody says "icing" these days.'

'Our method of icing is somewhat more traditional,' Pentti said. 'We take you for a drive in the beautiful Finnish countryside, out onto a lake, a hole in the ice and you go for a short swim. The ice refreezes very fast at this time of year. It's possible they would find your body after the thaw, but I understand that fish are particularly hungry in spring.'

'You're full of shit, Toivonen. You know as well as I do that you can't just hold me indefinitely. I'm an American citizen and I have rights.'

'Samuel Gordon possibly has rights, but the passport you are carrying says you are Benjamin Prentiss and last time we checked, he doesn't exist. So nobody will care if he disappears.'

'You Finns don't have the balls for that sort of stuff,' Sam said, though he appeared less confident.

'Of course, we could simply try you in an open court on the charges of entering the country illegally, being in possession of terrorist materials, explosives and weapons, and conspiring to create a coup in Russia.' Pentti looked at him over the top of his glasses. 'I'm not sure how good that would look on your résumé. Mind you, I doubt you would still be young enough to work if we ever released you. So the résumé question is rather academic, don't you think?'

He didn't wait for a reply, but turned and knocked on the door to be let out.

They waited for another twenty-four hours before visiting him again. When the cell door opened, it was Grammaticus. He had been thoughtful enough to bring a mug of reasonably warm coffee. Sam took it and paced around the cell.

'You need to do something to get me out of here.'

'Afraid not, old man. No can do.' He sat on the bed and patted the space beside him, indicating that Sam should sit. Sam kept pacing.

'The thing is, Sam, the Russians are exerting a lot of pressure on our hosts to toss you to the wolves. Of course, I went in to bat for you.'

'They're bluffing,' Sam growled.

'I wouldn't be so confident. They appear to have Zaikov and his facinorous minions on the run and feel that we'll all come out of this smelling like roses.' He looked around the cell. 'I wouldn't fret too much. It goes with the territory, doesn't it, winners and losers? Still, I hear that their prison system is very advanced. All the creature comforts provided; cable television, lectures, films and educational courses. Even the food is supposed to be rather good.'

Sam drained the last of the coffee and sat on the end of the bed. 'What about my colleagues?'

'Fickle things, we humans,' Quentin sighed. 'A deal has been done.'

'A deal?'

'They quietly leave the country with a glowing report about their assistance to the Finnish police. The alternative of disgrace, prison and so on, was enough to persuade them to remain silent. I must say, they're remarkably clever chaps. Every last word of their cover story, off by heart. Bravo, I say.'

'You're bullshitting me.'

'Alas no. As the old saying goes, those who bend with the wind, rise again when the wind stops.'

They sat in silence for a moment. Then Quentin cleared his throat and got to his feet. 'Well, must be off. A cup of tea and rather nice Finnish cakes await me.'

'Why did they not offer me a deal, Quentin?'

'Oh, they were going to, but when I heard it I told them that you would rather drink a crushed glass cocktail.'

'What deal?'

'Well, I'm certain you are not going to like it…'

'For fuck's sake, Quentin, just tell me.'

So he did.

It had amused him that the hotel in Vasil'eva Ulitsa was called 'Sampo'. On his first night there he had tried the restaurant and found it unsatisfactory, so after his sauna Zaikov headed to Rynochnaya Square and went into the Round Tower restaurant in the Vyborg tower. At the bar on the second floor, he paused for an over-priced shot of vodka then continued on to the third-floor restaurant.

He took a seat near in the middle of the room and ordered a bottle of vodka while he perused the menu. When the waitress returned with the bottle, she asked him if he would like to change seats.

'We have a cancellation, so I can place you by the window.'

'Fine. You are very kind.' She was also, he noted, delightfully plump and big breasted.

She ushered him away from the centre of the room to a seat with a splendid view over Vyborg. 'Salmon soup is good tonight. And I recommend the pork.' She opened then poured his vodka for him. 'My name is Olga, so just call me when you are ready to order.'

After a couple of glasses, he took her advice and ordered the soup to be followed by the pork steak.

Refreshed by the sauna, the brisk walk and now the vodka, Zaikov was in a mellow mood. Everything he had worked for was coming to fruition and within days he would no longer be a man in the shadows.

After his meal he lingered over coffee and waited until the few remaining patrons had left.

'I'm staying at the Sampo,' he told the waitress.

'You might need some help in finishing the vodka, maybe?'

He gave her his room number.

Olga turned out to be a lot of fun and when he eventually fell into the bed beneath her, he discovered she was as noisy as she was enthusiastically pneumatic. There was a lot to be said for a big woman, he decided, as he clasped her large buttocks; comforting and arousing at the same time. He couldn't reach the clasp on her bra, so she paused and with practised dexterity unleashed her breasts. They were mesmerisingly enormous.

'They build us big in the Ukraine,' she laughed when he finally got his breath back and gasped out an appreciative comment.

She had just climbed onto him for the second time when the phone rang. He gestured for her to be silent and answered it.

'Just to let you know the TV crew will be doing a walk-through in the morning,' his Saint Petersburg contact informed him. 'No cause for concern, and best you keep well away until they are finished.'

'Okay,' he said and hung up.

A hand snaked under his neck and jerked his head up.

'Bite my nipples,' Olga commanded. 'It makes me go all funny.'

He did, and she hadn't lied.

The Finnish film director, Ahti Kuula, looked at Heimo with an expression of utter disbelief. 'I've been dragged out of bed at God knows what hour, intimidated by the official secrets legislation, and now you want me to just sign away all rights for the pleasure of producing a piece of television how long? How long did you say?'

'Thirty seconds,' Heimo repeated blandly. 'Maximum.'

'And you have a second Russian second unit filming the actual location?'

Heimo nodded. 'Very professional, so I'm told.'

'And I get no credits, no official acknowledgment?'

'Correct.'

'And the Russians get no credits?'

'None.'

Ahti looked at Heimo as if he were an idiot. 'Can you give me one reason why I should agree to this? For God's sake, who on earth is going to watch thirty seconds of television?'

Heimo clasped his hands on his desk and leaned forward. 'I can give you a lot of reasons, but seeing patriotism isn't so fashionable, let me appeal to your ego. Who on earth is going to watch it? Everyone. Everyone on the planet with access to a television or the internet will see your work.'

The man did not look convinced, so Heimo went on. 'It will become an iconic piece of footage. Think moon landing. Think Dealey Plaza and the grassy knoll in nineteen sixty-three, the Berlin wall coming down November ninth, nineteen eighty-nine, the man and the tank in Tiananmen in eighty-nine. Your work will be part of history.'

'And nobody will know.'

'You will know.' Heimo sat back. 'So please just sign the secrecy forms and I'll take you through to see the script writer.'

'A Russian, I suppose,' Ahti said despondently, but he reached for the pen.

Heimo smiled, 'No, actually, she's British.'

For Nicole days and nights had become a blur. When she slept at all it was in a side office that had been vacated and fitted out with four camp beds. The conference room had quickly become overcrowded and unworkable so they had expanded into three rooms and taken up most of the canteen as well.

The original team was now scattered. Ilkka and Pentti had vanished into the night, and even when she pressed Heimo he was not saying what they were involved in. It was Quentin, who surprised her most. In Pentti's absence he took on overall management of the project, leaving Nicole to micro-manage the details. He displayed an intuitive sense of what needed to be done and when. There were moments when she was confused by the enormity of the task, and just at the right moment, Quentin would appear at her side with a quiet reminder that she had to talk to this person or that.

As the complexity of the operation threatened to become overwhelming, Quentin produced a flow chart of the tasks to be completed and scheduled meetings. When Nicole needed expertise and advice that was not on hand, he shunted the task of finding it to Heimo. Eero and Jukka, whose combat skills were not needed, took over catering and won Quentin over by sourcing a supply of Darjeeling White Peony tea. Nicole drank cup after cup of it as she sat through a series of meetings with Ahti Kuula intended to bring her up to speed with what was needed to make thirty seconds' worth of film.

It was four in the morning when Quentin woke her with the news that the footage shot by Ruskino in Vyborg had finally arrived.

'Get Kuula in and give it to him. He says he needs to find a matching background; and for continuity the sun has to be at the right angle.'

'Already done. I rang him and then despatched Eero to collect him,' Quentin said. 'However, the sun thing could be a problem. It's snowing again.'

'Then stop it, Quentin.' She tried to smile, but yawned instead. 'Actually, no, we need snow and sun. Whatever the weather is on Friday, Kuula needs to match it.'

'I'm sure he'll manage. Now, can I get you anything?'

'A new head, a fresh brain and twenty-four hours' sleep. What day is it?'

'Monday.'

'Christ, Quentin, we only have four days...' She lowered her head back onto the pillow, then raised it again as she remembered something else. 'Anja said she would be finished overnight. Ring her now and tell her it's morning. If she is finished, we need the truck and some men to collect it. And for God's sake we have to find Ilkka. We will need him for the explosives.'

Chapter Twenty-One

Eluding the security guards and crawling through the forest to the rear of the statue had been the easy part. Once under the large tarpaulin tent that totally surrounded the statue, they were safe from observation, but it was at that point that they encountered major problems. Access to beneath the statue was difficult, but not impossible. Set atop a huge granite boulder, the base of the statue was bolted to four concrete pillars reaching half a metre above the rock. There was only just enough space for Ilkka to turn on his side and wriggle between them.

He switched on the small LED headlight on his brow-band and looked up.

'A solid brass base around the circumference and then a narrow hollow core in the centre that goes up through the centre... and then...'

'Then what?' Pentti asked.

'Shit!'

'What?'

'Hang on...' He inserted his arm into the hollow space above him and then pulled it out again. 'No, not remotely possible.'

Pentti waited until Ilkka had wriggled free of the confined space.

'So?'

'Whoever put this together was really smart. The explosives and detonators are far up into the statue. And beneath them, out of arm's reach, is a steel grille that has been locked into place. There are two old-style FI grenades with their pins removed attached to the grille, and you can bet they are fitted with a zero-delay fuse. Christ! It is so fucking simple and low-tech it's embarrassing.'

Pentti shook his head. 'There has to be a way.'

'No. They armed this baby long before it was put in place. High-tech electronics, timers, pressure plates, you name it and I can usually find a way around it. But this is old school and would require removal of the statue, brute force and a hell of a lot of noise. And, of course, there is no saying that they haven't put other devices inside that I don't know about.'

Pentti thought for a minute, trying to remember something he had heard. Then it came to him. 'Can you shine the light up the statue?'

Ilkka removed his headband with the LED light and holding it in his hand shone it upwards. 'What are you thinking?'

'Remsu said something about the hammer.'

'It's not there,' Ilkka said. 'There is no hammer.'

'Can you climb up and take a look at the hands?'

Ilkka shrugged, replaced the light on his head and eased himself up onto the base of the statue. 'I'm standing on what I suppose is the lid of the Sampo,' he said. 'That's one for the memoir... if I live long enough.'

'Just take it easy and look inside the hands.'

Ilkka went on tiptoes and examined them carefully. 'Jesus! How did you know about this?'

'About what?'

'On the inner surface of both hands are contact pads. They're part of the structure, embedded in the metal and have wires running directly into the statue.'

'What would happen if you cut them?' Pentti asked, already anticipating the answer.

'Neither of us would get to write a memoir. It is a certain bet they are designed to detonate if they're interfered with.'

'But are they simply touch-sensitive?'

Ilkka examined them again. 'No, I would say not at all. They are designed to receive a small charge. Without that charge they are safe.'

'And they can't be removed?'

'No.'

'Okay, then we had better get out of here.'

'You go ahead. I am going to touch one of the pads, just to make certain.'

'No! I mean that, Ilkka.'

'And I'm going to test it, because I don't want Friday to come around and have a dead president on my conscience just because I didn't do my job. Now get the hell out of here.'

'Sorry. I'm ordering you down.'

Ilkka ignored him. 'Well, at least it's only the two of us…'

Pentti watched as Ilkka's hand reached for the left arm of the statue. This would be a very silly way to die, he thought, and despite himself, shut his eyes.

A split second later he heard Ilkka laugh and he opened his eyes. 'You could prod the thing with a stick, no problem. It's definitely not touch-sensitive. I should have put money on it.'

'If you had lost the bet I couldn't have collected,' Pentti said grimly.

They remained silent until they were safely in the trees and clear of the security guards. Ilkka sat on the snow, took out a cigarette and lit it.

Pentti watched him smoke for a moment then squatted in the snow beside him. 'That was a particularly stupid thing you did, and way beyond your brief.'

'Someone had to test it out.'

'Rendering the bomb inoperable was the brief, not seeing if you could set the damn thing off. Your conduct was reckless.'

Ilkka took a long drag on his cigarette, tilted his head back and blew the smoke up into the night, then grinned at Pentti. 'Tell you what, Pentti, what if I promise never to do it again?'

'Like I'd believe you.' He pulled out his phone and checked the time. It was one-thirty in the morning. 'Hopefully Sedov sleeps with his phone,' Pentti said as he dialled. It was answered on the second ring.

'The hammer; do you know where the hammer is?'

For several hours on the morning of the twenty-fifth, there was an unexpected lull in activity. The hiatus left Nicole feeling numb, empty and suddenly homesick. She couldn't recall having ever felt homesick before, but at that moment she would have given anything to be in the lounge bar of an English pub, beside a log fire, sipping a pint, then wandering home to her own bed in her own partially renovated house. She would get a cat, she mused. Not some overbred fancy variety, but an old-fashioned moggy with attitude and a penchant for laps. She had room for a cat in her life. Or would do if she ever got her life back. One thing was for sure, when she got that cat it wasn't going to be called Sampo.

Though she was exhausted and needed sleep, her brain refused to slow down, so she took a shower, dressed and went to check on how the various parts of the project were progressing. The trouble was that for the first time in days she actually had nothing to do. She and Grammaticus had been so efficient at delegating that she was now left with no option but to wander the building dropping in on the periphery of meetings where most of the participants were too engaged in their discussions to even notice her presence. The technical team were in a huddle speaking a language Nicole couldn't understand even though they were conversing in English.

She went in search of Grammaticus and found him deep in conversation with the hastily rounded-up group of Russian, Finnish and English media strategists, devising 'official' stories to cover a variety of outcomes. Nicole poked her nose in for a few minutes but found the spin-doctors' discussion of 'worst case scenarios' disturbing. It was not that the subject unnerved her, it was the tone; they might as well have been arguing over marketing soap powder and not the possibility of a great number of people being killed.

The editing was in the final stages and although she knew she couldn't contribute, Nicole sat in a darkened booth and watched the editor and director working, until Anti shook her by the shoulder.

'You fell asleep,' he said, and helping her up, ushered her gently from the room.

She wandered through to the canteen in search of coffee and found Heimo hunched over a table in conversation with Pentti. They looked up as she approached and gestured for her to pull up a seat.

'Welcome back,' Nicole said dryly.

'I was busy...' Pentti began and then simply shrugged.

'Stills from the footage of our tame international terrorist,' Heimo said with a glint of delight in his eyes. 'This should be more than enough to keep the bastard silent.' He pushed the pile of photographs over to her then reached for a Danish pastry from a plate in front of him.

The photographs were all of Sam Gordon. Sam with the explosives and weapons in the back of the van. Sam caught at the wheel of the van on CCTV footage. Security camera images of him passing though the Imatra check point into Russia, and close-ups of his passport showing his name as Benjamin Prentiss and of the Russian entry stamp. Finally, a telephoto shot of him parking the van at the Vyborg stadium.

'He's fucked,' she said quietly.

'And he hasn't seen it yet,' Pentti said. 'What do they call it in America, a show reel? Well, he has a choice, either he keeps quiet and goes home with a thank you note from our government or we show the reel.'

'Can't say fairer than that,' Nicole laughed. It was good to see Pentti in high spirits but there was something else on her mind. 'What's the decision from our friends in far flung places?'

'The Russians?'

'Of course the bloody Russians.'

'They are as concerned as we are about the initiating device.'

'The hammer?'

'Yes. Ilkka says that it must conduct a small electrical current, but the Russians are worried that the electrical circuit may be only one of two ways of initiating the explosion. They think that simply placing the hammer in position closes a circuit that is already primed.'

'Like turning on a switch?'

'Exactly.'

Nicole looked him in the eye. 'Do you think we should go ahead?'

'If it were my decision?' he paused, giving himself time to think. 'I would probably say no. I would cancel the unveiling of the statue and keep the President locked up in the Kremlin while Special Forces take care of known dissidents.'

'But it's not your decision.'

'No.'

'So? Where does that leave us?' Nicole asked, thinking that getting Pentti to have a flowing conversation was not a task she was cut out for.

Heimo wiped the crumbs from his chin and leaned on the table to look past Pentti. 'The President is adamant. We go ahead.'

'But technically we're not ready.'

'I think we're progressing,' Heimo said. 'Editing is nearly done. The tech crew in Vyborg have a cable patched into the TV feed, and the power and telephone team say they will have their systems locked in by tomorrow noon at the latest.'

Pentti laughed. 'And Sam Gordon delivered the van load of goods on schedule and without defecting.'

'He may regret that decision,' Nicole said. 'If word ever got out about his role in this he would be… God knows what.'

'Dead?' Pentti offered.

'Shame on you, Toivonen,' Heimo said with mock severity. 'How could you think such a thing of the Americans? They would never disappear one of their own.'

Nicole got to her feet. 'I can't sit upright much longer. I'm going to crash out for a while. Wake me if anything happens.'

Pentti frowned. 'It's only eleven-thirty in the morning. Whatever happened to a fair day's work?'

'For a fair day's pay, Mister Owl?' Nicole scowled. 'And I don't seem to have been paid in a very long time. So I'm sleeping on company time – so fire me.'

They watched her leave the canteen. 'A real asset,' Heimo said. 'I saw that in her from the start.'

'You bloody near nagged me to death to get her out of the country,' Pentti said. 'Still, she has been quite good.'

'Quite,' Heimo said, and reached for another Danish.

In the afternoon, after clearing everyone out of the conference room, they brought Sam Gordon out of the cell and gave him a seat directly in front of the monitor. Heimo sat to one side of the room, his attention focused on the contents of a folder on his lap. Pentti, exhausted, pulled out a chair and slumped into it with his eyes closed. Grammaticus, seemingly untouched by the long hours, remained standing, gazing out of the window at the sunshine. It had been a while since he had seen sunshine, and to his bemusement he had the irrational urge to go outside and experience it. He had mentioned it to Pentti, who reminded him it was minus fifteen degrees out there. Still, he thought, a walk would be pleasant.

'Showtime, Sam,' Nicole said quietly and pressed play on the remote control.

There was no sound, but the vision, cut together professionally, told its own story.

Sam had realised it was going to be bad, but not this bad. It was like a nightmare in which you saw yourself being ruthlessly and inexorably eviscerated, he thought, and the bastards hadn't missed a trick. From CCTV footage of his arrival at Vantaa to the final shots of him at the Avangard stadium in Vyborg, it was all there. The false passport, the close-ups of the van's contents, even the hotel receipts in the name of Benjamin Prentiss; everything in chronological order. If anyone in Langley ever saw this he was screwed. Dismissal? Certainly, and jail probably, though they might prefer the wet option – a road accident. It had happened before.

'Nice work,' Sam said bleakly when the screen finally went blank.

'Thank you,' Nicole said. 'It was my first production and I must say I'm rather proud of it. Of course, if we could have added the credits...'

Heimo got up and walked to the table. 'The thing is, Sam, what should we do with it?'

There was nothing he could say, so he shrugged.

'I'm afraid my superiors have mixed feelings about your future,' Heimo continued. 'Prosecution is a messy and protracted affair so the consensus is that we should expel you from the country and send a copy of our little movie to Langley.'

'So that talk of a deal was bullshit?' Sam said angrily.

'Not entirely,' Heimo paused. 'It appears your British colleagues may be a little more accommodating.' He glanced at Grammaticus. 'Quentin?'

'Sorry, I was just enjoying the sunshine.' He turned back from the window and crossing to the table, took the folder from Pentti. 'I have two documents here. One is the British Official Secrets Act. The other is a report detailing the splendid reconnaissance work you did on the Vyborg stadium and includes a series of photographs you took –'

'I didn't take any fucking photographs,' Sam snapped.

Quentin looked up from the folder and straightened his back. 'Mister Gordon, you took photographs. And splendid they are, most helpful. There is also an appreciative note from the Finnish and British authorities thanking you for your cooperation. I believe you'll find the report and addendums suitable to pass on to your colleagues in Langley.'

Sam looked at him. 'You Brits are unbelievable.'

'I'll take that as a compliment,' Quentin said benignly and laid the documents down on the table in front of Sam. He took a fountain pen from his jacket pocket and handed it to him. 'Now, if you would just sign here… and here.'

Sam read each page of the Vyborg report carefully, rolling the pen between his fingers as he did so. 'Humph, not bad.' He looked up at the faces around the table. They were all focused on him.

'So sign,' Pentti said. 'It's the best offer you're going to get.'

'And the little movie you just screened?'

'What movie?' Nicole said.

'It gets locked away where nobody will ever find it,' Heimo said, 'unless, of course, you step out of line.'

'Line dancing was never my thing.' He took the top off the pen, examined the nib and scrawled his signature.

'And this one,' Quentin said smoothly and slipped the next document in front of him.

'If I sign this, then it looks like I'm working for you.'

Quentin exchanged glances with Nicole, who nodded. 'Your CIA chaps will just think you have cultivated us, rather than the other way around.'

'You expect me to work for you as a double agent?'

'Of course not,' Quentin sighed. 'We would never be so crass. Simply a good working relationship.'

'And the upside,' Nicole chipped in, 'is you will actually be working with me.'

Sam swivelled around in his chair. 'You work for MI6?'

'As of...' Quentin consulted his watch, '... two hours ago. That's hush-hush, of course. Only one person in Britain knows about it at the moment and I'd rather like to keep it that way.'

'Christ!' Sam swore quietly. 'How can I turn down a chance to work with psycho-bitch?'

'I love you too, sweetie,' Nicole cooed and smiled as she watched him sign. Gotcha, she thought, we bloody well gotcha!

Pentti caught up with Nicole in the corridor outside the conference room. He looked flustered, she thought, and edgy.

'Yes? What is it now?'

He appeared embarrassed. 'I just wanted to say congratulations on getting the job.'

'I didn't *get* the job. It was given to me, or rather thrust upon me. Do you think I would apply to work with Grammaticus?'

'But you took the job?'

'That's classified.' She saw the crestfallen look on his face and stopped. 'Yes, Pentti. I took the job. Satisfied?' Christ, she thought, I've said the wrong thing again. 'Look, I'm sorry. It's very sweet of you to congratulate me.'

'I was going to ask you out to dinner to celebrate. We're all bracing ourselves for the next couple of days, and I've booked a table...'

'That's nice of you, but all I want to do is sleep.' She stalked off down the corridor without waiting for him to respond.

But she couldn't sleep. Stupid, she told herself, bloody stupid. The man was only trying to be nice. No, more than nice. She suspected he had warmed to her, if warming was possible in a country that since she had arrived most resembled the inside of a freezer.

She hauled herself out of bed and went looking for him.

Pentti was kicking himself. Right from the moment he had met Nicole, he realised she operated on a short fuse. Maybe it took a man like Ilkka, a bomb disposal expert, to handle her; he certainly couldn't. But, he conceded, there had been times in the last few days when he marvelled at her ability to focus on details that others overlooked. It was a good trait for a policewoman, but her people skills were a worry. It was obvious that she was going to be Sam Gordon's handler. God only knew how long that would work before one or the other demanded a divorce.

'Pentti?'

He turned around and found Nicole standing in a doorway behind him.

'Yes?'

'Look, I'm really tired and I'm sorry I was so abrupt.'

He walked over to her. 'It's understandable,' he said stiffly. 'We're all stressed at the moment.'

'I'm really sorry,' she repeated.

'Forget it. It's not a problem.'

'I wanted to say that I would rather like to have dinner with you.'

Pentti shook his head. 'I'm sorry, I cancelled the Savoy reservation.'

'Oh, I see…'

'But I can arrange something.' His face softened and he smiled. 'I'll meet you in the lobby at seven-thirty. I have my car.'

Nicole checked her watch. It was only just after three. 'That's great. I'll try and get some sleep between now and then, and Pentti…'

'Yes?'

'I promise to be on my best "*kulta*" behaviour.'

Nicole awoke with a start. It was seven fifteen and, remembering the Finnish penchant for punctuality, she scrambled into her clothes. Then it struck her that Pentti was merely being polite. He had cancelled the restaurant reservation with what seemed like unseemly haste. Had he been genuine he would have waited and checked with her again. Or maybe it was a cultural difference. She had turned his invitation down, but that didn't mean she didn't want to go. He could have tried to persuade her. He hadn't. He simply cancelled. Christ. What a mess. He was, she decided, the most annoying person and totally unsuitable for... what? What did she expect of him? No, the question should have been, what did she want of him, or with him? She hadn't a clue. But she decided what she really wanted was to see him outside the pressure-cooker environment of the last few days. So she finished dressing, paused to put on lipstick, and hurried down to the foyer. In the lift she checked the time again. It was seven twenty-eight.

'You look beautiful,' he said.

She mumbled a 'thank you' and got into the car.

They drove in silence for a while before she asked where they were going.

'I have to call in home for a minute,' he said.

'Home' turned out to be in Tapiola, a district of Espoo.

As they came into his apartment she realised that any notion she had entertained of a meal in some fancy Finnish restaurant was not going to happen. It was a beautiful apartment; but more than that, his dining room with its Aino Aalto club chairs, and Alvar Aalto clean-lined lighting fixtures, was awaiting her arrival. The table was set, the bottle of red wine had been decanted and she could smell the meal in the oven.

'You have no intention of taking me out for a meal...' she started.

'None,' he said flatly.

'I never asked you if you were married,' Nicole said, by way of conversation and to fill in the time until he decided to kiss her, as she suspected he would.

'Neither did I.'

'I'm not,' she said.

Pentti frowned. 'I've never told you about my wife and children.' He paused then his face relaxed. 'That would be because I don't have either.'

She punched him on the arm. 'I can understand that. I mean, who would want to marry a bloody owl?'

It was at that point he kissed her. It must have been around seven-fifty.

It was not until eleven that they dressed for dinner.

At midday on the twenty-sixth they assembled for a final briefing. Heimo, who had been involved in a long conversation with his Russian counterpart, was last to arrive.

'Well?' Pentti asked.

'He wants you all there,' Heimo said.

Pentti, obviously unimpressed by the idea, scowled, 'Since when did we agree to do everything Sedov wants?'

'Since the Presidents of our two countries agreed it should be so.'

'But I need to be running the operation from here.'

'I will be doing that,' Heimo said bluntly. 'This is non-negotiable, and in any case, from this point on our contribution on the twenty-eighth is limited to providing thirty seconds of television footage.'

'Thirty-two now, actually,' Anti muttered. 'I did a re-edit last night.'

'Thirty, thirty-two, whatever, my point remains the same.'

Nicole glanced down at her checklist. 'Has the footage been despatched?'

Heimo nodded. 'Both versions left this morning with the technical team who will co-ordinate with the Russian TV crew.'

Sam Gordon coughed politely and sat forward. 'When Sedov says "all", who does he mean?'

'Yes, Sam, you're going, along with Quentin, Pentti and Nicole.'

'Does anyone else find that odd?' Sam glanced around the table. 'What?'

'That he wants us all present.'

Quentin shook his head. 'It is a while since anything about this entire scenario looked anything else but decidedly odd.'

Pentti raised his hand. 'I'm sorry, but aren't we forgetting something? It was my understanding that we would close down the museum operation and arrest Remsu.'

'And get Auli Saarinen to a hospital,' Nicole added.

'And so you shall, but only after the broadcast.'

'Why wait?'

'Pentti, listen. It is imperative that Remsu thinks he has succeeded. He will see the television coverage and trigger the internet disruption as expected. Once that happens, Eero and Jukka will contain him until you arrive.'

'But –'

'That's an order. Now, I suggest you double-check everything and then get some rest. From now on everything is in the hands of our Russian friends.'

'Comforting,' Quentin muttered. 'Fucking comforting.'

'Do you think this is what Heimo meant by resting?' Nicole, flushed and breathless, pulled his head into her breast.

'No, this is what he calls inter-service cooperation.'

'An open and frank exchange of views?' she asked with a wicked smile.

'I'm not sure about open and frank, but the view is spectacular.' He nibbled playfully at her nipples.

'Do you do a lot of this, Mister Owl?'

'All the time. I'm considered to be rather a specialist in this area.'

'You weren't too shoddy in the other area...'

'Hush! You're supposed to be an uptight, frigid Englishwoman.'

'Uptight is fine,' she giggled. For a moment she remained silent, enjoying the closeness and the feeling of his hand stroking her stomach.

'I'll miss you,' Pentti said quietly.

'You'll be glad to get rid of me.'

'Not true.'

She pulled his head up and kissed him. 'You can't fool me. Right from the beginning you thought I was annoying and rude...'

'And pushy.'

'That as well. See, you will be glad when I'm gone.'

Pentti laughed. 'I see right through you, Nicole Parry. You're the classic... what was the term your writer, Le Carré, coined... a honey pot?'

'A honey trap.'

'I'm rather fond of them.'

Nicole rolled over and propping herself up on her elbows, looked at him. 'You know, there is an English children's story about a bear called Winnie-the-Pooh, and when he gets his head stuck in a honey pot his friend Christopher Robin says, "Don't worry, Pooh. We'll get you out."'

'And?'

'And Winnie the Pooh replies: "No hurry. Take your time."'

Pentti grinned and rolled her onto her back. 'Is there a moral to this story?'

'An immoral –' she started but got no further, as he had burrowed beneath the covers and begun gently licking her.

Later, smiling and satiated, Pentti was drifting towards sleep. 'I'm sorry you have to go back to London,' he murmured.

'Couldn't you be a bit like that man in the Kalevala?'

'Which man?'

'Lemon-kind.'

'Leminkainen...'

'And come and drag me into your sleigh from time to time?'

'Only if I can get my reindeer through British customs,' he stroked her face. 'Shh, sleep now.'

'But it's only just after four in the afternoon.'

'Hush. We need to sleep now and then there's plenty of time for more "resting" later.'

The early morning journey to Vyborg on the twenty-seventh was uneventful. There was little chatter and most of the way they drove in silence, each member of the team lost in thought, mulling over what the next day might bring. At one point Sam, in the back seat with Quentin, offered to drive. Pentti declined, saying that it stopped him thinking of what lay ahead.

'It's like being asked to do a high-wire act...' Quentin muttered morosely.

'Without a safety net,' Nicole concluded for him.

She had tried engaging Pentti in conversation, but each time he simply shrugged, nodded or grunted a reply, so she resigned herself to watching the landscape.

Shortly before they arrived at the Russian border, she switched the radio on and tried several stations without finding anything she liked. The tango music was on offer, but after a couple of minutes she had had enough and changed stations again. The reception wasn't great but she eventually found a deep-voiced male singer churning out mournful sounding lyrics.

'Great,' she said sarcastically and went to switch it off, but to her surprise Pentti reached over and turned it up.

'*Kun muistelen.* My parents liked this. They played it all the time.'

'It's a laugh a minute,' she said before she could stop herself. 'Sorry. I'm sure it's very nice.'

'Vesa-Matti Loiri, that's the singer.' Pentti grinned. 'Actually, I hated it.' He switched the radio off.

Orders had obviously come from on high, because the Russian Frontier police waved them through with nothing more than a cursory glance at their passports.

'Good to have friendly neighbours,' Pentti murmured and accelerated towards Vyborg.

Nicole rubbed the condensation off her window and peered out. 'It looks exactly the same as Finland. I don't know why, but I expected Russia to be different.'

'It was Finland, once,' Pentti said.

Their accommodation had the feeling of a dormitory masquerading as a hotel. Nicole didn't care. Pentti was off doing his secret owl stuff and all she wanted to do was catch up on some sleep. After a beer in the bar with Sam and Quentin, she excused herself and went to her room. She was asleep within minutes.

She awoke just after two and, with the rest of the team nowhere to be seen, she decided to do a little exploring.

'Where's worth visiting?' she asked the receptionist, a pimply-faced teenager who, to Nicole's surprise, spoke superb English, albeit with an American accent.

'Tomorrow's Kalevala Day so you should visit the statue of Väinämöinen in Monrepos Park.' She dug around behind her desk and produced a rather dog-eared leaflet. 'Here, it explains everything. Take a number six or number one bus.'

Nicole read the leaflet on the bus and found the English translation to be... she sought for a word. Charming? Quaint? No, idiosyncratic was better. The admission price was clear, sixty roubles; that was, unless she was a veteran of the Great Patriotic War, a person awarded the medal 'For the Defence of Leningrad' or had won the title 'Hero of the Soviet Union'. None of those seemed to apply but she wondered if she could bluff her way in by claiming to be a Hero of Socialist Labour. Surely working in the crypt at Hammersmith deserved such an accolade. She turned the page to the list of prohibitions and nearly choked to see that she was 'forbidden to breed' within the park. Well, she thought, there goes my afternoon's fun.

Having gained admittance, she followed a map that claimed it would guide her to 'multiple delights botanical' and carried a quote from a certain A Myer, who back in 1860 had written in the magazine *Son of the Fatherland* that: 'You will not find a stiff monotony, but at every turn open your eyes to new species.' Maybe it was true, but at the moment the omnipresent species happened to be snow.

It took her half an hour to reach the statue of the Kalevala hero Väinämöinen, and when she did she felt sorry for him, stuck on a giant granite boulder in a desolate setting. She also thought the sculpture was mediocre; nevertheless, she took out her phone and took a photograph. The time to visit the park, she realised, would be spring or summer. It was probably impressive, but right now it felt bleak and cold. She turned her coat collar up and began the hike back to the gate and hopefully a number six bus.

She had walked for ten minutes and detoured up a rise to what was described on the map as 'the Isle of the Dead', when she saw the man waiting on the path below her. She stopped and acting on instinct, crouched behind a rock. The man, wrapped in a warm coat with woollen hat, gloves and a long black scarf, was impatiently stamping his feet and clapping his hands together, trying to keep warm. He's not waiting for me, she decided, but still hesitated. There was something familiar about him that alerted her. Just wait, she cautioned herself. Carefully removing her gloves, she took out her phone and, selecting the zoom function on the camera, took a shot. She waited until it saved and then peered at the image. The man was now full frame, but his face was turned away.

She looked around for another path, but there seemed to be none. You are suffering from a bout of mild paranoia, she told herself, and decided to just walk down and continue to the park entrance.

It was as she stood up that she saw a second man approaching, and this time she recognised him. It was the Russian Sedov. She turned on the phone's video function and started recording as the two men greeted each other warmly, embracing then shaking hands. Nicole kept filming as Sedov took an envelope from his pocket and handed it to the man. The paymaster, she thought, handing over the cash.

For a minute or so the men chatted amicably then walked off together in the direction of the park entrance.

They had gone no more than twenty paces when to her horror she saw Sedov take out a pistol and calmly shoot the man in the head. Bending down, he retrieved the envelope, tucked it inside his coat, and without bothering to look around strolled off along the path as though nothing untoward had happened.

For a moment Nicole remained hidden, letting the shock and adrenaline dissipate. Then, checking that Sedov was out of sight, scrambled down to the main path and ran to the body lying face down in the snow. There was no doubt that the man was dead. It was not her crime scene, so she broke all the rules and rolled the man over. Nicole found herself looking down into the face of Andrei Zaikov.

'Christ!' she swore out loud.

She took her phone out again and took several photographs that captured the body, the head, the entrance and exit wounds and the still spreading blood on the snow.

Making sure she was unobserved, she hurried along the path following the direction Sedov had taken. She was some way behind him and only caught sight of the man as he exited the park and climbed into the back seat of a car.

By the time she reached the gate the vehicle was long gone.

'I hope you are enjoying your visiting of our natural park with sculptures,' the gatekeeper said.

'Wonderful,' Nicole said.

At the bus shelter she took a seat, catching her breath. For a moment she thought of ringing Pentti, but it occurred to her that she had no idea if their phones were secure. She turned the phone on and glanced at it only to find that ringing anyone was impossible, as she had no signal.

Chapter Twenty-Two

Quentin Grammaticus looked at her for a long time, weighing up her extraordinary story. For a moment it occurred to Nicole that in telling him she had made the wrong decision. Then Quentin got to his feet.

'We have been sitting on this bench for far too long. Let's keep walking.'

Glad to be moving, she fell into step with him.

'Coming to me rather than Pentti was the right thing to do.'

She shrugged. 'It is *his* operation.' She had so nearly burst into Pentti's room to show him the video and photographs. Then she had changed her mind, dragging Quentin out of the hotel and down Krepostnaya Ulitsa, where there were plenty of people and traffic and virtually no way they could be overheard. A couple of times she checked behind, but could see no sign of a tail.

For a few minutes they walked on in silence until they arrived at the Castle Bridge that leads to the Vyborg castle. Quentin stopped and gazed down into the water.

'He once asked me why rivers are not blue like they are on maps,' he said.

'Zaikov?'

'Yes. We decided it was because they were full of shit.' He peered sideways at her and lowered his voice. 'We keep this to ourselves. Now is not the time to use it, but trust me, it will prove valuable if things go our way tomorrow.'

'You mean, if nobody kills the President and the dissidents are captured?'

He nodded. 'If that happens, Sedov will become even more powerful, more important.'

'And we will have a hook into him?'

'Exactly. It is a situation very much to our advantage. So we keep it quiet.'

'Even from Pentti?'

'Yes.' Quentin glanced around and then smiled at her. 'Give me the phone.'

For a second Nicole hesitated, but then took it from her pocket and handed it to him.

He smiled. 'We've been standing here too long. We had better act like tourists and take a photo.'

He took a couple of shots of her on the bridge, then another of the castle.

'I do love holiday snaps,' he murmured as he tucked her phone into his pocket.

By dawn on the morning of the twenty-eighth the weather had cleared and all the indications agreed with the official forecast that the day would be bright, clear and, at only minus ten degrees, surprisingly warm. That was until just after mid-afternoon, when a storm front was due to pass through, bringing strong winds and fresh snow. Hopefully the weather would hold until after the Kalevala Day celebrations were over.

'And if the weather turns early?' Pentti asked, but nobody answered.

At eleven they arrived at the stadium to find a huge crowd already assembled and the entire area transformed from a snow-covered sports field to something approaching a fairground. Around the perimeter dozens of stalls had been set up, and men and women in national costume were selling hot food and drinks. There were toy stalls, a rather bizarre best dressed pet competition, a minia-ture Ferris wheel for very small children, and an area set aside for folk dancing.

'Christ.' Sam muttered as he surveyed the scene, 'if only they knew...'

'They don't,' Pentti replied, 'and neither do we, so I suggest you start looking happy.'

At around eleven-thirty, one of Sedov's men approached them with the news that he was their official minder and that they should follow him through security to a taped-off area of the main stand. They were not the first to arrive, and took their allocated seats at the back behind a row of men in a variety of military uniforms. The men nodded at them and continued on chatting quietly.

'Television,' Pentti pointed to the screen set to one side. 'I was getting worried we would miss the broadcast.'

'It's the one time I would rather see an event on TV than in the flesh,' Grammaticus said, glancing at the screen. An over-excited female reporter appeared to be holding an animated conversation with a dog dressed in leather breaches and a plaid tunic. Thankfully the sound was turned off.

'The President will be joining you after the ceremony,' their minder explained, 'when there is to be a mass folk dance by five hundred children.'

'It sounds worse than water-boarding,' Sam said bleakly, wishing he were anywhere else but Vyborg. His mood had been dark all morning and he confided to Pentti that he had a premonition that everything was going to go horribly wrong. 'That's why Sedov wants us all here,' he said, 'so that when it all turns to shit he can have us arrested or shot on the spot.'

'Then we had better hope it goes according to plan,' Pentti responded.

The local people appeared to share the Finnish punctuality gene and by five minutes to twelve had crowded into the stands on either side of the arena. As they did, the sound system crackled into life and an announcement was greeted with prolonged applause.

Away to the west storm clouds were gathering, but too far away to disrupt anything. It was just as well, Nicole thought, because it was now way too late to substitute the footage to match any change in the weather. At the moment the sun was shining brightly and only needed to do so for another few minutes.

'The President is about to take the baton,' the minder explained with undisguised glee as the audience cheered wildly. On the television monitor the scene shifted to outside the stadium and a close-up of the Russian President, stripped down, despite the temperature, to a singlet and shorts. He was running with the ceremonial hammer in his hand.

'Looks like a dress-code violation,' Grammaticus muttered, then glanced down to the front of the stand where some soldiers were forming an honour guard for some official cars that had entered the stadium.

Two sleek black limousines pulled up below them and Sedov and three other men emerged and proceeded up the stairs to the VIP area. Sedov gave Pentti a polite nod and then seated himself beside the empty blue chair that awaited the President.

Nicole checked her watch. It was exactly midday and right on cue the crowd erupted as the Russian President came onto the circular track beneath an arch of flags held by members of the local Vyborg Football Club.

Without hesitation he commenced a lap of the stadium, urged on by the crowd who were now on their feet as they applauded.

'Popular, isn't he,' Nicole observed.

'And fit, it would seem,' Grammaticus added.

Pentti was jumpy and checked his watch again. 'We are running two minutes late.' Away to his left he could see the mobile television broadcast van; several soldiers and a couple of police were guarding it. Hopefully the technical team inside were on top of the situation. So much depended on a single switch being flicked at exactly the right moment. 'This had better work,' he muttered.

'Relax,' Nicole said, despite the fact that she was totally on edge. 'He's got to get to the statue and then climb up...'

'*Paska!*' Pentti swore. '*Jumalauta!*'

'What?'

'Nicole... the climbing up...'

'So?' She stared at him; he looked suddenly terrified.

'Climbing up. What if I've got it all wrong?'

'Yes, you said –'

'When Ilkka climbed up to test the contacts in the slot for the hammer, he had to stand on the cover of the Sampo.'

'So?'

'What if it's a fall-back? What if they have only just armed it?'

She grabbed his arm. 'For fuck's sake, Pentti, what the hell are you going on about?'

'What if the lid of the Sampo is a pressure plate release mechanism, and when he steps on it that triggers the explosion? The whole thing about the hammer might be an elaborate distraction.'

'It's too late to do anything,' Nicole hissed.

Pentti realised she was right. Below them the President raced along the track towards the statue. Even if he tried to stop him, there was no way he could reach him in time.

As the crowd rose to their feet again, they switched their attention back to the monitor and the close-up of the President leaving the track and climbing to the statue. At the base he paused and, turning to the crowd, raised the hammer in both hands. It was a shot straight out of the Socialist-Realist filmmakers' handbook. No matter what else they said about him, Grammaticus thought, he certainly knows how to grab the maximum amount of media attention.

Nicole felt sick to the stomach. Down the end of the stadium, the President was just a tiny figure, alone against a backdrop of snow. But on the monitor, he was an heroic figure holding aloft the hammer that forged the Sampo.

He turned and vaulted onto the base of the statue and stepped onto the lid of the Sampo. Pentti forced himself to breathe. It was safe. So far it was safe. Without pausing, the President climbed to within reach of the hands of Ilmarinen. And with one last wave to the crowd, he began to slide the hammer into place.

The crowd went wild and at exactly the same moment there was a giant flash of light and an ear-splitting explosion.

On the monitor, the flash appeared as a wall of flame as the statue exploded, sending a shock wave that rocked the camera. For a second or two the cameraman lost focus and then regaining some semblance of control, panned around to the gaping hole in the forest edge where the trees had been torn to splinters and the snow blasted off the bare rock face. The camera zoomed out, not smoothly, but jerking as the operator fought to control it. The statue was totally gone. Nothing remained but some smoking twisted metal. For a moment the camera lost focus again and then tilted down to show the decapitated head of Ilmarinen half buried amidst some rubble. The camera remained on the head and then tilted up and back to the forest, where the splintered stump of a spruce was burning. The image flickered for several seconds before the screen went black and the signal was lost.

'Jesus H Christ!' Sam swore.

Nicole turned her attention away from the monitor and beamed at Sam. 'Your fireworks did the trick,' she said, but he was still gazing at the television and didn't seem to hear.

The inclusion and the timing of the fireworks had been her idea and, thankfully, worked perfectly. And, she admitted grudgingly, the shot of Ilmarinen's head had not been as over-the-top as she had argued to the director Ahti. The burning spruce image had worked as well. 'An image to remind us of an old film, *Tuntematon sotilas*, *The Unknown Soldier*,' he had claimed. She made a mental note to apologise to him. He had done an extraordinary job.

Pentti looked around to find Sedov standing by his shoulder.

'Stage one was impressive,' the Russian said. 'I particularly like the fireworks your American friend smuggled into our country. I hope you will reward him in a suitable manner.'

'Something like that,' Pentti said.

'In any case, a job well done.'

'Thanks to you,' Pentti nodded. 'If you hadn't told us where to find that damned hammer, we would not have been able to remove the batteries and we would be looking at a very different scenario. One that no amount of fireworks could have disguised.'

'Team work,' Sedov grunted.

'I hope you are as successful with stage two.' He shook Sedov's hand. 'Now, if you will excuse us, we have work to do back in Finland.'

Sedov shrugged. 'As you please. Though you may find it has been taken care of.'

Pentti glared at him. 'What do you mean, "taken care of"?'

But Sedov had turned away. 'Ah, I see our President is making his way back.' He glanced over his shoulder at Pentti. 'Drive carefully, Mister Toivonen, I hear there is bad weather on the way.'

Pentti ignored the remark, and taking out his mobile phone checked if the communication blackout was in force. He saw immediately that there was no signal so he gestured to the others to follow him.

As soon as they were out of the stadium, he turned to them. 'Sedov wanted us here so his people could deal with Remsu and the computers in the museum.'

Quentin frowned. 'But I thought Eero, Ilkka and Jukka were going –'

'Christ! We have to warn them,' Nicole said.

Pentti shook his head. 'There's no phone coverage, remember?'

'Then we have to get there fast and...' Quentin started, but the others were already running towards the car. Ahead of them was a long drive and the storm clouds were gathering in the west.

The effect in Russia, at least on the surface, was one of confusion. For the first time a majority of Russians found themselves without internet access and the major television channels were scrambling to make sense of the disrupted broadcast from Vyborg. Their first response was to blame it on a disruption to the power supply.

It appeared that the Distributed Denial of Service attack was spectacularly successful, reaching the highest rate ever recorded, some 400 gigabytes a second. The internet went down, but in doing so played into the hands of the Russian FSB, who with their own protected satellite links, now controlled almost every piece of information coming out of the country.

The FSB waited for two hours before they released the news that the attack on the internet and the hacking of a television transmission from Vyborg had been the work of a far-right extremist group. Anyone who doubted that simply needed to log on to any of the hacked government websites to be taken to the dissidents' website.

Out of the public eye the security services, the army and special police units, moved quickly into bases across the country. From Khankala, to the east of Grozny in the Chechen Republic, headquarters of the 42nd Motor Rifle Division, to the Lekhtusi early warning radar station outside Leningrad, the arrests took place with military precision. There was little resistance, and the only sustained fire fight outside the Moscow region took place around the Baltic Fleet headquarters in Kaliningrad.

Within two hours, reports from the Joint Strategic Command Centre in Yekaterinburg and the national leadership command facility at Lipetsk all confirmed that what they described as an 'attempted coup' had been suppressed and over six hundred people taken into custody.

Later it emerged that a large number of rebels had been killed in a concerted push into the command bunkers beneath the number two metro line in Moscow. Seventy-three dissidents succumbed to gas in a tunnel and another thirty burned to death when flame-throwers were brought in to flush them from an occupied bunker.

When television coverage of the celebrations eventually resumed, the viewers were taken back to Vyborg and the sight of an extremely happy President watching Karelian children perform traditional dances. This was followed by reruns of the President placing the hammer in Ilmarinen's hands and an interview in which he, with General Sedov at his shoulder, condemned the 'rebel scum and their foreign backers'. Sedov promised that every one of the miscreants would be brought to justice. Finally, the President thanked the people of the Russian Republics for their support and assured them he would be back in the Kremlin by nightfall and that internet services would return to normal by the following day.

The message flashed from Heimo in Helsinki was unambiguous. Stage one had succeeded and they should immediately initiate stage two. Eero, Ilkka and Jukka had been in position for two hours and the order to move on the museum came as welcome relief. A second message informed them that Pentti would rendezvous with them at the museum and was concerned that there might be interference from across the border.

'Russians? They would never dare,' Ilkka said.

'Driving time from Vyborg?' Jukka asked. 'How long until Pentti gets here?'

Ilkka looked at his watch and did a quick calculation. 'If they left straight after the main event, then they should be here between two-thirty and three.'

'Then I vote we secure the building and wait inside,' Eero said.

They drove directly into the car park at the front of the museum, entered through the main door and, like any casual visitors, purchased entry tickets. There was no security check and nobody took any notice of the three men or the sports bags they were carrying.

For a couple of minutes, they strolled around the ground floor and then Jukka nodded for them to follow him and went to the lift.

'Going down?' Eero asked cheerfully as the door shut. He took out his weapon. Jukka removed his Heckler & Koch UMP from his bag then located the button beneath the framed safety instructions and pushed it. 'Okay, earpieces in and all comms on channel one,' he instructed.

The sight that greeted them in the underground bunker was not what they had expected. There was no security and by the sound of the noise, a party was underway. The doors to the computer complex and central control room were wide open and they were able to walk straight in. At first nobody even noticed the three heavily armed men standing there, as the attention in the room was focused on a huge screen replaying the last thirty seconds of the Vyborg broadcast. They had the video looped so it repeated, and each time the explosion took place a cheer went up. At the centre of the room, seated in a large swivel chair was Kullervo Remsu, a broad grin on his face and a glass of champagne in his hand.

Eero took out his pistol and was about to fire a shot into the ceiling, but Jukka pushed his hand down. 'Let's not frighten the natives just yet,' he said quietly. He banged the butt of his weapon against the doorframe.

'Remsu!'

The effect was immediate. The party came to a halt as Remsu spun in his chair and faced them. He seemed totally unfazed by the intrusion and raised his glass to them.

'Come and join the party.'

Around him the dozen or so men and women of his technical crew seemed less confident and backed away from the line of fire.

'The party is over,' Jukka said. 'I have orders to take you into custody. The rest of you lie face down on the floor. Ilkka, wrist ties on everyone.'

The men and women obeyed without hesitation, but Remsu shook his head. 'Last time I looked, the scoreline was two-nil, in our favour; one dead president and one dead internet.'

'Then I suggest you change channels and take a look at Russian TV,' Ilkka said.

Remsu stood, put his glass down, then picked up a remote and flicked through the channels until he found *Rossiya 1*. The footage was a replay of the Russian President climbing the statue and slotting the hammer into place. There were several seconds of fireworks and then the President, beaming with satisfaction, was shown jogging back to the stands. The shot changed to a close-up of the President presenting a bunch of flowers to the organiser of the children's folk dancing performance. The text scrolling beneath the picture was unambiguous: *Coup defeated, plotters captured. Cyber attack thwarted. Internet expected back in service by midnight.*

Illka grinned. 'I agree on the score, Remsu. Two-nil, but unfortunately not in your favour.'

But Remsu wasn't listening. He sat back in his chair, an expression of bemusement on his face. Then he looked up as it dawned on him what had taken place. 'You substituted the vision.'

'Right,' Jukka said. 'Lovely bit of editing, very realistic.' He turned to Eero. 'Plasticuffs on his wrists now, please. There's a storeroom upstairs by the back entrance to the building. Pentti reported that it was lockable, so toss him in there while we do what we have to here.' He tapped his earpiece. 'Let me know when he's secure.'

Ilkka moved in behind Remsu, who put up no resistance. In fact, he didn't look even mildly perturbed by the situation. For a moment Jukka wondered if he was missing something. 'Hang on, see if he has a phone.'

Ilkka checked the plastic wrist ties were secure then went through Remsu's pockets and retrieved not one but two phones.

'Good, I'll take care of those,' Jukka pocketed them and gestured to Eero. 'Take him.'

'No!'

Startled by the voice directly behind him, Jukka spun around to find a woman standing in the doorway. It took him a second to recognise her from the photographs.

'I'm sorry, Miss Saarinen, but I have orders to make Remsu secure.'

'Then I go too. Where Kullervo goes, I go.'

He looked at her. Auli Saarinen looked healthy and her cheeks were flushed, nothing like the pale, sick woman that Pentti and Nicole had described.

'Suit yourself,' he shrugged and turned back to Eero. 'Take her along with you. When you have Remsu secured, I want you to get rid of everybody upstairs and lock the place down.'

'The staff upstairs? You want their details?'

'Yes, but then send them home with a story of a gas leak in the basement.'

He stepped to one side and watched as Eero used his pistol to prod Remsu along. The woman didn't attempt to speak to Remsu, seemingly content to fall into step beside him.

'Now Ilkka, we need names of everyone here, job description, everything. I'll call for transport, as I am afraid we are going to take them with us.' He pulled out his phone, but found he had no signal.

There was absolutely no resistance from the group of technicians and, after Ilkka recorded each person's details, Jukka directed them to take chairs and sit at the far side of the room. He had changed his mind about the need for wrist restraints, as it seemed that the sight of their weapons had been enough to make them realise that resisting would be a particularly bad idea. At least half of them appeared to be suffering from shock.

Suddenly a red light started flashing on the central control panel. Jukka turned to one of the older men. 'Why's the light flashing?'

'You ordered a lockdown. That indicates it's in place.'

Jukka frowned. Eero hadn't called as instructed. 'Ilkka, are you getting this?'

From the other side of the room Illka nodded. 'Loud and clear.'

'Eero. Eero. Are you getting this?'

There was no response. Then the man beside him tapped him on the arm.

'Excuse me. But if you are trying to talk to your companion upstairs, you can't.'

'Why?'

'The bunker is protected space. No radio waves out, no eaves-dropping in.'

'Shit.' Jukka paused for a moment. 'Tell me, what's your name?'

'Jorma Juntunen.'

'And what's your role?'

'I maintain the surveillance systems.'

Jukka pointed to a chair behind the main console. 'That's perfect. Okay, Jorma, I want you to sit here and keep an eye on the monitors. You assist me with that and I'll put in a good word.'

'All I want is a free Karelia…'

'You are not alone in that,' Jukka said, 'I just want you to watch the monitors and tell me if you see anything unusual.'

Jukka had returned to assisting Ilkka with recording the last of the details when the man called him over to the control console. 'You might like to see this.'

Jukka nodded for Ilkka to finish off and then went to the console. 'What?'

Jorma pointed at a monitor. 'Camera seven. Northern side. Six men. They came out of the forest.' He paused, then added, 'They don't look like Finns.'

Jukka felt himself stiffen. 'Ilkka. Here, now!' he barked.

Ilkka came quickly to his side and peered at the monitor. The black and white image was clear and showed six heavily armed men. Four appeared to have machine pistols and two were carrying what looked like rocket or grenade launchers. For about a minute they huddled on the forest edge and then they spread out, some going left, the others to the right.

'Camera five,' Jorma said, 'and camera eight.' He punched two buttons and produced a split-screen image from the two cameras.

'Huston, we have a problem,' Ilkka said quietly.

Jukka nodded. 'Christ, no wonder Remsu was so relaxed. He knew the Russians were coming to rescue him.'

'There's something else,' Jorma said. 'Camera one.'

The camera covering the car park at the front of the building had a wide angle lens, but even with the distortion there was no mistaking the blue Mondeo that had just pulled in beside their vehicle.

'Pentti.' Jukka took out his phone. 'I've got to warn him.'

Jorma shook his head. 'Didn't you hear what I said? No signals in or out of the bunker.'

'None?'

'Then I have to go out to him.'

'But you asked for a lockdown.'

'So?'

'So it will be an hour from when it was activated before you can open the front doors or use the lift.'

Ilkka grabbed the man by the arm, pulled him from the chair, spun him around and grabbed him by the throat. 'You're lying!'

But the man just shrugged. 'I'm telling you the truth. You can go out the back door, but with those men there…'

'Leave him!' Jukka snapped. 'We have a bigger problem. I don't think those men are intending to rescue anyone. Look what that bastard is doing.' He pointed along the bank of monitors to the far left. The picture from camera nine showed the sides of the huge gas storage tanks and a man attaching wires to what looked like a large amount of plastic explosive.

'It's too quiet,' Nicole said as she got out of the car.

Pentti nodded. 'I'll phone Jukka.' He took out his phone but for some reason the call failed to connect. 'Signal must be bad inside. I guess we just have to knock.'

Quentin and Sam climbed out of the back seat and stretched, both of them stiff from sitting so long.

'The weather was better in bloody Russia,' Sam quipped, pointing to the clouds that were now scudding overhead. The wind had picked up and while there were only a few flecks of snow in the air, conditions looked set to deteriorate. He reached back into the car and grabbed their jackets. He tossed Quentin's to him. 'Rug up, Quent.'

Quentin nodded his thanks and put the jacket on. 'Worse than Blackpool,' he muttered to himself. He turned to Pentti. 'So what's the drill, boss?'

'We break in if we have to,' Pentti said. He leaned back into the car and retrieved the pistol from the glove box. 'Nicole, take this, just in case.'

She took the pistol and slipped it into her jacket pocket. 'What about you?'

'Thanks to our VIP treatment on the border, my rifle is still safely in the boot.' He took the rifle bag out, removed the rifle and slotted the magazine into place. He was about to close the boot when another thought occurred to him. 'Sam, take the tyre lever, it might be a useful housebreaking tool.'

'And me?' Quentin asked.

Pentti laughed dryly. 'Quentin, just stick with me. We're breaking into a museum, not fighting a bloody war.'

They climbed the steps to the front entrance, but the reinforced glass looked impregnable with the tools at their disposal. 'We could probably blast our way in,' Pentti said, 'but for the moment I think we should keep that as a last resort.'

'So?'

'So we go around to the rear. There's a door beside some gas tanks. I think our best option is to see if we can force it open.'

He gestured them to follow and headed off down the steps and around the building to the right. But Nicole grabbed his arm and stopped him.

'Wait. This doesn't feel right. Eero, Jukka and Ilkka are inside and if they're not showing themselves there has to be a reason.'

Pentti nodded. 'I agree, but I don't see any alternative.'

There was no clear path around the side of the building and for the next few minutes they struggled through deep snowdrifts as the wind intensified, whipping the increasingly heavy snow into their faces.

The first door they came to was the solid steel one Pentti had seen before. Even if they could have forced it open, it would have taken an hour of digging to clear the snow and ice piled up against it. Pentti, who had forged ahead of the others, waited for them to regroup.

'Around the next corner there's the gas storage facility and the service entrance,' Pentti said.

'I would never have made a polar explorer,' Quentin gasped and paused to catch his breath.

Sam, exhausted from wading through the thigh-deep snow, didn't say anything, but flopped back in the snow next to Nicole.

'Fun,' she said darkly. 'So much fucking fun.'

Pentti let them rest for a couple of minutes and then, aware that the temperature was dropping and the wind picking up, got them to their feet.

'Around the corner of the building we should be out of the worst of the wind. Stick close to the walls as last time I was here the snow was not piled up like it is here.'

They rounded the corner and to their relief found that Pentti had been right. There were no snowdrifts in the lee of the building and they could walk at normal pace.

They had gone only a few metres when a volley of shots rang out.

'Down!' Pentti yelled and threw himself into the snow.

Another burst of automatic fire ricocheted off the building above their heads.

Nicole tried to reach her pistol, but found it was in the pocket beneath her.

'Stay down!' Pentti screamed. 'They're firing above our heads.'

Nicole saw some movement to her right. 'Pentti!' she yelled, but before she could say more a boot was planted firmly in the middle of her back, forcing her further into the snow. She twisted her head around and found the muzzle of a machine pistol was pointing directly at her head.

'Do as he says! Stay down,' said a voice from above her.

There was no chance to do anything. Out of the now thickly falling snow, dark shapes materialised as the man's companions joined him. One by one they hauled them to their feet, searched, disarmed and thrust them up against the wall.

The tallest of the men walked up and without warning slammed his fist into Pentti's stomach, knocking him to the ground. He stood over him and then kicked him. Pentti writhed in pain, unable to rise. The man signalled for his companions to haul Pentti to his feet.

'I have been waiting to meet you again,' the man said softly. 'You caused me a lot of unhappiness when you killed my friend Vladimir. I owe you for that.'

'Tesak,' Pentti grunted, suppressing the pain. 'Tesak, if you have a brain in that thick head of yours, you would leave now. This place is under surveillance and there is no way you can get away with anything.'

Tesak put his head back and roared with laughter. 'Stupid Finnish spook. Trust me, they can film all they like because shortly you and they will all be dead. Maybe you'll be blown up; maybe you'll freeze to death first.'

The figures of the Russians emerging like dark phantoms out of the snowstorm looked like a scene from an old-fashioned black and white silent movie. It was just as silent in the control room as Jukka and Ilkka stood transfixed as the Russians dragged Sam, Quentin, Pentti and Nicole along to the gas tanks and tied them to the pipes,

'Christ,' Ilkka whispered.

'What's that guy doing?' Jukka pointed to the top of the screen, where another man had made his way over to stand directly in front of the camera. As they watched he held something above his head.

'He's showing us the timer,' Ilkka said. 'I can't read it – the contrast is not good enough.'

'Bastards!' Jukka swore.

'Wait!' Jorma leaned forward, located a dial and turned it. The contrast on the image changed and the numbers became clearly visible.

'Thirty minutes. It gives them plenty of time to be out of here,' Ilkka said.

'How long is left on the lockdown?'

Jorma squinted at a small counter beneath the red flashing light. 'Twenty-five minutes, approximately.'

'What does approximately mean?' Jukka snapped.

'Sorry, there's some bug in the system and it's always been a bit variable. Maybe a minute or two either side, but basically twenty-five minutes.'

On the screen, they saw that the Russians had turned and were making their way back to the forest edge; a few seconds later they had vanished into the swirling snow.

Ilkka zipped up his coat. 'We have a window of five minutes between the lockdown ending and the detonation of those tanks. I have to get out there.' He turned to the technical crew. 'Listen, I can defuse the explosives, but I have to get out. There must be a way. If you know it, now's the time to speak up.'

There was silence. Ilkka was about to turn away when a young woman raised her hand. 'There is one way.'

Jukka gestured for her to come to him. 'Tell me.'

'Mister Remsu has a way out. It is very small, but he told me once that it connects to the old bunkers and trenches from the war. I know where you get in, but I don't know if you can get out.'

Jukka turned back to Ilkka and spoke quietly. 'Can you really defuse that thing?'

'Possibly. I can certainly free Pentti and the others.'

'What do you need?'

'Specialist equipment that we don't have; but a set of screw drivers, cutting pliers and a knife might be enough.'

'Tools are in the cabinet over by the wall,' Jorma said. 'Come with me.'

Jukka turned back to the young woman. 'What do you do here?'

'I'm an assistant nurse. I was looking after Miss Saarinen, but then she got better because she stopped taking her drugs.'

'Your name?'

'Hillevi Virtanen.'

'If you will show my colleague where this exit is, you may well have saved a lot of people's lives.'

'I don't want to die, sir, and I have never been in trouble.'

'You'll be fine,' Jukka said, hoping it was true.

'Let's go,' Ilkka called.

Jukka turned back to the others. 'Just sit quietly. There is no need to panic.' This time he knew it was not the truth.

Hillevi took Ilkka along a corridor and through a door leading to a small office with a single desk and chair. Switching on the light, she pointed to the far wall. 'He told me it shows all the trenches from the war.' She crossed the room to a large framed map and taking hold of one edge of the frame, pulled it away from the wall. 'Like a door,' she said as the frame swung out on a set of strong hinges. 'You'll need the chair.'

Behind the frame was a second sturdier wooden door that was secured by a single small bolt. He opened it to reveal a narrow tunnel drilled through the rock. 'Sneaky bastard,' Ilkka muttered to himself. Ahead of him the tunnel was pitch black. For a moment he thought he could see a dim light filtering in from somewhere several metres away, but realised it was only his eyes playing tricks. He turned back to the young woman. 'Please don't bolt the door, but put the map back in place. Tell my colleague I'll signal him from outside.'

Hillevi nodded and watched as Ilkka hoisted himself up and slid headfirst into the tunnel.

Chapter Twenty-Three

The conditions had deteriorated; the wind was now howling around them and the edge of the forest was blotted out by the driving snow. Pentti wondered if they were even still visible to anyone inside. The Russian who had attached the timer had made a point of holding it up to the nearest camera, which seemed to indicate that he knew people were inside watching on the monitors. The cold worried him, but it was a small concern compared to the certainty of being blown to pieces when the explosive charges were detonated.

Pentti peered through the snow to his left. Nicole was stamping her feet up and down, attempting to keep her circulation going. She looked up and their eyes met. Her face seemed devoid of any expression, as if she was no longer present. For a moment she held his gaze and then looked away.

'I'm sorry,' he yelled. 'This is all my fault.' He wasn't sure she could even hear him above the storm.

To his right Sam and Quentin were tied back-to-back to a large gas pipe. The timer had been placed above their heads but angled away from them so that they couldn't see the countdown. And none of them could get their wrists in a position where they could see their watches.

'Keep your legs moving!' Pentti yelled, but neither Sam nor Quentin gave any indication that they could hear him.

'I'm going to freeze to death before that fucking thing explodes,' Sam said loudly enough for Quentin to hear.

'They tell me that hypothermia is peaceful,' Quentin responded.

'I can't feel my fingers anymore but I think they're frozen to the pipe.'

'I would like a glass of Talisker.'

'What?'

'It doesn't matter,' Quentin said, deciding there was nothing to be gained by talking. He had not been dressed for prolonged exposure to the cold. Fortunately, he had put on his jacket when he got out of the car. But he hadn't expected to need gloves. It seemed a pointless line of thought. Even if had gloves he wouldn't need them for very long.

Sam, angry and frustrated, strained against the wrist-ties, using the pain as they cut into his flesh to keep himself alert. He jolted himself forward and screamed into the storm, 'This fucking sucks!' Then, knowing he was defeated, slumped back against the pipes.

He had crawled maybe five or six metres when he came to the end of the granite tunnel. The atmosphere had changed from dank cold to an earthy mustiness that suggested he had reached one of the trenches. Ilkka paused and felt around with his hand; then, confident in his judgment, slithered headfirst down onto wooden planks. There was a little light filtering in from somewhere ahead of him, but not enough to see clearly. He reached up and ran his hands along a ceiling constructed of rough-hewn timber.

The trench was about a metre wide, its walls made of split logs. The space was not high enough to allow him to stand up so he bent double and hurried forward.

A few metres further on he came to the remains of a wartime bunker. Broken bunk beds and a lopsided table were all that remained. From the bunker two more passages continued. One appeared to veer to the right and the other went directly to the left. He took the right hand one, but had only taken a few steps when he came to a dead end where the walls and ceiling had collapsed. He retraced his steps and took the other trench. It continued on for several metres and once again his way was blocked. This time it was not by a tunnel collapse but by snow. Ilkka knew that time was against him and that he had no other choice so, using a screwdriver for a tool, he began to dig upwards.

It took him five or six minutes but eventually he broke through to the surface, and scrambling upwards he managed to climb out of the trench. For a moment he lay on his back, gasping cold air. Then he got to his feet and looked around. The storm was at full force and his heart sank for he had no idea where he was, and in these conditions wandering in the wrong direction would be fatal, for all involved. Just go, he told himself. He strode forward and found himself on the edge of the forest. The driving snow was coming from his right. Was that west? He hoped so, because in that case the museum should be directly ahead of him. If not... but he dismissed the thought. He had to have guessed correctly.

The timer on the console indicated that there were fifteen minutes left before the lockdown ended. It had better be accurate, Jukka thought, or better still, a little slow. If the window of opportunity was only five minutes then they would need every second. He tried to remember how long it had taken the lift to descend. Less than thirty seconds. He had counted heads already, but he did it again. Thirteen people, including himself. Five in the lift at a time meant three trips up and down. Three times thirty seconds each way. Given turn-around time and getting people in and out... It was so tight. Allowing for a full five minutes, that gave them four minutes. But what if the opening and closing of the door took even a few seconds longer? His mind refused to do the calculation. And the front door? Would it just open or...?'

'Jorma. When the lockdown ends, is the front exit door automatically open?'

Jorma shook his head. 'No, but there is an emergency button on the right of the door frame that should open it.'

'Should?'

'It will open it,' Jorma said. 'It has to.'

Jukka thought for a moment then sat down beside him. 'Listen, this is what we do. In a few minutes I want you to assemble everyone beside the lift. Divide them into three groups. You have to be in the first group.'

'I should go last,' Jorma said flatly.

'No, I need you to get to the front door and open it. Then get people as far from the building as possible. I am going to come up with the last group and try and find my colleague, Remsu, and Miss Saarinen.'

'You won't have time –'

'Just do as I say,' Jukka snapped. The monitors still registered the same images. The near white-out conditions had rendered most of them useless, but camera eight, in the lee of the building, still showed the four captives tied to the tanks. They were snow covered, and worryingly, appeared not to be moving. There was no sign of Ilkka. He glanced at the timer. Twelve minutes.

There will be nothing left, no trace, no blood and gore. Vaporised. This close to the explosive charges and the tanks, there would be no... what was the phrase? No mortal remains. The cold was getting to him, he realised, creeping into his body, numbing him against everything, including fear. Ghosts, he wondered if they existed. Shades, shadows. Wraiths like the one stumbling, head down, towards them.

A hand jerked him, slapped his face and then twisted him sideways, and as the pliers cut through the restraints, pulled him free.

'Get the others,' Pentti said. 'Quickly.' But the ghost was gone.

He took two steps and nearly fell. Then a welcome burst of adrenaline kicked in. He was going to survive. He lifted his head and saw the others, free, massaging their wrists.

'Get as far away as you can, this place will blow in less than five minutes,' Ilkka yelled. 'I'm going to try and defuse it.'

'Remsu? Where the fuck are Remsu and Auli?'

'In the storeroom. Eero is guarding them. Jukka will try and get to them.'

'No! I'm going to get them. The rest of you get out of here.' Pentti didn't wait for a reply but, staying in the shelter of the building, made for the rear door. He had no idea how he was going to open it. He looked around trying to see what had become of the tyre lever, but it was gone, either with the Russians or buried beneath the snow.

'Keep going,' Nicole urged. 'Maybe we can alert them we're outside.'

It was no plan at all. 'Go away!' he screamed at her. 'There's no point in both of us –'

'Shut up!' Nicole yelled and pushed past him. 'The door… it's open.'

The door had been opened about half a metre before it had jammed against the snow. They ran to it and entered the building to find the storeroom door was open, smashed from the inside by a fire extinguisher that had then been left on the floor.

'There's someone inside,' Nicole said and swinging the door wide open, found Eero on the ground, conscious but groggy after a blow to the head.

'He did this?' Pentti asked.

'No, it was that crazy bitch.'

As Pentti helped him to his feet, Eero grabbed at his holster. 'Oh fuck! They've taken my pistol.'

'The Russians have explosives on the gas tanks. You have to get away from here fast,' Pentti said and pushed him towards the door. 'Get as far as possible. If Ilkka can't defuse it we have only…' he glanced at his watch, '…about three minutes.' He turned to Nicole, 'Come on, they can't have gone far.'

There had been many nights when the nightmare had woken him, sweating and feeling ill. In the dream he had fingers numbed from the cold or trembling so much he was unable to control them. And always there was a timer counting down.

In real life he knew that he had the skills to defeat most bomb makers, knew which wires to cut or which screws to remove to reach a battery or a detonator. In the nightmare the colour coded wires were always tangled bundles of green, yellow, blue and black, a deadly spaghetti mocking his fear yet seducing him into staying those few seconds longer. Seconds that always ended with him waking with a start. Yet the reality that confronted him was worse.

His fingers were numb but it was the wires that defeated him. Not only were there too many of them for him to recognise their individual role in triggering the device, but the designer had set the timer up with wires of a single colour. No colour coding, no indication at all of their function. Every wire was black. The detonation required no more than two wires; the others were booby-traps and decoys designed to render deactivation impossible.

Below the timer was a box, which he suspected contained a circuit board and which normally he would have unscrewed in order to examine the circuitry. But this box was a solid extension of the timer and it was a sealed unit. It was, he thought, a beautiful piece of work. He looked at the timer. Two minutes. He had no option other than to either abandon the building to its fate or blindly cut the wires. I will wake up in a moment, he thought. This is not real. One minute thirty. His numb fingers reached into his pocket for the pliers.

Outside, a gale was whipping the snow off the ground and swirling it through the air. 'There,' Nicole shouted and pointed to the fresh sets of footprints heading towards the forest. She glanced back at the building, but it was totally obscured by the blizzard. To her left she saw two shapes also stumbling towards the forest. Quentin and Sam. She stopped and turned to Jukka.

'Ilkka?'

'He's doing his job,' he said. 'Come on, I don't want to lose them.'

Along the ski trail to the lake, they were sheltered from the worst of the storm and the tracks were clearly visible.

They had gone twenty or thirty metres along the trail when the explosion tore the edge of the forest apart. Pentti dragged Nicole to the ground and wrapping her in his arms, rolled them both behind a boulder. The sound of the explosion was muted by the conditions but the shock wave and blast of heat ripped over their heads and for a few seconds a rain of blackened, burning and smoking debris fell around them like deadly snow.

Pentti kept her down, his arms tightly around her, until the last fragments of stone and shattered wood had stopped falling.

'Pentti...' she began, but her mind was frozen by shock and she had no words.

'Come,' Pentti said and pulled her to her feet. 'Nothing we can do back there is going to help anyone. We have to keep going.'

She knew he was right, but she felt numb, except now it was not from the cold.

Once they reached the lake, Pentti ran to the small hut that housed the snowmobiles, but it was locked.

'They're still on foot,' he yelled to Nicole, who was zigzagging back and forth, frantically searching for footprints.

'I've lost the trail,' she cried in desperation.

Out on the lake it was a total whiteout with snow both falling and windblown, thick as a sandstorm, obliterating everything.

'I can't see a thing,' Pentti called, struggling to be heard above the wind.

'Here! I can just make them out. But they are being covered by snow.' Nicole glanced over her shoulder to make sure Pentti could see her.

'Wait!' he yelled. 'If we go on, we could get totally lost on the ice.'

'They went in this direction. We just need to go straight ahead.'

'You can't just go straight ahead in this,' Pentti shouted. He knew how easy it would be for them to get disoriented and end up going in circles until they succumbed to the cold. He knew the dangers but he also knew that she was going to keep going. 'Hold on, we have to stay together.'

He stopped for a moment and attempted to wipe snow from his glasses. When he put them back on he could see much better, but he couldn't see Nicole. Straight ahead, he told himself. Just keep going straight.

It was, Auli thought, exactly as it should be. He had told her so many times '*me nousemme kostona Kullervon*' – we shall rise in vengeance like that of Kullervo's. But that was only part of the story. And it was not the proper ending. Not the ending that had been written so long ago.

He had risen in vengeance, but he was too ill-fated to survive it. Kullervo was the man who had loved her, the man who had stolen her memory and who had shamed the tribe. She supposed they had been a tribe. Not now, not anymore, no longer of the same blood. Time and events had scattered them as they were scattered now. Oblivious to her cries, Kullervo had gone ahead of her, a dark shape against the white; a wraith appearing and disappearing in the clouds of snow.

She struggled after him, fighting against the tiredness, cold and snow; following the footsteps left by some drunken angel. Some fool who should have allowed himself to cry instead of hate, to heal instead of fester. He staggered, so the footprints told. Then pushed on again, going the only place left to go, the centre of the lake.

She saw him ahead of her, wandering in circles now. Moving slower, so much slower, as the cold bit deep into his flesh, waiting to claim him.

She came close, stepping as she had so often done, into his footprints.

'Kullervo!' she called, but the wind stole the name from her lips and cast it across the vast white emptiness. 'Kullervo! Wait!' she tried again. But he did not look back.

She saw him stop, then tumble down into thick snow. He rose, sitting, for a moment his face tilted skyward, singing. The wind gusted around him whipping the freshly fallen snow off the ice like smoke, sending it away across the lake's surface.

Auli was closer now, keeping moving, knowing that the ice would claim her should she stop. Knowing too that she should return, but deeper down, knowing she must sing his last song for him, retrieve the words from the place deep inside her where they lay bound up in a box of memories.

It was too hard and the distance between them too far. Auli fell to her knees and though she had little strength left, forced herself to crawl over the snow towards him. The temptation of sleep reached out, seductive and alluring, a narcotic that she craved. But though it beckoned, offering peace and rest, she fought against it.

When she reached him, she rolled on her back in the snow, all her energy gone. Beside her Kullervo was saying something, mumbling to himself, and something told her it was important that she listened so she rolled on her side and strained to hear.

'Will this end it?' he asked, 'Will this take all the guilt away?' The questions were not directed at her, but to the pistol in his hand.

She wanted to say no, to tell him that death would take nothing but life. But instead she forced herself up and kneeling beside him in the snow, started singing. Her voice was a faint cracked whisper, and it took all her willpower to force the words past her frozen lips.

'*Kullervo, Kalervon poika,*
tempasi terävän miekan;
katselevi, kääntelevi,
kyselevi, tietelevi.
Kysyi mieltä miekaltansa,
tokko tuon tekisi mieli
syöä syyllistä lihoa,
viallista verta juoa.'[7]

---

7   *Kullervo, Kalervo's offspring,*
    Grasped the sharpened sword he carried,
    Looked upon the sword and turned it,
    And he questioned it and asked it,
    And he asked the sword's opinion,

For a moment he seemed to recognise her, or maybe it was the words drilled into him so long ago. He gazed at her face and started to speak. Auli leaned forward, trying again to catch the words.

'I saw my father die from his wounds, wounds he should never have had to suffer. I told my mother I would get revenge.'

'Hush now,' she whispered. 'That was another world and oh so long ago.' But he didn't hear.

'Do you care if I am guilty?' he asked.

She was about to respond when she realised that again he was not addressing her, but rather the weapon in his hands.

'Does a bullet care what flesh it rips apart?' He sank down into the snow and rolled his head toward her. A smile flitted across his face. 'It's supposed to be a sword.'

'I know,' she said, and holding his head in her arms began chanting slowly.

'*Miekka mietti miehen mielen,*
arvasi uron pakinan.
Vastasi sanalla tuolla:
'*Miks' en söisi mielelläni,*
söisi syyllistä lihoa,
viallista verta joisi?
Syön lihoa syyttömänki,
juon verta viattomanki.'[8]

She felt the cold taking her. There was more to sing, but the words froze in her throat. So she lay back and felt the large snowflakes

---

If it was disposed to slay him,
To devour his guilty body,
And his evil blood to swallow.
8 *Understood the sword his meaning,*
Understood the hero's question,
And it answered him as follows:
'*Wherefore at thy heart's desire*
Should I not thy flesh devour,
And drink up thy blood so evil?
I who guiltless flesh have eaten,
Drank the blood of those who sinned not?

land on her hair, her face and her eyelids, and for a time she drifted across the landscape that was claiming her.

She heard the shot as if it was something far away. She struggled to sit up and turn her head towards the petals of red flowers that had appeared upon the snow. Spring is coming, she thought. Part of her wanted to cry, but it was too cold for tears.

The debriefing had been going on for two days when they concluded that what needed to be recorded had been and what was best left in the shadows was left from the transcripts. They ordered drinks and were relaxing when a technician came in and handed a note to Heimo. He read it, thanked the man and turned his attention back to the others.

'It seems that things were not exactly what they seemed,' he said. 'Remsu's mobile phones had been used to contact a number we know rather well. I find myself wondering why Kullervo Remsu was making frequent calls to the Russian President's advisor, Alexei Sedov.'

Quentin shot a glance at Nicole and put a finger to his lips. Nicole nodded. Now was not the time to share what they had on Sedov.

Heimo continued. 'It's highly possible that the entire operation was being run out of the President's office.'

'You mean they recruited Zaikov and had him set up the entire show in order to flush out dissidents?' He shook his head in disbelief. 'They played us all for fools.'

Pentti shook his head. 'My guess is that they manipulated Zaikov without his knowing it. They ruined his FSB career and played on his disillusionment and groomed him with promises of future power.'

'A puppet unaware of the strings?' Nicole suggested.

'Elegant,' Quentin said with more than a hint of admiration, but whether for Sedov's strategy or Nicole's metaphor was unclear.

Heimo turned to Quentin. 'I understand that you and Nicole are returning to Britain tomorrow?'

'Unfortunately, duty calls.'

'I trust you know that we will be in your debt for a long time,' Heimo said with a grin.

Quentin laughed. 'I can assure you that Her Majesty's government will not take advantage of that situation.' He paused and looked around the table. 'That everyone survived the destruction of the museum is a credit to your officers.' He looked directly at Ilkka. 'The bravery displayed by all involved was exceptional. I will be making certain that an official record of those sentiments is conveyed from our government to yours. That we have all assisted the Russian President in gaining an even stronger grip on power, however, is an outcome we all may rue.'

Heimo nodded. 'True, but we now have a clearer understanding of what they are capable of.'

Nicole raised her hand. 'Can I say something?'

'Of course,' Heimo beamed. 'Without you, events would have taken place without our understanding and certainly way beyond the control we managed to impose.'

Nicole took a deep breath. 'I want to say that the inter-service cooperation has been outstanding, and I hope we can find ways of working together in the future.'

'Hear hear!' Quentin exclaimed. 'Outstanding.'

Nicole glanced sideways at Pentti; she could swear he was blushing.

Heimo coughed and cleared his throat. 'Maybe we can have one last piece of cooperation on another subject.'

Quentin nodded.

'This sculptor, Anja Kujola, is making a fair bit of noise about the theft of her statue and our subsequent destruction of her only remaining mould with which she could have reproduced it.'

Sam laughed. 'Give her a free copy of the footage of us blowing it up for the cameras.'

'I can see why you are a spook, not a diplomat,' Nicole grinned. 'But I have an idea which together we may well be able to pull off.'

Pentti grinned. 'Whatever it is, I vote for it.'

So she told them. There was no need for a vote as the agreement was unanimous.

'That was just a devious way of getting invited back to Finland wasn't it?' Pentti said later.

She looked at him, all wide eyes and innocence. 'Me? Devious? How could you think such a thing, Mister Owl?'

It was like coming up for air after a long dive in deep water. For the first time in months she knew *who* she was; the trouble was she had no idea *where* she was. Her memory was coming back. There were still gaps, but she had all the pieces and eventually she would fill in the jigsaw puzzle.

'You slept well.'

The voice was vaguely familiar.

Auli looked around and found Sirkka standing beside the bed, two cups in her hand. She remembered Sirkka.

'Coffee?'

'Where am I?'

'You are in my spare room, which is yours for as long as you like.'

'Spare room?'

'In Lönnrotinkatu.'

Auli looked puzzled. 'In Helsinki?'

'It was, last time I checked,' Sirkka joked. 'Cal had been giving you drugs that took time to clear out of your system. A detox, the doctor called it. Anyway, he seems to think you'll be fine in a day or two. And you are still recovering from hypothermia.'

'What?'

'You nearly froze to death. Luckily Pentti and the English woman, Nicole, found you and managed to revive you. The doctor said he thought the drugs may have somehow slowed your metabolism and that helped save your life. Anyway, there is no rush and when you feel up to it you can start work.'

Auli sat up, pulled the bedclothes around her shoulders and took the coffee. 'What do you mean, start work?'

Sirkka sat on the edge of the bed and sipped her coffee.

'Only if you want to, but I desperately need someone to teach a course next semester and I think you would enjoy it.'

'Me? Teach?'

'Advanced Kalevala studies for foreign students. I think you would be perfect.'

Auli stared at her. 'Me?'

'You. After all, you know every word of it.'

'If I can remember,' Auli frowned. 'My brain feels all screwed up.'

'Trust me,' Sirkka smiled, 'you'll be fine.'

At midsummer, they gathered in the forest near Punkaharju. A majority of the rubble had been cleared away, but under Anja Kujola's direction some of the twisted steel beams and blocks of masonry had been left as they were following the explosion. It was a haunting vision of ground zero that was, despite the destruction, alive and organic. The forest was already encroaching and lichens were growing on the stones. The hollow where the building had collapsed into the bunker had filled with water, creating a small moat around the site chosen for the statue.

Nicole found it strangely moving that, for years in the future, people would come here to the wilds of Finland, and down an unsealed road find a statue of Ilmarinen forging the Sampo. She stood close to Pentti, his hand firmly in hers.

Heimo stepped up beside them. 'So? What do you think?'

'It is a haunting image, both powerful and sad, and in this setting...' she paused, unsure of her mixed feelings. 'One thing is certain, it's much better here than in Vyborg.' She smiled at Heimo, happy to see him again. 'Tell me how you managed it.'

'I rang Sedov, as you suggested, and explained I was calling from Remsu's phone. I let that sink in then I told him that the loan of the statue was now over and we would like it returned. To his credit he didn't hesitate. He agreed that a statue of Ilmarinen was better suited to Finland, where it wouldn't create a shrine for Karelian nationalists.'

'Perfect.'

'I invited him to today's unveiling, but sadly he was busy running Russia. They say he may well be the next Prime Minister.'

'That wouldn't surprise me,' Pentti said.

They stood in silence until Nicole excused herself to go and take a photograph of the small plaque on the side of the moat in front of the statue.

The name of the statue and Anja Kujola's name were cast in brass above the date, while below it, in Finnish, English and Russian, was a single sentence: *Those who wield power for the sake of power and not for the common good shall be destroyed by the very power they wield.*

'Would you like a brochure? It's in English.'

Nicole turned to see a young woman dressed in Karelian national costume. The woman smiled at her. 'You don't remember me?'

Nicole grinned. 'Hillevi. Yes, of course I remember.'

'I was lucky, I wasn't charged.'

'I'm glad to hear that,' Nicole said.

'Is Auli okay?'

'She's fine. She's become a teacher.'

'That's good.' She pressed a brochure into Nicole's hand and lowered her voice. 'We aren't allowed to talk about what happened. In the brochure it says the museum was destroyed in an accidental fire. It doesn't say anything about the Russians or how we were rescued.'

'That's probably best,' Nicole said, 'sometimes it's nice to have secrets.'

She watched the young woman walk away and then took out her glasses and started to read the brochure. It told the story of the Sampo, its creation, its theft and its destruction. However, it failed to fully explain what the Sampo was. Nicole liked the fact it remained an object of mystery.

'You have new glasses,' Pentti said as he came up and put his arm around her shoulders.

'I needed them.'

'Listen, a couple of local politicians are going to give speeches and I think we should escape.'

'Where?'

'There's a little cottage near here that I've rented for the next few days.'

'Mister Toivonen, I hope you are not suggesting something inappropriate.'

'There is a sauna.'

She looked at him sternly. 'And who the hell is going to look after the security of the nation while you're romping around naked and sweaty?'

'What's that expression in English?'

'Which one?'

'The one about the owl that lost its voice?'

'Couldn't give a hoot?'

'That would be it.'

She punched him as hard as she could. 'You make a joke as bad as that again, then I am going to get on the first plane out of your bloody country.'

'Not while our security forces have hold of you.'

'And when will that be?' she asked.

'As soon as we get to the cottage.'

Epilogue

On Kalevala Day the following year, a very private ceremony took place in Helsinki. Pentti Toivonen and Nicole Parry were awarded a specially minted Kalevala Medal for 'services to Finnish culture'.

Later, over a glass of Koskenkorva, Nicole pointed out that Finland was probably the only country on the planet where an award for services to culture was made to individuals responsible for blowing up an artwork and a museum. Pentti's only response was to fill their glasses again.

'*Kippis,*' he said, 'here's to Finnish culture.'

Loppu – End

Sandy McCutcheon
Fez, Morocco
Kalevala Day, 2019